Ellen Edith Alice Ross

Violet Keith

An Autobiography

Ellen Edith Alice Ross

Violet Keith
An Autobiography

ISBN/EAN: 9783337030919

Printed in Europe, USA, Canada, Australia, Japan

Cover: Foto ©Raphael Reischuk / pixelio.de

More available books at **www.hansebooks.com**

AN AUTOBIOGRAPHY.

BY

MRS. ROSS.

———◆·◆·◆———

Montreal:

PRINTED BY JOHN LOVELL, ST. NICHOLAS STREET.

1868.

VIOLET KEITH.

CHAPTER I.

WE stood alone, my brother Willie and I, by the bed from which the body of our dead mother had been removed only a few hours before. Long years have passed since then, but every object in that large cold room seems as distinct as if I had never quitted it; the lofty bed with its long white curtains, the large windows draped in white, the crimson carpet, the dressing table with its service of white and gold; the large mirror, above which was suspended an old-fashioned woodcut of "the Pilgrim's Progress," on which Willie and I used to delight to trace the wanderings of Pilgrim, with eye and finger alike busy following him in his flight from the city of destruction to his entrance into the golden gate; and more vivid than aught else, is that long dread mark on the white sheet, made by the pressure of the coffin, that indelible mark which time has never been able to efface from my mind.

As we looked, our tears fell fast; it was the last trace of the dear mother, who, a few evenings before, smiled upon us and spoke so kindly, when we came to kiss her before going to bed. How well we remembered and how eagerly we repeated each word and look of that evening now. Ah! could we but once more feel the touch of that, then, white hand, smoothing down our hair as it used to do every night; but it could not be, she had entered into her rest; and for us, her beloved ones, the days of darkness were come. Darkness came on apace; with what different aspects this darkness comes, and how differently do we greet his coming. In happy cheerful homes he is welcomed with light and with song, the bright coal fire is stirred, crimson curtains are drawn snugly round, and children's bright faces look sweeter and brighter for the surrounding gloom. But to us, poor lonely children, in that cold large room, he came step by step, slowly and surely, enlarging each object as he enveloped it in his misty shroud, and making our hearts beat with a dread of we knew not what.

The rain which had fallen without intermission during the day, now increased almost to a tempest, while the wind passed by with a low moaning wail, as if a sick spirit were borne on its blast, and ever returning to raise the branches of the surrounding birch trees and dash them with a dull flapping noise on the dripping windows, the very elements had conspired to show us more forcibly our loneliness and desolation.

" We will always love each other, Violet."

I believe there are whispers of God to the soul; I do not think that the Holy Ghost is shown forth to us in the Bible merely to make up the number three in the Godhead; I believe there is a divine, penetrating life power, which comes from the Eternal Father upon us; I believe that our sense of truth, our thoughts, and our experience in this world, are influenced by the immediate touch of the mind of God upon our mind: and so it was that in the power of the Spirit these words passed from Willie's lips into my heart, kindling there a sense of perfect safety and protection, in the abiding love of my young brother, boy as he was.

How doth this divine emotion purify both those who exercise it, and those who receive its benefactions! By it God maintains the household. From its secret springs He nourishes the new generations of men. Even afar off from its source, it shines with power enough to guide the world, and lead men up the pleasant paths of civilization and peace. What, then, shall be its redemptive and educating power in that far off land of heaven, where our spirit's progress shall be ever onward and upward?

We know that in this world, love, like all the higher faculties of the soul, grows in power with exercise and age. A youth does not love his parent as a father loves his son; love is a thing of leaves, blossoms, and fruit, each in its order.

We sometimes connect together the manifestations of it, which we see in this life, to get a large view of what it will be in the future; even in this world, with our imperfectly developed faculties, we occasionally see in others, or experience in ourselves, that which gives us some conception of the divine power of love which we shall possess in the world to come.

Love is indestructible, there is nothing which love cannot do; it never faileth, never grows weary, nothing in the soul is superior, nothing equal to it; let love be an active feeling there, and all the other faculties come before it, and lay down their rubies and pearls at its feet; by its mighty influence we govern by a smile; all the higher feelings of our nature follow in the train of this mighty power, and open to it as the sunflower to the sun.

I put my hand in Willie's, and we passed from my mother's deserted room, into the drawing room with all its blaze of light and warmth, where my uncle (whom we had never seen until the preceding day) sat reading a newspaper, and did not acknowledge our entrance, by either word or look. While I now write, after a lapse of so many years, the scene I then saw is as fresh as yesterday.

My uncle, a tall, bony man, grey eyes, grey hair, hook nose, hard mouth, (I can find no other expression which will convey my meaning equally well,) sits in a large easy chair, at one side of the fire place, his crossed legs reaching half way over the soft rug, the remainder of which was occupied by a beautiful greyhound, whose handsome head formed a good contrast to the gaily wrought bunches of flowers it rested on. Poor Ponto, one of our trials on the morrow was parting from thee.

A chandelier hung from the centre of the room glittering with crystal pendants, blue and gold tea-china on the centre table, lace curtains, softly cushioned sofas, pictures, sculpture, and flowers, the pink blossoms of the camelia, contrasting with the white wax-like roses of the Cape jasmine, filling the room with its perfume. The flowers were my mother's especial care. I watered them next morning before our departure, my own tears falling fast while Willie stood by sobbing as if his heart would break.

Our uncle took us to Scotland where his home was, and placed Willie in the house of a chemist, where a hope was held out to him of one day becoming a Doctor, if he were steady and industrious, while I was sent to a ladies' school, that I might, as my uncle emphatically said, learn to be a governess, and earn my bread honestly. He talked a great deal to the lady preceptress of the necessity of my being taught as quickly as possible to earn my bread, as he termed it, in consequence of his being obliged to defray the expense of my own and my brother's education, and thereby injuring his own family, and absolutely depriving them of their birthright.

While he spoke, I felt myself a sort of culprit as I sat hud-
dled up in my travelling dress, and I thought then, what
afterwards I found to be the case, that he had impressed Mrs.
Moodie with a high respect for his saintly and generous character.

Upon my uncle's departure, Mrs. Moodie drew me towards
her, removed my travelling dress, smoothed my hair with
both hands, kissed my cheek, and spoke lovingly and en-
couragingly, gave me some fruit and cakes, and telling me I
would find several little girls of my own age there, brought
me into the school room.

The girls were just putting by their books for recess, as it
was called there, which means the hour in the middle of the
day when the day scholars go home to dine, and the boarders
eat their lunch and amuse themselves until the bell rings for
school again. For a few minutes all was hubbub and noise,
until the day scholars went, and then I found there were
fourteen young ladies of different ages in the room, all of
them intent on demolishing huge piles of bread and butter,
which, together with apples, formed their noonday meal.

Having satisfied their hunger, one of them observed me
sitting apart, my tears falling in large drops into my lap,
and coming up to me, she said, laughingly—

" Come Miss, what's your name, and I will introduce you
to your future friends ?"

Taking me by the hand, she led me to the table where
most of the girls stood, and rattled over in succession : Miss
Gordon, Miss Rose, Miss Brown, Miss Goodbrand, when,
seeing my look of misery, she stopped suddenly, and putting
a hand on each side of my face, drew it towards her own,
shutting one eye, and squinting in the most ludicrous manner
with the other, she drawled out—

" Cry, baby, cry, put your finger in your eye,"—until all the girls, and I among the number, shouted with laughter.

Miss Baird was the name of the young lady who had thus set me at my ease; she was a good-tempered, kind-hearted girl, who depended more on her neighbour's than her own exertion, for obtaining a knowledge of her lessons, and in every way took life as easy as possible; she was my best friend in these my most trying days, and I repaid her in the after time by regularly writing her French exercises for her. This was an easy matter to me; all my early days were spent in the south-west of France, we having only removed to England a year previous to the death of my mother. French was virtually my own language, and I spoke, read, and wrote French with a facility which I only acquired in English by hard study. My power in French was soon discovered, and made me very popular.

" Violet will sit by me," Miss Baird would say. " No she shan't, she'll sit by me," two or three other voices would call out simultaneously, while during the hour in which we studied our French lessons, I was made use of as a kind of living dictionary and grammar.

The greatest difficulty they had to encounter seemed to be their inability to distinguish the gender of inanimate nouns, and in consequence I was constantly assailed by such questions as " Is garden male or female ?" " Is the room a woman or a man ?"

Mrs. Moodie was a woman in whom the milk of human kindness flowed largely, well informed, and sensible, altogether more suited for the arduous duties she had assumed, than most people who undertake them. Her household consisted of fourteen young ladies besides myself, two governesses, one fat, good tempered, and young, yclept Miss Walker, the other Miss Forrester, thin, severe, and thirty-five, both performing their duties to the best of their ability.

The Sunday after my arrival Willie came to see me, was kindly received by Mrs. Moodie, and ultimately I was allowed to spend two hours in the garden with him every Sunday afternoon ; these Sunday walks were the white days in a life otherwise weary enough. It is the dull monotony of each day being so like the last, which makes a school-girl's life so weary. A girl in her father's house, however quiet and recluse the life they may lead, sees an occasional visitor, or goes out shopping, or sometimes visits a neighbour ; but the life of a school girl knows no such luxury ; Monday in one week is the exact counterpart of Monday in the next ; the same lessons, the same walk, taken at the same time, and at the same pace, even the same dinner ; we knew what we were to have for dinner quite as well as the cook, and I am sure we would all have hailed potatoes and salt with delight, merely because it was different from the constant round of beef to-day and mutton to-morrow. I had lived about six months in Ellenkirk, when one day after dinner Mrs. Moodie said, taking a letter from her pocket :

"You will all be glad to hear that Miss Hamilton will be among us once more in a few days ; she sends her love to all, especially Miss Baird and Miss Goodbrand."

"I am so glad," burst simultaneously from the lips of each of the young ladies so addressed.

They often spoke of Gertrude Hamilton as the best and prettiest girl in the school ; she was an acknowledged favourite, and Miss Baird and Miss Goodbrand were her class mates.

A day or two afterwards she walked into the school-room in recess, and was instantly surrounded by a troop of rejoicing girls.

She seemed about fourteen years of age, rather tall, well made, deep grey eye, sunny hair, and light step. I did not wonder that the other girls said she was so pretty ; she looked like a princess in the midst of our homely faces.

" These are the new girls ?" said she, interrogatively, to Miss Baird, as she turned towards myself and five or six others, and as we were named, gave her right hand to one. her left to another, until she had spoken a kind word, and given a bright smile to each ; it was evident she was the queen of the school. And so it was in her lessons ; her music was far above what any of us could attempt, she spoke Italian with its own soft cadence, German with the guttural accent of Herman, and French almost as easily as I did. She was an heiress and an only child, and yet the least selfish girl among us all.

She used to say that until she came to Mrs. Moodie's school at Ellenkirk, she had no home, wandering about with her father and mother, in search of health for the latter, which was never to come. From Rome to Florence, from Florence to Paris, and again on the German banks of the Rhine, no wonder she could speak the language of the French and German school girls she studied among, or deftly imitate the soft accents of the dark-eyed children she played with on the banks of the Po.

At her mother's death she was placed with Mrs. Moodie. where she remained until six months previous to the time of which I write ; she then went to spend with her father the remaining few months he was to reside in Britain, before going to join his regiment in Canada.

Our French and Italian master was a Roman Catholic priest, whose income, derived from a congregation of some hundred of the middling class, was so scanty as to oblige him to teach those languages, a perfect facility in which he had acquired during a residence of many years in the Vatican.

Mr. Forbes, such was our French teacher's name, was handsome, tall, and gentlemanly, with a composure and suavity of manner, which, to unprejudiced people, must have gone far to win favour. With the girls in Mrs. Moodie's school, the mere fact of his being a priest was sufficient cause of doubt and dislike ; he was nicknamed Guy Fawkes by one, Pope John the twenty-third by another, although what analogy existed between Mr. Forbes and either of these gentlemen, it would not be easy to say.

Neither Gertrude or I joined in these popular outbursts against the French master ; I did not because I had been accustomed to associate with Roman Catholics equally with Protestants, and could not conceive why the one was not as good as the other ; Gertrude, because she was herself a Catholic, and Mr. Forbes, besides being her teacher, was her spiritual director.

A few weeks after Gertrude's return to school, little Sara Douglas, a fine intelligent child of eight years of age, had measles, and was sent to a large room in one of the wings of the house to be nursed. Several of the older girls who had already had the disease, I among the number, took it in turns to amuse her as she became convalescent ; I liked this duty very much, and used to take the place of any of the others willingly ; by so doing I quite won her confidence.

One day she had a large piece of sponge cake, and drawing me towards her, and speaking very softly, although there was no one in the room, said, " take this key, Miss Keith, and in my drawer you will find a red box, bring it to me, if you please." I went to her room as she desired, and returned with a red painted box, about a foot long and half as wide, fastened by a little hook; she took it from my hand and smiled, saying:

"I will tell you a great secret; my brother James, who is now in the West Indies, made this box for me, and I am keeping all the nice things I get in it, and when I leave school I am to go to Jamaica to him, and I shall bring all the things I have and give them to him."

She then opened the box, and I found it contained a gingerbread cake, nearly large enough to cover the bottom of the box, on which appeared the alphabet in raised letters, an apple, and a penny. She gave a look of joyous triumph as I examined the contents of the box, but alas, upon touching the apple it was found to be a mass of rottenness. Poor little thing, how she cried, sobbing so bitterly. I had some painted and lettered lozenges in my own keeping, and slipping from the room, I returned with, and placed them in the box, five in number.

"Look," said I, "these are much nicer than the apple; beautiful red and white lozenges, and they will keep for years."

She looked at me as I spoke, and then at the lozenges, which I had arranged in a row above the gingerbread.

"O, Miss Keith, I will never forget you," she exclaimed, smiling gladly through the tears which still stood on her cheek, and then, as if shocked by her own selfishness, she hurriedly said, pushing the box towards me:

"O, I cannot take them, I am sure you were keeping them for your own brother."

"No, indeed; Willie brought me those last Sunday, and when you go to the West Indies you will tell James that I sent them to him."

We placed the sponge cake also in the box, fastened it up, and returned it to the drawer; subsequently she told me that

sometimes she was so impatient to see James, that she thought
of running away from school and going to the West Indies,
how glad James would be to see her, and how happy they
would both live together.

She showed me one or two of his letters, and I did not fee
surprised by her devotion to the loving heart which dictated
them.

At the end of the summer holidays, Sara came back as
thin and pale as she had been before fat and rosy, her black
dress telling its usual tale ; she put her right hand into my
left, and stood for a few seconds without speaking. I kissed
her thin cheek, and then she said in a soft low voice, without
either a sigh or tear:

"Brother James is dead; I will never go to the West
Indies."

Six weeks afterwards we were all assembled in the drawing
room, it was Friday evening, and we frequently spent our
Friday evenings there, as we had no lessons for next day ;
Miss Forrester was singing that most beautiful of all Scottish
airs, "Logie O'Buchan," and had just finished the line,
" They hae ta'en awa Jamie the flower o' them aw," when
we observed Sara fall gently down on the sofa where she was
sitting. Mrs. Moodie lifted her up exclaiming:

"Go for Dr. White, she has fainted!"

The doctor was with us in a few minutes. No, she had not
fainted ; she was dead! all efforts were useless—most surely
dead—died, as the doctor said, of disease of the heart; truly
he judged well, so she did.

A few weeks before this sad event, we were seated at
breakfast one morning, when Sara said, " Mrs. Moodie, may
I tell my dream ? I had such a beautiful dream last night.'

" Yes, Sara, tell us your dream."

"I dreamt," said the child, "I was standing by the drawing room window, when all at once the street was filled with angels, each having a crown on his head formed of stars; one of the angels, in addition to the crown on his head, had one in his hand; he crossed the street and went into Annie Maitland's house, and placed the crown he carried in his hand on her mamma's head: Mrs. Maitland then came out with the angel, and they all ascended towards the sky by a path formed of the clouds; I watched them until they were out of sight."

An hour afterwards we had intelligence of the death of Mrs. Maitland, which occurred through the night.*

The morning after Sara's death, her father and mother came to bring her to the place of sleep; Gertrude and I were arranging a wreath of white jessamine to place on the coffin; when they entered the room where we were, and where the body lay; such a contrast they were to each other; Mrs. Douglas, little, thin, and very like Sara, the very same sad face she wore since her brother's death; the father a sensual, eating and drinking looking man, about the middle size, fat, red faced, head and neck in one.

Mrs. Douglas walked up to the child's body without noticing any one, took one small hand in both her own, kissed the cold face just once, and then turned away, her pale lips rigidly compressed, evidently fearing her heart would fail.

The man looked at the body, not the face, it was covered. shut down the lid of the coffin with the spring, and raising it on his shoulder, walked out and placed it on the opposite seat of the carriage they had just left, and which was to convey them, together with their dead, again to the railway cars.

---

* A fact.

As her husband left the room, Mrs. Douglas asked, "where is Violet Keith?"

I was pointed out to her, and coming towards me, she put one cold thin hand on my shoulder, and pressed her pale lips to my cheek, and then passing from among us without uttering a word, entered the carriage which contained her living and her dead.

The deep eloquence of her touch on my shoulder and cheek, could have no rival in words; in my after life I never received such thanks; she, too, will die of disease of the heart some day.

After their departure, Miss Forrester packed up the child's clothes; while she did so, I carried the red box to Mrs. Moodie, who decided it was not to be sent to her mother. Mrs. Moodie opened the box in my presence; everything was there as it had been left months before, gingerbread, penny, lozenges, and sponge cake, with the addition of a small wax doll, about an inch and a half in length, dressed in a pink gauze frock.

We all, teachers, boarders, and day scholars, mourned very sincerely for Sara: the boarders, with the true demonstrativeness of school girls, wore black ribbon fastening their collars for a month.

In summer we spent our hour of recess in the garden, and a fine place it was for our plays or walks, as our dispositions or age might dictate ; a few flower beds surrounded the house, and then, stretching for two or three acres, were green fields and forest trees, together with the more artificial and useful beauties of arbours and swings, the whole surrounded by a high and thick hawthorn hedge, outside of which rose a stone wall eight feet high.

When we returned from the garden when recess was over,

one or other of the older girls generally brought a flower to be presented to Mr. Forbes or Dr. Byers, the music master, both of these gentlemen receiving such presents very graciously.

We did not know where Dr. Byers lived; he kept that secret to himself—he might have lived in paradise for aught we knew. I for one often wished him in heaven; I never was intended for a musician, and received more harsh words and sour looks for badly practised lessons in that branch of my education, than for all my other studies put together.

Mr. Forbes treasured our offerings; he had a great love for the beautiful, and certainly his home, if home it could be called, was not calculated to gratify his taste in that respect; his house consisted of four rooms, built two above two, against the back of the little chapel, in which he officiated. A high stone wall surrounded the paved court, in which not a blade of grass was to be seen.

One lovely day, during recess, we had strayed to the very op of the garden. When the bell rung for school, we ran as quickly as possible, so that we might be in the school room, as the rule was, ere the bell ceased ringing; and so we thought not of a flower for our teacher. Gertrude had a rose in her hand, it was true, but it was faded with the hot sun, and not fit to be given away. During the French hour, she continued to pick, one by one, each bud and leaf it possessed, until naught was left but a crushed pink blossom at one end of a brown stem, which she threw upon the table, when the lesson was ended.

It was my day to lay aside the books in the book cupboard, —this duty devolved on each of the elder girls in succession; and while thus occupied, I observed Mr. Forbes (who always took ten minutes after the hour in correcting the exercises) take up Gertrude's crushed rose, press it to his lips, and then carefully put it inside his vest.

My heart smote me when I saw him thus carefully lay up the crushed thing; and picking from a vase on the mantel shelf a beautiful moss rose full of buds and foliage, I laid it on the table before him. He thanked me with a smile, and seemed much gratified; an hour afterwards I found my beautiful rose on the table.

CHAPTER II

My uncle paid periodical visits to myself and Willie, at the end of each successive six months—in my case, to pay for my board, and impress upon me the necessity of studying night and day if possible, the sooner to relieve him of the burden, which pressed so heavily upon him.

The visit to Willie was to pay his tailor's bill, the amount being limited to three pounds in six months. Mr. Rexford allowed Willie his board for the service he rendered in the shop after the two first years of his residence there, yet notwithstanding, Mr. Keith never failed to urge him to improve his time, so that he, (our uncle) might be spared this heavy expense of three pounds per six months. We had twice a year an invitation to spend an evening at Haddo Hall, where my uncle's family lived; these invitations were always given by my uncle in person, and were by him limited to three hours, we being sent for at six, and returned to our respective homes at nine o'clock, by the same conveyance, his own carriage.

Haddo Hall was a large old house, built more like a Castle, than what we understand by a Hall; situated in the midst of a noble park, filled with fine old trees, which could only have attained their present growth in centuries; and a trout stream running through the grounds to the sea.

Haddo Hall came into our family by my great grandmother, who was the last of her race; an honourable and an heiress in her own right. Her picture hung there in the gallery, full length, dressed in white satin, with the long pointed

bodice and lace ruffles of the time ; she is represented standing in the recess of a deep oriel window ; the fingers of an
exquisitely shaped hand touching the strings of a lute ; which
with its antique stand occupies one side of the window. The
face is one of perfect beauty, with the square forehead and
small mouth betokening firmness and truth, a rich flood of
mellow light from the setting sun streams into the room, and
between the oriel and the sun, are seen pictured those very
giant pines and elms that now spread their great arms beneath
the wintry and summer sky.

The picture is a *chef d'œuvre* of Sir Joshua Reynolds, the
gem of the gallery, surrounded by knights in armour, with
the long curls belonging to the time of the first Charles,
statesmen, and officers of the reigns of the Georges, with
their ladies in crimson and gold ; but there she stands in her
quiet beauty far outshining all her compeers.

I never went to Haddo without passing part of my time
with her. It was no picture to me ; it seemed a living, breathing reality, in very deed my great grandmother ; there she
stood in all her dignified beauty, smiling sweetly on me, her
poor lonely grandchild ; and ever seeming to say " bear on,
bear nobly on ; " " what is right do it though the heavens
come down ; what is wrong do it not, though by so doing you
should gain a kingly crown."

Mrs. Keith was a gay, dashing woman, the very opposite of
her husband. She dressed well and saw a great deal of company. I never saw my uncle's family alone : there were
generally some English friends of Mr. Keith's or her own
relations, of whom the name seemed to be legion, staying with
them; I heard her say that nothing on earth could tempt her
to live at the Hall for one week alone, she meant with her
husband and family ; she was tall, fat, rather pretty, very

c

good tempered, and liked to see all around her enjoy themselves ; she was invariably kind to both of us ; while my uncle
as invariably received and dismissed us with a scowl.

Mrs. Keith played and sung well, and so did her eldest
daughter ; both ladies seemed to think that music was the sun
and centre of all feminine accomplishments. Lizzie, the eldest
daughter, was at the time I write of, a fine looking girl of
nineteen or twenty summers ; rode and danced well, dressed
with good taste, and was altogether a fitting bride for the
officer of the dragoon-guards, to whom she was engaged, and
who seemed to find more congenial employment, in attending
his lady love at Haddo Hall, than in the service of Her Bri-
tannic Majesty.

A boy of twelve years old, painfully like his father, and a
beautiful little girl of eight, made up the number of my
uncle's family.

During all my school life, I never spent a whole day at
Haddo ; although Willie and I would have given much to
wander for one day amid the old woods and by the clear
stream, where our father's young days were passed.

Mrs. Moodie sent for me one morning in my sixteenth year,
to ask me if I would like to learn Spanish ?

Would I like to learn ?   I had only been prevented from
doing so, by my uncle's decided refusal to pay the fees, and
for the last six months, Gertrude had regularly given me her
lesson of the previous day, before seven o'clock in the morning.

Miss Baird was to leave school, and Mr. Forbes had requested Mrs. Moodie to allow me to study with Miss Hamilton,
as he said her interest might flag if she learnt alone.   No, truly
her interest would not flag, but good Mr. Forbes had discovered
that I wished to learn the language, and hence the proposal.

These Spanish lessons were the most pleasant hours I spent in school; Gertrude and I were alone with our teacher and the governess, who always sat by while the masters taught. Mr. Forbes used to encourage us to ask him questions on any subject we liked, so as to make the time pass pleasantly, while we became familiar with the language. These questions with Gertrude always took a religious turn, and I naturally followed in the same strain. She used to say that theology was the only subject she cared to talk of, cared to study; everything else was only learnt as a part of this great whole, and in subserviency to it.

In these conversations Mr. Forbes took care to eulogize his own as the only true Church, out of the pale of which there was no salvation. A favourite theme of his against the Protestant Church, was to shew the blasphemy, as he said, of which it was guilty, in denying a purgatorial expiation of sin, thereby taking away one of the greatest attributes of God, namely, his mercy.

He would illustrate this by saying, " a man dies suddenly in unrepented sin,—if the Protestant creed be true, he cannot enter heaven; because he has not repented and obtained forgiveness of sin here below, thus making God less merciful than man : for what man is there who would not, if appealed to, say, let him be punished, certainly, but in the end let his penance and the prayers of the Church avail for his redemption."

The sophistry of this reasoning was not such as a school girl could combat; nor did it then occur to me, that the Deity may be, in truth, a more severe avenger of guilt than a humane and benevolent man would be, for this very reason, that he is infinitely more humane and more benevolent than any man can be. For who is it, even in this world, that beholds guilt with the

greatest indignation? Who is most intent on bringing the transgressor to punishment? Is it the unprincipled immoral man?
or is it, on the contrary, the good, the virtuous? The sensual
man would indeed shew great mercy to another sensualist;
the thief would reprove dishonesty with mildness; the murderer be a lenient judge of another murderer; in general the
man who had little regard for moral obligation himself, would
be far from thinking it proper that the crimes of others should
be visited with severity of punishment.   But as in a human
tribunal, the judge is cruel where the accomplice, or even the
by-stander would be humane, so the Judge of all the earth, who
cannot look on iniquity but with abhorrence, will indeed be
more severe, more rigorous than the most upright of mankind,
who, comparatively speaking, can look upon guilt with complacency and toleration.   The mercy of God is not the
mere animal sympathy, which cannot look at the infliction of
pain; it is not the indolence, which will not be troubled with
avenging; it is not the careless good nature, which overlooks
or forgets transgression; it is not the ignorance or perplexity,
which cannot discern the guilt; it is not the timidity, which
fears to commit wrong, and will rather take the safe side: it
is the deliberate, purposed, measured abatement of the claims
of justice in respect that the transgressor has repented, has
earnestly and sincerely desired that he had acted otherwise;
has deeply bewailed his infringement of the divine law, and
sedulously and anxiously sought amendment and pardon
through the blood of a crucified Saviour.

     To suppose that the Deity will, in any case, however tri-
fling, grant his pardon, grant the slightest commiseration to
sin, that is to say while it remains sin, I should also say *if it
really is sin*, after all allowances have been made for the ignorance and weakness of the agent and the constitutional infir-

mity of his moral principle, for everything, in short, that can palliate his guilt, while it has not been unmade, undone, (as it were,) again by repentance and amendment, is to suppose the Deity either weak in his nature or imperfect in his moral purity ; is to suppose either that he wants steadiness of purpose to execute his own laws, or that he hates sin with something less than a perfect hatred. "Let all the people fear him, " for he cometh, for he cometh, to judge the earth : clouds " and darkness are round about him ; righteousness and judg- " ment are the habitations of his holiness."

In Mr. Forbes we had an earnest teacher, one who did everything as unto the Lord. With him, earth was so small because heaven was so vast : man nothing, but God all. To him it seemed little were we to tread the thorny path of the desert with unshod feet all our lives long, so at last it led to God.

I have read somewhere of a strange speech that dropped from the lips of Epictieus, a heathen : "If it be thy will," said he, " O Lord, command me what thou wilt ; send me whither thou wilt ; I will not withdraw myself from anything that seems good to Thee."

And Priest Forbes lived out these words in his life ; what he believed the Lord had given him to do, he did it with all his might, his mind, and strength, and spirit ; from early morn until dark, he went from school to school, and from house to house, teaching to those he believed heretics the languages of the continent of Europe, every word of which flowed from his lips as if he were speaking his native tongue ; he dressed plainly, and ate the simplest fare ; and this was all done, not to serve for any earthly end, but that the money so earned might be given unto the God, whom he served, through that Church which he believed alone to be holy, catholic, and apostolic ; and that he, the humble instrument, might so tend to the glory of the Great Master. Our nature can make no perfect whole; here and there the circle will break. The bright sun as it comes bringing light and life to one-half the world, leaves the other in deepest midnight ; and so, incomplete by the very law of his being, this man, unselfish, earnest, devoted as he was, would draw the contrast, sharp as truth, between human frailty and the perfect law of God ; and had he lived in past days, would have swelled the procession of an " Auto da fe," with a spirit on fire from the excess of its own zeal. Well hath the poet said, " Fear is easy but love is hard," " he prayeth best who loveth best." I heard him say in speaking of the fires of Smithfield : " This was necessary, these men were burnt for the glory of God !"

Truly, God's glory is a wondrous thing, most strange in all its ways, and of all things, least like what men agree to call it. God is other than we think, his ways far above our ways ; far above reason's height, and only to be reached by child-like love. God's ways are love's life-long study, and love can be bold and guess, where reason would not dare.

The mind of Gertrude was a rich soil in which Mr. Forbes might sow, what he deemed, his good seed ; and doubtless it was to his teaching as her spiritual director, that she owed, in a great measure, the unworldliness of her character. The world had no charms for her, it lay all beneath her ; she lived in an ideal world of her own, beyond the fragrant hills of myrrh, the mounts of Bethel. From her Protestant mother, she had learnt to wait and watch for the coming of the Lord, which will yet burst with lustre on this long shadowy night. This part of her mother's teaching, her confessor, for reasons best known to himself, had left undisturbed, and thus she ever sat in her white garments, with her lamp trimmed; his bosom-

treasured word ever in her soul: " I come quickly." I have
seen her raise her eyes to heaven as if she then expected to
hear the joyful song, which will usher in the rising of the day
star ; for her the earth was full of greenness and beauty, the
heavens of joy and gladness, because she believed with the
most child-like faith that the marriage feast was nigh.

" Violet, do you not think Mr. Forbes the most spiritual
minded man you have ever known?" said Gertrude one day,
after he had given us a long dissertation on the perfect communion of saints which exists in the Catholic Church.

" I cannot answer your question," replied I, " I have known
very few men, scarcely one whose character I admire, and I
do not know if he is spiritual-minded or not."

" Then I do," replied she, " and you know that I am your
superior in all worldly knowledge ; I have mixed in the society
of grown men since my childhood, and I have never known
one I could at all compare to Mr. Forbes."

" You have probably never known a clergyman so intimately."

" Why, yes ; we all know Mr. Dusty very intimately, and
I always feel sick when we are to have a dose of him."

Mr. Dusty was the clergyman whose church we all, with
the exception of Gertrude, attended, and we attended his
church certainly, but nothing more ; I do not recollect one
sentence I ever heard the good man utter; hearing nothing
I could understand or appreciate, I preferred occupying myself with examining the bright ribbons and pretty bonnets
within my range of vision ; and I suspect my school-mates
were equally idle.

Gertrude's experience of Mr. Dusty's powers was confined
to certain short addresses given by that gentleman to Mrs.
Moodie's pupils at the end of each term, and consisted

mainly in praise of the performance of each young lady, whether her *forte* was Music, Drawing, Languages, or English; all came under Mr. Dusty's approval or disapproval,—he, good man, being supposed to be equally learned in all the branches taught in Mrs. Moodie's establishment as he was presumed to be in Latin and Greek. Fortunately for us, his good nature inclined him to pass lightly over our defalcations; and where he could, give unlimited praise.

"It is scarcely fair to compare Mr. Dusty with Mr. Forbes," was my reply. "Mr. Forbes is a learned man, he has lived on the continent, and possibly associated with the first minds of the age; Mr. Dusty, on the contrary, has probably never travelled beyond the city in whose university he studied; he has no opportunity of converse with minds better informed than his own, and most likely has never taken one step out of the beaten path of study his predecessor trode before him."

"Then, Violet, we shall take your uncle; he at least is a learned man, president of all the Literary Societies in town, subscribes to the Art Journal, the Athenæum, and I do not know all what else; he is also a rich man, and we all know riches give their possessor many virtues both negative and positive, he has also, to give him refinement of soul, what wealth cannot buy, a long line of ancestry; he is the child of many sires, renowned in tourney and in war, while on the other hand, Mr. Forbes is the descendant of some plebeian, he himself poor as poverty. Now, Violet, how goes the rest of the comparison? You shall finish it."

"No, Gertrude, I shall do no such thing; I owe, or think I owe, a debt of gratitude to my uncle, therefore I shall make no comparison, the result of which would be anything but flattering to myself as his niece; but tell me this, was it his spirituality which made Mr. Forbes put away your hand from his arm the other day so unceremoniously, or set down Minnie from the table so ungraciously."

The circumstances to which I alluded occurred a few days before; Gertrude asked a question relative to her lessons, twice; the second time, to draw his attention more forcibly to herself, laid her hand upon Mr. Forbes' arm; he immediately drew his arm from under her hand, and stood up looking nervous and frightened; (a very curious look for a cool man like him to assume), and then moved his chair almost a yard distant from her seat, while Gertrude stared in simple wonder.

Little Minnie was a niece of Mrs. Moodie's, who sometimes spent a day with us; she was a lovely little dark-eyed girl of three years, and a great pet with us all. On one occasion Gertrude and myself had carefully combed up her hair in front, in the way it is worn by French children, so that in Scotland she looked like a little boy. Minnie had a *carte blanche* to come at will through the house, and going into Mr. Forbes' class-room, he had never seen her before, and lifting her up, seated her on the table and kissed her, saying, " are you a good boy?" "Minnie's not a boy," said she very indignantly, while Gertrude and I simultaneously exclaimed, " It is a girl." He got up hurriedly, lifted the child, and placed her quite at the door of the room. When returning to the table, he desired us to recommence our studies, rather authoritatively.

I told this at the time to Miss Forester, who made a laugh of the whole affair, at Mr. Forbes' expense, and Gertrude, who was always his champion, did not like my allusion to it.

CHAPTER III.

THE time now drew near when Gertrude and I were both to leave school; with what different prospects; she to join her father, who was now with his regiment in Canada, to be the pet of a luxurious home, to know no law but her own will, the heiress of ten thousand pounds in right of her mother. In one short year this, to me almost fabulous sum, would be at her own disposal. Happy Gertrude, I used then almost to envy you, and wish so earnestly that one, only one, of those thousands belonged to Willie and I. It never occurred to me to think of the awful responsibilty attached to every thousand, every hundred, every pound; how the Lord at his coming, will exact an account from all those whom he hath made the stewards of his gold and silver, and how the voice of him who cometh from Edom, with dyed garments from Bozrah, the gentlest voice earth ever heard, will then shout in accents of thunder, reaching from the east even unto the west : " Inasmuch as ye did it not unto the least of these my brethren, ye did it not unto me." Marvel not, that while he was yet among us, he gave that solemn warning : " It is easier for a camel to pass through the eye of a needle than for a rich man to enter the kingdom of Heaven."

And I, where was I to go ?—I knew not whither, I only knew it must be abroad into the wide world, to seek that bread which, for eight years, I had been learning to earn. Yea, and so I will. " Thou hast, oh God, of thy goodness, prepared for the poor," and I will go bravely forth, trusting in thine own promise, " He that now goeth on his way weeping, and beareth forth good seed, shall doubtless come again with joy, and bring his sheaves with him."

Were it possible, I would gladly have taken a situation in Ellenkirk or the vicinity, but it was vain thinking of such a thing. The families in town, who could afford to keep a governess, preferred sending their children to Mrs. Moodie's, or some similar establishment, of which there were one or two in Ellenkirk. The neighbouring proprietors, who kept governesses, would never dream of trusting the education of their daughters to one who had not studied in either London or Paris ; although, if I may judge from the young lady to whose care my cousin Catherine's education was entrusted, it was not always an advantage having a governess from London.

During the past eight years Catherine had thrice a change of governesses ; each in succession, speaking a great deal of bad French, with a broad Anglo-Saxon accent. In one of my earlier visits to Haddo Hall, before I was wise enough or had sufficiently felt my own insignificance to know my greatest safety was in silence, I got into a scrape with my aunt on this subject, which, but for her unvarying good temper, might have cost me dear.

The way in which it happened was this :—Miss Howe, the governess, spoke almost entirely to Catherine in French ; very bad French, almost unintelligible, and so doing wished Catherine to reply : telling her first the words she was to use. " Très bien," which Miss Howe pronounced " Tray beang." Girl-like, without a moment's consideration, I said, O Miss Howe, we do not say " Tray beang " in France, we say " très bien." Miss Howe's face became scarlet, as with a flashing eye, she replied, " It is not of the least consequence how you pronounce your words ; Miss Catherine Keith is not to take you as a pattern in anything." Mrs. Keith, who caught these last words, and observed the excited way in which Miss Howe spoke, asked: " What is the matter ?"

It was explained to her that I had presumed to correct Miss Howe's pronunciation. She in her turn recounted the impertinence to her husband, who also had requested an explanation. I shall never forget the look of withering scorn, largely mixed with hatred, which the latter bestowed upon me. After a moment's pause, Mrs. Keith, evidently wishing to conciliate both parties, said: " When Miss Violet is a little older, she will understand better the difference there must be between the teaching of an accomplished young lady like Miss Howe, and that of a poor man like Mr. Forbes, who, of course, never had an opportunity of hearing Parisian French spoken."

Were it not that my uncle " held me with his eye " I would have answered that. It is now in the long ago. It was well I did not.

Willie and I had spent all our Sabbath afternoons together in Mrs. Moodie's garden for the last eight years, under the great elm tree, whose branches, drooping almost to the ground, formed a shade alike from summer's sun and wintry wind, until the turf seat, surrounding the giant bole, had more of home in it for us, than any other place in the wide world. Even when the snow lay thick on the ground, we would borrow a broom from the kitchen, and having swept the seat and trodden down a resting-place for our feet, we sat there until our fingers ached and our lips were blue with the cold.

The last Sabbath we sat there, we read from our mother's Bible, as we had done on every preceding Sunday; each of us reading a verse alternately.

We promised our mother, only a few days before her death, and again when she could only signify her wish for a reiteration of our promise by signs, that if ever we were separated, an event which she knew must soon take place, we would, if possible, read a portion of the Bible thus, as we had been accustomed to do from our childhood, each time we met. We kept our promise and we had our reward.

All our after lives were influenced and bore the impress of the hours spent thus in that hill-side garden, and we learnt in simple faith, not by man's teaching, but from our Saviour's own words, that he had left that glory which He had with His Father, before the world was; lived a life of weariness, pain and toil; and died a shameful death, that we might have life, and have it more abundantly, and that, as those men of Galilee had seen him ascend up into heaven, so in like manner would he come again, and of that day and hour no man should know; no warning should be given : that they would be marrying and giving in marriage, until the very hour when the voice of the great archangel shall proclaim, " Behold the Lord cometh with ten thousand of His saints ; and then those who wait and watch for His coming, will be caught up to meet Him in the air, and so be for ever with the Lord."

In those long years how tall and strong Willie had grown, and so handsome : on our visits to Haddo Hall, how often have I, with a feeling akin to triumph, compared him to our dwarfish looking cousin, who was to be the lord of the broad acres there, and now that we were to part, I felt how very desolate I should be without him ; he, the only living being to whose love I had a clear title.

Willie was two years my junior ; his medical studies would not be finished for four years to come, the winter months of which were to be spent in Edinburgh attending college. Through Mr. Forbes' recommendation I had obtained a situation as governess in a family living between Edinburgh and

Portobello; we would then only be separated for half the year, so that all things considered, neither of us had a right to complain.

Gertrude had gone to Canada some months before I left Ellenkirk, and I missed her every day, and all day long; we parted with vows of eternal friendship, exchanging locks of hair. The long sunny tress which thus became mine, I plaited to form a bracelet, and sometimes wound its length of two feet round and round my arm—in those poor days tied with a little bit of pale blue ribbon. In the after time it had a clasp of gold, her name on one side, and "Omni tempore" engraved on the other. "Omni tempore," verily so it was. Mrs. Moodie smiled rather sadly on witnessing our parting. "Foolish girls, I have heard at least a hundred such vows exchanged during the last twenty years; shall I tell you how many of these were kept?" "Oh! no," exclaimed Gertrude. "In Violet my faith has perfect rest, and I don't want to have it shaken."

CHAPTER IV.

"Morn on the waters and purple and bright."

How lovely and fresh everything looked and felt ; the breeze so cool and pleasant, as it came careering round the ship, setting ribbons and veils streaming forth like so many gay pennons. The long white trail, made by the engine of the steam-vessel, and the little baby waves on either side with their easy motion, seeming like things of life ; everything so new ; so like fairy land, or rather fairy life on sea. I felt as I threw off my neckscarf and held up my face for another bath in the sweet south wind, surely there is much happiness merely in living.

My time passed quietly and pleasantly by, at times watching the groups of ladies and gentlemen who paced the deck, chattering and laughing merrily ; at times reading Sir Walter Scott's Kenilworth—being the first novel I had ever seen—at last I became so interested in its pages, that, seated in the corner of one of the deck sofas, my parasol resting on my hat, so as to shield me at once from the rays of the sun, and the gaze of my fellow passengers, I was wholly unconscious that every one (except myself and the good-tempered looking old gentleman, who had succeeded at last in recalling me to what was passing around me) had left the deck for the dinner table. Under his escort I obtained a comfortable seat.

I should think we sat an hour at dinner, during which my old friend amused me by his piquant remarks on those who sat opposite.

" That fat lady with two bracelets on each arm is Mrs. Thorn, the wife of a grocer who lives in the High Street of Edinburgh. She has, doubtless, been visiting her friends on the east coast, and astonishing them with her grand display of jewellery."

" Those two young ladies in grey, are descendants of Robertson, the historian, and relatives of Lord B——, and evidently feel their own consequence. That young dandy who is doing the agreeable to them, is an advocate from Edinburgh, he is thought very clever, and is a rising man. You see he is quite smitten with the tallest sister."

As he spoke I looked at the descendants of Robertson with interest; they were pretty and lady like, the tallest very beautiful. Their companion did not look much like a dandy, but he did look clever and like a rising man, tall, rather slight, dark handsome face, finely cut features and firm mouth; he seemed indeed to look with interest on his pretty neighbour.

I saw them several times walking the deck together in the course of the afternoon, and fancied from the heightened colour of the young lady, that the attentions of the handsome advocate were not lost upon her.

Towards evening her sister left the deck. He offered his arm and they walked slowly up and down, while he talked so earnestly; what could he have said in those few minutes to make her cheek so like a crimson rose leaf, and her eye flash with such a pleasant light?

After tea the wind became chilly, so with my companion Kenilworth, I went to the saloon, and sat there by a pleasant fire, until the bell rung for us to go ashore.

On ascending to the deck, I found that the rain, which threatened to pay us a visit in the afternoon, had now come in earnest, and in addition everything around was black as the tents of Kedar.

With the aid of the stewardess, I soon found my luggage. It consisting of only one trunk, in which was stored all my worldly goods. I seated myself thereon, and awaited as patiently as possible, under the circumstances, for the cabmen, who, my friend of the dinner table told me, would come on board to be hired.

The old gentleman left the vessel at one of the intermediate ports, early in the evening, having first come to bid me a kindly good-bye.

I sat there for about ten minutes, and was getting tolerably wet, my tiny parasol serving only to protect my hat, while each whalebone point formed a miniature spout to conduct the rain which fell on the parasol round my back and shoulders.

As I sat thus, feeling rather forlorn, the two young ladies who were pointed out to me at dinner, passed closely by me, on their way to the gangway, accompanied by their handsome friend and another gentleman ; by the light from the lamps placed on either side of the gangway, I saw them handed into a carriage which one of the gentlemen entered, while the other raised his hat as they drove off.

The gentleman who was left returned to the vessel, and lifting up a leather travelling sack, was on the point of leaving a second time, when one of the brass clasps of my trunk (an old military chest of my father's) which had lost a nail, caught his sack—while disengaging it he asked, courteously, if I expected my friends to come for me ?

" No, I am waiting for a cab. I believe the men come on board to be hired."

" I shall call a cab for you with pleasure."

D

" Thank you very much," I said heartily, and in a few minutes I was handed into one.

" Where shall I tell the man to drive."

" Iona Villa, on the Portobello road."

" Ah !" replied he ; and his voice expressed surprise, " I too am going to the Portobello road, will you allow me occupy the vacant seat in your carriage ?"

" Certainly, with pleasure."

He handed his travelling sack to the driver, stepped lightly inside, and in a few minutes we were driving quickly on from Leith to Edinburgh, from Edinburgh to Portobello.

The handsome advocate, for it was he who was my travelling companion, did his best to make the time pass pleasantly, by telling me on which side of the way the various objects of interest we passed were situated. This was all that was possible, as the darkness was almost such as might be felt, relieved here and there by the light streaming from the lighted-up villas we passed.

As we neared Peirshill Barracks, popularly called Jock's Lodge, the sentry was calling the hour. The noise or the glare of the lights at the gate made the horse restive, and the driver was obliged to dismount and lead him for a few yards.

When just at the gate, my companion leant forward to the carriage window to look at his watch by the lamp light. As he did so, one of the sentries observed to the other, in accents more *fortissimo* than *forte :* " Gin I had that chap's face, I would hae a better-looking lass to court on sic a wild night, or else I wad bide at hame."

I can smile now when I recall the soldier's words, and the loud laugh of his companion, but it galled me then, and for many a day afterwards.

Iona Villa at last! How glad I felt; shivering with cold and wet, as I sat for the last hour and a half, it seemed as if we were never to arrive at my destination. At a glance, I saw a large house, lower and upper halls well lit up; as also two windows to the right of the door, and several others in the second and third storeys.

My companion stepped from the carriage and opened the iron gate of the parterre in front of the house, as if it was an old acquaintance. He had scarcely reached the house door, when it was opened, and a young lady, nearly as tall as himself, put her arms round his neck and kissed him, exclaiming, " I knew it was you, Robert."

He took both her hands in his own, kissed her cheek, and was back at the carriage-door again. All this passed in a moment; in another I was inside the hall, in a flood of light and warmth.

" Georgy, this is your new governess, Miss Keith," said the advocate ; (and, turning to me), " Am I not correct ?"

I bowed an acquiescence, feeling not a little surprised.

" Miss Keith, Georgy Scott, my little sister."

The young lady thus introduced to me was very tall, very slight, with a pale, sweet-looking, very young face.

She acknowledged the introduction, and then said : " Miss Keith, I am so glad you are come ; but you are quite wet, let Simpson take your cloak and hat, and come with me by the dining-room fire," unfastening my cloak as she spoke.

The dining-room, the door of which opened into the hall, looked very inviting ; a large fire blazing brightly, chandelier from the ceiling, shedding its light on the scarlet table-cloth, on which stood lighted wax-candles beside an open book.

" I am sure Miss Keith would prefer going at once to her

own room; she must be very tired, and it is nearly midnight."

These words were spoken by a young lady, whose presence I had not before observed. She formed quite a contrast to the other; under the middle size, well-proportioned, with a beautiful face, a little faded; such an expressive, earnest eye. Robert's sister; no mistake about that.

She took my hand, with a quiet, kind air, and led me up the broad staircase.

As I passed along, I observed that everything wore an air of comfort; but there were no superfluities, no pictures in the halls or staircases—no niche, with flower-vase or sculpture, as at Haddo; carpets, chairs, one table in each hall. On the table in the lower hall lay a small silver salver, for letters; nothing more. I thought, as we passed upstairs, if the beautiful is thought of here, it must be confined to the rooms.

My conductor preceded me to the third storey, where, opening one of the four doors in the hall, we entered a good-sized room, redolent of the perfume of mignonette, comfort and warmth.

"This is your room—I hope you will find it comfortable," said the young lady as we entered. " Simpson will help you to undress, and will bring you anything you may fancy. I would advise some sago or oatmeal gruel; either will most likely help to prevent your catching cold from your wet clothes."

I thanked her warmly, and bidding me good night, she left me to Simpson's care, whose nimble fingers soon divested me of my wet clothes. Bringing me my promised gruel, and a huge jug of hot water, that I might bathe my feet, she left me with a respectful good night. I had now leisure to examine my future domicile.

The first thing to be noticed was the bright, clear fire in a clean, well-brushed grate, and white hearth, shining brass fender and fire-irons; a large easy-chair, covered with white dimity, and drawn in front of the fire, to the left of which was placed a small round-table, on which stood a lighted wax-candle; a dark-coloured wardrobe, the drawers and doors of which were open, disclosing linings of newspaper, with lavender leaves scattered thereon; a small-sized bedstead with snow-white quilt and curtains; a toilet-table, also in white, with a larger mirror than had ever fallen to my share before; a new dark carpet, and, more delightful than all, a china bowl on the toilet containing a wealth of fresh wall-flower blossom.

What a nice room! what kind people! how different from the half-carpeted, cheerless apartment that generally falls to the lot of the governess, and which Mrs. Moodie warned me, with motherly kindness, I had to expect! how different from my own forebodings! "Surely the lines have fallen unto me in pleasant places;" "Thou hast dealt well with thy servant, O Lord, according to thy word."

I knelt by my little bed and thanked my Heavenly Father for all his loving-kindness towards me, and prayed for grace to walk in his ways and keep his charge all my life long.

CHAPTER V.

On awaking next morning, I found that my room had an eastern exposure, and the bright, morning sun was streaming through the window in rich golden radiance. The reflection of his beams had just reached the outer edge of a picture of the cup found in Benjamin's sack, which hung above the mantelshelf. I looked at my watch, so that next morning I might know the hour by my sun-dial.

It was six o'clock, the hour we all rose at Mrs. Moodie's. I thought of them all there, of dear Willie, who would be so lonely without me, until I was startled by feeling a large tear dropping on my pillow.

"This will never do," I mentally exclaimed, "how ungrateful I am," and jumping out of bed, I raised the window sash, so as to admit the fresh air, and there another pleasant surprise awaited me ; a green box fitted into the window-sill, outside, full of mignonette in full blossom, filling the air with its fragrance. This was but a little thing, but it made me ashamed of the discontented spirit I had indulged in a few minutes before.

It is these little things which make the sum of human happiness. " Whoso is wise will ponder these things, and they will understand the loving kindness of the Lord."

I had been dressed nearly two hours, had arranged part of my clothes in the drawers, and written a letter to Willie, when Simpson tapped at the door of my room, asking leave to enter. She stared at me.

" Oh! Miss, what made you rise so early ? I suppose you did not know what o'clock it was: it is only eight o'clock."

I pointed to my watch, which lay on the table ; it was my mothers, and she had hung it round my neck some weeks before her death, bidding me keep it for her until she was well again.

The watch diverted the current of the girl's thoughts.

" O ! Miss, what a beautiful watch and chain ! was it very dear ?"

" I don't know," replied I.

" It was given you as a present ?"

I nodded : she saw I was not inclined to be communicative, and stopped short.

" I have brought you a jug of hot water, but you have already washed. Miss Hariote desired me say breakfast is at nine ; and Miss Georgina will come to bring you to the breakfast parlour."

With nine o'clock came Miss Georgina, looking so pretty in her white morning dress. After bidding me good morning, she asked if I had slept well ? if my room was comfortable ? and hoped I had not taken cold ? all these questions were asked in a tone of interest, and augured well for my future happiness while in the house, from the spirit of kindness they evinced.

On going down stairs we turned to the left and entered a charming breakfast parlour at the back of the dining-room.

The family had already taken their seats at the breakfast-table. Miss Georgina, taking my hand, led me to a seat near her mother, introducing me with the easy air which betokens good breeding.

" Miss Keith—Mamma, Papa, my eldest sister, Miss Scott."

Mrs. and Miss Scott bade me a courteous good morning; while the companion of my voyage, Mr. Robert Scott, politely inquired whether I felt quite well after the soaking of the previous evening.

Mr. Scott stared but did not speak; did not even move his head in acknowledgment of the introduction. We sat at breakfast about half an hour, and during that time there were not three needless words spoken: "Do you prefer tea or coffee? do you take rolls or toast?" nothing more; not the least attempt at conversation; not a single remark of any kind.

While we were at breakfast, I had ample time to examine the room and its inmates. The room was rather large, the furniture dark green, the curtains, carpet, sofa, and chairs all a deep dark green: very pretty. Four large landscapes painted in oil; one placed above the mantelpiece, a woodland scene of great beauty, representing the stillness of nature at early dawn, the only living object being a stag that had come to drink from a stream, which, with mossy rocks and underwood, formed the foreground; an immense picture of Indian life in the woods, with all the gorgeous colouring of autumn, hung opposite, and completely covered the space above the sideboard. The two others were hung on the wall to which my back was turned. The other side of the room consisted almost entirely of folding doors, which opened into a conservatory. The doors were wide open, and the fragrance and beauty of the bright blossoms gave the parlour the air of a little paradise.

Mrs. Scott was a middle-sized elderly woman, certainly more than fifty years of age; very plain, eyes of the palest blue, grey skin very much wrinkled, dark brown hair mixed with grey, her face betokening discontent and fretfulness.

Miss Scott was a large stout looking woman, fat white face, a little marked by small pox, with a lymphatic expression, and the pale eyes of her mother, in whose sight, I afterwards found, she was the beauty of the family. Mr. Scott's face must once have been handsome; a square forehead and deeply seated keen brown eyes; a well formed mouth and nose, beautiful teeth, even and white; very gray hair. His three younger children had their beauty from him, but his must have been lost long ago, from the indulgence of bad temper, which was the characteristic expression of his face; his figure was large and heavy. He looked a hale old man beyond sixty years of age. Mr. Scott and his son had each a newspaper which they perused diligently during the whole meal: breakfast seemed to be quite a secondary consideration with them, it consisted of only tea and toast, and that taken in mouthfuls, at intervals, which seemed to mark the pauses in their reading.

Mrs. Scott was equally busy with some crochet work. Miss Hariote had a huge volumn to which she devoted almost her whole attention, eating sparingly. Miss Scott did the honours of the table, and I fancied enjoyed her breakfast as a sensible woman ought to do. Mr. Scott did not sit at table as people usually do at meals: he sat with his side to the table, with one arm laid from the elbow downwards on the cloth, both hands engaged in holding the newspaper; when he had finished eating, or rather drinking his tea (I do not think I ever saw him eat at breakfast), he folded his newspaper, laid it on the table, took off his spectacles, and put them on the newspaper; he then crossed his legs and hummed the Scotch air " Gin a body meet a body," beating time with his fingers on the table. In a few minutes he got up, lifted his spectacles and went into the conservatory, where he seemed to be examining several of the flowers with interest: from one of these he culled a tiny blossom, and as he walked from the room he said to his son, in passing, holding up the flower:

"See, Artty, I have been stealing one of your favourites."

His son looked up smilingly in his father's face with such an amiable expression—such a sunny smile—no wonder Miss Syme's eyes flashed with pleasure yesterday.

Mr. Scott spoke and walked with the look and air of a gentleman, notwithstanding his being dressed in a flaming red dressing-gown, which I have found to be a very trying article of costume even to a younger man.

Almost immediately upon her husband's departure from the room, Mrs. Scott stopped her crochet work, measured it on her finger, and laying it down, asked me if I thought I should like to live there?—a curious question, truly, to ask of one who had not as yet spent an hour of day life in their society; I, however, had no hesitation in answering in the affirmative; they all seemed pleasant people with the exception of the father, and with him I would have nothing to do. Besides, he might be very different from what he seemed—so many are.

"Dear mamma, how can you ask such a question?" said Miss Hariote, looking up from her book with a petulant, mortified air. "Miss Keith has not heard any one in the house speak a dozen words—how is it possible she should know whether she will like to live with us or not?"

"Georgy," said she, turning to her sister, "you had better not commence your studies to-day; Miss Keith must be very tired, and needs rest; besides, this is Saturday, and is always a holiday." Addressing herself to me:

"Miss Keith, are you fond of flowers; would you like to look through our little conservatory?"

"I love all lovely things: I will have much pleasure in paying a visit to the flowers—they seem so beautiful."

My pupil and I went into the conservatory. What a gem of a place, and without anything very rare or expensive ; soft, beautiful mosses and light wavy ferns forming a foreground of green and brown, in all shades ; next, wallflowers, the darker kinds of stock gillyflower, pansies and carnations, while above were several tiers of roses and camelias, in the greatest profusion; on either side hundreds of geraniums and salvias dazzling the eye by their scarlet and crimson-velvet beauty. Close to the parlour door were vines, planted on each side, and trained so as to meet over-head, and thus form a shade with their broad leaves and incipient clusters of fruits, grateful to the mosses and ferns which grew beneath, and love not the fierce blaze of the noon-day sun.

Unlike all other conservatories I had seen, there were here broad walks, quite six feet wide, in which were placed rustic seats, formed of the long, gnarled roots of forest trees ; and here, among the ferns and mosses, Georgy and I used to sit, with our French books, for hours, during those happy summer and autumn days I spent there : they were white days in my life then, and will be for evermore.

Quite at the other end, and just opposite the door opening into the grounds, was an artificial rock, formed of blocks of grey Aberdeen granite, clear Derbyshire spar, several large pieces of finely-veined marble from Portsoy, and red granite from Inverness-shire.

These were held together by earth sufficient to feed abundance of wild flowers; the digitalis, with its fairy bells, which are supposed to ring when the fairies hold their midnight revels; the blue and white hyacinth, lots of primroses, yellow and white, rose-tipt gowans, queen's clover and king's clover, with their tiny golden and brown blossoms ; the white convolvolus, clinging with earnest love to every sprig and spray within her reach, the flaunting scarlet poppy, and the little, blue-eyed veronica, so dear to us all by its old home name of forget-me-not. In the middle, and quite hid by the clustering wildflowers, was a jet not more than six inches in height, from whence sprung a shower of light, misty rain, falling on the rocks and flowers in a thousand living diamonds.

While I was admiring the varied colours of stone and flowers so skilfully heaped together, I picked a little spray of blue-bell, and asked my companion if she could tell me what family it belonged to ?

" You know botany, I am sure," said she inquiringly.

" But I am sure of no such thing," was my reply ; " you don't expect me to know everything ?"

" I am so glad you don't. I shall teach you all I know of it if you like ; it is such a pleasant study, and makes every step we take in the fields interesting to us."

Stooping down, she drew from the ground a little plant of blue-bell, carefully preserving the roots, then passing into the garden—if so it might be called—washed it in a little rill that ran among the grasses at our feet ;—putting the flower on her handkerchief, she skillfully divided its various parts, and beginning at the root, she passed on from stem to calix, petals, pistil and stamen, explaining everything in a more lucid manner than I have heard those do who pretended to lecture on the subject.

Was this the girl I had come to teach ? I mentally hoped she did not know French and Spanish equally well.

Outside the conservatory, and within a few yards of it, was an immense bowling-green ; such mossy green sward our feet pressed at every step; and beyond this, a broad belt of forest trees, skirting the bottom and both sides of the ground belonging to the house.

At eleven o'clock Simpson came to call Miss Georgina to take her music lesson; so, as I had not entered on my duties, I went to my own room, finished my English letter to Mrs. Moodie, and wrote in French to Willie. French was the language of our childhood and early youth, and after our removal to Scotland we always spoke to each other in French when alone. It would not have seemed natural for me to write to Willie in English.

At two o'clock I met the ladies of the family at lunch, which was laid out in the breakfast parlour, on two trays, each covered with a cloth pure as snow.

One tray contained two rather large-sized silver salvers, with a glass dish placed on each. In one of these were a pile of thinly-cut slices of bread and butter; in the other, water-cresses.

The other tray was occupied by small-sized china plates, on each of which were placed table-napkins and silver-handled knives, finely-cut glasses, and water in a white jug of Parian china, each side of which represented a scene from the mythology of ancient Greece in alto-relievo, cut so deeply as almost to stand out from the jug.

This, with little variation, formed our mid-day meal during the time I spent at Iona villa. Sometimes we had a plate of fruit in place of the cresses, always served in the same punctilious manner.

The old lady was chatty, asked me all she could think of regarding my voyage, and then, encouraged by the sound of her own voice, questioned me on my own affairs and my family; where my father and mother lived? what was my father's profession? how the expense of my education was defrayed, &c.; notwithstanding Miss Hariote's repeated expostulation of:

"Dear mamma, such questions must be painful to Miss Keith."

No matter, on the mamma went; another question, equally pertinent.

"My dearest mother, you do not think of what you are saying: we are such entire strangers to Miss Keith, this conversation cannot be pleasant."

She then turned to her younger sister, and said hastily, (I suspect to prevent a rejoinder from the mamma), "Georgy, if you have finished lunch, we will go out at once, as Robert has left a parcel with me to be taken to Mrs. MacIntosh's, and it is a long way to the village." Addressing herself to me—

"Would you like to go with us, Miss Keith?"

"Very much;" so away we went.

I found Miss Hariote very pleasant, very intelligent— she seemed to know everything, and I nothing. After trying in vain to draw me into conversation on the merits of books I had never seen or even heard of, she asked me, I fancy in despair: "What is your favorite style of reading, Miss Keith?"

I told her my time for the last eight years had been chiefly spent in learning languages, which I had again taught to others, my English reading having been entirely confined to the works of biography, history, &c., taught in Mrs. Moodie's school — I had also read a very few books on natural science, and that my nearest approach to light reading were the biographies written by Miss Strickland, Prescott, and a few others—that until yesterday, I had never seen a novel.

"What! you have never read a novel; never read Sir Walter Scott's novels?"

"No. I knew Sir Walter Scott as the historian of Napoleon, Swift, Dryden, and others, but as a novelist, no."

"You have a rich field of enjoyment before you," said she: "I almost wish I had never seen his novels, just that I might have the pleasure before me of reading them again. How did it happen that you never saw a novel?"

"Mrs. Moodie did not approve of young people reading works of fiction, and never permitted such books to be in the house."

"I dare say; I know that among Protestants those who are considered pious people look upon novel-reading as nearly allied to the sin against the Holy Ghost. I simply pity such people. There are novels written by Kingsley, Warren, Miss Muloch, and many others, which are calculated to do more good than all the sermons in the land; for this reason, that they are read by those who will not read sermons, nor indeed any religious books professing only to teach us our duty, or elucidate difficult points of doctrine or Scripture: no one can read Kingsley's Alton Locke, or Yeast, without every better feeling of his nature being aroused to sympathise with the poor and oppressed, whose cause he advocates so well. I hope Mrs. Moodie, in her zeal for the future well-being of her pupils, did not exclude poetry from her bookshelves?"

"On the contrary, she had a well-filled library of the works of the best British and American poets, and encouraged us in such reading both by precept and example."

"I am glad to hear you say so," was her reply; "a love of poetry is seldom acquired in after-life, and there is no feeling of our nature the indulgence of which is more calculated to refine and elevate the soul."

The utility of novel-reading was an entirely new doctrine to me. Mrs. Moodie and Miss Forester had both denounced novel reading, not simply as a waste of the time which our accountability as immortal beings renders it of the first importance we should employ to the best advantage, but as a style of reading decidedly demoralizing, and which would undoubtedly, if indulged in, leave its evil impress on our after-life. Mrs. Moodie and her elder governess had gained my entire confidence, because they had never, by word or look, forfeited my respect. The precepts they taught were well enforced by the example they gave. Few are such good judges of the characters of those they live among as children. In the presence of persons of our own age and station we are careful neither to say or do what will leave a bad impression, while no one would take the trouble to seem other than they really are to children or domestics. The day-scholars had frequently told us of the delights of novel-reading, and favoured us with specimens of the works they perused. These often consisted of love scenes, which either excited our ridicule or disgust; so that we had no temptation to break the rule imposed on us in this respect. I began to read John Halifax because I had no other resource from *ennui*, and I have read other works by the some authoress since, and have found in all good moral lessons—not one objectionable word or thought in any.

In due time we arrived at Mrs. MacIntosh's cottage, and were ushered into a room on the ground-floor, where we found her surrounded by some thirty pupils. Mrs. MacIntosh and her eldest daughter, Mary Ann, came forward and received us very graciously. Mrs. MacIntosh was the village school-mistress—a little, subdued-looking woman, wearing under her wig and white cap a pair of spectacles, which I found, when speaking, she always raised to her forehead.

Her daughter was fat and short, her plain face being set off by a quantity of beautiful black hair, which she made the most of, disposing of it in plaits and braids round her head and low forehead. She had small black eyes, which every now and then she lifted to the ceiling while addressing Miss Hariote, to whom she devoted most of her attention.

Mary Ann bustled about very obsequiously, placing chairs for us, and doing the agreeable to the utmost of her power.

Miss Hariote insisted that Mrs. MacIntosh would resume her duties, leaving us to the care of Mary Ann, expressing at the same time, her surprise at seeing her teaching on Saturday.

Lowering her voice almost to a whisper, and moving a little way from her pupils, so that they might not hear what she said, she shook her head very solemnly, and, I thought, sadly saying :

"You see, ma'am, there's always trouble of some kind; no such thing as rest in this weary world. The school was never in a better state : thirty-five scholars, and all paying their quarter pence quite regular, except the two you know of. Well, I take the most of it out in bread. Well, ma'am, just a month ago, Monday last, an old maid from Edinburgh, who can't speak good English herself, let alone learning others to read, and the grammar; and you know, ma'am, it takes experience to learn grammar. Well, as I was saying, she comes and hires a room opposite the door and puts up a board, and commences keeping school. Well, ma'am, this wasn't enough, but see how bold people will be; she goes right round to all the parents and tells them that she would teach for a shilling less in the quarter, and give the Saturday afternoons.

"Well, ma'am, some of the parents sent me word, that if I would not give the Saturday afternoons, they would send the children to Miss Wylie's, so you see, ma'am, I had to give in. The children is very troublesome at home, and it is very handy for the parents to have them here after dinner, when the passage and stairs is scouring; for you see you may shut the room door and keep them out, but you can't keep them out of the stairs.

"It makes our scouring late enough;" and she sighed as she turned to her pupils.

She spoke a few words in a low key; I fancied reproving them for various little pushes of each other, and half expressed laughs we were conscious of while she was talking to Miss Hariote, and then raising her voice a little, so that they might all hear, she said:

"Now any one who speaks or laughs, remember your corrections on Monday!"

Miss Mary Ann took up her mother's discourse just where she left off.

"Miss Wylie keeps up the blinds of the windows all Sabbath day; mother never lets ours be lifted, so it was only when we was going to church, we saw the sign: she put it up on Saturday night late. She is a very mean woman. She went to Mrs. Frazer, the merchant's wife, and asked for Maggie and Sarah to go to her school, but Mrs. Frazer is a very nice woman, and she wouldn't let them leave mother. Miss Wylie is a Methodist, and so is the Frazers, and the Methodists is very clannish, and stick together, and so Miss Wylie thought, for that, she would get Maggie and Sarah to her school; but she didn't."

Miss Hariote asked: "Has Miss Wylie got any scholars?"

"Oh yes, ma'am, she has; and she keeps them in very bad order. She had eight at first, and she got the two MacAndrews, last Monday: so that makes ten. They used to come to us, but it was very troublesome to get their quarter pence, and some-times they never paid at all: so mother did not care much when they went."

" It must be very unpleasant having her so near," said Miss Hariote.

" Oh! we don't like it at all; because her scholars are so unruly, but we can't help it. When they come out, it's just like a ragged school. Our scholars always sing a hymn be-fore they leave; but her's are let out sharp at four, like a lot of sheep, and they used to come close to the window, and screech and make a noise, and sing to mock our scholars; till, at last, mother was forced to go out and tell them that she would send the police after them."

" What did they say to that ?" inquired Miss Hariote.

" They had the daring assurance to call mother names."

The look of pious indignation with which the girl gave ut-terance to the appalling fact of the children, " calling mother names," so overset Miss Georgina's gravity, that she laughed outright.

Mary Ann got up and went to the window, smiling, as she did so.

" You are laughing at her sign-board ; mother was just the same, when she first saw it. She said if she could'nt pay for getting a better sign-board, she would write one for herself."

This remark seemed a relief to Miss Hariote, who was evidently annoyed by her sister's inconsiderate laughter.

Miss Hariote having given the parcel we brought, and delivered her message, we were about to depart when four o'clock struck. The girls stood up in two rows at one end of the room, while the boys, who were all children under eight years of age, ranged themselves on each side of the mistress, as they called Mrs. MacIntosh. Mary Ann whispered, " they are just

going to sing their hymn." The hymn they sung was one I ha[
never heard before, the simple words of which, to me, were ful
of beauty : the air sweet and plaintive. Several of the childre[
had rich, clear voices ; one girl sung clear and strong abov
every one else, and her voice was rich and sweet. I foun[
afterwards that the sweet singer was a daughter of th
mistress.

Mrs. MacIntosh led the singing, and did so with an earnes
devotion, which had its due effect on her young charges. Ther
is nothing so impressive or attractive as truth, and the ton
and air of solemn truthfulness which this woman's voice an
look expressed while praising God for his mercies, seemed t
pervade, with a holy influence, every one of those youn
children who joined in her song.

I felt a respect for this woman then, which every succec[
ing interview increased ; it needed no more than the tone of he
voice and the solemn yet joyful expression of her face, [
tell that she had found the " Pearl of great price," and w[
resting with firm faith on His promise, who hath said : " Ther
remaineth a rest for the people of God."

On our way home we naturally talked of the scene we ha
just witnessed.

" She is a good woman, and has endured many bitter trials,
Miss Hariote observed, " and the new school is, I fear, goin
to be another ; and one not very easily dealt with. Mr
Frazer, of whom she spoke, and several others have fancied, f[
some time back, that Mrs. MacIntosh's mode of teaching w[
too old-fashioned for the aspiring views of their young ladie
The village is not sufficiently large to support two, and if M[
Wylie can teach, I fear the days of Mrs. MacIntosh's scho
are numbered.

" Then she has kept school for a long time in the village ?

" Yes, all her life ; her mother, Mrs. Gibb, taught ' the young idea how to shoot,' when Mrs. MacIntosh was a girl, and she assisted her mother then as Mary Ann does now ; my brothers learnt their alphabet of her, and we all feel a deep interest in her welfare."

" She is a widow, I suppose ?"

" No, I wish she were; her husband is an idle, good-for-nothing fellow, who goes about pretending to be, what she really is, religious. He distributes tracts and holds meetings within a circuit of fifty miles, ostensibly for religious purposes, but in reality to induce the poor country people, who look upon him as a kind of saint, to feed him on the best they possibly can, with the addition of a dram, at least, after every meal. He also receives contributions for different religious purposes, which all find their way into his own pocket, and are useful for buying drams, and occasionally dinners, when they cannot be easily had otherwise. His clothes he buys in the village, and his poor wife's furniture has more than once been seized to pay such debts. When he is asked who provides for his wife and family, he invariably replies " Providence," and this has earned for him the cognomen of " Providence," by which he is better known than his own name.

Dinner was served at six o'clock, in the dining-room, of which I had a peep the night before, in passing through the hall. The side-board was loaded with plate ; on the table an epergne, corner, and side dishes of silver ; fine damask table-cloth and napkins; china dinner service ; everything perfect in its way. The dinner consisted of soup, roast mutton, and four kinds of vegetables; no pudding, no dessert; but in their place, bread and cheese, served on silver salvers. The dinner was always equally simple, unless (rare occurrence), we had company, then everything was in abundance.

The dinner passed almost as silently as the breakfast had done. Mr. Robert made some remarks about the weather, asked if his sisters had been out, and was answered by a simple affirmative.

Mr. Scott asked his son one question about a law-suit in which the latter was engaged; I have forgotten the question; the answer was, " No, it will not." The cheese was removed, and spirits of three different kinds put on the table ; sugar and hot water; the latter in a silver jug with a lid. Almost immediately Mrs. Scott rose, the young ladies and I followed, and Mr. Robert opening the door, bowed us out, with as courtly an air as if he was an earl; and we countesses in our own right. We went into the breakfast parlour, where tea was laid, and a bright fire diffusing warmth and cheerfulness. Miss Scott took from the drawer of a small table, in one of the windows, a piece of muslin embroidery, in which the pattern was formed by making holes ; and sitting down on one side the fire, devoted herself assiduously to this most popular of all lady-like employments.

Mrs. Scott drew her crotchet from her pocket, and seated herself in her large easy chair by the fire, opposite her eldest daughter.

Miss Hariote took from the side-table the book she occupied herself with in the morning; sat by the table, put both her elbows thereon, and resting her bent head between her up-raised hands, she neither spoke nor moved, except to turn the pages of her book, until eight o'clock. Georgy lifted the four pillows from the sofa, placed them on the hearth rug, and sitting down among them, Turkish fashion, related to her mamma, in the most comic manner, interspersed with comments of her own, all we had seen and heard in our walk and visit to the village school; mimicking to the life

Mary Ann s upturned eyes, and look of pious horror, while she told of the " daring assurance " of Miss Wylie's scholars in calling " mother names."

Mrs. Scott and her eldest daughter seemed to be much amused, and encouraged Georgy in this rather questionable use of her satirical talents.

" Oh ! mamma, if you had only seen the little dumpy thing, with her eyes searching in the ceiling for the stars, so that you could scarcely see anything but the white, and her toes absolutely turned in with religion, you would have died laughing; but," continued she, " it is rather dangerous laughing there. I incurred Mrs. MacIntosh's wrath long ago by laughing at one of her speeches, and she has never looked on me with a favourable eye since."

" How did that happen, Georgy ?" asked her mamma.

" I went there one afternoon, to bring Harry home : there was to be a donkey race that evening; and just before dismissing the scholars, she stood up and said, with one of her most solemn faces :—" I hear there is to be a donkey race to night; the races is a black place, and many a black man will be there ; and if you go there, my dear children, remember your corrections to-morrow."

She repeated this speech of Mrs. MacIntosh's with such a ridiculously sanctimonious air, that one could scarcely help laughing: her mother and sister certainly did not attempt to restrain their mirth.

Miss Hariote got up from the table, shut her book and laid it aside, saying, as she rang the bell for Simpson, to bring tea : " Papa has not gone out yet, and if he hears this noise you will not require to wait until to-morrow for your ' corrections,' Georgy."

Simpson entered with tea-urn and tea-pot, and Miss Hariotc busied herself infusing tea, desiring Simpson to tell Mr. Robert we waited for him. I had observed when we left the dining-room, that instead of going back to the table, he had immediately ascended the staircase, so that Mr. Scott must have been enjoying his toddy alone. As we sat down to tea the outer door opened and shut with a loud slam.

What a pleasant tea drinking we had. It seemed as if to make up for the way in which he lagged at dinner, old time had put on his swiftest wings. Mr. Robert had something pleasant to say to every one. He had in his visit to Aberdeenshire (from which he was returning when we met, so opportunely for me, on board the steam vessel), gone to see Braemar and Balmoral; and while at the latter place, had heard many interesting anecdotes of the Queen and the Royal family in their intercourse with the peasantry; these he told with such a quaint humour, and gave such vivid descriptions of the wild scenery at Braemar, that he seemed at one moment to transport us to the interior of some shepherd's hut, while in another, we were wandering among the craggy rocks, and listening to the wild tones of the bagpipe, as it sounded the pibroch of some old chieftain through the wild caves and glens of Braemar.

Georgy, whose sense of the beautiful in nature seemed to be quite as vivid as her sense of the ridiculous, sat with her eyes wide open, looking into her brother's face all the while as if she were drinking in every word he said, and was only reminded that she had neither tasted tea or bread and butter, by the servant coming to remove them at nine o'clock.

This used to be the time for retiring to rest at Ellenkirk; at Iona Villa it was evidently quite early.

Mr. Robert asked his sister Hariote some questions relative to her music, and then proposed that she should play for us : for this purpose we adjourned to the drawing-room, which we entered by the door on the left side of the hall.

Here everything was, as in the rest of the house, handsome, in good taste and in good order. The room ran along the whole side of the house, occupying the same space on the left as the breakfast and dining-room did on the right. It was divided by folding-doors in the middle : the first half, furnished in deep crimson, the other in rose-colour. We walked at once into the inner room, where the piano was placed—a grand square in a very plain rose-wood case.

Mr. Robert opened the instrument, ran his fingers over a few of the notes, and then, turning to the canterbury, asked Miss Hariote what music he would give her ?

" What you please," was her reply.

He put some sheets of music on the stand. Miss Hariote looked at the title page.

" Rossini, what made you choose that ? I have not played a note of his music for a year."

She touched a few chords in the same key as the music before her, and then playing softly, and rather slowly at first, increased in rapidity, with a firm light touch, until at last the music seemed to flash from beneath her fingers, with a brilliancy I had then never heard equalled. I have since heard much good music, but in no instance have I known a nonprofessional pianist, who excelled Miss Hariote Scott. She continued for upwards of an hour at the piano, playing the most difficult arrangements of Schubert's lovely airs of the " Earl King," and " Serenade." Spindler's " Spinlied," &c., the last so rapidly, yet every note clear, distinct, and strong as a silver bell. I had never heard music until then.

" And now to finish," said to Mr. Robert : " If you are not tired, we will have something from Mendelssohn—his Wedding March, will it be ?"

" No, you recollect the evening Ellen Syme astonished us all by playing it so well. I told you it would take three months' practice before I would venture to play it again."

" Oh! how stupid," her brother exclaimed ; " I quite forgot to tell you the Symes have come home ; I should not have forgotten such an important event. I found them on board the steam vessel when I embarked at Aberdeen."

As he said these words he stooped over the canterbury, arranging the sheets of music ; I fancied that his face might not belie his words. " Oh! fie, Mr. Robert, you have not increased the respect I had for you," and with such a truthful-looking lip and brow.

Georgy got up from the sofa, where she had been for the last half hour indulging in some day-dream, with eyes steadily fixed on the face of 'Rembrandt's Peasant Boy;' a highly finished copy of which hung in the room.

" Oh! Artty," exclaimed she, " how could you be so silly ? I should have liked so much to have gone to see them this afternoon."

Miss Hariote rejoined in calmer tones,

" Dear Robert, it was very careless; I am sure they expected us every hour ; we must go early on Monday, and give you all the blame."

" Aye, do. I shall contrive some how to make my peace with the young ladies."

"Has Ellen quite recovered ?"

" Yes, quite well again."

" And is she as beautiful as ever ?" asked Georgy.

I think so."

And he turned to the piano, evidently to get rid of being again questioned; and shutting it down, said playfully :

" You remember, girls, I keep Sunday, and a little bit of Saturday.

CHAPTER VI.

My first Sabbath among strangers, the first Sabbath I could remember without seeing Willie at least a part of the day. I could not see him now, that was true, but I could pray for him, pray that our Heavenly Father would set a hedge round his path, and keep him from the snare of the scoffer.

I had ever since my mother's death felt as if I was a sort of little mother to Willie, and I had entered on the battle of life, with more alacrity and good will, because the money I was to earn would materially assist in defraying the expense of his professional education, the burden of which our uncle had long ago warned him must fall on himself. For some years back he had received a small salary from Mr. Rexford, which would be increased after he had been a session at college, and so with economy, our united savings would suffice for the object we had in view. Our parting would not be for a very long time; a few years would soon pass away, and then Willie would know his profession and we would have a little house of our own, ever such a little mite of a thing, no matter how small : I could have a few pupils; and we would be so happy.

I was sitting at the open window with its sweet box of mignonnette, Mamma's bible open in my lap, dreaming all this over and over, when Simpson entered to say breakfast was ready. " Why, my watch tells me it is only eight o'clock." " Breakfast is always served at eight on Sunday morning." The same solemn meal as yesterday : just the same, except that Mr. Robert had a book instead of a newspaper; Mr. Scott had two papers folded on the table, besides the one he read from; perfect silence, which, after the first cup of coffee had been served, I ventured to break by asking Mrs. Scott whose ministry she attended.

"I and my daughters go to the chapel in————" said she, with all the stiffness and dignity the little woman seemed able to assume; why, was to me a mystery. A low "hem" from Mr. Scott attracted my notice to where he sat; he was looking full in his wife's face, with such an expression of drollery, his eyes twinkling with mirth. What could they mean?

I was wondering who was the officiating clergyman in the chapel she had named, not having courage sufficient again to break the silence, when Miss Hariote addressing me said:

"All of the family who go to church, except Robert, attend a Catholic place of worship; this is the reason we breakfast at eight-o'clock on Sunday morning, as mass begins at a quarter after nine. Mamma," added she, looking at her watch, "we had better go."

I got up from table along with the ladies, feeling rather uncomfortable about the way in which I was to spend my Sabbath; when just as we were leaving the room, Mr. Robert coming up to his mother, said: If Miss Keith will come to Free St. John's to-day with me, we can make an arrangement by next Sunday for her going to any church she pleases.

I accepted his offer with thankfulness, and promising to be ready at ten o'clock, the time he appointed, I sought my own room with a gladdened spirit.

I knew that Dr. Guthrie officiated in Free St. John's. Miss Forrester was a hearer of his during the four years she spent in Edinburgh previous to her residence in Mrs. Moodie's, and she spoke of him with love and respect. I recollected her saying that, during all those four years, she had never heard him preach a sermon which she had entirely forgotten; in every one there was something which, as she expressed it, she would " remember for ever and aye."

At ten o'clock the omnibus stopped at the door; we entered, and in due time descended therefrom within a few yards of Free St. John's. Dr. Guthrie did not preach, and the clergyman who officiated in his place, said nothing that struck me particularly then, or which I can at all remember now; but the subject he chose was the twenty-third psalm; one in which David expresses his strong trust, and tells of the goodness of the Lord.

> "The Lord is my shepherd, I shall not want.
> " He maketh me to lie down in green pastures.
> " He leadeth me beside the still waters."

And well might I join in his song with the sweet singer of Israel. He had also given me to lie down in " the green pastures, and by the still waters." That psalm did me good then, and it does now.

After service, my companion whispered that he always spent the interval between morning and evening worship with a friend, but that he would meet me again in church in the afternoon and see me home. I bowed my thanks, and in a moment more he was in the aisle talking to the Misses Syme.

The young ladies were accompanied by an elderly lady and gentleman, both of whom greeted Mr. Robert with great warmth. He walked down the aisle with the young lady who received so much of his attention on Friday. The aisle was crowded and they walked slowly. She was certainly very beautiful, her hair fair and shining, fell in long curls under her hat, the pale blue feather of which, falling behind her ear, contrasted well with her fair and clear complexion ; her mouth was well formed, her eyes blue and dreamy ; and then she listened with such a composedly happy air to all he said. A very pleasant friend, Mr. Robert, to spend the interval with.

I sat quietly in my seat until most of the congregation had retired, and then I left the church and walked slowly down one side of the street and up the other twice, so that I had a long walk before going into church again ; and no fear of losing my way.

Instead of returning by the omnibus, we, at my request, walked home. The afternoon was lovely, and my companion able to entertain a more fastidious listener than I.

We had the same silent dinner as yesterday, and went through exactly the same forms, only I observed that when Mr. Robert opened the door for us after dinner, he took his hat and gloves from the hall table and went out.

Immediately on going into the parlour, Miss Georgy piled her cushions on the hearth rug, lay down and went to sleep ; her mother and Miss Scott adjusted themselves in their easy chairs for the same laudable purpose, Miss Hariote took the book she read from the previous evening and sat exactly in the same position.

I rose from the sofa where I was seated, and saying to Miss Hariote I would spend an hour or two in my own room, and Simpson might call me when tea was ready, was on the point of leaving the parlour, when Mrs. Scott called me to her, and asked in a low voice :

" Where did Robert go between sermons ? did you see him speaking to any one ?"

" Mr. Robert left the church immediately after the blessing

was pronounced, and I remained until almost every one else had gone. I did not see him again until the afternoon, when he joined me in church. When service was over, we walked home alone."

While I spoke, Miss Hariote looked up from her book, listened attentively, and then, without speaking, resumed her former position.

In my own room I sat reading for some time, until the daylight changed to gloaming, which again, in its turn, was gradually fading into night. I felt very tired. I had no candle, and did not care to encounter the amount of trouble needed to procure one; and so, listening to the suggestions of laziness, I went to bed, and lay in a dreamy state, looking at the grey sky, through the uncurtained window, watching each bright star as the darkness brought them out one by one; and wondering, as each child of Adam has done for nearly six thousand years, if those great jewels of the sky contain beings, each having a heart filled with hopes and fears like our own.

I had been in bed for some time when Simpson entered.

"You are in the dark, Miss," exclaimed she; "I am so sorry I forgot to set your candle."

"No matter, Simpson, I have been in bed for an hour."

"And you have had no tea. I will bring up some for you. They always drink tea at nine o'clock on Sundays to accommodate Mr. Robert; he teaches Sabbath-school in Mrs. MacIntosh's, and it does n't come out till nine."

"Thank you, Simpson, but you must not bring me anything to eat. I never eat after going to bed, and I do not feel at all hungry."

The girl lingered in the room, remarked that the night was dark, and then that the moon would not rise until midnight.

She felt that I was lonely and a stranger, and would fain have done me a kindness if she knew how.

Next morning, after breakfast, I proposed to Miss Georgy that we should now begin our lessons.

"Very well," said the young lady, not more than half pleased, "we can go to the schoolroom; but I do not know where my books are, and I am sure the school room wants dusting; I have never entered it since Miss Watson left three months ago." .

She led the way to the second flat, and entered the room above the inner drawing-room, looking to the back. "Wants dusting." No indeed, everything in the same order and neatness as pervaded the whole house. The window was open, and the air came in balmy and pleasant through the fragrant leaves and light wavy branches of an immense birch and larch tree, both growing so close to the house, that their branches almost touched the window, on the outside sill of which was placed a large bird cage, fully three feet high, and long enough to fill the window, which was made like a French window to open in the middle, the cage being supported outside by a broad shelf fitted into the sill; and there sported in great glee two sweet little canary birds.

A window-seat covered with pale green filled the recess, while at each side were placed an oleander growing in a large green box, each box and flower so much alike, they seemed to be twins. The plants were taller than my pupil, and absolutely crimson and pink, with their fragrant blossoms.

"If you have not been here for three months, some one else has," said I, going up to the window, to inhale the sweet fresh air.

"Yes, Hariote has put her birds here," was the reply. The furniture was very plain, but everything that was

needed ; a large bookcase almost filled the bottom of the
room, and contained more books than I knew the names of ;
to these books I owe more gratitude for the instruction they
gave me, than to any living man or woman; a sofa, two
tables, some chairs, and a pair of globes, the best I had ever
seen ; on the walls were hung clear well-defined maps of the
four quarters of the globe, and several of the principal countries of Europe.

Notwithstanding Miss Georgy's fears, the books were found
at once ; the two she had been accustomed to use were Œsop's
fables in French, and Ollendorff's Easy Method. She had
no Spanish or Italian books, both of which languages I was
expected to teach her in conjunction with French.

I requested my pupil to give me a specimen of her reading
in French.

She read a fable with a broad Saxon accent, and *mal* pronunciation, such as no child of twelve years old in Mrs. Moodie's school would have done. I was rather pleased with the
deficiency ; she was evidently very clever. I knew from experience my own power of imparting information. I would
teach her, I had no fear of that. Oh that some one would
lend us a child just beginning to speak, for two years ! then
both would acquire a good accent ; but even as it was, I had
no fear of her being able to translate and read without *mal*-
pronunciation ; but as to teaching this young lady three languages simultaneously, oh no ! that was simply impossible in
the present state of things. When I agreed to do so, I was
under the impression that she knew French well.

I explained this to herself to her entire satisfaction ; it was
evidently a task, now it was come to the point, she did not
like at all.

F

"Pray, Miss Georgina, go and ask your mamma if I may see her for a few minutes."

Off she went, and almost immediately returned with her mamma; the latter, crotchet in hand, seated herself on the sofa, and commenced her work.

I began by explaining my pupil's deficiency in French, as delicately as possible. She interrupted me almost at once.

"You must explain all this, Miss Keith, to Hariote and Robert; it is a craze of theirs that the child should learn those languages; *I* cannot see what use she is to make of them; *I* never learnt either, and never felt the want of them; but as to her French, you must permit me to say she reads *well*. I myself have heard her read twice a week since her last governess left her."

"But you know, mamma, Miss Watson said I pronounced badly, and that I had a horrid accent," said Georgy, deprecatingly.

"I differed from Miss Watson in that, as in most other things," said her mother, as she swept out of the room with what she intended to be an air of great dignity.

I must have looked what I felt, very much perplexed.

"Shall I go for Hattie?" asked Georgy, with a look and tone as if the pity she before entertained for herself was now transferred to me.

"Pray do," said I, scarcely knowing what to expect, but feeling certain of one thing, that if Miss Hariote's appreciation of language was equal to her mother's, there was but one line of conduct left for me to pursue, and that was at once to resign my situation. It would take twelve months' hard study entirely devoted to French, before my pupil could have advanced far enough to be in a position, with regard to her knowledge of that language, to warrant her in commencing one other, far less two ; and as to beginning both at present, what nonsense ! how could they be so foolish ? If I could be capable of going on as was proposed, and receiving money for instructions which I knew were useless, I would be virtually picking their pockets. A common thief would be less guilty. It would be nothing less than a course of deceit persevered in from day to day. No! And I went in spirit back to the picture gallery at Haddo, and looked in the face of my great-grandmother, and I heard her spirit say, " Do it not, though by so doing you should gain a kingly crown." No ! If I must go, where is it to be ? and how am I to go ? I had exactly twelve shillings in the world : how far would that bring me ? how long would it buy food ? These were serious questions, and made me shiver. Where was I to find another situation, and among such people, so kind, so considerate. I might never find such another. Even so, at all risks, no !

I had plenty of time to think over all this, and fully to make up my mind, half an hour having elapsed before Georgy returned accompanied by Miss Hariote.

" I hope you will excuse me, Miss Keith. When Georgy came to call me, I was surrounded by six or eight of Robert's Sunday School scholars ; it is more a ragged school than anything else. He has occasionally to provide shoes, hats and frocks, and I am his almoner; so this must plead my apology." Saying this she sat down as if she was prepared to give me her entire attention.

I explained to her candidly how matters stood, and that, under existing circumstances, it would be impossible for me to fulfil my original engagement. I spoke for at least ten minutes, and explained as simply as I could the difference be-tween the languages and the degree of mental effort required for the acquisition of each. She heard me patiently to the end, and then said :

"Miss Keith, we are quite sure of your ability to teach what you agreed to do, and we are also certain of your integrity. Father Forbes, whose knowledge of your acquirements and character extends over a period of eight years, and to whose kindness we are indebted for procuring your services, has perfectly satisfied us on these points ; and I can speak for Robert as well as myself, when I say that we are willing to do in this matter as you think best. Three years hence we intend going to the continent for some time, part of which will be spent in Spain and Italy, and we are anxious that Georgy should at least be able to make herself understood while there. Pursue the plan you think best for the end in view."

What a relief! While I spoke, and during her reply, my cheek burned and my heart beat with various emotions, the predominate of which was fear lest her reply would have been the very opposite of what it was.

" So standeth the Lord round about his people."

I had been six weeks at Iona Villa ; every week-day seemed the sister of the day before, and every Sabbath the brother of the preceding. Georgy was getting on with her French famously, better than I had anticipated. Instead of the half-lazy manner in which she used to ascend the staircase to the school-room at ten o'clock, she now went up with a light springy step; and one day, when finishing her lesson, she said " I will know French well in a year." How happy it made me to hear her say so ! Another proof of her progress —Mr. Robert generally came home at five o'clock, and occasionally spent a few minutes in the schoolroom, where Miss Hariote always sat in the afternoon, before six. He always talked French, which he spoke well. At first she could not understand a word that was said; latterly she could tell the subject of conversation, and even repeat whole sentences, translating them into English.

One evening the Misses Syme were at tea; Miss Ellen was singing the little ballad of ",Pescator del onda," which she did with great pathos and beauty. Mr. Robert was standing close behind her chair, and regardless of the vicinity of Georgy, who he fancied could not understand what he said, spoke a few words in French, which tinged her cheek with the same rose tint I had once before seen it wear.

Next day Georgy said, " did you see Ellen Syme blush last night when Robert spoke to her in French after she sung ' Pescator ?' "

" Yes, I observed she did."

" I'll tell you what he said; I understood it all."

" No, you certainly must not; it was not intended for your ears or mine; and therefore you are bound in honour not to repeat it. Your brother most likely would not have said what he did, if he thought you understood French well enough to comprehend his meaning."

" I know he would not; but I knew their secret long ago, although they do not think so."

" Well, Georgy, you must keep their secret, whatever it is; it is always the sign of a well regulated mind, when we cannot only keep our own secrets but those of others."

A few days after this conversation, just as we sat down to our lessons in the morning, a most unwonted clatter of feet on the staircase made us both look up. Georgy's eyes sparkled, and turning her head a little to one side, she seemed all eyes and ears; we were not long in suspense, in a moment the door opened with quite a noise, and a handsome boy of thirteen or fourteen years of age burst into the room, accompanied by a large Newfoundland dog.

"Oh! Harry. Oh! Don," burst in the same breath from Georgy's lips.

The last named gentleman put both his forepaws and great curly head on Georgy's lap, leaving the impression of the former in mud on her light coloured dress.

"Oh! Donny, you pet, you darling, you bad boy, why did you stay away so long? How did you get a holiday, Harry? where did you find Don?"

All this seemed to come from her lips at once.

"Uncle brought him into town three days ago, and desired me to send him to Artty's office, but I knew we were to have a holiday to-day, so I kept him to bring myself. There's always some good thing happening, so one of Gibson's youngsters kicked the bucket, and to-day is his funeral; so we have a holiday. Maitland lives next door to Gibson's house, and he says it's the small pox, and the other youngster is sick, so perhaps we'll have another holiday next week.

"Come, George," continued he, "you must ask Miss what's-her-name to give you a holiday too. Come, hurry up your cakes; I can't wait," and he took hold of her arm as he spoke.

"May I go, Miss Keith?" asked Georgy.

It was a hopeless case, she must go of course, and off they went, and Don with them. What a mess the floor was in; the dog must have passed through all the puddles between this and the high school of Edinburgh.

A few minutes after they left the room, Simpson entered armed with brush and pail, scrubbing cloth, &c., her face crimson with anger.

"I never saw such a boy as that Master Harry is. I wish he was in Greenland; it's always the same, he never comes home that he doesn't make a mess of dirt from top to bottom of the house ; and that abominable dog come home again. I never saw such a house ; between boys and dogs, no two hands could keep it clean ; but they can just look out for some one else, I would'nt stay another year for double wages."

She delivered all this in rather a loud key, while endeavouring to erase the marks of the dog's feet from the carpet, and was interrupted by Mr. Harry entering in a great hurry, to possess himself of a large ball of cord, which he took from one of the drawers of the table, that went by the name of Harry's drawer, and in which all his precious things were stowed away.

He turned round on seeing Simpson, whom he did not observe on entering.

" What a nice chap, that mason of yours is, Simpson," said he. I saw him to-day at a new house they are building near the Calton Hill, and he's coming down here to-night after six with a lot of pieces of brown and white marble he's been keeping for me.

Simpson's face changed in a moment, it seemed as if the sun shone out in the darkness of night.

" I am sure he's not my mason, Master Harry."

" What a wopper ! did'nt I see you walking with him on two Sunday afternoons, when you got leave to come up to church to Edinburgh."

" It could'nt have been me, Master Harry."

" Get out. Perhaps it was'nt you that was speaking to him at Watt's door, the day you brought my clean clothes, and I asked him to keep the marble for me."

Simpson laughed and blushed as she gathered up her implements of labour, saying :—" Oh ! Master Harry, you are so funny. I declare the house has no life in it, when you are not at home."

Harry seemed pleased, so was Simpson; she evidently would not leave her place this time. After lunch, Georgy came up to the schoolroom, and throwing herself on the sofa declared she was too tired to go out again.

"What lazy things girls are," exclaimed Harry impatiently, "they are always tired or something else. You are tired for nothing, and I walked down from Edinburgh, and I'm not tired."

And he walked from the room rather slowly and sulkily. In ten minutes he was back again, calling out :—"George, George, come and see this ; get a paper, hurry up."

Georgy seemed to know what was coming ; she sprung up from the sofa, and put a newspaper on the table, which was immediately filled with mud, water and worms taken from the young gentleman's pocket. Georgy put her pocket handkerchief on the table, lifted the paper with its contents into it, and both hurried from the room. What they were to do with the worms I could not then even guess.

The table-cloth was quite wet and rather dirty, and I was obliged very reluctantly to call Simpson to repair the mischief. To my surprise she took off the cloth saying good humouredly :—" Is'nt Master Harry stirring ?"

What a change since the morning !

Towards five o'clock both Georgy and Harry came in ; one lay on the sofa, the other on the window seat, completely tired out. Miss Hariote having given up the window seat, which was considered her property, for Master Harry's accommodation.

By and bye Mr. Robert joined us.

" What, Harry, you here ?"

" Got a holiday ;" replied he laconically.

Mr. Robert opened a flat japanned box he carried in his hand and displayed a quantity of beautiful sea-weed.

" I was down at Leith to-day, and gathered these myself," said he, handing the box to Miss Hariote.

While we were admiring its contents, he inquired :—" How goes your Latin, Hall ?"

" Oh bother," was the reply.

And then sitting up on the seat, as if the idea had just struck him, he said :—" Did you gather that sea weed for Ellen Syme ? I saw you pass our house twice with her last week."

Mr. Robert bit his lip ; he will doubtless choose another direction for his walk in future.

" What o'clock is it, Hattie ?" Master Harry asked this question in a particularly ill-tempered tone of voice, and then turning to me without giving Miss Hariote time to answer him, said :—" You see, Miss Keith, I have no watch. Alec. Chalmers and Johnny Maitland, and lots more of the boys have watches. Artty has one locked up idle, but he won't give it to me, although it's of no use to himself."

" Artty had to work for his watch, and he thinks it best that you should do so too," said Miss Hariote ; and then looking at her watch, she added :—" It is half-past five. Why do you wish to know ?"

" I want to know how long it will be before pa comes."

" I thought so ; will you ask him to give you some money for me when you are getting your own ?" said his sister with a comic expression.

" 'Deed I won't," was Master Harry's reply, as he sat, his hands in his trowsers pockets, kicking his heels with vehemence against the window seat, and becoming perceptibly more irritable every five minutes ; presently a carriage stopped at the door, and he jumped from his seat calling out :

" Crikey, here's pa ;" and was gone from the room in a

moment; we heard him give a great shout of merry laughter
as he exclaimed,—" I knew it was you, pa!" and then Mr.
Scott's staid deliberate step on the staircase, accompanied by
Harry's noisy clatter of feet and tongue, laughing and talking
louder than ever I had heard in the house before, even in
Mr. Scott's absence, and in his most awful presence! The
noise accompanying his solemn self even into his sanctum
sanctorum, the door thereof left open, and Master Harry, his
hands in his coat pockets, performing in the door-way a dance
of joy, by dexterously hopping on each foot alternately, while
the other kicked the boot of the dancing foot. " 'Twas
strange, 'twas passing strange." Mr. Robert got up to shut
the door of the schoolroom which young hopeful had left open,
observing as he did so, " That is our Benjamin."

A very handsome Benjamin he looked, as he entered the
dining room with his father. His face had been carefully
washed, and his hair brushed from the perspiration and dust
it had acquired in the many labours of the day; his suit of
coarse grey cloth changed for one of invisible green, which
set off well his bright cheek and dark eye.

His father was evidently very proud of him; he behaved
well at table and talked little until the cloth was removed, but
that little made the dinner pass off very differently from the
usual way.

While the cheese was on the table, he gave his papa a description of various school feats, which the latter seemed to
enjoy, drawing the boy out now and then by a leading question,

" What did you all say, when you were told of the holiday?"

" We didn't say anything. Oh! Dido, you should have
heard the shout we gave; it made the old school ring."

After dinner he searched his father's pockets in order to

find a shilling, which he said he must have; his father evidently enjoying the boy's coaxing, told him he had no money ; nothing daunted, Harry continued his search until his industry was rewarded by half a crown.

Seven o'clock struck. " Oh, crikey," he exclaimed, " what'll I do ? Old Watts 'll be mad. You are going to town to-night, pa ?"

" No, my boy."

" Oh, yes, though ; Watts 'll be in a towering passion ; I should have been home at seven."

" I am tired ; Robert will go with you."

" No, I shan't have him, he's such a sulky fellow ; you must come, pa."

A great deal more of this ; at last Harry won the day ; it was decided the old man should go, and away they both went to the great distress of Georgy.

To comfort her, in parting, Harry whispered, " I am going to get a watch."

That evening Miss Hariote rung twice for tea before Simpson appeared ; when I went to my room I had no candle, fortunately there was a bright moon ; my bed was unfolded, and I had no water to wash with ; before Harry went away, I saw him intrust Georgy with his pieces of marble.

Perhaps the mason took tea with the young ladies in the kitchen.

CHAPTER VII.

In the beginning of July Harry came home for the holidays, two or three of which were occupied by him in turning Georgy's head, and making a noise, while Miss Hariote, the mainspring of the household, ordered new clothes, put buttons on his shirts, &c. After these arrangements were completed, Mr. Scott and he went for a tour through the Western Isles; what a relief! how he did, to use Simpson's expression, " turn the house up-side down;" yet it was not a relief to all the inmates of Iona Villa; his mamma declared Harry had brought life to the house, and taken it with him when he went, and Georgy cried for half a day after his departure.

We were to have an evening party; I fancy Mr. Scott's absence being considered an advantage, and so it was; on former occasions when we had company in the house, the members of his own family seemed to be afraid lest even a laugh should be heard.

On the afternoon of the day on which the company were to arrive, Mr. Robert came into the school room, with a newspaper full of flowers for his sisters to wear in their hair.

The conservatory was his own property, built and kept at his expense, and no one ever cut the flowers without his permission.

A lovely bunch of pink china roses for Georgy; dazzling scarlet geranium, with its round green and brown leaves, for Miss Hariote; crimson camelias for Miss Scott. He laid these on the table, each on a sheet of paper, telling me to whom they belonged. There still remained a quantity of rich starlike jasmine, so pure and white; these must be for his mother; how much better to have given them to Georgy!

He lifted up the sprays, and placing them lightly and gracefully together, came over to where I sat, and half-bending over my chair, he said: "will Miss Keith wear those flowers in her hair?"

"How beautiful, how very kind," I said, almost involuntarily.

The company consisted of the Misses Syme—we never had company without them—their brother, tall, handsome and gentlemanly; our neighbours Dr. and Mrs. Nelson, and six or eight others.

Tea was served in the outer drawing-room, from china which had been in the family for sixty years; Georgy looking very pretty with her pink roses and pale blue silk dress. Miss Hariote wore black velvet, with her geraniums placed quite at the back of her head. How handsome she looked! not tired and faded as she generally did, but bright and joyous; not so lovely as Ellen Syme, but far more intellectual looking. If I were a man I know which I would choose. When tea was over they all went into the conservatory, and hence to the bowling green and shrubbery. I remained in the conservatory; I well knew that the governess was nobody, and I felt happier sitting with my Aytoun's "Bothwell," (which Miss Syme had brought for me to read,) hid in the vine which was now full of broad leaves and purple fruit. The conservatory was so much higher than the grounds, that I could see over every part of it, and when tired of reading I amused myself by watching the others as they strolled in groups of two and three about the grounds.

Young Syme was doing the amiable to Georgy, making a wreath of daisies and doing his best to make her wear it, not that he cared for the raw young girl of sixteen, not he, but he was amused and would have been very pleased if she cared for him. I would have given something to put a stop to his nonsense; I knew how it would be; she certainly would not attend to her lessons for a week to come.

While I was watching Georgy and her beau with anything but good humour, Robert and Ellen Syme entered the conservatory; he led her to a seat, and taking a ring from his pocket, lifted her left hand and put it on her finger, and then raised the white hand to his lips—what a blush! it absolutely extended from shoulder to forehead; she must have expressed a wish for some water, as he took a tumbler from one of the flower shelves and went to the spring in the grounds to get it filled. When he was gone she took off the ring (how it sparkled,) and pressed it to her lips, looking so happy. So she might, she had drawn a prize in the matrimonial lottery.

Don came in through the breakfast parlour, snuffing about and searching for Georgy, whose particular property he was, straight through the conservatory he went, to the bowling green, where Georgy sat on the upper circle, her pretended swain at her feet; through the brook Don went, and then dripping wet as he was, bounded up to Georgy over her lover. Alas! for the dress-coat, white vest and spotless shirt, spotless no longer; Georgy shrieked with laughter, she had no command over herself.

"Oh! Don, you bad boy," said she, bending her head over the dog in a fit of uncontrollable laughter.

"O Donny, Donny, you must be whipt."

Her companion looked ferocious; she bent over the dog's head shaking with laughter. Mr. Syme said a few words and immediately left her, coming through the conservatory in a sadly bespattered condition.

" An accident has happened," said I, as he passed.

" Yes," he replied rather sharply, having evidently lost his temper, " if people keep such animals loose, they should not invite company to their houses. Will you have the goodness to bid good-bye to Mrs. Scott for me ?"

You did your mistress a good turn to-night, Don, and in return I will forgive you the next time you come into the school-room during lessons.

I joined Georgy in the bowling green, and told her Mr. Syme's message to her mamma.

She then told me the whole story, mimicking her *ci-devant* lover to the life, until she made me laugh as heartily as herself.

During the evening we had a great deal of music ; Mrs. Nelson played well, and so did her husband ; Miss Hariote also played more than plain well ; Ellen Syme was asked to sing.

"No," she said, "she could not, she was so tired, but she would rest and then sing after all the others." And so we had Meyerbeer, Thalberg, Gottschalk, Mendelssohn & Blumenthal, for nearly two hours, until every one felt at least a little tired ; each piece was beautiful, but we had too much of it. At last Ellen Syme went to the piano, put her fingers on the keys, but scarcely touched them, and sung in her best style, soft and low, the Scotch ballad " Wha's at my window, wha, wha ?" The effect was magical, there was perfect silence ; and before she finished every gentleman in the room was behind her chair.

One of the guests was a Mr. Erskine, whom I had never seen before at the house, although I recognised him as a gentleman who, several weeks previous, entered a shop in Edinburgh, where Miss Hariote and I were making purchases, and accompanied us in our walk home, almost to the door, much to my annoyance, as I was very tired, having, as part of my duty, accompanied Georgy in her constitutional walk of the morning, and then done quite a large amount of shopping. I anticipated riding home in the omnibus, but my companion, contrary to usage, decided otherwise, and I, as governess, had no voice in the matter.

I did not recognise him at first as the same person, he looked so different in dress to what he did in the shooting coat and grey unmentionables he wore when I first saw him. Perhaps I was in a bad humour from having to walk instead of ride home, but that day he did not, in my eyes, look much superior to Simpson's mason. He seemed very much at home; Robert and he called each other by their Christian names. I also heard him address Miss Scott and Georgy in the same manner, but he seemed to have no place in the old lady's good graces. He evidently wished to conciliate her and made several advances, which, however, she repelled with the affected pomposity which she chose occasionally to assume, and considered dignity.

After Ellen Syme had finished her Scotch song, she was besieged by the gentlemen to sing another, which she did at once with taste and sweetness.

Several of the gentlemen seated themselves near the piano. Mr. Erskine took possession of the corner of a sofa beside Miss Hariote, who was amusing herself with a solitaire board; close by his elbow was a little table, on which stood a vase of flowers and a chess board; these I was endeavouring to occupy myself with by placing and replacing the men. Mr. Erskine was certainly not attending to the music, although

he was one of the most earnest in asking for the song ; he
kept talking to Miss Hariote in a low voice all the while, and
just as Miss Ellen was enjoying her second triumph of loudly
expressed praise, he took from the vase a single pansy (popularly called heart's ease) and putting it on her hand rather
than in it, said, in the same low tone, but so clear I could not
help hearing :

" Hattie, will you give me this ?"

She answered not, by word or look, but her dark eye-lash
lay for a moment on her cheek, and her lips quivered. I
knew, I knew.

And so great, tall, broad Mr. Erskine, with his large
hands, large feet, and high cheek bones, was Miss Hariote's
lover ; well, there is no accounting for taste, but then why
was she not Mrs. Erskine ? He was not a man with empty
pockets ; oh no, not the least look of that ; then what can
be the meaning of this ? It seems a mystery.

It is said, " there is a skeleton in every house," and I
used to think Mr. Scott's bad temper was the skeleton in
ours, but no, it is not that which makes Miss Hariote's face,
now so bright and radiant, in general tired and faded.
Neither is it Mr. Erskine's religion that is the bar to their
union. I heard Miss Hariote say she would marry the man
she loved, whether he were Protestant or Catholic.

Some days afterwards Miss Hariote left the book she was
reading in the schoolroom, and Georgy, in moving it from
the table, let it fall, when from its pages dropped a pressed
pansy. I lifted the book from the floor, and in doing so
observed that it was a Protestant Bible, and presented to her
by J. E.

The party was on Friday ; on Saturday afternoon Miss
Hariote proposed to Georgy and I that we should accompany

G

her to Mrs. MacIntosh's, where we had gone with her the first Saturday I spent at Iona Villa.

I was very pleased to go; Mrs. MacIntosh had impressed me very favourably the first time I saw her, and I was glad to renew the acquaintance. The path chosen was one which passed through the fields and beltings of wood a long way behind the houses; the afternoon was lovely, and as we passed a field of beans on our way, the soft west wind sent its fresh breeze in our faces laden with perfume from the fragrant blossom ; the birds sang a song of praise on every hedge and tree, and even Don, staid and grave as he generally was, seemed to have imbibed some of the sprightliness and joy which pervaded all nature. Sometimes a rabbit would cross our path, when he would immediately run after it, frightening the poor little thing almost to death ; but it was only a bit of doggish fun. Back he would come bounding to his mistress' feet, to walk quietly by her side until the next rabbit made his appearance.

Mrs. MacIntosh was engaged with her school when we entered ; everything exactly as we left it the last time we were there, three months before ; every boy and girl in the very same place they occupied then. We were placed in the same part of the room, on the same chairs. We might almost have fancied we had closed our eyes for half an hour, and dreamt the events which had taken place in the interval.

I was sorry to observe a few more lines of care in Mrs. MacIntosh's anxious-looking face. The hymn sung and the children dismissed, the mistress came herself to entertain us.

" I hope," said Miss Hariote, " you have not lost any more of your scholars ?"

" Not as yet, ma'am," was the reply, " but after the play I would not wonder if I did."

"You do not give long play; the high school boys have had theirs for a fortnight back."

"I dare say, ma'am, that's very good for quality children, but the parents here would put up with no such thing. I never give but eight days, and Mary Ann and me was considering if it would not be better to give no play this year."

"Why not? You seem quite worn out, and it will be a great relief for you to have a rest for even a week."

"That's very true, ma'am, but you see, Miss Wylie has sent her niece to learn music more than a week ago, and she is to be back before Christmas, to teach it in the school. So you see it won't do to trifle with the parents this year."

Miss Hariote seemed to be lost in thought.

"Would it not be possible," asked she, "to have Katie taught music? She would soon learn."

"Oh, Miss Scott, you don't know what you are speaking about!" and the poor woman smiled bitterly as she spoke; "there is no one teaches music here; and if there was, it costs a pound in the quarter to learn, and where would that come out of? and if she was learnt to-morrow, where is the piano to come from? They say the cheapest piano you can buy, to be anything like the thing, is ten pounds; and if every article we have in the world was made a roup of they would not draw ten pounds, no, nor eight. Oh, there is no use speaking about it."

It was very evident it had been talked over, and all the fors and againsts considered before our arrival.

There was a long pause, during which the poor woman leaned back in her chair, and put her left hand over her eyes, as if she communed with Him who is a very present help in every time of trouble.

She was the first to speak.

" This young lady goes to the Catholic church with your-selves, I suppose ?"

" No ; she goes to Free St. John's with Robert."

" Oh, I am glad of that."

Another long pause, and then she added :

" There's a great want of teachers in the Sabbath school— a hundred and sixty scholars last Sabbath, and only seven teachers, and not all very regular. Mr. Robert takes thirty himself. And you know no one can do justice to thirty ; and by rights he shouldn't teach at all, but just look over the other teachers."

No one answered. Another pause.

" I daresay the young lady would think it too far to come down this length to take a class ?"

The young lady now answered for herself.

" No, indeed, it is only a pleasant walk. I should like very much to have a class."

" Oh ! my ! Mr. Robert will be so glad ; it is well I thought of speaking."

It was well for me she did ; such listless, useless Sabbath evenings as I had passed since I came to Iona Villa. The Sabbath was only a day of rest there—not the Sabbath of the Lord, honorable, no holy convocation to the Lord there. I spent my Sunday evenings in my own room, reading my Bible ; but this would be very different—I would be doing something useful—I would be employing a small portion of my time in the Lord's vineyard. While I was talking to Mrs. MacIntosh about the hours the school assembled, and whether my class would consist of boys or girls, I found Georgy had left her seat, and upon looking round the room, I saw her at the further end, just behind Mrs. MacIntosh, her hat off and replaced by what was evidently Mrs. MacIn-

tosh's Sunday cap; one that I observed hung on a nail by
the window as we entered. There she sat, her hands crossed
on her lap, while mimicking to the life every uplifted eye
and shake of the head, which the poor woman, unconscious of
being an object of ridicule, was indulging in.

I looked what I really was, very much displeased, when in
a moment she threw up both her hands to the ceiling, sent
her eyes after them, squinting at the same time, and shaking
her body alternately backwards and forwards, or from side to
side. The effect was so irresistibly, ludicrous, that I was
obliged to withdraw my eyes lest I should laugh outright.

On Monday morning, before we commenced our lessons, I
spoke to her gravely and earnestly on the subject, pointing
out the evil effect indulging in such habits would have on
her own mind. She sat perfectly still all the time I was
speaking; and when I had finished, she took up a pencil and
amused herself by sketching on the cover of her French
exercise-book. When examining the exercises for correction,
I found there a pencilled head of Mrs. MacIntosh, with an
enormously exaggerated cap border placed on the body of a
little fat boy with short legs, his hands stuffed in a pair of
pockets nearly as large as himself! I fear my lecture had
not much effect.

That Monday morning was a white day to me. I received
letters from both Willie and Mrs. Moodie; that from the
latter enclosing one from Gertrude, the first I had received
since she left Scotland. She did not like Canada—she had
found no one, with the exception of her father, she cared to
be intimate with, and longed for the time when the regiment
would be ordered home.

Willie I heard from every week. His letter was just as
usual, full of hope, and gave me an account of all the little

chit-chat in Ellenkirk. Mrs. Moodie's, if not so dearly welcome as the others, was of more importance. She wished to
know if I was satisfied with my situation; if not, she would
give me ten pounds more than my present salary if I chose
to take Mr. Forbes' place in her establishment. Mr. Forbes,
she regretted to say, was to leave Scotland in November,
and he had recommended her to offer me the situation, in
case I was not happy in my present home.

My dear good teacher! how much I owed to his kindness, when my uncle became pale with rage at the proposal
that I should learn Spanish, and thereby increase his expense
a few pounds yearly, dear Mr. Forbes proposed that I should
receive my lessons for nothing. It was to him I owed my
present situation, and now, in case my present life was not a
happy one, I was through him again offered a home, where
my school-days passed so calmly by.

I wrote to Mrs. Moodie in reply, telling her how I was
placed. After I had been two months here, Mrs. Scott, or
rather, Miss Hariote, in her mother's name, had engaged me
for three years. Their kindness had been unvarying; from
the first moment I entered the house I never, in one instance,
was made to feel that I was the governess; so that my
leaving my present home was out of the question.

The latter part of Mrs. Moodie's letter gave me a little
trouble ; Willie and his cousin, the half-dwarfish heir of
Haddo, had a fierce quarrel some time before. Of course,
my uncle considered Willie entirely in fault. The consequence was, that the latter was formally turned out of the
house, and told that he never should enter it again. My
uncle's rage must have made him forget what was due to
himself, in his character as host, even although his guest
was a boy and a poor relative ; as, when sending him away,

he endeavoured to make Carlo, the Irish retriever, chase Willie from the grounds.

Fortunately Carlo and Willie were intimate friends; besides our visits to Haddo, Willie had many opportunities of seeing the dog. My uncle's man came into town three times a week for letters, papers, &c., which were left at Mr. Rexford's shop; on these occasions he was always accompanied by Carlo, who became a great favourite with Willie, and the sequel will shew that the affection was mutual.

When Willie heard my uncle setting the dog upon him he turned round and held out his hand, which the dog immediately licked, fawning on the boy. My uncle, seeing this, came to Willie, and with an oath, struck him a blow on the head, which almost stunned him. Carlo, a large, powerful animal, in a moment sprung upon my uncle, seized him by the throat and pulled him to the ground. Willie, although half-stunned by the blow, walked quietly away. Poor Carlo paid for his affection with his life.

CHAPTER VIII.

NEARLY three weeks after our last visit to Mrs. MacIntosh's, Miss Hariote offered to accompany Georgy and I in our afternoon walk, if we would agree to take the direction of the village ; her presence was always an agreeable addition, whether in the school room or in our rambles ; so we gladly assented.

Miss Hariote carried a large music book under her arm, and Georgy asked her if she was going to take lessons from Miss Wylie's niece ?

" No, indeed ; I am a more important person than you think ; I have been installed musical governess to Miss Katie MacIntosh for a fortnight back, and I am happy to say my pupil improves so rapidly, that I have seen fit to advance her a step ; hence my bringing this book."

" If you are to be good girls," continued she, archly glancing at Georgy, " perhaps I may allow you to hear her perform some day soon."

" I do not know," said I, " if Georgy and I can go to Mrs. MacIntosh's together for a long time to come. But where did you get the piano ?

" John Erskine gave it to Mrs. MacIntosh," said she, and her colour rose just a little as she said so. The Erskines lived here when he was a boy ; John was one of Mrs. MacIntosh's scholars when she was a girl not older than Mary Ann is now, and he feels a great interest in her welfare ; he gave the piano very willingly.

" What a horrid old maid you are, Miss Keith," said Georgy.

" I know it is because I made fun of Mrs. MacIntosh's cap that
you won't go there ; you should have heard how mamma and
Mary laughed on Saturday evening when I told them about
it.   Mamma says that you are just cut out for an old maid.''

" Then, Miss Keith, you and I will take up house together,"
said Miss Hariote. " I shall teach music, and you languages ;
and we will do it in no small way; we will commence in style
and make a fortune."

" So, you have decided on being an old maid, is this your
deliberate choice ? "

" I am not sure that it would be, were the choice in my own
power, but we are not allowed to shape our own destiny.   I
wonder whether we will be able to do so in the spirit land;
our non-ability to do so here, is surely part of the discipline
of life." I thought of what she said, but made no reply ; it was
an interesting subject.

" Here we are at Mrs. MacIntosh's," said Miss Hariote. " I
suppose this, to you, is Tom Tiddler's ground, where you
cannot enter, so good-bye."

Georgy was rather sulky on our way home; she liked to
visit the school ; besides the amusement of seeing the village
girls ply their tasks, and hearing Mrs. MacIntosh talk religion,
as she called it, she liked a little gossip with Mary Ann, more
so with Katie, which she had contrived to indulge in on our
former visits.

She walked very slowly and perfectly silent, quite an unusual mood for the young lady ; no matter, the day was lovely, the air was cool and pleasant, the birds as gay, and the
flowers, trees and grass as beautiful and green as ever. I had
plenty of company, and the lesson would do the damsel
good.

Our greatest troubles only endure for a time ; in the evening Georgy's star was in the ascendant. Harry returned from his tour, as noisy and boisterous as ever, and Mrs. Scott decided that, for the few days intervening before his return to school, Georgy should have holidays, not one lesson until the day after Harry's departure.

The Misses Syme came to pay a half hour visit that evening, accompanied by their brother. The young ladies were frequent visitors; they often walked down from Edinburgh in the fine summer evenings, and returned (always accompanied by Mr. Robert) ere the daylight left us.

They were general favourites; every one, from Mrs. Scott to Georgy, felt pleased when the Symes made their appearance, even Harry; it was very evident Ellen Syme had found out his soft side, as well as his brother's, although in a less ratio.

Young Syme proposed, as a pleasant way of passing one of Harry's remaining holidays, that on the morrow, we should hire donkeys at Portobello, ride down to Joppa, take lunch there, gipsy fashion, under the trees, and return in the evening.

Mr. Robert, who would of course have to bear the expense, seconded the motion, so in ten minutes, to the great delight of Georgy and Harry (I suspect also to the delight of older people,) it was fixed as the laws of the Medes and Persians. The Misses Syme had come in a light pony phaeton driven by their brother, so Mr. Robert had no excuse for seeing them home, and said to Miss Hariote after their departure, "that he was glad he had not to go with them, he felt so tired." How is it that people, who are otherwise perfectly truthful, think nothing of telling fibs on such occasions? And Miss Hariote too,—her reply was, " I dare say,"—she did not " dare say," she knew as well as he himself did, he would have liked very much to go home with Ellen Syme.

It was arranged that our party were to meet at Portobello at twelve o'clock precisely; it was now only ten; Georgy and Harry were amusing themselves in the belting of wood, which surrounded the house, and Miss Hariote and I were busy in the schoolroom making some white seam for Harry, which I had volunteered to help with.

While seated thus, everything in and around the house wrapt in such perfect quiet, that sitting at the open window, we could hear the rippling of the little brook, as it wound its way lazily along, past the bowling green to the conservatory; even a bee humming in the birch trees would attract our notice—when suddenly there arose such an uproar as I had never heard before, either there or anywhere else. It seemed like Bedlam let loose, slamming of doors, knocking about of furniture, stamping of feet, swearing the most appalling oaths, loud shouting, all mixed up in the most shocking and pandemonium like confusion. Just as the noise commenced, Miss Hariote became pale as death, let her work drop to the floor, and almost flew from the room, taking care, however, to shut the door in her retreat.

I could hear the dining room door burst open, then a loud crash as if a quantity of things piled against it had fallen in; afterwards the door shut with a loud slam. The noise then died gradually away; the loud talking, however, continued at intervals after the rest ceased.

What in the world could be the meaning of all this? Any where, under any circumstances, such an uproar would be most disreputable, but in an intensely respectable house like Mr. Scott's, a house where the master looked up in angry surprise if the servants jingled the plates noisily in carrying them from the dinner table. What could it mean?

Whatever it was, I was not to know; the house returned to

its old stillness, the brook made itself heard again, the wild bee sung her song undisturbed in the birch tree ; and the ticking of my watch, as it lay on the table, seemed to say ; " see, how time is hurrying on into eternity."

I should have liked to hear what that noise was. We sometimes have little temptations as well as great ones. I had one then. Half an hour after the noise ceased, Simpson came into the room, and busied herself in dusting the furniture ; she had evidently something she was very anxious to communicate, and at last began by asking :

" Did you hear the noise downstairs, Miss Keith ?"

" Oh ! Simpson," said I, looking at my watch ; " will you run out to the belting, and tell Georgy that it is past eleven o'clock, tell her to hurry, I fear we will be late."

About half past eleven, Georgy and I descended to the lower hall, where we were joined by Mr. Robert and Miss Hariote, who came from the breakfast parlour, the former looking very grave, the latter pale as death.

We found Harry walking up and down the path in front of the parterre in great impatience.

" I know we will be too late," said he ; " I should not wonder if all the donkeys were engaged," and a great deal more to the same purpose ; but when we arrived at Portobello, the donkeys were not engaged, but all waiting to be so. The Symes arrived on the ground almost at the same time. John Erskine was there too, looking so well ; he came forward, shook hands with Miss Hariote and Robert, talked and laughed for a few minutes, and then lifting Miss Hariote into the saddle, as if she were a baby, stalked off with her, both looking exactly like Joseph and the blessed Virgin, as they are exhibited to us in old Roman Catholic prints, only the Scotch Joseph had a coat and trowsers, instead of the flowing robes his eastern prototype wore.

Mr. Robert, of course, took charge of Miss Ellen Syme, Mrs. Nelson's brother of Miss Scott, and thus matched, away they all went. Dr. and Mrs. Nelson, Georgy and Harry, had been the first to leave the ground. So I found myself alone with young Syme.

He seemed to have some misunderstanding with the owner of the two remaining donkeys, and with true womanly curiosity, I walked towards them. As I came within hearing, young Syme said in a very angry tone.

" Do you know who I am ?"

" O aye," returned the man, " I ken vera well wha ye are : ye'er ane o' thae clerk lads frae Auld Reekie, wha come down here ilka ither whip, an hire donkeys an dinna pay for them.

" Oh ! stuff," said the offended lad, looking at the same time very silly ; " I am Mr. Syme, son of Alexander Syme, clerk of the Session Court."

The man had a tin jug, full of water, which he had just taken from one of the many boys by whom we were surrounded, and turning with mock respect to young Syme, his small eyes twinkling with a peculiarly comic expression, he said :

" Are ye though ?" and then lifting his bonnet with one hand, while with the other he raised the jug of water to his lips, he continued, " my service to ye, Maister Sim ; an I'll be obliged to ye to gane hame an tell ye'er mither nae to lat ye down here anither foreneen, wanten siller tae pay for ye'er ride : for my certie, gin ye hae na ony siller, ye'er lass or you either wonna ride the day."

Understanding how the matter lay, I took my purse from my pocket, and placed it in the lad's hand ; he took from it sufficient to pay for the use of the donkey until five o'clock ; and away we went after the others as fast as possible.

A happy day we all had. Mr. Erskine and Robert sent down the lunch from Little John's, and he took care we lacked nothing. Harry filled both his pockets with the good things, to the great amusement of Georgy and Ellen Syme. This done he was in great good humour, and displayed his watch to the admiring multitude; a very nice watch it was, a silver lever, with chain and key and seal.

"Where did you get it, Harry?" asked his brother.

"In Glasgow. Pa and me went through almost every shop in the town before I could get one I liked."

"And did you find it in the last shop you went to?"

"No, we had to go back to a shop we went to the first day: pa knew it was a good one, and wanted me to take it at once, but I would'nt, so we just tried every shop we could find, and at last we had to go back to that one after all. You should have heard some of the chaps," continued he, "how they tried to cram down pa's throat that their watches were the best ever was made. Pa just stood and heard all their lingo, and then said to me, 'well, Hal, will you have it?' I always said no; so out we went, and off to some other shop."

We had a great proof of Harry's good humour; he lent his precious watch to Georgy, as he said, just for an hour or two; the possession thereof was no sinecure, he was constantly cautioning her to be careful.

"George, take care, you will break the glass of my watch," and again, "George, if you go on in your rough way, you'll break the main spring of my watch." At last before half an hour had expired, it was demanded again.

"George, you must give me my watch, you'll be sure to break it, and pa 'll go mad at me for lending it to you."

At last Harry announced that it was nearly five o'clock, and each gathering the precious things collected in the course of the day, in the shape of wild flowers, shells, geological specimens, &c., we mounted our donkeys, and after delivering them to their respective owners, we were in due time dressing for dinner at Iona Villa.

CHAPTER IX.

It was late in October, the weather fine and dry, the trees were becoming almost bare, the flowers all gone, and the grass withered, but what of that ? it was a happy time for me.

And now the last week of October had come ; next Monday would be the first of November, and the weather was cold and raw, but what of that ? it was the happiest time of all the year for me.

The twenty-fifth of October, such a disagreeable morning ; fine drizzling rain ; damp and cold even in the house, and I had to go to Edinburgh ; perhaps every afternoon this week. I looked from the windows : what a lot of mud ! the path-way fully an inch deep, and the business which called me to Edinburgh was my own, so I must not think of spending six-pence a day riding up and down in the omnibus ; not I, I was not so foolish, I had plenty to do with my money, and my donkey ride to Joppa, in August, cost me five shillings, so I must save now, and what did I care for the muddy roads and streets, and the drizzling rain ? I was never so happy in all my life. Oh ! that it were one o'clock ! Georgy's music master came at one on Monday and Thursday, so I would have an hour longer in Edinburgh to-day ; an hour longer for my search and preparations. How long the time seemed ! would one o'clock never come ?

And what was the cause of all this happiness to the poor little governess, who in general had to seek for happiness in the light reflected from the joys of those around her ?

I had a letter yesterday from Willie, telling me he would be
n Edinburgh on Saturday, in order to commence his college
duties, in the beginning of November; he said he would
arrive by the railway, at five o'clock, would go to a hotel
until Monday, and then find himself some cheap lodging.

No, indeed, he would not go to a hotel, where he would
not be very comfortable at best, and where he would have
to spend so much useful money; I could find a lodging for
him, and I was sure Mrs. Scott would not object to my going
one or two afternoons to Edinburgh to make a search.

I wrote to him that I would be at the railway station when
the train came in on Saturday evening, and if possible would
hire a lodging for a week, and when he arrived, he could
decide whether it would suit him for the winter or not.

I despatched my letter, and before dinner told Miss Hariote
that I expected my brother, and would like to have one or two
afternoons to myself, that I might search for a home for him ;
did she think Mrs. Scott would have any objections ?

" Oh no," was her reply, " on the contrary, I think mamma
will be very glad to have an excuse for taking Georgy with
her while paying her autumn visits : I shall settle it all for
you."

And so she did, as she did everything else, with the greatest
kindness and consideration : I was to have every afternoon
this week, and the whole of Saturday for myself. I was con-
strained to say, as I did on a former occasion in this house :
" Surely the lines have fallen unto me in pleasant places."

How few governesses were placed as I was. Mrs. Nelson's
governess had three little girls under twelve years of age to
instruct in English, French, and Music, to which Georgy added
in giving a list of Miss Grant's duties " General Fascination."
Miss Grant was expected to superintend the toilet of the

H

young ladies ; not to assist them, but to see that it was properly accomplished ; take them to walk twice a day, and see them put to bed.   And she received thirty pounds while my salary was forty.   How would it be possible for Miss Grant to leave her charge every afternoon for a week ? and yet she was not worse off than most of our class who teach for twenty pounds ; and probably had never been asked to perform a single duty which was not specified in her engagement.

I was dressed in my thick boots, cloak, and felt hat, and proceeding downstairs to commence my travels, when I was met by Miss Hariotte on the stair-case.

" I was going to seek you," said she ; " there is a card which Robert gave me for you this morning ; it is the address of an old lady with whom a friend of his, who left town last week, lived.   Robert says he thinks your brother would be very comfortable there, and it may save you trouble in searching for a place."

I took the offered card with thanks, and read, written in a clear strong hand, ' Mrs. Livingston, No. 9, St. Bernard's Row.'—This was certainly a great relief.   I had been cogitating with myself all the morning, how I was to find a lodging, and after it was found, how I was to know whether it was a respectable house or not, and a great many more hows ; here they were all solved in a moment ; doubtless this was an intensely respectable house, or Mr. Robert's friend would not have lived there : the only doubt I had, was it not probable that the rooms would be too expensive for us to pay for ; I would see.

On my arrival in Edinburgh, I began to inquire my way ; and I think I must have entered at least six or seven shops for the purpose.   I always received the same answer.—' It is a long way off, go to the end or the middle (as the case might be,) of this street and then turn down to your left ; you had better ask your way again, it is a long way off;' and so it was, I was tired enough before I reached my haven of rest : however, there it was at last—St. Bernard's Row ; and here is No. 9.

I knocked, and the door was opened by a neat looking young girl of about sixteen years of age.

" Is Mrs. Livingston at home ?"

" Yes, ma'am ; walk in."

I was shewn into a nice clean parlour, with a bed-room attached, the door of which opened from the parlour. I saw at a glance everything was new and handsome ; although on a small scale, it was too good for us ; all my walking this day was for nothing, that was evident.

Mrs. Livingston entered, most surely the mother of the girl who opened the door.

"I came to ask if you have a parlour and bedroom to let."

" Yes, the one we are in, and that is the bed-room," and she moved her hand in the direction of the inner room as she spoke.

" What do you charge for it ?"

" For a gentleman, who is in an office and sees no company ; a pound a week, for a lady and gentleman, twenty-five shillings."

" The rooms I want," said I, " are for my brother, who is coming to attend college; I got your address from Mr. Robert Scott—he knew the last gentleman who lived here ; but these rooms are too expensive for us—I knew they were so, when I came in ; but I have walked almost from Portobello and am glad to sit down, otherwise I do not think I should have remained."

" You must be very tired after so long a walk ; do rest yourself as long as you like," was her reply.

" Do you know of any one else who has a small parlour and bed-room to let, not nearly so large as this, and plainer furniture ?"

" What price does your brother wish to give ?"

" I cannot tell; we do not know the price of lodgings—perhaps you could tell me,—we wish to get rooms as cheap as possible ; we do not care how plain they are, so that the house is respectable."

" Well, I know a place that I think will suit, provided you do not object to living in a land ?"

" Oh! not at all."

" Well, my husband's aunt has a nice little parlour in the third land, above Mr. Wilson's shop in the High Street; the bed-room is not very large, that is true—just a little mite of a place—but she is a very clean, decent woman, and keeps the Sabbath well, and that's a good example for a young man ; and it's cheap, only five shillings a week."   •

" That would be the very place for us," said I ; " are you sure it is to let ?"

" She was here at her tea on Sabbath night, and it was not let then, and I am sure she would like your brother ; it's mostly divinity students she has. You see they're mostly in straightened circumstances, and they like a cheap place, and they're quiet and she's quiet, so the one does wi' the ithir."

As she continued to speak, she unconsciously adopted the broad pronunciation, which was most familiar to her, and flowed most naturally from her lips.

" My brother is not a divinity student, but he is very quiet, and if the rooms are not let, I feel sure the old lady would like him."

I looked at my watch, it was four o'clock—I must be home before six—and I rose to go.

"You are very tired," said my hostess ; " it is a long way to walk; you had better take the omnibus—it will put ye down two or three doors frae my aunt's for threepence."

I was glad of the suggestion ; we went to the door, the omnibus was just passing. Good-bye! Good-bye! I was inside, and on my way to the High Street.

I asked the conductor to put me down as near Mr. Wilson's shop in the High Street as possible. The third land above Mr. Wilson's shop—that was all the address I had. In the hurry of getting into the omnibus I had forgotten to ask, and Mrs. Livingstone to give, any other; however, I would find her out—I knew the old lady was Mrs. Livingstone's husband's aunt.

I had not long to wait; by and bye the conductor signed to me to come forward, saying at same time, " Come awa, lassie, here's ye'er place—ye'er gaun to auld Mrs. Livingstone's, at bides aboon Wilson's shop, are nae ye ?"

I assented, and was set down, as Mrs. Livingstone styled it. I had learned the old lady's name from the speech of the conductor; she also was a Livingstone.

It seemed a long way up to the third land, which in plain English means a landing, ascended to by a common stair— each flat forming a separate dwelling, shut in by its own outer door. I knocked, and the door was opened by a clean-looking young girl, dressed in a white cotton jacket and black petticoat. This boded better for me than the smartly-dressed girl at the first Mrs. Livingstone's. " Does Mrs. Livingston live here ?"

" Yes, mem, come in."

I could not see very well where she meant me to go; the

little entrance hall had no other light than was afforded by fan-lights above the doors inside,—and the daylight was fast fading into night. She thought of this herself.

" Wait, mem, I'll get a candle."

She opened one of the doors from within, which issued a stream of light, and presently returned with a candle in a small, bright brass candlestick.

" Tak the leddy in here, Jean," said a voice inside, and I was ushered into the room in which the speaker was seated. She was an elderly woman, dressed in a black gown, and wearing a widow's cap.

" Sit down," said she, pointing to a chair at the opposite side of the fire to that she herself occupied, scrutinizing my face as she spoke with a keen searching glance from a cold blue eye, the expression of which was anything but flattering to my self-love. I daresay that I presented rather a strange appearance, wet and weary as I was; I sat down utterly tired out.

" What's ye'er wul," asked she, and the tone of her voice was as cold and repelling as the expression of her eye.

" Have you any rooms to let? your niece, Mrs. Livingstone, in St. Bernard's Row, directed me here.

" Aye, we hae twa; but we dinna tak leddys."

" It is for my brother I want the rooms."

" O weel, even so; I aye like ane o' the young ministers; we dinna tak a' body here."

I saw she was unfavourably impressed with me, and I thought I would try the strength of Mr. Robert's name, it was possible she might know him. I felt dispirited and sick at heart; I had ate nothing since morning, and felt weak and tired.

" Mr. Robert Scott, the advocate, who sits in Dr.

Guthrie's church, sent me to Mrs. Livingstone. My brother
is not a divinity student, but he is a quiet, good boy; he
has never been in Edinburgh before, and I am anxious to
obtain a home for him with some respectable people; but
we cannot afford to pay a high price."

" Aye, sae ye ken Maister Robert Scott," said she, relaxing a very little. " He's a vera decent gentleman—
he's ane o' our deacons; what way dae ye ken him?"

" I am governess to his youngest sister, and I sit in
Dr. Guthrie's church," replied I.

" Ye sit in St. John's kirk, do ye," and her voice and
face both softened visibly as she spoke; " are ye the young
leddy who sits in Maister Scott's pew and aye comes in
lang afore the rest i' the afternoon to read her bible?"

" I always go early to church in the afternoon," said I,
very thankful to see the turn things were taking.

"They're decent folk, thae Scotts, I reckon," observed
she, as if she were thinking aloud rather than speaking;
" he's a gude lad, Maister Robert; maybe ye wad like to
tak a look at the rooms? Jean, light anither candle."

The girl did as she was bid, and then preceded her mistress and I into a small parlour, one of the doors of which
opened into the room in which we sat.

The room we entered was like that we had just left,
scrupulously clean, a table in the middle, on which lay a
bible, at least a foot and a half long; another at the foot
of the room, on which were placed several large books in
good condition; and above these a set of deers' horns, six
chairs, a carpet reaching within a yard of the wall, a hearth-
rug made from a piece of the carpet, with a black fringe
round it, a brightly-brushed grate, fender, and fire-irons.
On the mantle-shelf were placed several china tea-cups, and

above hung an oil painting, so dark, that it seemed impossible to say what the painter meant to represent. Mrs. Livingstone took the candle from the girl's hand, and held it up to the picture, saying, as she did so, "That's my gude man."

Opening a door opposite that we entered by, she shewed me the bed-room; it was indeed what her niece said, a "little mite of a room," but neat and clean; a white counterpane on the bed; white curtains on the window; a chair, a little dressing table, a little basin stand, and a little looking glass.

"It's but a wee place," said she, as she held up the light that I might see it better, "but it just does well enough for a lad at the skulle, and he can pet his claes into the drawers ben in the room."

I had not observed that piece of furniture, but on leaving the bed-room, there it was at the side of the room to which my back was turned as I entered : above the chest of drawers stood a cupboard with glass door, well stocked with china and glass ware.

"The rooms are very nice," said I, as we again entered the family sitting room, with its bright fire and cleanly sanded floor, "and I am sure my brother will like them; what is the rent ?"

I used to get five shillings in the week ; but we wonna fight for the price ; it disna mak muckle for two or three bawbees up or doun. Wha's gane to pay the rent? is't the lad's father ?

"No ; his father is dead long ago ; but you will be sure of the rent, we will pay it between us ; if Willie likes the room we can give the rent in advance every week, and I will pay for the first week now, if you will let me have the room," said I, taking out my purse for the purpose.

"Pit ye'er siller in ye'er pouch, my bairn," said she with a grim smile ; " dinna be sae ready ge'en ye'er hard wan baw bees tae folk ye ken naething about."

" Ye'er aw weet," remarked she, taking hold of my cloak as she spoke, and evidently observing my dripping condition for the first time ; " tak aff ye'er weet claes and sit doun at the fire side, an tak a cup o tea; we was just gane to tak ours when ye cam in."

I looked at my watch, it was nearly six o'clock ; I could not be at home in time for dinner ; I was wet and weary, and felt very glad to accept her invitation.

Mrs. Livingstone took off my cloak and hat, giving them to the girl with instructions to hang them on a chair near the fire, placed a foot-stool inside the wide fender, and made me place my feet thereon.

This done, she busied herself for a few minutes in arranging the tea table—the tea I could see was already made, one side of the hob being occupied by the tea pot, the other by the tea kettle—she drew the table close to my side, seated herself opposite, and lifting the tea-pot from the hob placed it on a plate on the tray. Then placing her hands reverently together, she asked a blessing on the meal.

A very nice meal it was, nice black tea, white sugar, white fresh bread, honey, thin oaten cakes and fresh butter.

" You have given me a tea fit for a prince," said I, while I did ample justice to the good things set before me ; I had tasted nothing since breakfast, and I felt faint and hungry.

" Weel, its easy to gee a gude cup o tea, vera lettle will do that," replied she, pressing me to eat and seeming to feel a real pleasure in seeing me do so.

I felt a little ashamed of making such inroads into the oaten cake, and told her I had ate nothing since breakfast.

" Have a care o' us," said she, "and what for did ye no ?"

"I was anxious to find a home for my brother, and I did not know but it might take several days to find one."

" Na, weel then, that coo's aw; as gin there wasna twa lodgings for every lad at's tae pit in them," and she laughed heartily as she spoke.

" An whar does your mither bide ? I reckon your young brither is wi' her the noo."

" No, my mother is dead nearly nine years since. My brother is living with a Doctor in Ellenkirk, where I came from ; and it is to study medicine that he is coming to Edinburg."

She sat looking at the fire as if wrapt in thought, but made no reply.

When we, or rather I, had finished eating, the girl, at a sign from her mistress, came forward and stood by the table, while the latter returned thanks ; she then removed the tray to a table at the other end of the room, where she before had sat knitting, then rubbed up the table until it shone, and seating herself by the tray, commenced her supper.

I looked at my watch, it was after seven o'clock, I shewed it to my hostess, saying " it will be late before I get home."

" A weel, ye canna help it for ance : I'll pit on my shawl, and gang down to the omnibus we ye mysel'." I was selfish enough not to refuse her offered kindness ; the night was dark, and I doubted very much if I could find my way to the place from where the omnibus left for Portobello without some such help.

My cloak and hat were by this time quite dry, and the old lady insisted on putting a worsted scarf round my neck. Having dressed herself in a close black bonnet and shepherd-plaid shawl, we sallied forth, Mrs. Livingstone having first given strict injunctions to Jean, not to open the door to any one in her absence ; saying as she departed, " gaen ye do, ye'll maybe be murdered ; as the lassie in the cannogate was, last winter was a year." The girl did not look as if she was likely to open the door to any one.

My kind conductress waited until she saw me safe in the omnibus ; and said as she took my hand in parting " pit ye'er feet into het water whan ye gang to ye'er bed, my bairn," and the good will o' Him wha dwelt in the bush be about ye."

CHAPTER X.

As I alighted from the omnibus at the little iron gate, which divided Iona Villa from the highway, I felt a little uneasy about the lateness of the hour. Comparatively speaking, I was a stranger to those I lived among; this was the first time I had gone to Edinburgh alone, the first time indeed I had ever been out alone, even to the village, since I became an inmate of Iona Villa; and I did not know in what light these fastidious people might view my remaining among entire strangers to such a late hour; however, as Mrs. Livingstone philosophically observed, there was no help for it.

When ascending the broad steps in front of the door I could not help contrasting my feelings and situation then, with what they were seven months previous, when I first passed over the threshold. What a lonely being I felt myself then, uncertain of the people I was to meet, or those I was to live among; separated from the only living thing to whose love I could lay claim; and now had I not much cause for the fervent thank God which rose from my heart to my lips. In another moment I was in the lighted hall, the darkness and damp outside, the light and warmth within, exactly as it was on the night I first entered its precincts; strange too, as I glanced at the dining room, the door was open, the glass chandelier lit, scarlet cloth, candles, and open book on the table!

Almost before Simpson had time to shut the hall door as I entered, Miss Hariote and Georgy came to meet me from the little parlour.

" I am so glad you are come ; what kept you ? we were afraid you had lost your way, or some accident had happened," burst almost simultaneously from the lips of both.

" I shall tell you all, by and bye," said I, as Miss Hariote pressed my hand, and Georgy touched my cheek lightly with her lips, laughing as she did so.

" I have had so many adventures, I have lived a year since one o'clock," and seeing a shade of anxiety pass over Miss Hariote's face, I added, " and such a pleasant year too."

Simpson took my hat and cloak ; and Miss Hariote hurried me up-stairs, in the same kind way she had done the evening I first saw her.

There was my own room in all its comfort, the first fire of the season replacing the birch boughs I had left in the grate when I went out. The large white chair in front of the fire, the little round table with the candle, all as I had first seen them.

Miss Hariote and Georgy had both accompanied me to my room, and e'er five minutes had elapsed, I had exchanged my wet boots for a pair of thin slippers, and was seated in my large chair relating my adventures to an eagerly listening audience of two. I had just finished my story, when we heard the gate and then the hall door open, and Mr. Robert's voice making some inquiry of Simpson.

" Goodnight," said Miss Hariote, as they both rose to leave the room, " I must go to give Robert his tea. Go to bed as soon as possible and dream of old Mrs. Livingstone. As they left the room, the hall clock struck nine, I had never known Mr. Robert take his tea so late except on Sunday; he must have dined in town.

Simpson, with her usual kindness, brought me the hot water Mrs. Livingstone recommended, and which I would not

have thought of asking for myself, and told me, very gravely
" that they (the cook and herself) never thought to see me
again ; Edinburgh was such a dangerous place at night, and
Sandy Robinson had been down with pieces of marble for
Master Harry in the evening, and he said he was sure you
would never be heard or seen again, because the young doctors are all coming into the college next week, and there is
always a great lot of folk murdered the week before they
come in—they murder them to sell their bodies to the doctors
—and he told us there was a young leddy just about your age
murdered just this day last week in a house in the Gallowgate,
where some men was drinking, and two of the men was taken
up for it, and was in the Calton jail waitin' their trial."

Having delivered this long speech she sighed, whether for
the young lady, the men in the Calton jail, or myself, I was
not exactly sure, it is possible she did not know herself.

" Good-night, Simpson, thank you for all your kindness."

" Good-night, ma'am," and she shut the door, leaving me
to my meditations.

And very pleasant they were : with all its fatigue and little
annoyances, had it not been, as I said in the morning, a happy
day for me ?

In the first place, I had found a home for Willie, and such
a nice home too. I liked that old woman even already, although she was so grim and uncivil at first, and then it was
so cheap, only one pound a month, thirty shillings more would
buy his food; why, I could pay all that myself, and I was
sure with Willie's savings, we would have money to save after
paying college fees, and buying books and clothes.

Oh yes, no fear, he would get on nicely ; this was the first
step to our cottage home.

What a long time it seemed to be until Saturday—this was

only Tuesday night—Wednesday, Thursday, Friday, three long days—well, they will pass away,—I will go up to Edinburgh to-morrow, see the rooms again, and pay one week in advance ; perhaps too, I could make some little improvements, but I must have a care. I must not offend Mrs. Livingstone, who doubtless considers her arrangements as the very best which could be made ; no, I would not risk offending her, I would take care of that.

I had another cause for happiness, which I had not at all anticipated, the kiss Georgy gave me in the hall was a proof I had now at least a small corner in her heart. I had certainly sought her love by every lawful means, but she had been a spoiled child all her life ; if her faults were observed by Miss Hariote or Mr. Robert, they were taken not the slightest notice of ; I fancy under the popular failing, that as she grew older, she would correct them herself. In the opinion of the Mrs. and Miss Scott, the young lady was as near perfection as it was possible for a human being to be, and as to her father, he seemed never to interfere with either person or thing in the house, saving only his darling Harry, provided everything was kept still and in perfect order.

Georgy had naturally a fine mind, but it was full of weeds from over indulgence ; I had never shrunk from the disagreeable duty of pointing out her faults, and as far as I would be allowed, correcting them ; under these circumstances, I could hardly have expected to gain her love. There was surely much cause of thankfulness in this.

I had indulged my pleasant meditations so long, that it was now nearly eleven o'clock, and taking my bible I opened it at a chapter Willie and I used often to read together:

" In my father's house are many mansions, if it were not so I would have told you. I go to prepare a place for you. And if

I go to prepare a place for you, I will come again, and receive you unto myself; that where I am, there ye may be also."

I sat thinking of all the great promises which were contained in these few lines: not only a house not made with hands, eternal in the heavens, but also lest we should be weary, and faint by the way, when all was ready for our exception, he would come again, he himself to bring us home. "I will come again," —no ambiguity there,—the eternal promise,—his own words, —fast and sure,—though the hills be removed,—most surely he shall come again.

The fire had become hollow, and taking the poker, I broke the outer crust, and made the fresh coals above fall into the red fire; this made such a dazzling blaze, I was fain to shut my eyes for a few minutes, to escape from it. While I sat thus, I began thinking of Dr. Doddrige's wonderful dream, and presently, I was with him passing through the regions of space, treading on the blue and grey clouds, as if they were firm earth, swiftly onward and upward, away and away; I staid with him as he paused in his aerial ascent, over the great city of London, and I heard the words in which he prayed for grace and pardon to be given to that countless multitude passing to and fro beneath, in all their worldliness and folly. In a moment I was away, far away from the heavenly messenger, the blue sky, and light and air; I was lying in a deep dungeon, dug in the bowels of the earth, surrounded by thick darkness such as might be felt. I was confined there for some offence, of which I was quite guiltless; and it was darkness evermore; and days and months passed away, and I was still there, surrounded by that black darkness; only once in a long time a faint ray of light came from above, and a mysterious hand let down a pitcher of water and a morsel of bread. How earnestly I seized the pitcher and drank, that I might cool my lips, hot with fever in that cold damp dungeon, and after a long countless dark time, knowing nought of day and night; when my heart and flesh were failing me for fear, came one in the guise of an angel of light; but I knew he was an emissary of darkness, and he said " Curse God and die," but the hand that was ever under, about and around Dr. Doddrige, appeared to me there even amid the darkness, and I knew the evil one lied, and a sweet low voice whispered in mine ear, " I will come again." " Behold I come quickly, and my reward is with me," and the evil one looked in my face, and he saw no fear or faltering there, and he fled away, screaming, into the outer darkness.

I awoke to find myself stiff and cold, the fire out, and the candle flickering in the socket.

My watch was on the table and pointed to four o'clock; how my head ached and my lips burned! I drank a long draught of cold water, put out my candle and went to bed.

I tried in vain to sleep ; my feet and limbs were stiff with cold, while my head and hands burned as with fire ; how often in the weary tossing of that dark morning, I said, " would that it were light."

At last the daylight came, and with it Simpson, bringing with her my usual jug of hot water.

" Oh, Miss Keith," said she, " your cheeks are like fire."

" I dare say," replied I. " I feel as if I had taken cold, but when I rise I will feel better.

I arose and tried to dress, but I could not; the room swung with long sweeps, backwards and forwards ; beneath my feet my head reeled, and it was with difficulty I reached my bed again.

I lay there all that day and the next, scarcely conscious of anything, except the blessed coolness of the wet cloths,

I

which kind hands were every now and then putting on my head. On Wednesday night the fever left me, and I was then conscious of the care and attention which was bestowed upon me; everything which kindness could suggest.

An old servant who had married long ago, and was now a widow living in the village, where she and a grown up daughter kept a little shop, was sent for to nurse me well again; a better nurse never was, so quiet and gentle; no whispered gossip, that most annoying of all sounds to a sick ear, just enough of attention, everything that was needed and no more, no needless tormenting " well, how are you's," how often I said mentally, if ever I am sick again, I should like you, Mrs. Wilson, to nurse me.

After eight o'clock that evening, Georgy came into the room, smiled and kissed my forehead, and laying a daisy on my pillow, she noiselessly left the room again.

"Mony a gowan she brought you these twa days," said the nurse, " they are aw as muckle taen up about you as if you was their ain sister; Mr. Robert came twice yesterday, and twice the day, to the head of the stair, and signed to me to come and tell him how you was, and very glad he looked whan I tell't him the night at ye was better; and Miss Hariote—but there's nae use speaking about her, she was aye gude, gude tae aw body, gentle and simple.

On Thursday I awoke, feeling so well that I wished to get up, but my kind nurse made me lie still until after breakfast; I then rose and sent for Georgy to give her a lesson; she came at my request, but would " have no lesson; " she said her mamma had told her she was to have no lessons until Wednesday next, she had no holidays when Harry had his, and she was to have them now. I knew the meaning of this.

In the afternoon Miss Hariote came to sit with me, bringing her work; she had in her hand a bunch of pink roses tied up with moss.

"Robert sent you these," said she, laying them on my lap. How beautiful the delicate blossoms and pale green moss looked lying on my white muslin dressing-gown. "Ellen Syme was here yesterday, and sent you her love; she wished to come up to your room, but mamma feared she might have disturbed you."

I answered by a grateful look. I was still weak and weary, but I thought how handsome they both, Robert and Ellen Syme, were, and I inwardly prayed that she might equal him in mind as well as in face and form; and that both might be among those "whom the Lord will count, when he maketh up his jewels."

I told Miss Hariote that I intended to meet Willie at the railway station on Saturday evening.

"I fancy it would be of no use trying to dissuade you from doing so," was her reply. "I will see what arrangement Robert can make for your going there without injuring your health. It is a very precious boon to us all, but in your case it is doubly so; your brother's advancement in life, everything seems to depend on your health.

How true, everything indeed; what would become of Willie if I were to die now, or worse, to become sickly and useless? it made me think that speech of hers.

Before she went to dinner, Miss Hariote made me come down to the schoolroom; I was very pleased to do so, being heartily tired of my own room; as I entered, I observed a large easy chair placed beside the fire; the chair did not belong to the room and was evidently brought there for my sick self. It was not such an unpleasant thing after all being sick here.

By and bye my dinner was brought in a tray covered with a fine white cloth ; how I enjoyed that dinner, and then my walk afterwards up and down the room.

I was quite strong, as much so as before my illness, and .my spirits rose to an unwonted pitch as I thought of what would be this time to-morrow. I had an almost irresistible inclination to sing Willie's song of " Scott's wha hae wi' ·Wallace bled," as I paced up and down the room.

What would the good people below have thought if I had indulged my fancy ? how it would have electrified haughty, silent Mr. Scott!

When I went down to breakfast next morning every one expressed themselves glad to see me. Even Mr. Scott looked up from his paper, and said, " You have had a sick bout, Miss Keith, you must not get wet again." Quite a long speech for him.

Before leaving the room after breakfast, Mr. Robert said, addressing himself to me :

" If you will allow me, Miss Keith, I will be here at half past four to take you to the railway station."

" Thank you very much," I said heartily. It would be dark at five ; I still felt weak and did not like the idea of waiting in the railway station alone. I was very glad therefore to accept of Mr. Robert's kind offer.

With half past four came Mr. Robert ; I went down to the hall and was handed into a carriage ; this annoyed me, why go to that expense, we could have gone in the omnibus ; if he made, as Georgy said, plenty of money, I knew he had plenty to do with it ; Mrs. MacIntosh had enlightened me on the subject.

" How old is your brother, Miss Keith," he asked after we were seated.

" Eighteen ; he is younger than I."

" So I should suppose, from this being his first year at college." No compliment there to my youthful appearance.

" He must be taller than you ?"

" He could look over my head last year."

—The railway station.—I was handed from the carriage and into the waiting room, Mr. Robert finding me a seat away from the draught of the door. I found several ladies there, and I knew from the snatches of conversation I heard, they were on the same errand as myself.

We sat for a few minutes, when my companion said, " I think the train must have arrived, from the bustle outside, although I did not hear the whistle ; I will go and see ; do not leave your seat until I come ; I will be back in a few minutes."

I kept looking in the direction of the door, but the room was so large and so dimly lighted, while people entered and retired in such quick succession—such confusion: laughing, talking, and shaking hands, that it would have been impossible to recognize any one at the distance I sat from the entrance : what a sea of faces, hats and bonnets, moving backwards and forwards. I did not see Mr. Robert enter until he was by my side. I looked up in his face, my heart beating audibly ; dreading, yet expecting him to say : " your brother has not arrived," when a clear well known voice at my back and close to my ear said, " Es-tu là, ma sœur ?" In a moment, I was back in the home of our early days, in the old chateau on the banks of the Gironde, where playing our favourite game of hide and seek, I would wrap myself in the thick folds of the damask window curtain, or some other, to me, impossible to be found place, when a little curly black head and bright eye would peep slily in just at my shoulder, saying clearly and merrily, as it had now been uttered, " Es-tu là, ma sœur ?" and I involuntarily exclaimed, as I was wont in our old French home, " méchant."

What a revulsion of feeling; how handsome he looked! and how proud I felt as I introduced him to Mr. Robert. I think he must have grown a foot since I saw him last, and he was so gentlemanly, I felt he was inferior to none, superior to most I had met since we parted, chemist's boy as he was.

We moved towards the door, when Willie looking sharply round, called out "Carlo, Carlo;" and in a second my uncle's Carlo, who I believed to be dead and buried, came pushing his way through the crowd.

" Willie, who is this ?" I asked in amazement.

" Don't you know Carlo, uncle's Carlo."

" Yes, I know him, but I thought he was dead.

" Nonsense, who told you that ; you see he's not, and he's mine now," and he added laughingly, " I will tell you Carlo's history by and bye, it is quite a romance."

We entered the carriage, and I sat with Willie's hand clasped in both mine : Tuesday was my happiest day then, this was my happiest day now.

" I have got you such a nice little parlour and bedroom," said I, " but the bedroom is no bigger than a cupboard."

" If it is cheap enough all the rest will do."

" Then I think that will do ; but Carlo, I fear your land-lady will object to Carlo.

" I hope not; if so, she must kick me out along with Carlo, we must be together."

The carriage stopped at the common stair leading to Mrs. Livingstone's land ; Willie left the carriage first, then Mr. Robert, who in handing me out said, " I shall not leave town for some hours, and will call for you at nine o'clock, if that is not too early." " How very kind and good you are," said I, and in my happiness and gratitude I clasped his offered hand in both my own.

He looked earnestly in my face ; a look of such powerful meaning. I put it by in my heart, and kept it there, and years afterwards, in a time of great trouble, when his very name had become almost a shadow, I took it out, looked at it, and was comforted.

We ascended to the land, lighted on our way by one miserable lamp, which hung midway in the staircase, and served just to make the darkness visible. The door was opened by Mrs. Livingstone in person.

" How's aw wi' ye ; come in ; this will be your brither," said she, in a tone of voice which of itself gave a hearty welcome, " come awa in, sir," and she measured him with her eye from head to foot, evidently surprised ; and added, " I thought he was a laddie, but he's a young man." Willie looked very pleased and drew himself up to his full height.

" Will you show me your door-mat, Madame ?" (Willie's French stuck more closely to him than mine did,) looking at the same time for such a piece of furniture.

" It's just inside the door," said our hostess pointing it out, " we aye tak it in, in the gloamin ; there's sae money orra folk gangs up and down the stair, it might be taen awa."

The mat being found, Willie called Carlo, and shewed it to him, when he, with great doggish sagacity, brushed all his four feet.

" I taught him to do that myself," said Willie, evidently proud of the feat.

" Na weel then, that coo's aw," said Mrs. Livingstone, " but come ben ye'er surely caul, and Maister Scott tillet me at ye've been in yer bed sine ye ware here."

We entered the parlour that was to be Willie's, not passing through the sitting room as I done done, but by a door opening from the landing; it was the very picture of comfort on a small scale; a small but bright fire, the tea pot on one hob, the kettle on the other; on the table a tray containing cups and saucers, sugar, &c., outside the tray fresh bread, butter, eggs, and last but not least, a glass dish containing preserves.

"Pit aff your things in the chamber there, and come to the fire side and tak your tae."

A behest and invitation which we most gladly obeyed.

"Fess ben the eggs, Jean," said her Mistress; and presently Jean appeared bringing in a plate of fried eggs in addition to those already on the table; and acknowledging my acquaintance by a slight smile and a curtsey. Mrs. Livingston made tea for us, during which she said to Willie, "I gae Jean twa shillins and gart her buy as muckle tae and sugar and white bread and butter and eggs, as will serve ye for a week, an ye can buy meal on Monday, an fa'an Jean bakes our ain bread, she'll bake for you. I put down the jam o' my ain to welcome you, but young lads dinna need jam ilka day."

"No, indeed," said I; "Willie wishes to live as cheaply as he can," and turning to him, I said, "the rent is only five shillings a week, and I am sure we can pay that; but, (to Mrs. Livingstone) how much will it cost us for coals?"

"It wonna cost ye ony thing, nor his drap milk either; I get my milk frae ain o'my ain bairns, at bids out at the meadows, an I aye hae mair than I can had my face to: bit ae' thing, I dinna like ye'er dog muckle, we aw his mainners, he'll file the house whiles, an' I canna abide a fule house."

"Let Carlo stay until Tuesday," said I, "and by that time we may perhaps think of some place to put him."

"Je ne resterai pas sans mon chien," said Willie.

"What's ye'er wull?" inquired she, turning her head to one side, and then quickly added, "I whiles think I'm grown deaf." After a pause, she returned thanks, and taking the eatables from the table, locked them in a corner cupboard, which I did not observe in my former survey of the room, while doing this she observed :

"Their kind dacent folk, thae ye bide wi'. Mr. Scott came here seeking ye, about an hour after I came hame on Tuesday night ; he was down at Bernard's Row, and they sent him here ; he said he was feart ye had lost the gaet, and he came again on Wednesday and tald me ye was in your bed, and bade me be sure an' keep the room for the lad."

We were now left alone ; and after Willie told me the state of his finances, which were much better than I could have at all supposed, he asked how I heard of the dog's death. I told him of Mrs. Moodie's letter, and repeated what I knew of the story.

"All is quite correct as far as it goes," said he, "only that my story begins where Mrs. Moodie's ends, she having obtained her information from my uncle."

"After the dog pulled uncle to the ground, the whole inhabitants of the house came hurry-scurry out to the lawn, attracted by his cries, which were loud enough in all conscience. A thought struck me—I knew I would never enter the house again ; I cared little for that, but a desire strong as death came over me—I must go and bid goodbye to my great grand-mother's picture. I had come to be nearly as fond of it as yourself, after you went away ; and I think I wanted to show uncle I could go into the house whether he would or not. At all events, I walked straight up to the front door, up stairs and round to the picture gallery; the ladder was there which they used when dusting the pictures; I placed it by the picture, went up, and kissed the face; I then descended at my leisure, and going along the gallery went out by the left wing; on coming out the coast was clear, but at a little distance I saw James Robb, who goes for the letters, and another man, I think the coachman, dragging Carlo between them; I whistled to Carlo and they let him go at once, so away he came with me; however, after we were a quarter of a mile from the gate, Jamie came running, almost breathless, calling to me to stop.

" ' I mun tak the dog !' said he, ' the master ordered us to kill him.'

" I asked if he had hurt my uncle—you should have seen the queer expression of his face; uncle is a harsh master ; none of his servants like him, and I fear satisfaction was the predominate feeling of his mind as he said—

" ' Weel, I canna say that I think he's much hurt, but his long-tailed black coat is torn in repacks ; I wadna gie three pence for't to make garters, and I hae orders to kill the dog and bury him, and never let the master see bane or hede o' him again.'

" ' O Jamie,' said I, ' give me the dog and I'll give you a shilling for him; I am going to Edinburgh very soon, and I will chain him in the back court until I go ; no one shall ever see him here again,' and I offered him the shilling.

" The old man looked at me for a moment, and then said with some emotion :—' I'll give ye the dog, Master Willie, but no for your siller, I winna tak that, but for your father's face that sets on your shoulders an' looks at me through your een ; I carried him about in my arms mony a day, and gin he was

livin' now you wadna need to rin like that frae your grandfather's place, an its my thought that gin he was lookin' up
that's beneath the ground, yon proud peat up at the Hall
wadna hae sae muckle siller to ware on that ill faurt loon o'
his.'

" 'Tak the dog, Master Willie,' said he, letting him go,
' but for my sake dinna let him be seen or heard of; gin ye
do, I wanna be lang o' getting my leave frae the old place
whar I served your grandfather lang afore your father or
the master we hae now was born or thought of.'

" ' Fare ye well, my bonny lad,' he continued, ' and when
ye gang to Edinburgh mind ye come o' gentle blood, and
dinna be drawin' up we aw the common trash that's at the
college, but keep yoursel to yoursel, fear the Lord an' be an
honest man, and there's nae fear of ye.'

" When Jamie went off I came home with Carlo, whistling
' Scot's wha hae wi' Wallace bled ' every step of the road.
I told Mrs. Rexford all about it, and she laughed heartily.
The doctor had been sent for to see my uncle, and when he
came home I told him ; all he said was to take care I would
not allow Carlo to be seen. I asked if uncle was hurt.—
' No,' said he, ' not his body, but his coat was, as Jamie
Robb said, not worth threepence to make garters, and if your
uncle is not hurt he was dreadfully frightened, which amounts
to much the same thing.' "

Faithful to his promise, with nine o'clock came Mr. Robert;
he asked Willie to occupy a seat in his pew on the morrow,
and accompany us home to dinner ; to this Willie gladly assented. Mr. Robert's plaid was spread on the seat of the
carriage for me to sit on, and wrapping me round as if I were
an Egyptian mummy, he said :—" There is no fear of your
taking cold this time !"

On the morrow after the second service Willie came; I had not seen him since the evening previous, as feeling too weak to go to Edinburgh, I went to Mrs. MacIntosh's pew in the village church, which I had done on one or two former occasions. I took him into the conservatory, and was pleased to see with what interest he examined all the plants ; it was a lovely afternoon, the twilight creeping in upon the day. Into the bowling green and round the belting we went ; there was a little nook there that Georgy called her bower, where the spring rose that fed the brook in the shrubbery. The gnarled roots of a giant elm had formed an alcove over the little shallow pool with its clear pebbly bottom, scarce a foot in diameter, where the spring gurgled up. Among the elm roots above, yet near enough the pool to be mirrored there, grew a single plant of wild violet, while out and in through the great roots, and completely covering the bank above up to the bole of the tree, an abundance of long-trailing moss and curling lady fern, had made their home ; these overshadowed, and would have quite hid the violet, but for her blue eyes which were ever bending forward to look down into the clear water, that she might see her own fair form reflected there.

I brought Willie to the great elm and shewed him Georgy's pet.—" The pretty little thing," said he, " how lovely she will look in the bright moonlight when the stars come peeping in to see her admiring herself."

These few words were to me cause of deep thankfulness; they told me his soul had entered the " chambers of imagery," and that wandering in the wide labyrinths and drinking from the pure fountains there, he would never long to tread the miry ways, or thirst to drink from the polluted and troubled springs which form the enjoyment of so large a portion of his compeers.

I felt a little uneasy as to how Willie might behave at table : when only ten years of age there was no fear of his making any mistake ; we had been carefully trained in this as in everything else, by a loving mother, but I had not dined with him since we came to Scotland, and I was not at all sure as to the etiquette of the table; we are so much the creatures of circumstances that we generally imitate the habits of those around us, even when we degenerate by so doing ; however, by the time the cloth was removed, I was perfectly at ease on this score. After dinner we spent an hour in performing the promise we had made to mamma, and which we had not forgotten when we met last in Willie's new home.

We spent the evening in Mr. Robert's] Sabbath school, where Willie agreed to take a class, and we bid each other goodnight at the gate of Iona Villa, he going full of hope on his way to Edinburgh, and I entering my happy home with a light and thankful heart.

CHAPTER XI.

WILLIE passed his examination with credit, and was admitted as a medical student; that was cause of thankfulness, although, until after he passed, and I saw him in such spirits because he had done so, the possibility of his failing had never occurred to me. Drawling, dreary dark November came and went with its short wet days, and December came and passed away likewise, with its bright smiles and Christmas cheer.

One morning, early in January, I called Georgy to her lessons twice before she came; and at last when she appeared, her eyes were red and swollen with weeping. "What is the matter, child?" I asked.

"Papa is in one of his rages about nothing; I would rather be dead than live in this way."

"What were you doing to excite your papa's anger?"

"Oh! nothing that need have displeased any one: I was plucking a few roses in the conservatory: I heard Robert say in the morning, that he thought there were worms in the soil, and so I thought I would turn them out to save him the trouble, so that was all the reason; he called me a wasteful Papist like my mother; I am sure mamma is much better than him."

"Were you potting the roses with that dress on?" I asked, and I looked at the violet coloured merino she wore, soiled with earth on the skirt and sleeves.

"Yes," was her answer, "but I can brush that off," she added, as she saw my eye resting on her earth stained dress, and with her handkerchief she made several ineffectua attempts to remove the marks, at last giving it up for a bad job, saying as she seated herself:—" I wonder mamma ever married him, he's so ugly : and when mamma was young, she was perfectly beautiful."

I had my doubts about that, but said nothing.

" Dont you think papa awfully ugly ? " asked she.

" No, I certainly do not ? "

" Well, Miss Keith," said she hastily, " every one else does : and mamma told me herself, that she could never have her picture taken correctly, because her features were too good ! "

I fancy she must have thought I looked rather sceptical, as she continued with heightened colour :

" And Mary says that she remembers mamma one of the most beautiful women in Edinburgh ; but of course papa's temper has changed her very much ; Mary says so ! "

There must indeed have been a wonderful change in both complexion and features.

That night when going to bed, I wished to drink, but as there was no water in the room, a very unusual neglect with Simpson, I preferred suffering a little from thirst, to wandering downstairs, and perhaps encountering Mr. Robert, who always sat up late, or worse still, Mr. Scott, whose temper seemed not to have recovered its equilibrium since the affair with Georgy in the morning.

In the middle of the night, however, I awoke so parched with thirst, that it seemed as if I must drink or die, so putting on a dark dressing gown and slippers, I went down to the parlour without a light, as I knew I could find the water, by the light from the hall, which was always left burning.

When I reached the parlour, I found there was no water on the side board—(Simpson's mason must have been at Iona

Villa to-night) taking a tumbler I went into the conservatory, certain of being able to quench my thirst at the fountain there. As I finished one of the most delicious draughts of pure water I ever tasted, I heard loud footsteps tramp tramp, in the hall, and in a second Mr. Scott entered the parlour, and passed from thence into the conservatory, with a candle in one hand and a carving knife in the other.

"Damn them, the papist set," said he, as he entered. "I'll teach them to spend my money that way."

I was in the shadow of the fountain, and I remained perfectly still, almost paralyzed with fear; he placed the candlestick on one of the garden chairs, and then going to the front shelves containing the roses, cut down every one, equal with the pot, throwing them to the ground as he did so, and then stamping upon them in his rage, swore the most horrible oaths, as he stamped, again and again, on the broken roses: at last snatching up the candle he exclaimed, "damn them, I'll fire the house about their ears," and in another moment he was gone. What was I to do? he seemed as if he were capable of this or anything else he might take into his head to do in his present state of frenzy; if I waited for five minutes, it might be too late, the house would be in a blaze; in a second I was at the foot of the staircase on my way to arouse Mr. Robert, but before I had time to ascend one step, I heard Miss Hariote speaking, in a clear low voice; and looking up, I saw her standing on the last step of the stairs, her hand upon her father's arm as he stood two steps below. I stood looking up, feeling as if I were transfixed to the spot! she spoke for a few minutes, her hand still resting on his arm, and then taking the candle from his hand, she walked slowly into his room, he following at the same pace.

I remained standing there until I was thoroughly chilled,

fearing to go up stairs lest I should meet Miss Hariote coming from her father's room : I would not on any accoun that she should know I had seen this sad exhibition of the poor man's ungovernable temper.

At last I was so cold, I could wait no longer, and treading as softly as possible, I was in my own room and in bed in a few minutes.

Poor girl; what can keep her in that room so long? I had rather be the governess than Miss Hariote Scott.

Next morning I glanced into the conservatory as I sat down to breakfast; everything there was in its usual order, only there were stocks of different bright colours where the roses were wont to be : three days later the rose trees appeared again and in full blossom, we had benefitted by the change, those that were destroyed had only green leaves.

One morning it rained so heavily that Georgy and I could not take our usual walk, which at this season of the year we always did in the morning ; on our rising from breakfast, Mr. Robert proposed, as we could not go out, that Georgy and I should each take a pair of scissors and remove the dead leaves from the plants, which exercise would form a good substitute for a walk

We very readily agreed to do so, and set to work at once, leaving Mr. Scott and his son seated at the breakfast table.

As we commenced our labours, Mr. Robert said, addressing his father, " you must see about Harry ; Mr. Watts has been at my office twice lately, and I have tried my influence without success."

" What is the matter now ? What has Harry been doing, or rather, what is it that he won't do ? no tying together of cats tails again, I hope. "

" Oh no, but the old story of the Latin resumed ; Mr.

K

Watts says it is perfectly impossible to get a proper translation or a well-written exercise from him; he has tried punishment in all its forms with no effect; would it not be better to lay aside the idea of bringing him up to the law?"

"No," said the old man, and rising from his chair he paced up and down the room with a heavy tread, his hands thrust into his pockets, and his scarlet dressing-gown waving to and fro behind.

"No," twice, and such a determined no. "Here is nothing for a man to do now, except the law or the church: you would make a better parson than Harry yourself, Artty: besides every black coat in the country is expected to know Latin, although the half of them don't know more about it than Harry does."

He stopped short in his walk, looked at the floor, as if he became suddenly sensible of something extraordinary in the pattern of the carpet, and then, raising his head, and turning to his son, said in a tone of voice I should not have fancied at all if I had been in Harry's place :—" Bring him down here to me at five o'clock."

And he strode from the room, with the firm step and erect gait of a man of fifty.

After both father and son had left the room, Georgy whispered almost below her breath, as if she feared the vine leaves overhead would repeat her words, " I should not like to be Harry to-night."

With five o'clock came Mr. Robert, accompanied by Harry, the latter going at once to his mamma's room, where, however, he only remained a few minutes, having found there no elucidation of the mystery of his being brought home so suddenly.

He then came into the school-room very unceremoniously,

and without shutting the door or speaking to any one, seated himself on the window-seat, with his back to the window, and his hands in his trowsers' pockets ; this elegant mode of disposing of his hands, I found he copied from his papa, and after sitting thus for a few minutes, said with a very ill-tempered look and voice :—" George, what's up with pa now ? Artty sent one of his chaps to school for me, but like him he would not tell me a word about it."

And he kicked his heels with vehemence against the side of the window-seat, as I had seen him do on a former occasion.

Georgy told him all about it, that is all she knew, repeating faithfully every word her father and brother had said in the morning.

" Well," said he, his face scarlet with rage, " after that anything : if Bob is'nt the deceitfullest fellow in all the world, and I asked him twice coming down what it was,—that beats dickey ; and him at the beginning and the end of it himself ; what business has he coming down to clash on me to pa ?"

After a pause, during which he kicked the window-seat with more violence than ever, he said :—" I wont stay at school any more, George, I think I'll run off."

" Where to, Harry ?" asked Georgy, pale with terror at the mischief she had made.

" Don't know : perhaps off to sea with some of the ships."

" But your always sea-sick, Harry," suggested Georgy.

" Of course I am, and is'nt that just what he wants ? would'nt he laugh, if he got me out of the way off to Calcutta or somewhere, and pa all to himself."

" Oh," continued he, beating the carpet with one foot in a half kicking sort of motion ; " if Bob is'nt the meanest dog out, I don't know who is : first to clash all the stories he can scrape up to pa, and then bring a fellow down and not say a word about it beats all; let him come past the high school the first snowy day, wont he catch it, Dido! I'd just like to have a shy at him."

"But if you go to sea?" said I.

"What's your business?" said he, getting upon his feet, "do you think I'm going to sea to please you or Bob either; its like you, always poking in church with him."

"I'll tell you what I'll do, George; I'll provoke him, see if I don't; to-morrow night is Friday; so I'll ask old Watts to let me go to the Symes, and I'll tell Ellen Syme every word, and if she'll mind him after that she's as mean as himself."

"The very thing," said Georgy, "I would if I were you;" and they both laughed; the mirth, however, was put a sudden stop to, by Simpson coming to desire Harry go to his father in the dining-room.

"Tell him I've got to wash my face and hands first," said he, suddenly recollecting that this was necessary.

When we came down to dinner, Harry was standing on the hearth-rug sharpening his pencil; he must have found it difficult to succeed in making a point, as the hearth inside the fender was literally covered with little chips of wood.

Mr. Scott was sitting in the large leather chair opposite, his head leaning on the back, his legs crossed and his arms resting on the projecting side of the chair; between the finger and thumb of his right hand, he held a long gold pencil case, which he turned up and down slowly and at regular intervals; he kept his eye steadily fixed on the boy, and said as we entered:—"Now, Hal, you know I can keep my promise, be it for good or evil."

During dinner Master Harry gave sundry very angry glances at his brother; at last finding that it was impossible to control his temper without some little outburst, he kicked poor Don, who was streched at full length under the table, and turning to his father said, in a quick manner and with flashing eye:—" Pa, will you make Bob keep his feet to his own side of the table ?"

His father looked under the dining table, and having satisfied himself that Mr. Robert's feet were where they ought to be, hemmed in reply.

" After dinner, Harry and his father went to Edinburgh, the former coming first to bid good-bye, Georgy whispered softly:—" What did papa say ?"

" Not much," was his reply; " Bob missed fire this time ; but I'll never speak to him again all my life, he's too mean."

We were to have a great dinner party, a gentleman's party, it was to be, but a very great affair. Lord B——, was in Edinburgh—he and Mr. Scott were great friends in their younger days, and as Lord B. resided in France, only visiting London when his parliamentary duties called him there, and seldom coming to Scotland, they had not met for years —and the party was given for him.

Dr. S—— also was to be an honoured guest, that is, if he came, a question which would be doubtful up to the hour of cause. The rest of the party consisted of gentlemen holding the same situation as Mr. Scott, among whom was Mr. Syme and others of high standing in the law.

I assisted Miss Hariote in writing the invitations, and very carefully they were done—plain cream laid paper, the envelopes not of a very small size, and sealed with an impression of the family arms in red wax.

In addressing the cards, I found that John Erskine, advocate, was one of the invited guests.

There were ten guests, which, with Mr. Scott and his son, made the proper number of gentlemen : twelve, Mrs. and

Miss Scott were to dine at table; if all the guests came, Miss Hariote was not to make one at the table, if one only did not arrive, she must fill the empty chair; if two were wanting, she was again relieved from the duty; but if three, then she must be there; the numbers must be equal on each side of the table.

If we lived plainly in general, everything now was to be in profusion, and the best which could be got.

The salmon was one of the first and finest of the season, so large that I wondered where the saucepan would be got to boil it, or the ashet to put it on when boiled.

When the day came, every invited guest came with it; even Dr. S—— was there in time to hear grace said; dinner was at seven, and the Misses Syme and two Misses Campbell I had never seen, were to come at eight to help the ladies of the family to entertain their guests.

The Misses Campbell were pretty girls, tall and well made, with blue eyes and fair hair, the latter a little tinged with the national colour: they were easy and pleasant in their manners, and evidently great favourites with Mrs. and Miss Scott.

Mr. Erskine and Mr. Weimes were the first to leave the dining-room, and by degrees we were favoured by older and brighter lights.

I watched each face as its possessor came into the drawing room, anxious to see the lion of the evening, Lord B——; when he came, I knew him at once before he was pointed out to me: there was the same peculiar looking nose, the same truly Scotch face as I possessed embossed on a card half a foot square, presented to me in my school days, as a prize for my knowledge in English history.

Next in interest was Dr. S——; he was a short stout

man, who very evidently paid little attention to the duties of
the toilet ; an immense head ; strongly marked features ; with
beautiful eyes and a great quantity of fine hair ; his mouth
most expressive ; at one moment firmly set, at another full of
tenderness and again of drollery.

After tea, which consisted in most cases of a cup of
tea being held in the hand, one or two little sips taken, enough
to moisten the lips, and then placed on the table, we had a
little vocal music. Miss Ellen Syme sung " a wee bird cam to
our ha door," as usual, very beautifully, the Misses Campbell
sung one or two Jacobite songs, duettes, with great applause ;
but a Gaelic song, the air of which was arranged for the piano
as a duette by the young ladies themselves, and sung in parts,
was received with an approbation which must have been very
flattering to the fair performers. Nearly all the gentlemen
were Gaelic scholars, or at least understood enough of the language to comprehend the meaning of the song. Later in the
evening Miss Elizabeth Campbell translated it for me, it ran
thus :

> " Oh ! my lovely Mary, thou, in thy beauty, dost far outshine
> All the other maids who wander in the glen ;
> Oh ! my beautiful love, elegance is thine."

One or twice during the evening I was annoyed by Mr.
Weimes staring very unceremoniously in my face ; I changed
my seat to no purpose, his eyes were still upon me : at last
Ellen Syme, who sat next to me, said with a smile :—" Miss
Keith, you are a fortunate girl, you have made a conquest of
Nabob Weimes."

I answered by some pleasantry, and almost immediately
after Mr. Robert, advancing towards me, accompanied by Mr.
Weimes, begged leave to introduce him.

I felt exceedingly awkward, and was not relieved by Ellen

Syme, rising from her seat by my side, and taking Robert Scott's arm, saying, as she did so :—" You will give me a few roses, won't you ? look at my poor flower, how the heat of the room has withered it."

In my eyes her bouquet was fresh and beautiful, but away they went through the hall to the conservatory, which was lighted up for the occasion, and was doubtless a more pleasant place for a promenade, than the crowded drawing-room ; particularly as Miss Ellen was sure there to have the conversation of her handsome lover all to herself.

Mr. Weimes took the seat on the sofa vacated by Miss Syme, and almost immediately said :—" I have sought an introduction to you, Miss Keith, to ask if your mother's name was Violet de Sallaberry, and also, if your father was a Colonel in the East Indian Company's service."

" My mother's name was Violet de Sallaberry, and my father was a Colonel in the East India Company's service ;" and I looked in his face for an explanation of his motive in making the inquiry.

" I was your father's groomsman," was his answer,—" and I had also the pleasure of being one of your earliest acquaintances. A dear sister, whom I lost six months ago, was your Godmother. Your father and mother, soon after their marriage, went to live on the banks of the Garonne, and I hired a house there also, to be near my old friend, where we spent two happy summers, at the end of which my business required my presence in India, and we never met again. Your likeness to your mother is so striking, that on finding your name was Keith, I felt convinced you could be no other than the daughter of my old friend."

Mr. Weimes sat by me the whole evening, and gave me his arm to the supper table, asking me many questions about my mother, and telling me several interesting anecdotes of my parents during their residence at Lamotte, in the early days of their married life. I often thought of the vivid pic. tures he drew of their happy days, and repeated them to Willie, but his being present at my mother's marriage and my baptism I quite forgot ; no I did not forget, thank God for it, there is no such thing as forgetting ; a record once written on the memory is never obliterated ; there it is safe ; and wave upon wave of our every day life comes, each bringing its portion of sand and debris, until the loose sand becomes a solid rock where the earth accumulates and the grass grows, and we pass over it, but one day the rock is shivered to pieces, and lo ! the little unthought of pebble is there round and smooth, not one red or brown streak lost.

And so, these words of his, which seemed forgotten almost as soon as spoken, came to me in my greatest need, in my sorest trial, filling my soul with joy and gladness, turning my captivity as the waters in the south.

At supper Lord B—— asked Mr. Syme his opinion on some right of way case, which had been tried in the Court of Session, and on which their Lordships were to deliver judgment in a few days.

" You must ask Robert Scott, he is junior counsel for the defendant," said Mr. Syme.

Lord B—— then requested Mr. Robert to give him an idea of the leading facts of the case.

He at once complied, speaking with great eloquence for fully ten minutes, during which not a finger was raised, scarcely a breath drawn.

The great statesman sat eyeing the speaker, one hand placed on the table, his head bent a little to one side and forward, his keen eye never for a moment relaxing in its intense look of attention ; not a muscle of his face moved.

I looked from Lord B—— to Mr. Scott; there the old man sat, all eye, all ear; his thin lips firmly pressed together; his whole frame dilated with the pride he felt in listening to his son's eloquence.

When he had finished, no one spoke for full half a minute; at last Lord B—— said,

" Mr. Scott, why don't you go to the English bar ?"

I do not know what Mr. Robert's answer was, or if he made one, but immediately a hubbub of voices arose each declaiming against such a proceeding.

Miss Hariote's eyes were filled with tears of joy.

Ellen Syme's whole face glowed with happiness as she looked at her handsome and eloquent lover, his words flowing forth in their beauty, diamonds and pearls and emeralds entrancing these men learned in all the learning of the Egyptians, with the power of his intellect—she had good cause for happiness—he was handsome, learned, eloquent, and much more, he prayed while other men talked, and while others cast their gifts into the treasury, his left hand knew not what his right did ; when the eye saw him it blessed him, and he caused the widow's heart to sing for joy.

We had another demonstration, and a very painful one, of Mr. Scott's ungovernable temper, a few weeks after the dinner party.

In the paddock behind the shrubbery was kept a dear little shaggy Shetland pony, which, as well as Don, was Georgy's private property. Popity was a general favorite and possessed a large share of his mistress's affection, and helped to give her healthful exercise as well as amusement in her play hours.

We used to feed him with biscuit, gingerbread, in short, anything we had to give. Popity was always ready to eat, and so knowing was he, that on seeing any of us at the paddock gate with outstretched hand, he would come running to us in his helter-skelter way, eager to receive our offerings.

Poor Popity was too knowing ; when the gate was left with only the latch keeping it shut, he would open that most unceremoniously, and walk into the forbidden ground of the bowling green.

Now, although the green was never used for the purpose which its name would imply, yet Mr. Scott liked to see it smooth and nicely kept, as he did everything in and around his house, and Popity's feet made most unseemingly marks on the closely shaven grass, and more than once he trod down the early crocuses, as they came up with their golden and purple heads and shiny green leaves, above the brown cold earth, to make us glad, and he did not spare even the little snowdrop, which, with no guardian leaves to keep her safe from the cold damp earth, seemed to hang her fair young head, asking for the protection nature had denied her.

I must confess Popity's offences in this respect were many and most provoking. At last Mr. Scott brought home a padlock, which was to replace the sliding bar used for fastening the gate in addition to the latch.

Mr. Scott fastened the gate himself with the padlock attached to a chain, and hung the key in the porch of the back door leading to the bowling green, informing us all that he had done so, and, that the first time he found the pony in the shrubbery, he would shoot him.

The key had been in use about a month, when one morning Miss Hariote, Georgy and I were seated in the school room ; (it was Georgy's hour for French reading, in which she was now very proficient,) when suddenly we heard the report of a pistol ; Georgy clasped her hands together, and pale with terror cried out ' Popity.' We all ran to the window, and sure enough there lay poor Popity in the bowling green, a long dark streak from his neck, telling but too surely his hours were numbered. Mr. Scott was walking slowly towards the house, examining the pistol which he still held in his hand as he walked along.

The look and air of intense rage which Georgy's face and whole form presented as she left the room with erect head, staring eye and dilated nostril, I shall ever remember.

Miss Hariote and I hurried out after her ; she had already thrown herself on the ground beside the dying pony. Poor fellow, he knew that she was there, and made an ineffectual effort to stretch his head towards her ; she put one arm over his neck and laid her fair young head on the pony's, sobbing as if her heart would break.

" Popity, Popity," she said, in a low and bitter tone, as if her last hope had fled. Poor Popity tried twice to raise one of his fore feet in answer to the kind voice he loved so well, but it would not be, that little shaggy foot will never rise again. Georgy raised her head for a moment, lifted the foot and put it in her lap, and then laid her head down as before on Popity's, and long after his heart had ceased to beat, and no breath came, no muscle moved, and he was dead, dead, she lay there, and no persuasion that Miss Hariote or I could urge were of any avail to make her move from the body of her pet. Poor child, it was her first great sorrow, and perhaps as bitter as any she will ever feel.

" I will go and bring mamma," said Miss Hariote, and going into the house she returned in a few minutes with Mrs. Scott, who, with Don's assistance, succeded in making Georgy leave poor Popity's body, and go into the house, from whence they both departed an hour afterwards in a close carriage with valise and bandbox.

Miss Hariote told me her mother was very fierce when she heard of the pony's death, having been quite ignorant of all that had occurred, until her daughter went to call her.

Miss Hariote added, " I am sure they have gone to Roslin ; my aunt lives there, a sister of mamma's, whose two youngest girls are about Georgy's age. We will not see them for about a week at least."

CHAPTER XII.

APRIL had come with its smiles and tears, and with it the, to me, rather curious announcement that Miss Scott was to be married.

The happy man was a Mr. Murray, a Catholic gentleman, who frequently visited at Iona Villa, and who always paid particular attention to both Mrs. and Miss Scott, and who, I knew, was a particular favourite with the former, but the idea of Miss Scott's having a lover, never once entered into my calculations.

When Mrs. Scott informed me, which she did with her usual dignity, of the approach of the auspicious event, she said, " Mary has been particularly fortunate in her choice of a husband—rich, of a good family, gentlemanly manners, very much attached to herself, and, above all, a Catholic;" and speaking at Miss Hariote, she added, " a Catholic woman, who, after twenty years of age, marries either a Protestant, a Jew, or a Mahomedan, or, in short, any one outside the pale of the Catholic Church, must have, as Bishop Mac-Donnell observed last Sunday in his beautiful sermon on the duty of confession, a heart harder than the nether millstone, and deserves the anguish which will wring it."

Mrs. Scott must have married before her twentieth year.

Mrs. Murray to be, was to have a carriage, an old family mansion in Fifeshire, and a handsome town house in George street, Edinburgh ; and in addition to all this, Mr. Murray being a widower, she would have four children under twelve years of age to welcome her home.

Miss Scott and her mother were in town every day buying and giving orders for the wedding, which was to be a very handsome one, Mr. Scott's heart having been opened in an unwonted degree by the unexpected good fortune of his daughter. The marriage was to take place as early in May as possible, and the happy couple were to spend, at least, three months on the continent, visiting friends of both families in Rome and Florence.

On the first of April I had a long letter from Gertrude; it contained the sad intelligence of her father's death; she wrote on the subject just as I would have expected her to do, full of the hope of a glorious immortality. "It is only parting for a short time," she wrote, " when the Lord will come he will most surely live again; have we not the express promise that we who remain will not prevent those who are asleep, and then shall we rise together to meet the Lord in the air, and so shall we be for ever with the Lord."

They were settled at Algona, one of the first cities in Canada, at the time of her father's death, and by the advice of Mr. Forbes, who was one of the parish priests there, she had entered the convent of St. Bride as a boarder.

Her description of convent life was very beautiful; the nuns so amiable and sympathising, so full of good works.

Attached to the convent was an hospital for the sick and aged, which, at the time she wrote, contained one hundred and ten old and infirm people, whose bodily and spiritual wants were attended to by the good nuns with the care and attention bestowed by children on their parents.

There was also an educational establishment attached to the convent, where some twenty-five young ladies were boarded and educated. Their English governess, who was required also to understand French well, the young ladies being, with few exceptions, French, had a salary of seventy-five pounds a year; she was to leave them in the vacation, which took place in July, and in September; if I would like to come to Canada for a few years, Gertrude was sure that she had interest sufficient with the Superior to procure the situation for me. Gertrude said she would remain, at least, three years in the convent, perhaps she would never leave its walls; convent life was the nearest to life in heaven we could conceive of on earth; she pressed me very much to come to Canada, and urged every reason she could think of: I would see part of another quarter of the globe at no expense to myself, I would make as much money in one year as I could make here in almost two, and so be better able to help Willie, and I would be with one I loved well, and who had been the companion of half my life; and a great many more ands.

I saw all these advantages: I would again be an inhabitant of the same house with the one who, next to Willie, for eight years of my life, I loved the best in all the world, and who still held her place in my affections, and ever would; again, with that large salary, I could afford, besides helping Willie as much as I did at present, to lay by a sum each year, which, at the end of three years—and Willie would have finished his studies then—would suffice to purchase the furniture needed for our cottage. But it was impossible to think of such a thing. In the first place my engagement did not terminate for two years to come, and even if it did, I was too happy in my present home to think of leaving it for any pecuniary advantage, unless, indeed, it were absolutely needed for Willie's education.

To leave Iona Villa, and those there I loved so dearly, the only true home I had known since my mother's death! Oh, no, no; the very thought of such a thing, made my heart beat with accelerated pace, and with a fluttering painful motion I can scarcely describe; go to Canada and not see Willie, and those around me, who were so dear, for three years. Oh, no; when Willie and I have our cottage, I hope it will be in Portobello, or in the nearest Suburb of Edinburgh, so that I may teach my class in the same Sabbath-school and sit in the same pew in church; I wish for as little change as possible.

I answered Gertrude's letter, telling her of my present engagement and my future plans, and I begged of her to write to me often, and tell me all about her convent life. I wrote my letter between dinner and tea, and had just finished when Simpson came to call me.

As I entered the parlour, Mr. Robert, who had not dined at home, came into the room with a newspaper in his hand.

"I have good news to tell to-night," said he, "Harry Enderby has got his company."

"Is that all?" said Miss Hariote. "I do not see how much good that is going to do."

"Well, will this satisfy you?" said he, and unfolding the newspaper he read as follows:

"At Enderby Hall, on the twenty-second March, Sir Ernest Enderby, Baronet. The estates and title descend to his nephew Captain Henry Enderby, of her Majesty's Royal horse guards, blue.

Every one seemed transfixed with astonishment, and very agreeable astonishment; at last Miss Scott asked,

"But where is his son?"

"He died about a month previous to his father, from the effects of a fall from his horse."

"Oh! I am so glad; what does Ellen say?" did you see

L

Ellen?" came from the lips of each of the three young ladies almost at once.

"I have seen Miss Ellen Syme, and she says very little, but she looks as happy and as beautiful as ever."

"Did you see Mr. Syme? and what did he say?" asked Mrs. Scott.

"I saw him certainly, and I find he looks with quite a different eye upon Sir Henry Enderby, to what he did on Lieutenant Enderby; they seem to be two distinct persons; on receiving my letters, I went to Mr. Syme's, and found them at dinner, and Mr. Syme in the old way insisted on my sitting down to table with them, although I had dined at the club; I knew very well how it would end, so at the risk of frightening Ellen I said, 'I only called to give Ellen a note. I received in a letter this afternoon.' Ellen's face became as white as the table cloth, and she looked as if she were petrified with fear. Mr. Syme's face had exactly the look we see in the close black cloud, before the thunder storm bursts, and turning his face so as to look full in my eyes, he said:

" ' Mr. Robert Scott, may I ask who your letter was from?'

" ' Certainly, sir, from Sir Henry Enderby.'

" ' Sir Henry Enderby, who is he?'

" ' Why, don't you remember Harry Enderby, who two winters ago won all the girls hearts; he is now Sir H. Enderby of Enderby Hall, in the county of Suffolk, and as he wished me to deliver a note to Ellen from him, I thought there would be no harm in doing so; ' and I handed him the newspaper with the black border, portioning off the account of the funeral procession, folded outside so as first to meet his eye.

"He took the paper from my hand, and at the same time kept his eye on the note I handed to Ellen, he then rubbed his spectacles, put them on ; and I suppose from the time he took, read the account of the grand way in which Sir Ernest was gathered to his fathers twice over; he then returned me the newspaper, saying,

" ' He's a lucky fellow that; I remember him well—a tall, thin, slip of an awkward looking lad.'

" ' Pardon me, sir,' said I, ' my memory brings me the likeness of a very handsome soldier.'

" I looked to see how Ellen took all this, but saw only her chair, so handing her father a letter I had for him, I said :— ' Sir Henry has also addressed you, sir.'

" He took the letter from my hand, and put it on the table, without saying a word; I looked for the answer in his face ; I might as well have looked on a sheet of blank paper ; as on the face of the cool calculating lawyer."

" Miss Scott," said Mr. Robert, addressing his elder sister, who always made tea, " having now satisfied the curiosity of all the ladies present, I will, if you please, take a cup of tea."

During tea, Ellen Syme, and her fortunate lover, formed the principle topic of conversation.

" I am so glad,—Ellen is so amiable,—she will be quite a great lady, they will be such a handsome couple," was echoed on all sides. During all this, I felt perfectly overwhelmed with surprise, it so upset all my former speculations on Miss Ellen Syme's love affairs, although it explained satisfactorily, what had before appeared to me her very openly displayed preference for Mr. Robert ; she certainly rose in my esteem, as even under the impression that an engagement subsisted between them, I had formerly considered her as sadly want- ing in maidenly reserve.

I was twice conscious of Mr. Robert's eye resting upon me

with a peculiarly searching expression; so much so, that it made my cheek burn even to pain; perhaps my face did not possess the useful quality which he evidently appreciated so highly in Mr. Syme's, and that he was reading there the strange thoughts that were passing in such quick succession through my brain. I hope not.

The time appointed for Miss Scott's marriage was the second of May, and it was now drawing very near; I had determined beforehand to ask a holiday for myself on that day. Fortunately it was Willie's birthday, so that gave me a good excuse for wishing to absent myself. How I dreaded the usual question of, who is that?—and its reply,—only the governess.

The happy day arrived, and having obtained Mrs. Scott's permission, who, it struck me, seemed very much pleased by my making the request, I was on my way to Edinburgh before eight o'clock in the morning.

As I opened the hall door in going out, I met Mr. Robert, who was returning from the walk which he took every morning before breakfast.

"Miss Keith," said he in a tone of surprise, "why so early abroad?"

"This is my brother's birthday, and I am going to Edinburgh, so that we may spend it together; he does not expect me, so it will be a pleasant surprise."

He opened the little gate for me to pass, and following me out, shut the gate and accompanied me on my way to town.

"It still wants twenty-five minutes to eight," said he looking at his watch; "the air is so balmy, it is a punishment to remain in the house; if you will allow me, I will be the companion of your walk."

I gladly assented, and proposed that we should take the

way through the King's park. Although I often went to Edinburgh, this path was to me untrodden as well as classic ground; when either of the Misses Scott were with me, we always rode, and when alone, I had feared going through the park lest I should miss my way.

Almost as we set out my companion said :—" I surprised you the other night, when I told my sisters of the good fortune of Sir Henry Enderby."

" You did indeed," I replied. " I had given Miss Syme quite a different person as a lover."

" And to whom did you assign the fair lady ?" he inquired.

" Why, of course to yourself."

" To me!" said he in a voice which he intended to express surprise, but instead, it told me plainly enough, he had received the answer he expected, and he laughed so merrily, looking in my face as he did so, with that earnest expression of eye I had seen him wear once before. " To me! how very preposterous. Ellen Syme would feel like a caged bird by my side ; Ellen Syme, the beautiful moss rose courting the sun's rays, shewing its dazzling beauty in the noonday light and flinging its delicate fragrance on the passing breeze, would soon wither and die buffeting the waves of fate, and walking in the sunless by-paths which my love must tread ; she herself the sweet violet, hiding her head in her own lowly leaves, keeping her perfume for the touch of the loved one, and smiling alike in tangled brake or woodland dell."

My face felt so hot, I had to untie my bonnet and throw it as far off my head as propriety would permit; we had arrived at a hollow, where the ground was still soft, and the turf wet, from the wintry rains not having yet dried up ; some kind hand had placed large stones at regular distances, so that with care, the mimic swamp might be passed in safety.

Mr. Robert gave me his hand, to assist me in crossing, and walking in front himself, I passed over without even soiling my shoes; when we got to the smooth dry grass again, he still kept my hand, as if to help me along: I tried to disengage it from his, but he still kept it firmly, saying laughingly, " you will fall if I let you go alone."

" Ellen Syme," said he, resuming the subject we were talking of before we came to the swampy ground, " will, as she has ever wished to do, braid her sunny tresses with sparkling gems; my love must gather the pure pale jasmine or the flower of the mountain side to wave in her bright hair. Ellen Syme will shine in her own stately halls, the brightest there, but my wife must trim the midnight lamp, and soothe with her sweet smile the grave student who has to ascend the hard steep path of the law in the battle of life. And as a help mate, given of the Lord, share with me one hope, one fear, in the efforts I shall make all my life long to glorify the God of Israel."

He paused for a few seconds, and I tried to disengage my hand, but he held it more firmly than ever, and walking so far a few yards he said :

" The day your brother arrived in Edinburgh, you took my hand in both your own, and now I want you to give me this one, to give me a right to put a ring on it,—to call it by my name for evermore."

Was I in my senses,—could I have heard aright ?—I felt as if I occupied some giddy height, from which I was about to fall ; was it possible that he could seek me for his mate. I the little plain girl, whose eyes and pale brown hair were the only things those who loved her best had ever noticed, the little brown sparrow, with just enough of knowledge to pick up the crumbs necessary for its daily food,—whose fate was to spend its life hopping about the eaves where its nest was built;—and he, the glorious mountain bird,—the bright eyed forest king—with his dazzling plumage of scarlet and gold,—he whose path lay on the tops of the lofty pines, and the highest peaks of the snow capped mountains,—and along the rushing river, whose breast the prow of the mariner had never ruffled,—he who knew everything,—the names of all the birds,—every flower of the field,—every tree of the wild wood—he the learned man—the great lawyer, whose voice grey haired men listened to with respect, and whose advice was asked by all his peers—the good Christian whose praise was in all the churches. It could not be reality. It must be a dream, from which I would awake and feel so desolate.

CHAPTER XIII.

"Many happy returns of the day," said I, as Willie opened the door of Mrs. Livingstone's land for me.

" Ma chère sœur, " replied he, kissing my cheek as he spoke. Carlo also came to welcome me, putting his head in my open hand as I held it out to him ; poor fellow, he had soon reconciled Willie's landlady to himself, with what she called his good manners.

" I did not expect you to-day, Violet; how could you come ?" inquired he.

" Well, my brother, I did not wish you to expect me ; and I came because I wished to spend your birthday, in your home, with you ; and this being Miss Scott's marriage day, my presence was not at all needed there: so now I want some breakfast," and I put off my cloak and bonnet, sitting down quite tired as I did so.

" Breakfast !" said Willie smiling, " it is past ten o'clock."

" Nonsense," replied I ; " I left home at twenty minutes to eight." I looked at my watch as I spoke, and lo ! 'twas half past ten.

" You shall have breakfast notwithstanding the lateness of the hour," said Willie. " I have had none myself; I did not feel as if I could eat in the morning ; but I can now."

He went into Mrs. Livingstone's room, and returned accompanied by his landlady.

" How's aw wi' ye, Miss Keith ?" said she, in her usual kind tone of voice, which, since we became friends, had changed wonderfully from the frigid accents I first heard her speak in, " and sae ye hanna taen onny meat the day ; that's nae a gude fashion to come out i' the mornin' fasten'."

I told her my reason for leaving home so early ; adding, " I came through the King's park, and up the Canongate, and spent more time there than I should have done."

" Aweel, that's nae wonder, its a bonny place ; mony a hearty hour I pued the gowens there, whan I was a young lass ; and mony a happy day I clamb Arther's seat wi' him at's awa ;" and as she spoke she glanced sadly enough at the picture above the mantle-piece.

"Sae it's your birthday," continued she, addressing Willie, " an ye'er nineteen the day ; well, my bonny man, pray to the Lord to gie ye grace, ilka year, to serve him better ; and then your birthdays will be waymarks in your path, that ye'll look back on wi' joy and rejoicing."

She gave us a nice breakfast, and because it was Willie's birthday the glass dish was filled with honey.

" I maun gang ben the house," said Mrs. Livingstone, after putting the breakfast on the table, which I was rather surprised by seeing her do, as in general, the girl did everything under her orders ; " I hae latten Jean gang to see her friens for twa or three months ; I dare say ye ken that my son here (looking at Willie) is gane awa the morn for sax months, and sae I'll jist red up the house and gang the day after ; I hae a visit o' my ain to mak' as weel as younger folk."

After breakfast, I brought a cloth and warm water from the kitchen, and washed the tea cups, put them in the cupboard, wiped the table and swept up the crumbs.

Willie was really to go on the morrow ; he had been for some time back in correspondence with a Doctor in Perthshire, who kept a chemist's shop, and he had concluded an engagement, by which he was to receive fifteen pounds and his board, from May to November; the preceding evening he had received a letter requiring his immediate presence, in consequence of the departure of his predecessor; this was very sudden, but we knew he might be sent for at an hour's notice, and everything was ready a week before; not a shirt button less, not a sock with a hole the size of a pin head.

And now we sat down to calculate our debts, and what we had to pay them, I had drawn my quarter's salary on the thirtieth of April, ten pounds; and there were three bills to pay, the bookseller's, the grocer's, and the tailor's, these were found to amount to eight pounds, leaving two pounds to pay travelling expenses; the sum in hand would not only suffice for that, but leave a little pocket money for Willie.

" I have a birthday present for you," said I, producing our mother's bible, which I had brought with me; you know Willie the half of this is mine; and I give you my half as a birthday present."

We then read it together in the way prescribed by mamma as we had always done. Willie took the bible in both his hands when we finished reading, and said, " I don't like to take mamma's bible from you, Violet, it seems as if you had a better right to it than I."

" But," replied I, " I have made up my mind that you will take it, so you must not say another word on the subject."

" What must be must," replied he; " when I arrive at my new home, I will devote part of my money to buy a new cover for it. "

I almost screamed with horror, a very unusual thing for me to do, my nature not being demonstrative. " Willie, a new cover, I would not know mamma's bible if it had another cover, it would never be the same to me." Taking it from his hands, I shewed him that it was glued to the boards.

" Poor mamma," said I, " did this herself ; I recollect well the day it was done, not long before her death ; Oh ! no, it must never be taken off."

The cover in question, though certainly shabby and a little worn, was one of black leather, and was quite good enough to last for years to come. and I could not bear to have mamma's work undone.

Late in the evening Willie walked home with me to the gate, and we bid each other good-bye there. " The train for Perth started at twelve o'clock at night ; if the hour had been earlier I would have waited to see him off, but at that hour it was impossible. I have always heard that when friends part, the one who remains feels more deeply than the other : with us it was the reverse, when I left Ellenkirk I felt very bitterly parting with Willie, to come among strangers, and he was comparatively composed ; now he wept like a child, while I, although very sorry to part from my brother, felt calm and hopeful.

"It would only be for six months," I urged. "In November he would be back again in his little parlour. He was quite a pet of Mrs. Livingstone's, and she had assured him that if Prince Albert hired it for the summer, he would have to vacate it before the first of November." It was of no avail talking thus, he would not be comforted, but came back twice to bid me good-bye again over and over : The second time he said :

" Violet, I feel as if we would never meet again, when I come back, I am sure you will be dead."

" Oh Willie," replied I laughing, " what a foolish boy you are : I too have my presentiment as well as you, and mine is that I shall send for you before November to be bridesman at my marriage."

I could not make him smile; I kissed him several times and told him he must go, and at last, when I prevailed on him to do so, he turned at every few steps he took to look at me as I stood at the door. When I entered the house I went to my own room, opened the window and looked out, and there, in the pale moonlight, was Willie, standing on the pathway, looking at the hall door, as if he expected me to emerge from it.

Tears came into my eyes, but they were those of sympathy rather than of sorrow; I knew it was best he should go to learn his profession, and that by spending six months in the country, his constitution would be made stronger for his winter studies and as for his presentiments, I smiled in very joy when I thought how different in all probability the issue would be. I was in the midst of the most delicious day-dream; fanned by the light wings of the perfumed breeze, and wearing lilies and roses in my hair which had no thorns.

I watched Willie from my window until he moved away; he walked slowly on his way towards Edinburgh, turning once or twice, as he did so, to look at the house; I stood gazing after him until his figure became less and less distinct in the moonlight, and at length disappeared entirely.

When I could see him no more, I came in and shut the window, and then I knelt by my bed, and prayed our Heavenly Father to keep him by his right hand and his stretched out arm, until we should meet again.

Next morning Georgy presented me with a piece of the wedding cake, which had been consigned to her care for me.

The bridal had gone off with great eclat, the bride looking remarkably well, as brides always do, and had gone off in high spirits in a carriage and pair of her own.

We were to have a long walk that morning, as Georgy had no taste for lessons after the festivities of yesterday. We had long talked of a walk to the King's park, and as we did not wish to return until the hour for lunch, we bent our steps in that direction.

In our walk we encountered a number of gypsies; they were gathered round a fire, which was lit outside their tent: above the fire hung an iron pot, suspended from a hook which was attached to three poles fastened into the ground; from the pot issued a strong smell of onions and boiled fowls, while at the edge of the fire in the ashes, were dozens of eggs. There were three women and seven children; two of the former were occupied in caring for and adding to the contents of the iron pot, while the other, a large, handsome looking woman, with the dark penetrating eye characteristic of her race, sat a little distance from the fire, knitting; her seat consisted of a bundle of straw, on which was placed the harness and other accoutrements of the donkey, who was grazing beside his crazy looking cart, which latter was almost filled with tin pans, kettles, milk dishes, &c.; an immense pile of fir and pine branches were beside the cart, from which the women in attendance on the pot replenished the fire. We went up to them and spoke to the children, and were instantly deafened by the whole calling out at once "ge's a bawbee, lady, ge's a bawbee." One of the women at the fire came forward, calling to the children, "lat the leddes alane; had ye'er whisht, had ye'er whisht, or else ye'll get ye'er sairen," and she slapt one or two of the children on the head, upon seeing which the whole retreated behind the cart.

The woman then lifted up the shafts of the cart on two pieces of wood, which seemed to be kept for the purpose, and

asked us to sit thereon ; the seat was rather elevated for our
views, but not wishing entirely to refuse the offered hospitality, we leant against it.

The woman, who sat knitting, asked Georgy if she would
like to have her fortune told ; I at once objected, but Georgy
begged so hard to allow her have it done, telling me that whenever the gypsies came to Iona Villa their mamma always gave
them money to tell the fortunes of herself and Harry, when
he was at home, that at last I consented, truly against my
better judgment. Georgy gave her a shilling, and the woman
looking at her hand said, " Deed, my leddy, I've little to tell,
ye'll hae very little sorrow all ye'er days, ye'll get a handsome
husband and a rich, and he'll hae mair land than ye can ride
round on a summer's day ; and all the tears ye'll ever shed,
will never sink deeper into your heart than that," and as she
spoke she placed the point of her forefinger on the fat
shoulder of one of the little children, the impression of which
formed a dimple that was gone almost as soon as made ; she
then turned to me, saying :

" Will ye lat me tell your fortune, my leddy ? "

" Oh no," said I, " I know my fortune very well."

" That ye dinna," said she, shaking her head, " gin ye
kent what I ken ye wadna stand there sae light o' heart."

" It is very curious that," said she, looking in my eyes, as
if she saw there what she spoke of ; " the sun's shinin sae
bright on ane side, that aw thing looks like the red gowd an
the lavcrock's singing his sweetest sang up in the blue lifts ;
an' on the ither side, the cluds are as black as the mirkest
night can mak' them, an' rollin the ane ower the ither like the
waves o' the sea, and there they are up yonder fu to over
flowin, wi' the caul win' an' the loud thunner, and down aneath
is your bare head."

I turned away with a shiver; I knew well why I had secured such a dark doom ; but I would have far rather I had
given her the shilling, and thereby bought her silence. That
woman's ominous look, dark eye, and uplifted finger, would
cross my mind's vision, resist it as I might, like a dark shadow
sweeping over a bright stream, and make me shiver with an
undefined dread of I knew not what.

The first Sunday in May was a bright Sabbath day, and the
sun set among the grey clouds in the west with an unwonted
amount of gold and crimson.

As we went to the Sabbath school at seven o'clock, Robert
repeated some of those beautiful lines on the Sabbath, which
Graham has left us. It was easy to realize his description in
the scene around.

As we came home Robert pointed out a cottage, a little
further removed from the road than the others, a porch in
front of the door, and bow windows on either side, round which
clustered, in wild profusion, jasmine and honeysuckle, while
underneath lay plots of closely shaven grass, the whole enclosed by a fence and gate of trellis work.

I had often before noticed it in passing, and admired its
look of quiet home comfort.

" That is mine," said he ; " will you be contented with such
a lowly dwelling for your home ? "

I did not reply in words ; my heart was too full of happiness
to allow of my giving utterance to my feelings in speech ; but
in my inmost spirit I thanked the great All Father for the
true heart that was to give me such a pleasant home.

Early next morning Robert left home for an absence of
six weeks, his clients' business obliging him to go with the
Lord's Justiciary on their northern circuit, and as soon after
his return as the arrangements could be made our marriage
was to take place.

With the exception of Mr. Scott, the family were aware and approved of Robert's choice; they all called me Violet, and dear Hariote frequently addressed me in playfulness as her "little sister." Mr. Scott was not to be informed until after Mr. Robert's return from the north. I did not know what was the meaning of this, and I did not ask ; I was perfectly willing to trust all else to him to whom I had trusted myself.

Before going Robert promised that he would write to me twice a week, and that his letters would lie at the Portobello post-office until called for. " You must go," said he, " for my letters yourself; every Monday and Thursday, if I am alive and well, you shall receive a letter."

On the following Thursday Georgy and I went to the village post-office, and there was my dear letter and also one for Mrs. Scott.

When we came home, I found a letter from Willie waiting for me on the hall table. I was rich to-day ; I went to my own room, shut the door, locked it, and without putting off my hat, sat down to read my letter.

Robert began by giving me an account of the work awaiting himself and his brethren, the advocates attached to the circuit court. They had made a list of the number of persons who were to stand their trial; the number was greater than usual, and what was also an unusual occurrence, there were more than one accused of the crime of murder ; they had also made a synopsis, as far as they had materials, of the course which led to each particular crime, and in all, without a single exception, the huge demon, who stalks unmolested through the length and breadth of our fair country, a sword in his red right hand, slaying, as he goes hurrying on, from palace to cottage—from the sheltered home of him who ministers at God's Altar, to the stately halls of our senators—placing one within the stone walls and iron bars of a jail, causing another to pass by with averted head, lest those who were wont to be the companions of his midnight carouse should recognize him in his tattered robe and crownless hat, and laugh in their mad folly at his present degradation ; and the last worst phase of all, consigning hundreds of his votaries, whose name is legion, some from their homes of luxury in our finest squares and crescents ; others from dens of misery in filthy alleys, such as our well-cared-for household dogs would abhor to enter, and alas ! alas ! not a few from the green lanes and sunny cottages of our rural villages : all alike consigned by their fell master whom they have so sedulously worshipped, to dishonoured graves, there to await the coming of the Lord, when they will arise to call on the mountains and rocks to fall on them and hide them from the wrath of the Lamb. And the name of the demon who thus rules his tens of thousands with an iron rod, and with such a full assurance in their very heart of hearts that the end will be destruction, is " STRONG DRINK."

I have his letter now before me, and have copied from it almost verbatim ; I will now continue in his own words : " When I was a boy a year younger than Harry is now, John Syme and I were boarded with Mr. Watts, and attended together the high school. For many months a pretty little fair haired boy, about eight years of age, came regularly every day to the school gate, in order to receive the morsels left by the boys after eating their lunch, which most of them did in the school park : bringing bread, sandwiches, cakes. &c., in their satchels for the purpose. The child, unlike his class, had always clean hands and face ; he was very fair, but pale and delicate looking, with a broad high forehead, round which his fair hair clustered in rich curls ; he was a great favourite with us all, and we dubbed him 'bonnie Charlie.'

"Bonnie Charlie, poor fellow, was very ragged ; never, even on the coldest day, a shoe or stocking on his feet ; he never asked for clothes—only for the remains of our lunch—but at various times we brought him clothes, trousers, jackets, caps, shoes and stockings. Charlie received all without manifesting any great pleasure, brought the clothes away with him ; and that, in every instance, was the last we saw of them : not one article of anything given ever appeared on Charlie ; and when we asked where they were, he would hang down his head, say his mother took them, and that was all we could get out of him.

"At last we tired of giving him clothes that were to be of no use to him, and we resolved upon another plan ; so having from the wardrobes of several contributors obtained a whole suit of clothes, we took Charlie inside the gate, stripped him of his rags, and dressed him in his new clothes, a full suit, from the crown of his head to the sole of his foot : what a difference a few minutes had made ! such a transformation ! bonnie Charlie looked quite a gentleman. The poor little fellow smiled with evident pleasure, as he looked at his legs and arms, dressed perhaps for the first time in decent clothing ; he took off his cap, looked at it, smoothing the cloth, and then put it on his head again ; he did this several times, as if to convince himself of the reality of his having such a fine cap of his own.

"At last, tired of admiring himself in his new clothes, he proceeded to make a bundle of his former rags, in order to bring them home. To this we decidedly objected, saying we had only given the others in exchange, and that we should most certainly keep the rags for ourselves ; Charlie was very unwilling to go without them, saying, almost with tears in his eyes: ' Im feart to gang hame wantin' my ain claes, my mither i'll gang mad at me, leavin' them.'

" One of the boys made a bundle of them and sat down upon it ; Charlie tried in vain to obtain possession of it, making many ineffectual attempts to push the boy from his seat.

" ' I say, gi'es my claes, I'll get a licken gin I dinna tak them hame,' said he, giving another push, but with little avail. At last we took a summary mode of putting a stop to his entreaties ; two or three boys took hold of each garment and literally tore it to shreds.

" Next morning we congratulated ourselves on the work of destruction we had made as being quite successful when bonnie Charlie made his appearance in his new clothes.

" ' Was your mother angry for the loss of your tatters, Charlie ? ' we inquired.

" She didna say muckle aboot it,' was his reply ; but alas ! in four or five days at most, Charlie came as usual, but his new clothes, as we called them, were gone ; and in their place,. a pair of trousers and coat fully as bad as his former rags, and which had evidently been the property of a boy twice his size ; the tails of the coat and half the legs of the trousers being cut off to enable the present wearer to walk with them. We all raised a shout of indignation.

" ' Where's your new clothes, Charlie ? ' was asked by at least twenty voices at once.

" ' My mither wadna lat me keep them,' was all he would say ; and when questioned as to their whereabouts, he would invariably reply :

" ' I dinna ken, I dinna ken. '

" We asked him where he lived.

" ' Ye couldna fin out whare I bide, ' said he, evidently

not wishing to give the desired information ; ' its owre far awa, and its nae easy to win at either : '

" However, we were not to be baulked thus, so we determined to follow him home—at least some of us would do so, and John Syme and I were appointed by general consent to do the work : we asked Charlie if he would come at four o'clock.

" ' Its no easy to do that, said he, shaking his head."

" ' But we'll give you some gingerbread if you'll come, Charlie ; ' ' I dinna ken, may be I'll come ; I'll try.'

" ' You'll get six penny rolls, besides the gingerbread, if you'll come ; will you come now, Charlie ? '

" ' Weel, I'll come,' said he, as if all difficulty was removed ; and sure enough with four o'clock came Charlie, basket, long coat and all. The school was out, as we termed it, and so going outside the gate we gave Charlie his promised rolls and gingerbread ; and in order to prevent his suspecting our intention of following him, we continued talking as long as he would stay, asking him to come on Saturday and shew us the way to his home. He would not promise, he said, as if he wished to put us off; ' may be he couldna win out on Saturday, maybe ye wad forget to come yursels on Saturday, when ye dinna come to the skule : at ony rate, I hae nae muckle time, I winna promise to come;' and saying so he bounded off like a young deer, his long ragged coat fluttering behind the little creature in the evening breeze.

" We ran after him as fast as we could, having hard work to keep him in sight, his shoeless feet running along the pavement at a far swifter pace then we could do. Down the street we went, then across to another, then down again, where our feet had never before trode, until at last he entered a miserable dark court, ' where the light came only from a narrow strip of sky up far overhead, between the two black looking stone walls formed by the houses on either side ; far down the court he went and entered a door, which was only attached to the doorpost by one hinge, and consequently hung awry. Charlie entered another door inside, close to the bottom of a staircase. We kept out of sight of the inmates of the house, and yet so close to the door as to be able to hear what was said inside ; as to seeing, it was too dark for that in the court, although up at the high school it would be broad daylight for two hours to come.

" ' Whar hae ye been aw the afternoon, ye ne'er-do-weel? said a woman's voice inside, in no gentle tones.

" ' See, mither!' said Charlie in reply, look at that; I've aw thae cakes o gingbred and sax rolls."

" ' Hae ye nae ony siller ?' asked the woman, her tone of voice a little modified. We had by this time, favoured by the darkness, got inside the door close to the wall, so that we saw all that was going on ; a large rather young-looking woman, with a very red face, was standing close to the only window in the place, which shut out as much light as it admitted, being covered with dust and cobwebs ; she held the gingerbread in one hand, and in the other the basket Charlie always carried.

" Charlie stood before her, his face turned up to hers, but his back being towards us, we could not see whether in hope or fear as he replied.

" ' Na, mither, I didna get aw bawbee; ye ken I had to come hame rinnin aw the road to lat you out.'

" ' That's like your tricks,' said the woman, with a great oath, as she threw the gingerbread and the basket into the dirty window-sill, and struck Charlie such a hard blow on his head as made the little thing reel to the wall. ' You just geid threepence for thae bits o gingbread for yoursel an'

Geordie to ate ; its little ye care, gin ye stap ye'er ain stam-akes fue aneuch, what comes of the puir mither 'ats i'the head o'ye baith, an hae's na a drap or a bit to pit in her mou ; bit I'll learn ye ' (another great oath and a slap) ' to play thae tricks on me.'

"While saying this, she gathered up the gingerbread and rolls which had fallen from the basket while she was chastis-ing Charlie, and putting some dry crusts that also formed part of its contents on the window-sill seized the now re-plenished basket, and a small tin pail, and went out swearing vengeance against Charlie as she did so.

"We stood close up to the wall and in the shadow, so that she passed without observing us. When she came into the ad-ditional light afforded by the outer door, we saw that her cap was dirty and crushed, and the rest of her clothes as old and ragged as Charlie's.

"When she had fairly gone we came forward to the window to comfort Charlie ; he was sitting on the ground, with one little hand pressed to his head, where he had been struck, and crying bitterly, although without making the slightest noise. We endeavoured to comfort him in our own peculiar way.

"'Come, Charlie man, don't cry ; never mind her,' and we tried to raise him as we spoke.

"'Whisht, dinna speak sae loud ; ye'll waken Geordie,— what for did ye come here ? I'm sure I didna want ye to come.'

"'Who is Geordie ? and where is he ?' we asked.

"Come, an I'll lat ye see him, but dinna mak a noise, he's my little brither,' said he, seemingly reconciled to our pres-ence now that the ice was broken and we had seen the poverty of the land. While he was speaking he went to the other side of the room, and there, in a cradle, the top of which was entirely gone, and the sides patched with pieces of boards in all directions, lay a boy so emaciated that his head presented more the appearance of a skull with skin drawn over it than a living being. As we came close to the cradle he opened his eyes, large blue eyes they were, and must once have been beautiful; but now it was easy to see the glaze of death was fast drawing over them:

"I had seen death once before; a favourite dog had been accidentally poisoned, and she took a long time to die, lingering for days in her agony. Hariote and I tended her carefully, fancying we could cure her, and I knew well, when I saw it again, the look which came over the eyes of poor Juno.

"'Geordie, my bonnie man, look what I hae for ye,' said Charlie, taking a piece of apple from the depths of his trouser's pocket, and biting off the skin before putting it to the child's parched lips; 'tak a bit, Geordie, its rale nice,' said he, trying in vain to put the apple into the child's mouth. His eyelids closed over the great blue eyes, and there was no mistaking the look of the face. John Syme had never seen death, but, (he told me afterwards) he knew him now as well as if he had been familiar with him years ago.

"'Geordie's deein,' Charlie almost shrieked; and flew rather than ran out of the house, calling out as he went, 'mither, mither, Geordie's deein.'

"In a few minutes he returned again in the same haste as he had gone out, and going to the cradle, lifted the dying boy in his arms, keeping the thin dirty blanket around him as he did so, and sitting down upon the floor, placed the child in his lap, supporting the dying head with one arm, while the other was clasped across his legs; as he raised his brother from the cradle, we observed that he was nearly as tall as Charlie himself.

"'Oh Geordie, Geordie, winna ye speak ta me,' wailed Charlie. 'Oh, Geordie, speak to me jest ance, is there ony thing at ye wad tak?'

"And then, turning to me he said, 'gie me the bowl wi' the water, 'ats in the window.'

"I went to the window and found there a bowl with a piece broken from the side, containing a little water; we tried in vain to get a little into the thin lips which were fast closing in death.

"'O Geordie, Geordie,' sobbed Charlie, as again and again he kissed the worn cheek on which his tears fell, and which, in his deep sorrow, he seemed to be unconscious of.

"All at once the child raised his eyes to his brother's face with a bright joyous glance—no death there, no death glaze—now life most abundant was beaming from eye and brow; the thin rigid lips relaxed into a smile such as those angels wear, who always behold the face of the Father.

"'Oh! Geordie, ye'er better,' cried Charlie, his accents ringing with joy, as he kissed the wan face over and over; but even while he did so, the heavy eyes closed, and the thin jaw fell—all his troubles were over,—it was well with Geordie.

"As the little spirit departed with the ministering angel, who had waited, unseen of mortal eyes, so long besides Geordie's poor cradle, the mother entered, the empty basket on her arm, and the pail in her hand; the latter evidently containing something precious, from the care with which she placed it in the window-sill.

"'Come here, mither, and look at Geordie; Im feart he's decin,' said Charlie, never removing his eyes from the child's face for one instant.

"The woman had been drinking,—our olfactory nerves told

us that—but she was by no means drunk ; only what we Scotch
so graphically call greetin fu'.

" She came forward to the place where Charlie sat, and taking the child's body from his arms, prest it to her breast. ' Na,
he's nae dead ' said she, her tears falling fast, he's only
taen anither o' thae fits ; puir bairn, he's like mysell, deein wi'
cauld an' hunger, a saw the puir folk dee, an' the gentles hae
mair mate an' claes than they ken what to mak o' !' looking
at us as she spoke; and then added : ' What took ye here,
young gentlemen ?'

" She did not wait for an answer; looking at the child the
little motherly feeling she still retained was again excited,
and she begun to wail over him : 'My puir bairn, he's as
cauld as ice, my puir wee Geordie. Shak up the bed, Charlie.'

" Charlie went to the corner of the room next the fireplace,
and busied himself in arranging a filthy looking bed, which
lay on the floor, without either sheet, blanket, or pillow ; and
from various apertures, in which protruded part of the straw
and chaff of which it was composed, having made it as even
as possible, he took the mattrass from the cradle and placed
it close to the wall to serve as a pillow. While he was making
the bed the woman went to the window-sill and took a drink
from the pail, keeping the dead child all the while wrapped
in the piece of blanket in a reclining posture on her arm ;
she then laid down on the bed, and spreading a piece of her
tattered dress on one side, she placed the child's body upon
it, and putting her arm below her head, she pressed it closely to her bosom, endeavouring to restore warmth to the little
dead limbs. We watched her as she lay weeping and wailing
over her troubles in a voice which every instant became more
indistinct; our patience was not long tried; I should think
in three or four minutes she had wept herself to sleep. We

then endeavoured to persuade Charlie to come home with us. I do not think either of us had a very definite idea of where we were to bring him to, but we might as well have talked to the wall ; he would not listen to us.

" ' Na, na, I'll never leave my mither an' Geordie ; what wad they dee wantin' me ; there's naebody to win bread for them bit me.'

" ' But Charlie,' we urged, ' if Geordie is not dead, (we had not the heart to tell him the truth at once) he will soon die.'

" ' Nae maitter gin he war dead the morn, I'll never leave my mither; she never begs or gathers sticks for hersell; she wad dee o' cauld an' hunger.'

" ' I'll come to the school the morn,' said he, evidently wishing to get rid of us ; ' I'm rale tired the night, an' whan ye gang awa I'll steck the door and gang to my bed at my mither's back.'

" Thus dismissed, we left him, and on emerging from the court, we were rather relieved to find it was still broad daylight.

" On our way home, each took the other's hand, and made a vow, boys as we were, that whiskey should never pollute our lips, or when we grew to be men, and had houses of our own, should it ever pass threshold of ours, and that the money thus saved should be scrupulously laid aside to aid in purging from the land the accursed thing which had wrought all the woe we had witnessed that day.

" I must finish Charlie's history up to the present time, although I have far outstript the limits of a reasonable letter, and perhaps have taxed both your time and patience.

" For three days Charlie came not to the high school, and the fourth being Saturday, John Syme and I went to fish him out, as we termed it; we had a half holiday, and by permission of Mr. Watts we were to pass the afternoon and evening at Mr. Syme's house in George Street.

"When we arrived at Charlie's miserable home we found it fastened up, but by dint of wiping the glass of the window with our pocket handkerchiefs, we could discover that the room was quite empty—dirty bed, cradle, all gone.

"We were at our wits end how we were to obtain any trace of Charlie. The outer door still stood open, hanging by its one hinge, but on the opposite side from Charlie's door was a dead wall; true, there was the staircase, a narrow ladder-looking affair, very dirty, of course, with a black wall on each side, and a thick rope doing duty as a bannister; we determined to ascend the staircase and see whether the inhabitanst of the upper story could not give us some information about Charlie; as we were about to go up, a man entered the doorway with a sackful of chips on his back.

"We asked him if he knew what had become of the woman who lived here?

"'Gin I ken far the wife is the noo wha bade but there? O, aye, I ken that weel enough, but what dae ye want wi' the wife, my young masters?' and he eyed us suspiciously as he spoke.

"'We want to see her little boy!' said John Syme.

"'Weel, my man, the wife's i' the jail for murderin the laddie 'at ye'er seekin, and a bonnie little chap he was, wi' his white head; he had used to beg for bits o' bread an' the like, i' the new town.'

"'She was a drunken wife that: I heard say 'at they were decent folks once, but they baith drank afore the man died, an' sine, fan she was left her lane, she never halted; she drank the claes off the callant's back twa or three times, 'at the gentle folks i' the new town gied him.'"

" The man went up the stairs with his sack, and we turned, sick at heart, into the court again.

" As we walked slowly from the court, we looked into every window we passed, all nearly as dirty as poor Charlie's; when about to emerge into the street, a clean window attracted our attention; we looked in as we had done with the others, and wonderful to tell, there stood a geranium plant in a wooden box.

" John Syme put his face close to the window, with a hand on either side, so that he might see all that was inside besides the geranium, and after a second or two spent in examination, shouted at the top of his voice, ' bonnie Charlie!' We rushed into the house *sans ceremonie*, and truly there sat bonnie Charlie in ' living flesh and blood.'

"He sat at the side of a cheerful fire in a clean swept house, with clean, decent, although very poor looking people, his head bound up with a white cloth, and his arm in a sling.

" We did not ask him a question, but we told him we had come to the court on purpose to see him, and we gave him the cakes and oranges we had brought for him, and all the pence we had in our pockets.

" The poor fellow was very glad to see us, and at parting said : ' Will ye come next Saturday ?'

I promised we would, but John Syme said : ' I think, Charlie, we'll come back to-night,' and so we did.

" When we went to George street we repeated all our story to Mrs. Syme—every word and look we could recollect of both visits—and after dinner Mrs. Syme sent for a carriage, and taking John and I with her, went to see Charlie; she sat down beside him and spoke to him as she does to every one in trouble—with the kindest look and voice ever woman had—gave him a little basket full of delicacies prepared expressly for himself, and a suit of Alexander's clothes, who was two years younger than Charlie, but quite as large.

"Mrs. Syme also paid the woman who had kindly taken him in twice the amount of board she would have asked for him, promising to pay a similar sum each week.

"The woman was prevailed upon with great difficulty to take the money; she said : 'he's hearty welcome, puir laddie, to a bit and a sup we our ain bairns, and my gude mån says he'll share wi' the lave ; we'll never miss what he gets ; we kent his mother weel whan she was a young lassie nae bigger than our Jean, and a bonnie bairn she was, and her father an' mither rale decent folk, and weel to do, and whan she was aughteen years auld, there was nae a bonnier or better lass in the gate 'aen, and proud was the auld folk o' her, for they had nae bit hersel; but she married a lad wi' a bonnie face and little grace, and her father stood out lang against it, but it had to be—she wadna want him ; ilka ane man dree their werd, and for a while he was sober enough, though now and than he wad tak a drap mair than was good for him, but after the auld folk diet he broke out aw thegether, an' sine we began to notice at the hous an' the bairns war vera ill reed up, an' I kent brawdly at Phemie was takin' it hersel, and twa year past at Whitsunday, Sandy fell fae a hous they were buildin i' the new town, an' he never spoke again ; puir man, he had been drinkin' i' the mornin' afore he gaid to his wark, and after that Phemie never did a good turn, but drank on aw the time ; she lost aw heart, an' she never halted till she sellt ilka thing at was in the house, and sine she took Charlie frae the charity school whare he gaed wi' our bairns, an pat him out wi' a basket to beg, and this is the upshot o'tt.'

"Bonnie Charlie was ultimately taken into Mr. Syme's family, not as a menial, but to receive an education equal in every way to that given to Alexander Syme, their own son, who, as I said before, was only two years younger than Charlie. Which of the two have profited best by the care bestowed upon them, you will be able to judge for yourself, when I introduce you to Mr. Gordon, a licentiate of the Free Church, who was once 'bonnie Charlie.' His poor mother died in prison, where she was sent by those who prevented her from killing Charlie on the day his brother was buried; she had no trial, dying before it came on, in that most terrible of all deaths, the drunkard's madness; may the Lord have mercy on her soul."

There was only one line more in the letter, but that line made my breath come faint and quick with very happiness, and I lifted up my soul in accents of gladness and praise to my Heavenly Father for the strong true heart that was all my own.

CHAPTER XIV

WILLIE'S letter gave me much pleasure ; he was very happy. Doctor Macdonald's family consisted of himself, his wife, and two grown up daughters, both over twenty years of age ; they were good people, and their household was a pleasant and cheerful one.

The Doctor seemed pleased with what Willie could do, and he was doing his best ; Carlo was quite a pet, and Willie was already warned that he would not be allowed to take him to town in November. He had never felt so much at home as he did now since we lost our own home in the long ago.

This day was to be a memorable one : Georgy was to begin her Italian lessons. Some time previous Hariote regretted in my presence having neglected her Italian since she left school ; and I proposed that she should read Italian with me every day, and also sit in the room while Georgy took her lessons, for her reading would be an advantage to Georgy, as it would accustom her ear to the accent of the language.

Georgy had taken her lesson, and found it so easy that it put her in great good humour. The book Hariote chose to read from was " *Tasso's Gerusalemme liberata,*" and she had proceeded as far as the words " *Vede Tancredi aver la vita a sdegno,*" when Mrs. Scott, contrary to all precedent, entered the room.

I had never seen her in the schoolroom before except on one occasion, and then she came at my own request ; we were all taken by surprise, and rose simultaneously to offer her a chair. I saw from the important air she always assumed on such occasions that she had something to communicate which she considered of great consequence ; seating herself exactly in the middle of the sofa, and keeping her body so upright, that not a crease was to be seen in skirt or waist, she, with a face of great gravity, commenced :

" I have received a letter from Robert, and he sends his love to you all :" a long pause, and then ; "Violet, my dear child, under existing circumstances, I think you should not confine yourself to the schoolroom ; you had better be enjoying yourself in the open air," and a great deal more to the same purpose. I forget what she said ; I only know it made me feel very uncomfortable at the time, and I think Hariote and Georgy felt equally so.

I begged she would leave us to pursue the course we had laid out. I had never lived an idle life, and if I were obliged to do so now I would be most unhappy.

She still insisted, talking a great deal with most oppressive kindness. I felt nervous and hot, as if there was not enough of air in the room.

At last Hariote rose and went down-stairs ; presently Simpson came to say some one wished to see Mrs. Scott in the parlour ; doubtless it was Hariote, who had taken this method of putting a stop to this ill judged show of kindness : what a relief !

Some days afterwards Mr. Scott, addressing Mrs. Scott at breakfast, said : " By the bye, I have ordered a carriage for you and the two girls to go to Roslin, it will be here in an hour."

They were all much pleased ; they always were to go there. I was also pleased to be alone ; it was the day I expected my second letter, and I would have all day to myself to answer it, and if it were as long as the first, it would take no little time to read it twice over.

I put on my hat after breakast to go to the village post office for my letter, and had scarcely reached the hall door when Hariote came running down-stairs.

" I have been to your room in search of you; you will go with us to Roslin ? I am sure you will enjoy yourself."

" Another time," I answered, " I would be very pleased to go ; to-day I had more than one letter to write, and wished particularly to do so." It was easily settled, Hariote was too polite and too unselfish to be exigent.

I went quickly to the village; it was a lovely morning, warm and sunny, yet not too bright, the little garden plots in front of the villas (which form almost a continuous line down to the village) looked radiant with beauty in their spring attire of auricula, polyanthus, wall flower and violet, while the hawthorn hedges, loaded with white and pink blossoms, scented the morning air with their rich and sweet perfume.

I fancied the grass looked a brighter green under the clear dew-drops ; the flowers more lovely, and the birds were more abundant, and sung a louder and sweeter song than I had ever known ; all nature seemed to keep holiday, and to be as happy as I was myself.

The post office reached, I inquired " Have you any letters for Iona Villa ?"

" No, ma'am ; Mr. Scott was here by eight in the morning and got them all."

" How provoking : had you a letter for Miss Keith ?"

" Yes, ma'ma ; Mr. Scott got it also."

How annoyed I felt; what could have made him go to the village post-office ? During my residence in his house I had never known him go to the village for any purpose. I felt very

N

uneasy, yet I knew not why; and turning to the lad, who gave out the letters and who now had gone to his work at the opposite side of the place, I asked.

"Did Mr. Scott bring letters to put into the post office?"

"I think not; if he did, he must have put them in outside," was his answer.

"Good morning," said I, in as cheerful a tone as I could assume, recollecting that by these questions I might give food for village gossip, but could by no means help myself to solve the problem which puzzled and annoyed me so much. I walked lazily home, wishing now I had gone to Roslin, or better still, had gone to the post-office in the morning. Mr. Scott would not be at home until five o'clock, perhaps not then; when Mrs. Scott went to Roslin with Georgy on the occasion of poor Popity's death, Mr. Scott always dined in town, and then it occurred to me again and again, what could be the meaning of his going to the post-office? What could he mean by not giving me my letter?

The sun was by this time high in the heavens, and the heat, together with the dust rising in light clouds from the dry road, made me feel nervous. .I sat down under the shade of the hawthorn hedge beside a little spring, which in summer was quite dry, but now ran pure and bright out and in among. the grass at my feet; after resting a little, I laid my hat on the bank, and kneeling down, put my face close to the spring, and drank the true wine, made of God, that which gives strength to the body and vigour to the soul; what a difference that little rest in the shade and that drink of clear water made; I could reason now; I could understand that it was very possible Mr. Scott went often to the village for his letters; he was an early riser, and might go there every morning for ought I could tell, and as to his not having given me mine, most probably he put it in his pocket and forgot all about it; yes, this must be the reason, and no matter, whatever it was, I should have my letter in the evening.

I walked on until I came to the cottage, which was to be my own home in the happy time to come; I passed so swiftly along in the morning that I had not noticed it; now I lingered for a few minutes by the iron railing in front. The grass had been shorn since I saw it last, and was now dazzling to look upon in the bright sunshine, with thousands of gowans lifting their red-tipped, star-like heads to the morning sky.

The window of the room opposite which I stood was made so as to open in the middle as a door, and reached to the ground; it was wide open, and I could see the white marble mantle-piece with mirror reaching to the ceiling, a table with flowers, pictures on the walls, and over all a glow of purple and gold, a very *beau ideal* of a cottage home, such an one as a few months since I had never dreamt of calling my own.

I looked at my watch as I arrived at the gate—it was past ten; how quickly the time had passed, and yet it seemed to be a long time to wait until six o'clock for my letter; however, I would begin my answer, and tell of my disappointment, and how beautiful the cottage looked, and I would write to Willie—the time would pass.

As I walked through the hall, I was surprised and not a little pleased to see Mr. Scott had not yet gone to town; there he was, walking up and down the dining-room, dressed in his red dressing-gown, with his hands set deep in his pockets, apparently in no gentle mood.

I was debating with myself whether I would at once go and ask for my letter, or send Simpson to make the request, when Mr. Scott came to the dining-room door, and stood in the doorway, drawn up to his full height, his grey hair, which in general he wore combed to one side and flat, was raised from his forehead, his colour heightened, and his eye looking excited and angry.

"Miss Keith," said he, speaking rather louder than he usually did, " I wish to speak to you," and saying so he moved from the doorway so as to let me pass ; he then shut and, I think, locked the door.

He motioned me to take a chair by the sideboard, which was on a line with the door, and waiting until I was seated, he took an open letter from his pocket and threw it on the table, saying as he did so :—" Miss Keith, did you expect a letter from my son this morning ?" and he fixed his eye upon mine, as if he would read my very soul.

I replied firmly enough, " I did ; " although feeling, I scarce knew why, considerably frightened.

He came up to where I sat and stood exactly in front, and very close to my chair, his hands still in his pockets, and bending his body so that his face almost touched mine, he said, still speaking in a louder voice than usual, but very distinct and slow :—" Young woman, are you not ashamed to tell me that you have entered into a clandestine correspondence with my son ?"

I answered now with perfect firmness : " I am never ashamed to tell the truth. I have entered into no clandestine correspondence with your son ; if I had done so you could not have obtained possession of his letter to me, which I see now on the table, and which you have opened."

While I spoke, he walked up and down the room in short turns, his eyes absolutely burning with rage ; when I finished he came close up to me, holding his clenched hand so near my face as almost to touch my eyes.

" You tell the truth !" he roared rather than spoke; " you, whose whole life has been a lie ; you, who never told the truth except by accident, you infernal liar."

As he said this, he shook his clenched fist in my face, almost on my eyes, grinding his teeth in his rage. Strange to say, I felt little fear, but I felt my blood run hot in my veins with indignation, and if my strength had been sufficient, I would have crushed him to the earth.

I leant on the back of my chair, and threw my head as far back as possible, so as to get away from his hand and face ; perhaps my movement recalled him a little to himself; at all events, from whatever cause, he became calmer, and drawing himself up to his full height, he stood erect, his shoulders and head thrown back, and his hands resuming their old place in his pockets.

" Now madam," said he, " you will tell me before you leave this room, when this cursed marriage took place, and which of your damned parsons had a hand in the precious job ? '

" What marriage do you refer to ? " I inquired calmly.

" What marriage do you refer to ? " said he, mockingly, mimicking my voice in a lower tone than that I used, and then, as if his passion had returned, he added, in his former loud key, but without manifesting the same violence, and speaking slowly :—"I refer to your marriage with my son, you insolent jade."

" I am not married to your son," said I firmly.

" You are the greatest liar out of hell," said he, and again he clenched his hand and put it close to my eyes.

I pushed my chair as far back to the wall as I could, and looking him full in the face, I said in a calm, strong tone, my eye never quailing for a moment under his steadfast gaze :—" If you believe me to be a liar, what purpose will it serve your asking me questions or I answering them ?"

"Aye !" said he, almost in his natural tone of voice, " you have enough of mother wit, but in the midst of it all, you have forgot that I have read that letter, and know its contents," and he kept his eye fixed on mine as if watching for the least shadow of falsehood.

"I do not know what is in the letter," was my reply ; "but I know there can be no allusion there to an event which has not taken place ; neither do I forget that you have read the letter ; and were you not Robert Scott's father, you should answer to your brethren of the law in Edinburgh for the crime you have committed in opening my letter."

"Well, my young woman," said he, in a quieter tone than he had yet used; " as to your threats of vengeance they are not worth the breath you spend in making them; I, as Ro- bert Scott's father, am at perfect liberty to open any letter he writes except his business letters, while he is an inmate of my house."

"And now," continued he after a pause, " if you tell the truth as to your not being married to Robert Scott, you may thank your stars ; you are the fourth young woman, who in as many years, have left the situation you now hold, to be married to him: whether he married them or not, the devil knows, we don't ; but we saw no more of them ; and now, my young woman, you pack off from this, bag and baggage, to-day; and if ever I see, or hear, of your prowling about here, or in the village [and here he produced from his pocket, the pistol he killed poor Popity with, a small silver, pretty-looking thing] by the Heavens I'll blow your brains out with this pistol ; and if I catch your snivelling cur of a brother here, I'll dispatch him also. And mind what I tell you ; I am tired of all the disgraceful conduct that has been going on in my house for the last four years, with young women," (and while he spoke, his face expressed the abhorrence he felt, more than even the words he uttered) " and I have come to the firm resolution, in weal or woe, to put a stop to it, and I warn you if I find you writing to Robert Scott or holding any communication with him, and I have twenty pair of eyes in Edinburgh watching you, by the Lord, I'll shoot him."

When he had finished speaking, he went to the door, either unlocking it or taking off the cheek bar, and then went to the mantle-piece and pulled the bell ; walking up and down until Simpson made her appearance.

" Simpson," said he, in a quiet composed tone of voice, " Poor Miss Keith has received a letter, glancing at the one on the table as he spoke, which obliges her to leave this in as short a time as possible ; go up stairs and pack up her traps as quickly as you can, and bring them here ; she is too much excited to be able to do so herself."

Simpson had not much to do ; there was very little to pack, and in less than five minutes my trunk was in the hall ; it used to lie almost empty, with the key in the lock ; I had not sufficient clothes to fill the large chest of drawers that were in the room.

She brought me the key, which she handed to me with a look of respectful sorrow.

" Bring me my coat, Simpson," said her master, " I will see Miss Keith into town myself."

Simpson looked at him in evident admiration of his kindness and condescension.

His coat was brought ; he was helped to put it on, his hat and stick handed to him, and Simpson was by the gate hailing the omnibus in less time than I have taken to write it.

My trunk was lifted on the top, Mr. Scott and myself
inside, and the omnibus on its way to Edinburgh in a few
minutes more ; if its seats and sides could speak, how many
tales of cherished hopes, crushed in silence, and wounded
hearts from which beneath a calm face the life blood is dropping, they could tell.

I was seated at the opposite side of the omnibus from my
old home, and I looked at it until the last rod of the iron
railing, the chimney tops, and last of all the great elm tree
at the bottom of the bowling green, which towered above all
the rest was lost to view.

I can scarcely tell with what feelings I looked upon these
objects for the last time : my brain was in a whirl; I tried in
vain to collect and form into order my scattered thoughts;
it was impossible—sorrow, indignation, anxiety, anger, would
each in turn present itself, and clamour loudly to be heard ;
and I fear uppermost of all was abhorrence of the man seated
opposite me, and on whom I looked, with alternate feelings,
of dread and contempt.

The great clock of St. Giles was striking twelve o'clock
as we arrived in Prince street ; Mr. Scott offered his hand to
assist me in descending from the omnibus : I was now in the
free air of God's heaven, and brave men passing every
moment, any one of whom would have felled him to the earth,
gentleman as he called himself, and clerk of Session Court
as he was, had he lifted a finger against me ; and so trusting myself to the protection of God's noblemen, the masons
and carpenters, who were passing to their homes to eat their
frugal dinners, I said in a firm voice, and looking him full in
the face :—" I would not pollute mine by touching hand of
yours, after all the falsehoods I have heard you utter this day,
to be made the heiress of all the land that lies around Edin-

burgh." He did not answer me; but he gave me such a look of hatred, of deep detestation, that haunted me in my dreams for years after, when the Atlantic Ocean, with its wild winds and its three thousand miles of waves, rolled between me and the land that contained his sleeping dust.

CHAPTER XV.

I ASKED the man in charge of the office where the omnibus halted, to take my trunk until I should call for it; he at once had it put inside the counter.

I must now seek a home where I could rest and think what I was to do. In all the great city, with its thousands of human beings, in hearts of each one of whom flowed less or more sympathy with their fellow creatures, I knew not one to whom I could apply for the advice I so much needed. As I stood looking into the crowded street, I could not help asking myself, is there one among all those passers by so lonely and sore at heart as I?

I had given all my last quarter's salary to Willie, leaving myself with only five shillings; this would have been quite enough for all my wants until the end of July, had I remained at Iona Villa; now it was all I had to procure food and lodging until I found another situation.

Had Mrs. Livingstone been at home I knew that I might have rested there for a week until I could hear from Willie, or Mrs. Moodie, or in truth I know not what; I only knew I had my bread and Willie's to win, and I must seek a place to win it in; and, worst of all, my once hopeful spirit was gone, and in its place my heart was full to overflowing with misery and distrust.

I asked the man in the office if he knew of any cheap and decent lodging, where I could go at once. He answered in the affirmative, and gave me the address of one in the neighbourhood.

It was like Mrs. Livingstone's, in a land. I knew it was the woman who kept the house who came to the door, a decent-looking, well-dressed young woman, with a clean pretty baby in her arms.

I asked her if she could give me a room for a few days.

" Yes, come in."

She showed me a room far above my means.

" What is the rent of this ?"

" This room, with the litle bed-room, is ten shillings a week."

"That is too expensive for me. Have you a bedroom you could give without a room ? I wish to live as cheaply as possible."

" No, she had no other."

" Do you know of any other place you could recommend ?"

" No, she had only come to this part of the town a few weeks since, and knew no one."

What a mystery is the human heart ;—I knew that Robert Scott was virtually as dead to me, as if the grass grew green above his head. From the moment I was aware of his conduct to those three young girls, who, most likely, he had falsely deceived and left, I made an inward vow that my lips should never utter a single word in reply to word of his; that my hand should never pen a line, or my head bow in acknowledgment of any attempt he might make in explanation ; yet I would fain have had these rooms, from the windows of which I could see him each day as he went to his office. His father need not have held out such dire threats of vengeance as the penalty of my ever speaking or writing to his son : no fear of my doing either. Oh ! no, never. But the blow I had received was too recent, too sudden to snap the silver cord which bound me to him ; it was broken, but not severed. I knew it would be in the far future, but now my heart was too sore, I could not tear him from it, all bleeding as it was.

I turned away to renew my search; I thought of Mrs. Livingstone, St. Bernard's Row; perhaps she could tell me of a cheap place. I would go there and try.

I looked at my watch, it was one o'clock: what a long day it had been: it seemed as if I had lived long years since the morning.

The sun shone with a fierce heat; the day was very close, and my head ached with every footstep I took, as if it would burst. The hot rays of the sun seemed to be lying on my head. I had forgot my parasol on the hall table, and I missed it now, small as it was.

St. Bernard's Row at last. I rapped, and Mrs. Livingstone herself opened the door. She recognized me at once, and smilingly asked me to walk in.

I told her my errand.

" Rest yourself a little," said she, " the day is very warm, and you look so very tired; I will try and think of some place." How grateful I felt for her kind looks and gentle words. Oh if we only knew how much good a little smile, a kind word, may do to those bruised hearts hid under calm faces we are constantly coming in contact with, we would be less chary of these cups of cold water, and the blessing we bestow would come back seven-fold on our own heads.

I was glad to rest. It was half-past two by Mrs. Livingstone's time-piece. I looked at my watch; they nearly agreed. I must have walked at a snail's pace.

I sat nearly an hour. Mrs. Livingstone gave me an address in Pitt street, to which I bent my steps.

There was a stay-maker's sign in the window; it was down in

the area. I knocked at the door, which was opened by a nice looking young woman.

"Have you any rooms to let?"

"Yes, I have one nice bed-room."

"Is it cheap? I cannot pay much."

"Yes, it is only six shillings a week."

I looked at it, a large room, and a nice clean looking bed. I would be so thankful to lie down. I had not six shillings to give; but I would write to Willie, and by the end of the week he would send me all the money he had. I knew he had not spent his pocket-money, or he would have told me so; my food need not costme much.

"I will take the room for a week."

"Very well, ma'am; I always require the money in advance."

I explained how my finances stood.

"She was very sorry," she said, "but they had lost so much money by giving the lodgings without the price in advance, her husband preferred having them empty."

The woman looked sorry, as she said she was, looking hard at my face, she continued:—"You look tired and sick-like. If you will wait for a half hour, I will make you a cup of tea."

I thanked her, "No, I could not take anything, but did she know of any other place equally cheap?"

"Yes, one in the same street; number twenty-three. She is a lone woman,—she can do as she likes,—she has no one to control her."

I tried this place also. The landlady was a woman past fifty: thin, very wrinkled, sharp looking.

"Have you a cheap bed-room to let?"

"I dinna tak weman," was the reply, in a thin, ill-tempered voice and scrutinizing look.

" I am so sick I would be very thankful to get in for only one week ;" and as I spoke, I felt so ill, I leant against the door-post.

" Weel, ye maun gang wi' yer sickness to some ither place, we dinna keep nane o' yer kind here," and she shut the door.

What was I to do, I was almost fainting with fatigue, and my head throbbed as if the veins in my temples would burst. I walked on a little further,—I came to a street running parallel with George street; I walked along scarcely knowing why : I felt parched with thirst,—there is a baker's shop, —I can have a drink of water there perhaps.

" Will you have the goodness to give me a drink of water ?" I asked a clean-looking young girl inside the counter.

" Surely ; sit down, ma'am."

She brought me a glass of clear delicious water, and presented it with a smiling face. How grateful I felt for that smile !

" You look tired, Miss ; will you take a seat ?"

I looked the thanks I was hardly able to speak. I sat a long time ; my limbs seemed glued to my seat.

" Do you know of any lodgings to let here ?" I asked the girl.

" Yes, three doors above this, they let rooms. Would you not eat one of these warm buns ?"

" Thank you, no ; I am not hungry." I was not; I felt as if I should never care to eat again. That girl was a good Samaritan. I bade her good-bye, and went in the direction she had pointed out to me.

A servant girl came to the door in answer to my knock. I asked my usual question. The girl turned her head inside the dark-looking passage, and said in a loud key :—" There's a leddy here wants the rooms, mem."

The mistress came forward, a large dirty-looking woman, wearing a thick muslin cap, and hair that looked as if it had not been combed for a week.

" Did ye want them for yersel'?" she inquired.

" Yes, only a bedroom, no matter how small."

" Come in, ye'll see what we hae."

The rooms were in keeping with the lady of the house, dirty and untidy.

" What is the price of the bedroom alone?"

" Weel, ye can hae it for seven shillings, an' that's nae dear; but I maun hae the siller afore han'."

I told her it was rather too much for me to give, and I could not give the money for a few days. I would receive it by post in six days at most.

" Nae, I canna gie the room; I winna wait for sax hours."

When I came out to the street, a large drop of rain fell on the stone pavement, and then another and another; at last it came in earnest, a heavy shower. I stood in a doorway until the rain lightened a little, and then I tried other lodging houses, all with the same success: every one must have the money in advance.

I was wet as well as weary now; the street lamps were lit, and I began to ask myself whether I might not have to remain in the streets all night, and if so, where I should sit down. I felt quite prostrated in mind and body. The last house I had gone to, the woman told me if I went to the Old Town, I would find a cheap lodging there. I thought of Mrs. Livingstone: there might be another like her there; and, weary and sick as I was, I bent my steps towards the High street.

The night was very dark, with a drizzling cold rain. The lamps were lit, but seemed not to give half their usual light.

Just at the entrance to the High street, I stood by a lamp post, leaning against it for a few minutes, my limbs trembling with fatigue. Two women passed with large bundles on their backs, and walking quickly, yet with a hard tread and unsteady motion, more like that of a half drunk man than a woman. When they had passed a few yards, one of them addressed the other loud enough for me to hear, but in a language I did not understand; and the speaker, turning sharply back, peered under my hat; the light from the lamp fell full on her dark eyes and handsome face, as she said with a wicked triumph in her eye and voice, which thrilled through my every nerve :

" Ye widna believe me yon day, my leddy; bit the rain's come noo, and the win' 'ill blaw loud encuch afore the morn's morning; bit it 'ill no halt the rain, an' the storm winna be ower for mony a lang day." So saying, she rejoined her companion, and was lost in the darkness. It was the gipsy woman of the King's park.

I turned to resume my search with a shudder, and sought the house I had been directed to in the High street. I received there the same response as I had met with all along; it was in a land, and the staircase was very wide, and had scarce any light, the lamp being placed in the first flight. By sitting close to the wall, I would not be observed by those going up or down; they would naturally hold by the bannister. I would sit down and rest at all events.

I thought over the events of the morning, what Mr. Scott had said of his son—was it not possible it might be false, false as the story he told Simpson so unblushingly in my presence ? Such a man would not hesitate to vilify the character of his son, if it suited his own convenience.

But, on the other hand, it occurred to me that on one or two occasions, when Georgy spoke of her former governess,

Hariote had stopt her by a look. The last, Miss Watson, was only four months in the house, and Georgy spoke of her as one who had done her duty. How was this to be accounted for? And young Syme, on the day of the donkey ride, told me with a peculiar laugh, that Miss Watson sat in Robert's seat in church, and that he always accompanied her in her visits to her friends in the interval of public worship ; and, more convincing than all, a testimony against which there was no appeal ; one that to me was " confirmation strong as proof of holy writ" was the truthful and earnest look with which Mr. Scott made the accusation against his son. Alas ! look which way I would, it was all too true.

Where were the roses and lilies now ? The fierce north wind had come—and the cruel biting hail and sleet beat upon my roses, and there they lay, withered and dead at my feet. They would never bloom again. I could not bear to see them lie there, soiled with the black earth and splashed with the cold rain. I lifted them up, and shook off the mud from the poor crushed blossoms, and pressed them, all wet as they were, to my hot brow. Alas ! they were full of great thorns, and made my temples bleed.

Two men passed up the staircase. I kept close to the wall, and, coming in from the comparatively lighted street, they did not see me. They each held by the bannister of the staircase as they went up. This roused me from my reverie. I put my hand over my eyes, and leant on it for a second or two, trying to think what I should do. I knew it was impossible to pass the night there ; when I heard a whisper in my ear, as distinct as if breathed by human voice, low yet clear, say, " The Lord is in heaven yet," and my soul answered, " Verily so he is—I will call upon him in the day of trouble, and he shall deliver me."

o

And there, in that dark staircase, I knelt and prayed to the God of Israel, that he would set a light on my path, and provide me a shelter, where I might lay my weary head. I arose from my knees comforted, and sure that the Lord would send me an answer in peace.

I went into the street, and it immediately occurred to me that I could not be far from Mr. Wilson's shop.

I knew Mr. Wilson well; he was a relation of Mrs. Livingstone's, and Willie and I had purchased from him the few articles of clothing we allowed ourselves. I would go there; most likely he could direct me to a lodging for the night. I had a strong conviction that my troubles for the night at least were ended.

In two or three minutes I was in Mr. Wilson's shop. He was putting up the shutters.

" Miss Keith," said he in surprise, " you are late in Edinbro' the night."

" Yes," said I, " I am to spend the night in town, and have come to ask you to recommend me to a lodging."

" Ye'll surely gang to Mrs. Livingstone's," said he, looking still more surprised than before. " She'll tak it vera ill if ye dinna; no for the sake o' the siller, but ye used to be sae thrang."

" But you forget," replied I, " Mrs. Livingstone left town the morning after my brother went."

" O!" said he, as if he now understood what I meant; " ye didna hear, at she fell down the stair an hurt hersel the night ye'er brother gaed awa? he was na five minutes out o' the house whan it happened; it was a gude thing at I was there or else there widna hae been a livin' soul to lift her up; she was feart to sleep in the house, her leafu lane, and bade me come up whan I shut the shop."

" I am very sorry to hear that, and I would have come in to town on purpose to see her, had I known of the accident, which I did not."

" Aweel, its ower true though ; and she was laid up for aught days, or mair, and her dochter cam up fae the meadows to notice the hous an' tak care o' her mither ; but she's hame again, an' Mrs. Livingstone's weel ancough noo, an' she'll be real pleased to see you, I warrant ; come awa, I'll light ye up the stair mysel."

And taking up the lantern, which was on the counter already lit, he turned off the gas, locked the shop-door, put on an iron bar with a padlock, locked it also, and in a few minutes I was seated by Mrs. Livingstone's bright little fire, my wet cloak and hat hung up to dry, my muddy boots off, and my feet in a pair of Willie's old slippers, resting on a footstool placed inside the old fashioned round fender.

In a few minutes more, she gave me a cup of weak tea, with a piece of biscuit floating in the tea-cup. " Drink that, my bairn," said she, in her kind motherly way, " ye'er nae like as ye ware hungry, but ye'er very like as ye'd fastit ower lang." She had defined well ; I certainly did not feel hungry, but I was sick and faint from want of food.

When I had drank the tea, she took the cup and saucer, washed and put them in the cupboard, took up her knitting and sat in her easy chair on one side the fire.

" An noo, my bonnie bairn," said she, " ye'll tell me what brought ye to Edinbro' sae tired an' weary at this time o' night."

I did not answer for some time, and my companion sat beside me quietly knitting, manifesting not the least symptom of impatience. I had made up my mind that no one should ever know from me of my engagement to Robert Scott ; I would fain have buried my reminiscences of him deep in my heart, as a thing never to be spoken of. I thought, then, it was impossible for me ever to know happiness again; but it was not a part of my nature, to throw the shadow from my own life, on that of another, and I would fain have put his image in the innermost recess of my heart, and piled the autumn leaves and wintry snow so high above it, that those who knew me best, and to whom I was most dear, would never suspect it was there.

But I was placed in a peculiar position by coming to Mrs. Livingstone's house, at the hour and in the way I did. Had I left my situation at my own request, and on good terms with my employer, it was not likely I would have gone, without at least having provided myself with a temporary home. I was without sufficient money to pay for food and shelter for even one week; and I wanted advice as to how I should proceed in order to procure another situation, as much as I needed the home, the kind words and kindlier looks which Mrs. Livingstone had bestowed upon me.

During the time all this was passing through my mind, she sat knitting as if her breakfast on the morrow depended upon her work being finished in a given time, and as if she was perfectly oblivious to my presence.

At last, I told her the truth, all the truth, my engagement to Robert Scott, the time at which that engagement was to be consumated, his mother and sister's being cognizant of the same, and lastly I repeated every word I could recollect of the violent scene in the morning.

I watched her narrowly as I spoke; towards the end of my recital she knitted so quickly I could scarcely distinguish which needle she used; when I had finished, she took her spare needle, stuck it behind her ear, as a clerk does his pen, and

laying her knitting on her lap, locked one hand in the other,
and put them above it, sitting for some minutes without speaking.

" Weel, my bairn," said she, at length, " ye ma'an c'en put
a stout heart to a stae brae : but gin I ware in your place I wad
na gee ower muckle heed to what a man like auld Maister
Scott wad say, clerk o' Session Court though he be ; a man at
wad tell sae mony lies to his ain servant lass in your very
face, wadna care aie bawbee to tell a dizen mair gin they wad
sair his ain purpose : an nae doubt it wad gang sair against
the proud stamacks o' thae Scotts to lat their auldest son
marry the governess.   And for the twa young leddies at was
ilka ain o' them sweethearts o' Maister Robert Scott's, I
dinna believe aye word o't : its vera like what the generality
o' young men wad dee, an' little doubt the auld man was
minden on his ain ongaens in his young days, whan he made
up that lee ; but its nae like young Deacon Scott : na, na, its
aw aye lee frae tap to tail : but there's aye thing ats clear
anaugh to me, the woman folk are jist as far against ye as
the auld man is, gin it ware nae sae, what for wad they gang
aff to Roslin at a minute's warnin' like that ; they never gaed
afore sae sudden, did they ?"

" No, that was very true, but I would stake my existence
on the truth of Hariote Scott's character."

" Weel, may be ye wid, bit I wadna stake my twa feet
atween this an the kirk door on nae sich thing ; what for did
na she speer at ye in the mornin gin ye wad gang wi' them,
an nae wait till ye had on ye'er bonnet an' was maist out at
the door to seek ye'er letter ; an' faw tell't the auld man at
ye'er letter wad be there, but the young lassie at ye took to
the post office wi' ye the first time."

This seemed all very good reasoning, but I knew Hariote

and Georgy too well to suffer a doubt of their integrity to exist in my mind for one moment; and I said so very decidedly.

"Weel, weel, ye'll hae your thought about it, an I'll hae mine; but the upshot o't aw is, that ye man gee the young man up for a while at ony rate."

"I have made up my mind to give him up for ever."

"Weel na, I wadna dee that either. Maister Scott is nae bound to be answerable for aw his father's rampageen an' lees: but it wadna dee for you at aw, to marry him the noo, contrary to aw his folk's wul; ye'er nae sae auld yet, bit ye can wait for twa or three years, an be a better wife for the waitin'; and gin Deacon Scott be the godly man I tak him to be, he wonna brak his word to you for aw his folk can say or dee." And gin ye faw in wi' a gude place i' the new toun, an nae doubt but ye'll do that, ye'll aye be seein ilk ither, at the kirk on Sabbath, an that i'll keep ye baeth frae forgetten; and in the course o' Providence, something i'll turn up afore lang."

"I do not wish to remain in Edinburgh if I can possibly help it. The threat contained in Mr. Scott's last words before we left the house would be ever in my thoughts. I could not pass along the street without fancying myself watched by some of his spies, and the violence of his temper is such that if he were roused I could fancy him shooting his son with as little hesitation as he did Popity." And I told her the story of poor Popity's death.

"Na weel than, did I ever hear the like? the auld haythen at he is, at never sets his feet inside a kirk door. But its a great difference, my bairn, shootin a poney and shootin his ain auldest son: na, nae fear o' that, he jest said that tae frighten ye, and I'll tell ye anither thing, at 'ill haud him frae shootin' his

son mair than ony thing else ; gin he did it the day, he kens
brawly, nane better, that in aye sax weeks after, he wad be
hangit himsel on the streets o' Edinbro' : na, he'll nae try that
trick, I'se warrant ; he has ower muckle regard for his ain four
quarters."

As she said this, she stirred the fire, which was now getting
low, and raking the cinders together, put a peat upon the live
coals preparatory to resting it for the night, and again sat
down to wait until the peat would kindle a little before putting
on the coals.

" An' his twenty pair o' een ats watchin' you," continued she,
" O ! the sinfu' lein man, theres nae aye 'ee, bit his ain ougly
guilty cockles, an' afore this time next year maybe they'll be
lien caul an' dark aneath the kirkyard moold.   O sirs," continued she, sighing deeply, " isnae it awfu' an auld man we ae
fit i' the grave to pit sae muckle sin on his soul for naething, to
pit eternity in comparison wi' a wheen havers.   Oh ! me, me."

She then rose, and going to the other side of the room returned with the Bible, which she put in my hand, saying, " Ye'll
read the word o' the Lord, in the forty-second psalm, and then
we'll commit oursels to the keeping o' him, wha slumbereth not,
an' we'll pray to Him to create a new heart in the puir auld man,
that I'm sair feart never prays for himsel."

And she did pray earnestly that there might be a new heart
and a right spirit created and renewed within him.

I slept in Willie's bed, and I praised the Lord with my
whole heart, for his great mercy in giving me a bed to lie on and
a shelter over my head.

CHAPTER XVI.

I AWOKE next morning with the early dawn; perhaps the unwonted noise in the streets, so different from the perfect stillness I was accustomed to, broke my rest e'er the physical wants of my nature were satisfied.

In the beautiful home I had left but yesterday, where I was so happy—happier than I had ever been before, happier than I could ever hope to be again—my day was ushered in by the wild bird singing his song of praise, or the winds stirring among the green leaves of a huge oak, whose branches almost touched my window pane. A robin had built his nest in the ivy and jasmine which covered the eastern wall of the house, where my window was placed ; I used regularly every night to scatter crumbs in the box of mignonette which filled the window sill ; and the robin and his mate, who knew well where to find their morning meal, repaid me by singing there their sweetest matin hymn. Here, the noise of heavily laden carts passing over the paved streets, and the loud shouting of the carters, were the sounds that were ringing in my ears. I was only half conscious, my eyes still shut, but my heart was oppressed with a feeling of such intense woe as I had never felt before, and in all my troubles have never felt since.

A sense of utter desolation, some dire calamity, I knew not what, oppressed my soul, as if the gates of hope were for ever closed, and I cried out in my misery, " would God it were morning ;"—the sound of my own voice awoke me to perfect consciousness; I opened my eyes, and lo ! " t'was morning,"

I could not at once comprehend where I was, and why; but when I did I knew that although I had suffered a sore trial, and one that would not lightly pass away, the effects of which I then fancied I would carry to my grave, yet I also knew my trouble was not of my own seeking; I feared not the searching eye of the great all Father, and I could still, in firm faith, plead the precious promise, " when thou passest through the fire I will be with thee, and through the rivers, they shall not overflow thee."

When I met Mrs. Livingstone at breakfast, I told her of the offer I had received from Mrs. Moodie long ago.

I knew she had found a governess, but not one who suited her, and that she was now on the out look for some one to fill the situation after the vacation, and would, I felt sure, gladly give it to me, were I to write to her asking for it. I also told her the reason I had for wishing for the present at least to be away from that part of the country.

I then spoke of Gertrude's letter, and the salary I would receive were I to go to Canada: the teacher in the convent there would not be required until the first of September, and by writing now, there was every probability of my obtaining the situation.

The old lady seemed lost in thought for some time; at last she said:

" As to your gaen back to Ellenkirk, I think ye are weel out o't or any ither place at your uncle wad be in; its ower easy seen he disna like aye bit o' ane o'ye, an he's a great gentleman, an' ye'er a puir fatherless an' mitherless lassie, sae its better for ye to had out o' his road, folk will hearken to the like o him' at wonna to you, and gin ye'er nae near him he'll forget you, and if he shouldna, his ill word 'ill do ye nae scaith."

" But," continued she, after a short pause, " gin ye ware nae frightened to gang sae far awa's America, I think ye wad mak a good job o' that : afore three years ware ower ye wad hae a pouch fu' o siller to help you to begin hous-keepin' wi' ; an I'm nae feart gin Maister Keith has ony chance at aw, but he'll haud up his head wi' the best o' them yet." She stopped for a few minutes, and then again continued :—" But its a far gait for a young lassie like you to gang her lee fu lane ; I doubt ye wad be ower fearet; deed its nae reasonable to think o't."

" No," said I; " I would not be in the least afraid to go, and I think I would like it very much ; I would remain three years, and come home when Willie has finished his fourth year, but then it is impossible for me to think of that ; and I explained to her exactly the state of my finances.

She reached over her hand for my tea-cup, from which I had drank my tea, and placing it beside her, said :—" Aweel, gin that's the only thing that keeps ye frae ga'en ye'll nae bide at hame for that ; I'll lend you as muckle as will tak you there, and twa or three bawbees for bye; it wonna dee for you to gang there wi' an empty pouch : and gin you like, I'll gar Andrew Wilson write to a frien we hae in Glasgow, and tell him to send word whan the first ship is gaen to sail, and what will be the price o' the passage ; and afore the answer comes ye'll hae time to mak up your mind if ye'll gang or no."

To this arrangement I most readily assented, expressing my sense of gratitude for the kindness : Mrs. Livingstone then took up my cup, and looking into it, said :—" There's a journey as plain as a pike staff in the bottom o' ye'er cup. When I was a young lass we used aye to look at ilka cup o' tae we drank, (but we didna drink tae ilka mornin' or night either then;) gin we ware only gaen doun to the meadows the morn's mornin like, we had try gin there was a journey in our cup.'

"Oh! sirs," continued she, and her face assumed a sad earnest expression, "thea ware blithe days; but aw the folk that read the cups wi' me then are cauld and quaet noo."

After breakfast Mrs. Livingstone put on her shawl and bonnet, saying, ' I am gaen doun to the office for your kist, and I'll speak to Andrew Wilson tae write to Glasgow; and for bye that I've twa three errands o' my ain; sae it will be weel on to twal o'clock afore I win ham; and ye'll mind, my bairn, an' nae open the door to ilka ane at chaps: jest speir " faws there" first. There's a wheen orrow folk frae the Gallowgate and there about, at comes roun regular to the lands (that they ken there's nae men folk bidden in), big stout chields wi' sticks in their hands; and its vera easy to lat them in; but its nae sae easy to get them out again: sae just keep the Smith's fingers atween you an' ony ane at chaps till ye ken wha it is.'

Having, as she thought, frightened me into keeping the door securely locked in her absence, she departed, returning, however, in less than ten minutes, and as she knocked at the door, called out, " its me."

The reason of my kind hostess's return was to bring me some writing paper; taking the keys from her pocket she opened her bureau, and bringing therefrom pens and ink, laid them before me, saying: " I came back to gee ye that; I thought ye wad be tired aw the forenoon readin' your Bible and Pilgrim, sae I brought ye a sheet o' paper to write to Maister Keith on; and ye needna tell him ower muckle about yeersell; jest say ye left ye'er place, ye needna say gin ye left it wi' ye'er will or against ye'er will; puir lad, there's nae reason for pitten his head through ither wi' a

thing that i'll be sae soon mendet. Sae noo gude day to ye,
for a while, and tak care ye keep the hallen door fast steeket."

I was very glad to receive the writing materials; under
any circumstances I should have quite dreaded passing a
whole forenoon without employment for either my head or
my hands; but at present, I knew that activity of mind and
body was my best resource; that the greatest help I had in
endeavouring to recover my usual tone of mind was constant
work.

I felt more deeply now, even than yesterday, with all its
anxiety and mortification, the woe and weariness that was so
surely my future lot. I could not all at once banish the
image of Robert Scott from my heart, the all unworthy lover
of four young girls in succession as I knew him to be; every
look he had ever given me, almost every word I had heard
him utter, were engraven with a pen of fire on my soul; even
when I believed him to be the affianced husband of another,
he occupied no common place in my esteem; since first I knew
him, he had been my *beau ideal* of all that was good and
great in man. I tried earnestly to say in my soul, "I was
dumb and opened not my mouth, because thou didst it," but
it would not be, I could not, not yet. I new well that the
promises were shining like countless stars above my head;
but I saw them not for the black clouds which intervened
and obscured their light. I felt as a sapling shivered and
bent before the rough tempest; whenere I essayed to raise
my head, the thoughts of what had been, came, and it was
beaten down, down. I was as one striving to walk on the
stormy sea; but as each strong wave came up heaving in its
angry might, I sank where'er I trode. I knew God's covenant stood sure as ever, but I could not clasp it to my
breast and say: 'for me, for me.' My faith's flame quivered

almost to extinction; I strove to walk in my own strength, and weakness was thrilling through every nerve; my only consolation lay in thinking that soon this bitter life would be ended, and then man's wrath would be harmless; then, no false one could be arrayed as an angel of light; there, we shall know, even as we are known,—and then the question came sharp and strong as a poisoned arrow, " who should I best like to meet there?" and I lay down on my face and wept bitterly.

The great clock of St. Giles chiming eleven woke me to consciousness; the indulgence in unavailing sorrow would never do; I was a responsible creature, placed in a state of probation; I, even I, cipher as I am, have work to do for God, and thinking of the past will do me no good, but it will totally unfit me for obeying the direct command, " whatsoever thy hand findeth to do, do it with thy might."

I wrote to Willie, and in doing so, took Mrs. Livingstone's advice. I told him I had left my situation at Iona Villa, but that I expected soon to get another ; that some time since I had an offer of one, with a salary of seventy-five pounds, which I then refused, but I believed it was still unfilled, and I meant to apply for it : the only draw back was, if I obtained this situation with its large salary, I would be obliged to live at a distance from Edinburgh, so that we might not be able to see each other during the three remaining years of his student life ; however, this would seem but a small sacrifice when the time came for us to commence our life's journey in earnest, and we found ourselves possessed of quite a little sum to begin with.

With what different emotions we write, and those we write to read ! Little would poor Willie think while reading this letter, so replete with hope, that while my pen traced these pleasant words, my life blood was dropping, dropping.

I also wrote to Mrs. Moodie, and after telling I had left Portobello, in consequence of a misunderstanding with Mr. Scott, I told her of the offer I had received through Gertrude, and that I had some thoughts of accepting it. I wished her to give me the advice I knew she was so willing to bestow on all her old pupils, and I told her why I would not like to go back to Ellenkirk. I need not have done this, she knew it well.

Gertrude's letter was not so easily managed; I had said too much of my happiness in my former letter when I refused to go to Canada; she would not be satisfied by my merely saying I had left my situation. I told her I had left from the force of circumstances, over which I had no control, and through no fault of mine; that my leaving Iona Villa had cost me the bitterest tears I would ever shed, but that, were it in my power, I would not again return to my former pleasant home. I offered, if the situation of English governess was vacant still, to fill it to the best of my ability.

I had finished my letters as Mrs. Livingstone came in. Gertrude's was the last, and the reminiscences it called up were not calculated to raise my spirits. I dare say I looked what I felt.

The good woman sat down on a chair opposite to me, as if she were very tired, and without putting off her bonnet or shawl, folded her hands together, and looking me full in the face, said:—" Sae' my bairn, ye are nae willin to lippen yoursel to the Lord yet."

" Be strong and of a good courage, be not afraid; neither " be thou dismayed, for the Lord thy God is with thee, whi- " thersoever thou goest."

She spoke those words, not with the broad pronunciation she generally used, but just as they are written; only with her strong accent, and in a solemn manner, which said as plainly as words could have done. " I have a message from God unto thee." And so it proved in very deed, in spirit and in power ; it did not take away the sting which rankled in my bosom, but it took away all fear ; I was ready to go forth, trusting all to him whose blessed words she had used.

I untied Mrs. Livingstone's bonnet and shawl, folded the latter, and laid both in the drawer from which I had seen them taken.

" That's a gude bairn," said she, smiling kindly upon me ; " and noo Maister Wilson's letter is aff to Glasgow, and we'll hae an answer the day after the morn ; and after dinner ye'll need to gang yoursel for your kist, they wadna gee't to me nor thanks ; sae we'll baith gang doun in the afterneen and tak it up in a cab."

In a couple of days Mr. Wilson received an answer to his letter. The sailing ship *Winged Zephyr* was to sail in a fortnight, with accommodation for ten steerage and six cabin passengers, the price of the passage was ten pounds in the cabin ; that of the steerage four. There were steamships sailing every fortnight, but in those the price of the passage was nearly double that of a sailing vessel.

Before deciding finally, I waited for Mrs. Moodie's letter. It came in due time, and strange to say, a letter from Gertrude inclosed in it.

Mrs. Moodie approved highly of my going to Canada. She wrote thus : " Besides making more money than at your age you could hope to do here, you will receive very material advantage yourself in associating with highly educated and refined women such as nuns who conduct educational establishments for the higher classes are ; they are almost without exception the daughters of the aristocracy of the land which they represent; and by mixing familiarly with French ladies of their rank, you will unavoidably acquire the best and purest style of the language, which, I have sometimes feared, you prefer to your own; and, which is now almost the universal medium of communication on the continent; and apart from any consideration relative to yourself, I should rejoice at your being with Gertrude."

Gertrude's letter was written for the acknowledged purpose of again urging me to accept of the situation which I had already refused, but which I now was so anxious to obtain. By the date of her letter I saw that she could not have received my reply to her last.

She described her life as being happy and tranquil beyond what she had ever imagined possible in this world, previous to the happy time when there will be no sin, no sorrow, when each will love his neighbour as himself.

There was an immense hospital attached to the convent, and her description of the unremitting efforts of the good nuns, and their unwearied labours in their attendance on the sick and aged, was certainly one of the most beautiful pictures of self-denying benevolence that pen could draw; their simple and child-like faith, their sincere affection for each other, and implicit obedience to their Mother Superior, were themes she delighted to dwell on. They were to have a bazaar for the benefit of a poor monastry of the order of the "Passionists," and the diligence of the nuns in working for it amounted to absolute hard labour, rising at four o'clock in the morning, and working busily in the intervals of worship and their usual every day duties, until eight o'clock in the evening; and this not for a few days, but for six weeks at once. And all so cheerful, so unostentatious; none taking credit to themselves for their good deeds, but each esteeming the other better than themselves ; each anxious she should be allowed to do the most to exercise the greatest self-denial.

I read both Mrs. Moodie's and Gertrude's letters to Mrs. Livingstone, saying, as I concluded, that I now felt almost glad at the prospect of going to Canada.

"Aweel, my bairn," observed she, (alluding to Gertrude's description of convent life) "that's aw. vera gude, and I dinna doubt bit thae nuns aften lead better lives than them that has had the word of the Lord in their hands sinc they could pit twa words thegither ; and doubtless the Lord has his ain among ilka tribe an tongue, but dinna lat them mak a Catholic o' you, my lassie ; that was ae thing I didna think o' afore : gaen in among them is jist like setten your feet on the edge o' a precipice ; ye'll need mair care in half a dizin steps there than ye wad need in sax mile on the high road ; ye hae a clearer light than they hae, and ye ken that aw the good deeds ony sinfu creature can do, atween the rising o' the sun and the gaen down o' the same, will stand for naething in the great day o' the Lord. Nae doubt aw the good works we can do are necessary to let the world ken that we are the servants o' Him wha has said : ' Inasmuch as ' ye did it unto one of these my brethren, ye did it unto ' me.' But there's a great danger o' placing our trust in these filthy rags of our own righteousness, and forgetten the weary steps that were ta'en for three and thirty years in auld Jerusalem, and the precious blood that was shed on Calvary for us lang ago."

It was finally decided that I should go. Mr. Wilson wrote to Mr. Brown, his Glasgow correspondent, to take a cabin passage for me on board the *Winged Zephyr*, which was to sail from the Clyde on the tenth of July. It was now the eighth, and on the morrow Mrs. Livingstone and I

P

were to go by rail to Glasgow, and remain all night in the house of her friend Mrs. Brown.

Mrs. Livingstone went out in the afternoon, leaving me at home to prepare tea and pack my trunk in her absence. I had all my letters in one packet kept together by two bands of elastic : Robert Scott's letter was among the rest, and I took it out that I might burn it; there was no good in keeping it, but much evil. The sight of this letter, I felt sure, would for years to come be sufficient to awaken thoughts and feelings which had better far lie buried deep in some unfathomable abyss, never again to rise to the surface.

I walked to the fire place and held it above the fire I had made to boil the tea kettle, when a thought struck me, I will look once more, only once, at the signature. I opened the letter, I would only look once and then burn it. I read the first and last paragraphs. No, I would not burn it : what use would there be in doing that? I would never look at it again, only this once, but I would not burn it. I sat down and read it all through. And then I laid it at the very bottom of my trunk, that it might be quite out of sight.

It did me no good reading that letter; my cheek burned, and my spirit wandered on the mountains of vanity all that evening, and far into the night.

CHAPTER XVII.

WE were not to leave Edinburgh until eleven o'clock, and I had laid aside the morning for Willie's letter, which was still unfinished. I had to tell him where I was going, and had delayed it as long as possible. I knew well the pain this letter would give to the one who loved me best; but I was doing what seemed best for us both; he was the only one I had to live for, and if it had not been best for him as well as for myself, I would not have gone. I told him all this, and expatiated as largely as possible on the benefits which the money I was to win in Canada would bestow on us both when his studies were finished; then said I had parted with Mr. Scott on bad terms, that both he and Mr. Robert had behaved ill towards me, and that for the future it was my wish that neither he or I would have any communication with the family. We were not likely to come in contact with them; our respective paths in life lay on each side of a broad river; theirs, by reason of their wealth and position, lay high up on the broad, green table land above, while ours, even after we had succeeded in passing across the stream, must for a time at least, be with slow, careful steps among the thick brushwood, by the pebbly shore and occasionally the marsh which skirts the border of the stream. It was possible we might never meet again, except in the street. Simple recognisance there was all that was necessary.

I had written to Gertrude and Mrs. Moodie the previous evening, and I now put all three letters aside, to put into the post-office at Glasgow.

By eleven o'clock we were on our way to Glasgow, where we were kindly received by Mr. Wilson's friend, Mrs. Brown.

Mrs. Brown was the widow of a clergyman, who had come to Glasgow with her only son on the death of her husband.

They occupied the half of a house, consisting of a parlour, three bed-rooms, and kitchen; a young lady lived with them, who taught music, and who Mrs Brown introduced as Miss Watson from Edinburgh.

Miss Watson, before our arrival, had consented to give me the half of her bed, Mrs. Brown being to share hers with Mrs. Livingstone.   Mrs. Brown was a woman of about forty years of age, very pleasant and well informed ; her son, Mr. James Brown, was tall and handsome, with a bright eye and thoughtful brow ; he might well have a thoughtful brow ! he, with his eighteen or twenty summers, at most, was the principal support of his widowed mother, she having besides only twenty pounds from some fund.

Miss Watson was five and thirty certainly, perhaps more ; but she dressed handsomely and youthfully, and probably looked younger on this account ; her face betokened sense and much sarcasm ; she spoke a great deal, but everything was well said and to the point ; she was cheerful withal, and had the rare gift of making those around her fall into her own mood.

After dinner Miss Watson took me, as she said, under her own wing, that she might shew me the lions. We walked about two hours, during which she pointed out each object of interest we came to, and told me all about what it was, or was to be : talking and laughing all the time, and making me do so also, as far as the laughing went, although it must have been in sympathy, as in truth, I scarcely knew for what, my thoughts being far away with dear Willie among the hills of Perthshire.

Before entering the house on our return home, we went into the bookseller's shop, which formed part of the same building, and was under the rooms occupied by Mrs. Brown. Young Brown was there behind the counter, and seemed with his quick eye to be looking everywhere at once ; Miss Watson told me that though only nineteen years of age, he filled one of the most onerous situations in the shop, and that his mother paid a mere nominal rent for the flat she occupied, all the rooms of which were large and handsome, Mr. Pringle, his master, considering he received a benefit equal to the rent from young Brown's living on the premises.

After tea, Miss Watson seated herself on one side of a window-seat, raised a step from the floor, and projecting from each side of the window, so that those occupying it had their faces to each other, and also saw all that passed on the street below. She invited me to take the opposite side, and drawing some tatting from her pocket, divided her time equally between it and the passers by, making the most piquant remarks on the latter.

All at once she dropped her work, threw up the window-sash and looked out, exclaiming " As sure as a gun that's Robert Scott." She continued watching some one going up the street for fully five minutes, she then shut down the window, and resumed her seat.

" That gentleman who has just passed is the brother of a young lady to whom I was governess for a few months a year and a half ago ; he has been and is a good friend to a brother-in-law of mine. I cannot think what has brought him here, I saw his name some eight or ten days ago, on the list of advocates attached to the Northern circuit."

Robert Scott so near, what of that ? he was nothing to me, or ever could be ; I felt my blood run cold through every vein.

"Put off that sad face of yours," said my companion, giving me a shake as she spoke. "Canada is in reality to us governesses not further off than London; were we in the latter, we could only come home to see our friends at the year's end, and we would have to work for half the sum you are to receive; if you tire of Canada you can come back next year, pay your passage, and have fifty pounds in your pocket to live on for a year, if you wish to do so. Going to a convent in Canada is part of the romance of governess life; if you live in single blessedness until you are as old as I am, you will see romance enough to fill a volume. Part of the romance of my life is connected with the gentleman I looked after just now, and I will tell it to you to make you laugh."

"The family live at Iona Villa, a house with an acre or two of ground near Portobello; they are not rich, but as proud as Lucifer."

"I know them" said I; "I lived there."

"You, is it possible?" how long were you there? when did you go there? when did you leave?"

I smiled at the eager look and tone with which these questions were put; "You must give me time to answer your questions one at a time. I left Iona Villa nearly a fortnight past, and I was nearly fifteen months there."

"Fifteen months!" said she, holding up her hands and eyes, "and you are not a petrifaction yet; if you could live fifteen months at Iona Villa, you need not fear to live in a convent. I never saw such a stiff, silent set; I would not live a year there for a hundred pounds, but I need not say that, they did not put it in my power to stay; I was sent away, whether I would or not. "I must tell you all about it. Oh it was such rare fun!"

"To begin properly, you, my hearer, must bear in your

mind's eye what Mr. Robert Scott is : young, handsome, intellectual, one who a very few years hence will be at the top
of his profession, and on the death of his aunt, passing rich.
Now you must look at me : nearly ten years his senior ; never
had the least pretentions to beauty in my youngest days ; I
know French pretty well, and music indifferently ; these are
the extent of my attainments ; have not a penny in the world
but what I earn.

" Now for my story. Mr. and Mrs. Scott, who often dis-
agreed upon other subjects, agreed on this, that these attractions of mine were too great for their handsome son to resist,
and the two eldest young ladies, who are themselves fast
waning into the sear and yellow leaf, saw the affair exactly
in the same light ; so one day I was sent for, to speak with
awful Mr. Scott in the dining-room, and was there informed by
him that he had discovered all the arts I practised to entrap
Mr. Robert Scott, as he called him : that he, as Mr. Robert
Scott's father, must tell me he could never give his consent to
his son's marriage with one, who at best was only a little above
a servant, and therefore it was necessary I should leave his
house within half an hour. I know he intended I should be very
much overawed ; but he reckoned without his host there. I
told him, (staring him in full in the face while I spoke) I was
never happy for one day in his house, and that I would be very
glad to get out of it, that residing there seemed to me like living
in a church-yard with the grave digger, he himself representing the latter important personage, and that I would be
very happy to go whenever he paid me for my year's service.

" It was with great difficulty I could make him hear me
to the end. He interrupted me several times, but I was
more than a match for him. He had a strong will, but I had
a stronger ; he talked loud and fast ; I spoke in a low voice,

and drawled out my words as slowly as possible. What a fury the old gentleman was in! how he stamped and swore, assuring me over and over again I should never touch a shilling of his money. I saw his aim; he was not only desirous to keep his son, but his money also; but I was no child, and told him so. The chambermaid, who, by the by, was a particular friend of mine, had warned me long before that he had turned away two of my predecessors without paying them; but they were young girls, and were easily frightened. I thought of this, and said:—' Old man, are you not ashamed with your grey hairs to cheat people in the way you do. I am aware you cheated the last two governesses who were here; but I am—'

" He stopt me there. Oh, what a noise, calling servants, ringing the bell, stamping, flinging chairs out of his way. Depend upon it, that man will kill some one, and be hanged for it yet. However, the end of it was, I only received four months' salary before I left the house; but Mr. Robert paid me for the whole year, whether out of his own pocket or not I cannot tell.

" What made them take this wild idea into their heads it would be hard to say, unless it was that Mr. Robert used to go with me to see my poor brother-in-law every Sunday, between the services. My poor sister's husband, John Lillie, was a schoolfellow of Robert Scott's; he is now miserably poor, and has been paralyzed for upwards of two years. If he had been an honest man, he would never have known the poverty he has suffered. And I did not wish these proud Scotts to know that John Lillie was my brother-in-law; and when they were told by the Misses Syme that Mr. Robert accompanied me every Sunday forenoon out of church, I begged of him not to tell where we went to; he still goes every Sunday to see John, and does much more for him than that. I hope the old man and the sisters think he comes to see me still. How you got on with them for fifteen months is beyond my comprehension. Miss Hariote Scott, who really rules the roast at Iona Villa, is the most disagreeable old maid I ever met."

" I am surprised to hear you say so," I replied; " when I lived there I loved Miss Hariote as if she had been my sister, and I will ever respect and esteem her highly."

" Well, I suspect you are more of an old maid yourself than I am," said she, laughing; " and the point of affinity between Hariote Scott and you must be silence ; you are quite as silent as herself."

Next morning Mrs. Livingstone paid ten pounds for my passage, and she insisted on me taking a draft for five more. This I did not wish to do, as I really had no use for so much money, but she would not listen to anything I had to say.

We were to go on board at four o'clock, the time appointed for the vessel to sail being five.

Miss Watson had gone out to give some music lessons, and Mrs. Livingstone came into her room with me, so that we might spend the remaining time together.

She spoke long and earnestly, warning me of the danger I was in of becoming a Catholic, if I did not pray and strive against the influence which, she said, she was sure would be brought to bear on me. She seemed now to have quite a fear of my going, and twice proposed that I should not go. We would, she said, remain in Glasgow a week, and go home again, or I would go with her to the braes of Ballquider, where she was to visit her only sister, and spend some months.

But I would not hear of remaining at home. I had thought myself into going, and I was now as anxious to see Canada as I was averse to leaving Scotland a few months previously.

How little we can judge by the feelings of to-day what those of to-morrow will be!

There was one thing I must do before leaving Scotland, and I had delayed it to the very last moment.

In the event of my never reaching Canada, Mrs. Livingstone could not be paid the money she so generously advanced to me, for many years. Poor Willie, unaided, would find it hard work to educate himself. How was he to pay fifteen pounds. It would indeed be a long time ere he could do that.

I had nothing to give as an equivalent except mamma's watch, which she had hung round my neck so shortly before we parted for ever. It cost me a pang to part with it, but what could I do? I had nothing else, and there must not be even a chance of Mrs. Livingstone losing her money. I had recollections of jewels, which mamma told us were sent to her as a marriage gift by our paternal grandfather; and we also remembered our father's watch with its gold chain and seals, the great object of Willie's childish ambition; where were they? Perhaps some day, when my position would be different, I would ask uncle that question.

But the present must be thought of now. I knew it would not be easy to make Mrs. Livingstone take the care of my watch into her hands; but it must be done. I could not leave Scotland unfettered otherways.

" You must keep mamma's watch for me," said I, putting it into her hands; " if we were to be shipwrecked I should lose it, or it might be stolen from me."

She looked hard and grimly in my face; that old woman could read my very soul.

" Keep your mother's watch! Na, I'll no do that; you must never part wi' it, till you part wi' yoursel'."

" But by your keeping it for me, I will be more sure of it than if I had it in my own possession. I am only going to remain in Canada three years ; and if I lost it during that time, it would cause me great pain. Besides, if I never return, you will give it to Willie. If I leave it in Canada, who there will take that trouble ?"

" Aweel," replied she, " there's twa sides to ilka question, an' gin ye hae honest folk about ye, they wad sen' your watch hame at any rate. Bit nae matter ; I'll no keep it, sae let's hear nae mair about it."

Mrs. Livingstone and Miss Watson went into the cab, which contained my luggage, and Mrs. Wilson and I were to walk to the ship. I was to have quite an escort to see me on board.

I suspect that this arrangement was made by Mrs. Livingstone for my particular benefit, as Mrs. Wilson entertained me, during the whole of our walk, with various accounts of the many artifices Roman Catholics resorted to, to obtain proselytes.

The wharf was absolutely covered with packages, boxes, carts, loading and unloading, carriages, etc., and out and in through these we had to pick our way to the ship. A small steam vessel was about to start, and the passengers were hurrying towards her. Two gentlemen on their way to the steamer passed us so closely that the handle of an umbrella, which one of them carried under his arm, fastened in the hood of my cloak ; and he, unconscious of what stopped his progress, in his efforts to disengage his umbrella, threw me over one of the packages. His companion and he both came to the rescue : the latter helped me to rise, and asked me if I was hurt, in a voice that thrilled through every nerve. I looked in his face—it was Robert Scott. I knew I could not be recognised. I had a green crape veil tied double over my face. I murmured some indistinct response lest my voice should betray me. He again said some words of apology, and was gone.

I was transfixed to the spot, and stood watching him until he passed along the way leading from the wharf to the steamboat, and was lost to my sight in the crowd on board.

"I fear you have been hurt," said my companion."

"No, I feel giddy, that is all."

I felt giddy enough, but not from the effects of my fall; the wharf and all its various burdens, the vessels with their decks crowded with human beings; the very earth and sky swung backwards and forwards in long sweeps; I sat down on one of the bales at my side; it was well I did, in a moment a noise surrounded me, as if a cataract were pouring its waters on my head, and then the whole world whirled round and round in rapid whirls, and I the centre.

Mrs. Wilson removed my veil and bonnet, some water was thrown on my face, and by degrees, the skies and earth, ships and wharf, steadied themselves down into their old places.

Before we went on board the ship, I placed my watch in Mrs. Wilson's hands, telling her to give it to Mrs. Living-stone on the morrow.

The *Winged Zephyr* was a small merchantman, that also carried a few passengers; there was a poop cabin on deck, the small saloon of which was lighted from the top; at each side of the saloon were two doors, each opening into a small cabin, in which was a bed and sufficient room for a trunk at each end.

Besides my own trunk, I found another in the small cabin allotted to me, which Mrs. Livingstone said she had brought from Edinburgh, packed with a few necessaries for the voyage.

Before we parted, she took me aside and told me, should I
be disappointed in my expectations on my arrival in Canada,
to write to her, and she would immediately send me money
to bring me home, and she made me promise to pray night
and morning for grace and strength, to keep in the faith of
my fathers, and that I should never bend my knees but to
the God of Israel, whom they worshipped in my native land.

I bade Mrs. Livingstone good-bye with many tears ; she
blessed me as if I had been her own child, and prayed that
my soul and spirit might be kept blameless unto the coming
of the Lord.

I liked that old woman well, and I had cause. With reverence be it spoken, she showered her benefits upon me as the
Lord sends the rain on the dry ground.

CHAPTER XVIII.

My travelling companions in the cabin were a lady and gentleman from the Northern Highlands, who, with their two little children, were on their way to seek a home in the west; they were pleasant, kind people, and shared with me the little luxuries they had stored for the voyage with no sparing hand.

The steerage passengers consisted of a woman from the Western Isles, with her two little girls, going to join her husband, who, as a common laborer, had landed in Montreal two years before with half a crown in his pocket, and now had a couple of well furnished rooms to welcome her to, besides having sent her so much money every month, as enabled her, during these two years of absence, to save ten pounds. These ten pounds she had in gold, and carried in her bosom, carefully folded in a piece of newspaper, over which was again folded a piece of printed cotton, the whole being placed in the foot of a stocking. She and I became very friendly during the voyage, and it was towards the end that she showed me her pose; she said that from the day he went away, she had never bought a shilling's worth of clothes for herself or the children, with the exception of shoes.

A young, well-dressed widow from Glasgow occupied the sleeping berth next to the Highland woman; she had also two little girls, and went to fulfil a matrimonial engagement, and whose intended husband, she took care to tell, was to come from Kingston in Upper Canada, to Montreal, to meet her, and also told, to show how she was valued, that it was her lover who had sent her the money to bring herself and her children to Canada.

A young girl and her brother going to their parents, who had preceeded them. This girl was the admiration of us all ; her industry was untiring ; from early morn until the light failed her, she sat on deck or on the last step of the ladder-like staircase, leading down to the steerage, knitting lace, which she intended for sale when she arrived. Before she left the vessel she had accomplished a task of twelve yards.

Next, a shoemaker from Upper Canada, who was returning from a visit paid to his friends in Scotland, after an absence of twenty years ; a very great man was the shoemaker, a little pompous, and no wonder, he had become a man of wealth and consequence. The house he lived in was his own ; he employed two men to work for him ; he had a hair-cloth sofa and chairs in his parlour; and he had only come out in the steerage, because he considered all money spent in travelling was wasted ; when we arrived at our place of destination we had nothing for our money. Although he had a just sense of his own importance, and liked to be spoken to with deference by his fellow passengers in the steerage, whom he evidently considered his inferiors in the social scale, yet he was a kind-hearted body, and regularly shared the comfortable breakfast and dinner he cooked for himself, with one of the others, always selecting those who seemed most to require a good meal.

And last, though not least in inches certainly, was a Glasgow weaver, who having quarrelled with his wife, had left Scotland in a pet. Poor man, we had scarcely set sail when he amused every one on board by his bitter lamentations at his own folly, in having, as he expressed it :—" Left the land where he was bred and born, to gang amang haythens and Catholics and aw kind o' folk. Oh!" said he, with almost a groan of despair, " gin I were at hame the nicht, I wadna flyte wi' the wife, gin she was as fu as the Baltic, and cawed me aw at ever was cawed ane."

The poor weaver was a great lank fellow, at least six feet high, with legs and arms so long and thin, that they seemed out of all proportion to his body ; and as he walked up and down the deck, giving vent to his lamentations and swinging his long arms to and fro, with every step his unsteady wavering legs took, the younger part of his audience laughed outright.

We had tea soon after we set sail, and when the tea things were removed, Mrs. Lessely placed her work-basket and key tray on the table, giving it quite a home look.

Her two children were pretty and good ; the little girl fair, with long flaxen hair ; the boy, a merry, black eyed, curly haired fellow, little more than a baby.

Franky, as he called himself, was soon a pet with every one ; even the sailors had a word or two for Franky, as he went along imitating the swing with which they walked, until he was as perfect in it as themselves.

Captain Russel, the sailing master, was a little, stout, fair haired man, with a quick eye and a turned-up nose ; he was activity personified, and we very soon observed that when his orders were executed in a slovenly manner, he went at once and did the work over again himself, with a quickness and precision which none of his men possessed. The captain, as we called him, was always in great good humour when we had, what he called, a spanking gale, and we called a hurricane, with the wind blowing in our favour.

Mrs. Lessely was very sick for three or four days, so during that time I installed myself head nurse, and got to be quite an adept in my profession, and a favourite with the children.

Mrs. Lessely was not alone in her sickness, every passenger on board, with the exception of myself and children, were sick for two or three days, and in consequence, the decks seemed quite deserted, and presented a very different appearance from the evening in which we set sail. The shoemaker was the first to recover, and on the forenoon of the third day, gladdened our eyes by appearing on deck with his frying-pan, with which he wended his way to the cook-room, a little place on deck two or three yards square, from which in due time he issued, still carrying his frying-pan, now filled with a most savoury mess of ham and eggs, with which he descended to the steerage, declaring he would soon cure the others and have them on deck again.

I was fortunate enough never to feel sick for an hour, no matter whether we had fair weather or foul, I was always well, enjoying the cool sea breeze on deck.

By degrees our sick passengers all appeared, with the exception of the eldest child of the widow ; she, poor little thing, seemed never to have power to rally from the weakness which the sickness left. The captain was most kind and attentive to the child, carried her on deck in his own arms, gave her medicine himself, in case her mother would not do so properly ; in short, did all it was possible for him to do, but in vain. The child sank by degrees, and at last died on the seventh day.

There was a coffin made, and the little girl's body decently laid out in it, as it would have been on shore.

When it was to be sunk, the passengers and crew were all called on deck, and Mr. Lessely read the beautiful service of the Scotch Episcopal Church, (to which he belonged) for the burial of the dead at sea.

Mr. Lessely was a tall handsome man, of grave aspect, and his appearance accorded well with the solemn words he uttered. I have seen few clergymen whose looks accorded so well with their sacred office, as Mr. Lessely's did.

The coffin was placed on a long plank, which was slightly fastened to the bulwark of the lower deck.

Every one stood uncovered, and with quiet attention and reverence, when he pronounced the words :

" We commit this our sister's body to the deep, in the sure " and certain hope of a blessed resurrection to eternal life ; " through Jesus Christ our Lord."

The fastening of the plank was removed, and the coffin let slowly down among the waves, there to rest until the sea gives up her dead.

It was an impressive scene. The broad blue sky, without a single cloud, above our heads. The deep green sea, with its rolling billows all around ; and we, a handful of wanderers, on the deck of our frail bark, lifting voice and eye to the Creator of all this immensity, and consigning our dead to the keeping of the sea—in firm unwavering faith—that our Lord at his coming would bring her also.

Mrs. Lessely's little girl wept as if her mamma had died and been consigned to that fathomless grave. The mother of the child, and the young sister, looked on with grave faces, but unmoved. No one wept but little Mary Lessely.

On our arrival at Quebec, several French women came in boats alongside the vessel, selling fruit and flowers. Mary begged her mamma to buy her a bunch of white china-asters, which, on receiving, she untied, and let fall, one by one, over the ship's side, watching them as they floated with the tide out to sea, until they were lost to sight.

I asked her why she had thrown away her flowers?

" I have not thrown them away," was her reply, " I have sent them all down to poor little Bessie's grave !"

There were among the crew two English boys. Jack, a bright, handsome boy, about sixteen years of age ; he had been on the ship for two years, and was a favourite with captain, mate, sailors, every one.

The other, a tall, stout fellow, evidently the 'black sheep' of the ship. Tom, as far as he dared, disobeyed orders, and quarrelled with everyone. Jack sometimes played with the children on deck, and on such occasions Tom invariably tried to make them fall, by placing an unseen rope in their way, which he had the dexterity to pull in such a manner as to make the whole tumble. Every one disliked Tom, and Tom returned the feeling with interest.

When we were about ten or twelve days out at sea, a storm arose towards evening, which increased during the night to a perfect hurricane.

I was lying awake listening to the roaring of the sea, as it dashed its angry waves with giant fury against the side of the ship where I lay, and the loud voice of the wind, as it came in gusts, sweeping through the bare rigging, and across the decks, when suddenly there arose a loud noise, I fancied quite close to my ear. Stamping of many feet, several loud, angry voices, clanking of chains ; and now as I listened, I could distinguish the clear, silver sounds of a woman's voice, as if in fear and used in entreaty. It instantly occurred o me that the ship had struck on a rock, and Willie's parting words and sad face were before my eyes in the darkness, and ringing in my ears distinctly, amid the noise of jarring voices within, and the wild war of elements without.

I had turned with contempt from the gypsy's prophecy; and in three short months, how bitterly did the sharp storm of adversity break over my devoted head.

And when Willie wept with the sad presentiment which unmanned him, and drew tears from his eyes, I smiled, with no dread of the future, knowing in my present path was fullness of joy. Were those sad words of his, that I held so lightly, now about to be fulfilled?—"My sister, my sister! when I come again, I will not meet you, you will be dead?" All this passed through my mind in half the time I have taken to write it. I slipped on my gown and shoes, and pulling back the door of the cabin, I saw by the night-light, which hung in the saloon, that a door in the back, which I had never seen used, was now wide open, and the space behind filled with men; among whom I recognized the captain, second mate, and Tom; the latter with his hands chained together.

Tom and the captain seemed both frenzied with rage. Mrs. Lessely was inside the saloon, but close to the door, dressed in a white dressing-gown, her hair braided quite off her face, and rolled up into a large shell-like knot behind; her hands were clasped and uplifted in a beseeching attitude—she seemed to be speaking and acting under the greatest excitement and fear.

I stood as still as possible, glad to find it was no shipwreck which occasioned the uproar that alarmed me so much. I could scarcely distinguish what any one person said, but I could gather from the whole that Tom was put in irons for disobeying the captain's orders, and was to be confined in the hold, where they were about placing him, by means of a trap door, (opening close to the saloon door, already referrred to) when Mrs. Lessely came to plead for Tom's pardon, evidently impressed with the idea that he was to suffer death, or something very near it.

The second-mate was standing close to Tom, his hands grasping the culprit's arm, and his face as pale as death ; he looked as if he were trembling with fear ; if ever I saw abject fear pictured on a human face, it was on that man's. I think had the captain desired him to kill the boy, and it could have been done at Tom's back, he would have done it. The captain was struggling with Tom, while the latter, a great giant in comparison to the captain, was only prevented from battering the little man's brains out with the hand-cuffs and chains attached to his wrists, by the grasp the second-mate had of one shoulder, and the steward of the other.

Captain Russel was stamping, talking to Tom, and at Mrs. Lessley, swearing that all the women in the world should not save him, when Mr. Lessely appeared at the door of his own cabin. He came forward, and seeming to understand it all in a moment, took his wife by the arm, and drew her gently away from the scene of action. He was talking to her in a low voice, and I heard him say as he passed my cabin door :

" If the captain were interfered with, it might lead to a mutiny on board, an hour hence."

How these words of Mr. Lessely thrilled through my every vein ; they effected an entire revolution in my opinion ; before hearing them I was decidedly a partizan of Tom's, now I was willing the captain should have his way.

Mr. Lessely made his wife go into her sleeping-berth and lie down, he seating himself on one of the saloon seats close by.

Tom was forced down the ladder into the hold, and was, I believe, for several hours hung up by his chained hands.

CHAPTER XIX.

The darkness and storm passed away together, and the morning rose bright and clear; everything so calm; not a breath of wind stirring, and only by the swell in the sea, whose white crested billows came with a quicker dash, and climbed higher up the ship's sides than before, were we reminded of last night's tempest.

Not so the temper of the captain: he took his meals in the saloon with us, and always sat at the head of the table; in general, he was good humored and chatty; but that morning he maintained a dignified silence, which did not at all accord with his red hair and turned-up nose.

However, Mr. Lessely took Captain Russel's side of the question, and looked upon his wife's interference as a most grave offence.

It appeared that the storm came on so suddenly, that all hands were required on deck; and upon the captain desiring Tom to go into the rigging to arrange something there, he refused, and this was the cause of all the trouble; Tom was now in the hold, and was to remain there for the rest of the voyage.

The Glasgow weaver played the flute very sweetly, and we used to get him to come up on the poop deck and play for us every evening, to the great delight of the children, who absolutely screamed with laughter at the faces he made while playing.

Poor fellow, he never failed to give us a dose of his unceasing lamentations, after the happy home he had left in the Cowgate of Glasgow, and the good wife " who was sitting her lane there."

When the weaver came on board, he was very wrath against his wife; after we set sail and he found we were fairly off, he still blamed her a little ; but distance and time had endowed her with every virtue—she was now an angel, suffering all sorts of privations from his waywardness and folly.

" O Sirs !" he would occasionally burst out with, " what an idle wratch am I, idlein' awa my time, doing naething a' day here, and my puir wife sittin' maybe at hame wi' neither fire or meat i' the house !   An' sic a gude wife as she; there is nae ane in a' the Cowgate 'at can beat her at makin' bannocks or langkail."

On his making this speech, the little lace knitter, who, in her quiet demure way, liked a little mischief, and was besides a privileged person, having been a neighbour of Sandy's in that happy place, the Cowgate of Glasgow, reminded him slily that his wife occasionally indulged in something stronger than langkail."

Sandy was now angry, and replied in sharper accents than I thought he was capable of using :

" Gin she does, she does na mair than her neebours ; there is nae a wife in the gate end, 'at doesna tak a dram whan she can get it; and whan my wife takes a drap, she aye gies siller for't, but mony a wife i' the Cowgate pawns her good man's sabbath coat for drink ; puir Jannet, she wad long look at it afore she wad do that."

And the poor man sighed heavily, as he recounted the good qualities of the injured woman he had left to mourn his absence in the Cowgate.

The Upper Canada shoemaker was a wit in his own way, and to amuse the ladies in the steerage, told the weaver that, if the captain liked, he could hail a passing ship, and send him home—it was in vain for the captain to declare the thing was impossible, it could not be done, Sandy was assured that it was a matter of every day occurrence; and if he would persevere, no doubt the captain, wearied out by his importunity, would finally hail a ship and send him home.

When the morning was chilly, Mrs. Lessely and I used to walk with the children on the lower deck, as it was more sheltered than the poop.

One morning while thus taking our constitution walk, as Mr. Lessely termed it, we were amused by listening to a conversation between the shoemaker and his butt Sandy.

There was a sail in sight, and the shoemaker calling Sandy's attention to it, declared he knew it was a ship bound for Glasgow; the ship in question, was, at the time, so distant, it appeared like a toy.

"Now's your time, Sandy man," said the shoemaker, "pluck up your courage and speak to the captain like one who knows what he's about, and my word to you, at the rate that ship's going at, you'll be in Glasgow in six days."

"Think ye that, man?" said the other, doubtfully; "it has ta'en us fourteen days to won this length;" and saying so he formed the fingers and thumb of his left hand into the nearest approach he could make to a spy glass, applying it to his eye in order to have a better view of the said ship.

"So it has," said the shoemaker, "but don't you know that there's a current in the sea, the very same as in the rivers and burns that run down to the sea; and the current runs from America to Scotland, so we have to sail against the current, and that ship is sailing with it."

"Deed," continued he, looking very wise, "I wouldna say but you would be in your ain bed on Saturday nicht, if ye take the right way about it."

" I would do muckle to be in my ain house on Saturday nicht," said the tall, lank weaver, bending even more than he usually did, and looking on the deck at his feet as if he would read there whether such a blissful consummation were possible, and the best way of accomplishing his purpose.

" Well," said his friend, drawing himself up to his full height of five feet, and pacing the deck backwards and forwards within a length of six yards, his thumbs stuck in the arm-holes of his vest, and his shoulders thrown back, so as to give full breadth to his ample chest ; his figure, unlike the generality of his craft, making up in breadth for what it wanted in length ; " well, if you tell the captain that right or wrong you're bound to sail with that ship, he'll be forced to put you on board ; but take no ither body's name in to it, or he'll ken you know nothing about it yoursel ; the law is on your side, but if he thinks your na just sure o' that, he'll gar might make right, and keep you on board his own ship whither ye will or no."

The shoemaker spoke as much English as he could ; he thought it a more dignified and genteel language than his native Scotch ; but when he was very earnest, the broad pronunciation and accent of his mother tongue would slip in, whether he would or not.

Sandy threw off his listless air in a moment, rubbed his hands, and nodding his head to one side with the wisest look he could assume, said :

" My faith, he'll nae trick me that gett ; gin its the law as ye say it is, and it stan's to reason as it is sae, he wonna gar me bide wi' him for a' his cuteness."

As he spoke he became more confident and bolder in the defence of his right, and added, with great decision, striking his clenched right hand into the open palm of his left as he spoke :

" I wadna bide here anither nicht gin he wad gie me his wecht in red gowd ; but I am only spendin' time here ; I'll jest rin down and pit the flute an my bit traps thegither, an' maybe ye'll keep a gude look out on the ship, 'at she'll nae gang by whan I'm down the stairs." He spoke in a hurried manner as if he had now learned the value of time, and discarded his old lymphatic air and slow drawling mode of speech.

" No fear of that," replied the shoemaker ; " I'll no lat her pass ; but pack up your things wi' all the speed ye can, for its better for you to settle wi' the captain afore the Glasgow ship comes too close, for you see there will be a boat to get ready to put you on board."

Sandy scarcely waited to hear the shoemaker's reply, but hurried along the deck and down the ladder staircase leading to the steerage, with more the air of a man than I had ever seen him wear before.

Twice Sandy's head appeared above the ladder, inquiring " Is she near yet ?"

" Nae yet."

In a few minutes the head popped up again.

" She's nae near han' yet, is she ?"

" No, no," said his friend, nodding his head significantly, and continuing his walk up and down the deck.

" But stick ye to your last, and close the boot in a crack."

He must have been thinking of his own " profession," as he termed it, while he meant to hurry the weaver in the preparations he was making for departure.

At last he ascended, dressed in a clean shirt, brushed shoes, and a better suit of clothes than I had supposed him possessed of. What a difference, almost a metamorphosis !

The unshaven, half silly looking, flapping about creature of the morning, whose clothes always hung about him as if they had been put on with a pitch-fork, looked a decent respectable man, with a degree of energy in his tread and gait that was most marvellous.

He had a brown paper parcel under one arm, which looked as if it contained the flute and music books, while in the other he carried a large carpet bag.

The rest of the steerage passengers followed him up stairs, several of whom were evidently impressed with the idea that the weaver was going to leave them.

" You havena forgotten anything, have ye ?" inquired the shoemaker.

" Na, na, I counted them aw ower three times," replied Sandy ; his face shining with soap and joy, and his mouth in a broad grin from ear to ear.

" There's nothing but change in this world, on the sea as well as on the land ; little did I think whan I fried the ham and eggs this morning for us baith, that one o' us would be on the road to Scotland afore nicht." And the rogue put on a serious face and heaved a sigh, as if for the unstable nature of all things, friendship included, here below.

" Aweel," replied his dupe, trying to twist his face into an expression which he meant to be in sympathy with the shoemaker's sigh, " the waft an' the warp, man part in time, and sae man we, but freins will meet whan the hills winna ; and I'm sure I'm muckle obliged to you for aw your kindness, and gin ye ever come back to Glasgow, baith me an' the wife will be rale glad gin ye'll come an tak ye'er kail wi's i' the Cowgate ; we haena a gran house like yours, but its aye clean, an' we hae plenty to eat and drink, and that's nae a tale at awbody i' the Cowgate can tell."

The shoemaker was very proud of his house, and a favourite theme of his was describing his fine furniture, and the fine dresses of his wife and one daughter, who was his only child, both of whom he took care to make known early in the voyage, were as well dressed as any ladies in Kingston; and it was doubtless some reminiscence of these glowing descriptions which made Sandy warn him in case he should pay them a visit, not to expect such finery in his humble home.

As he finished his speech of thanks and invitation to his friend, the captain came up in the leisurely manner he walked the deck in fine weather, with his hands clasped behind his back.

I think he must have understood what was going on, his light blue eyes twinkled with merriment, and his whole face was lighted up with fun.

" What's ado now, Sandy ?" said he, standing, sailor fashion, his legs wide apart, and putting his hands into his trowsers pockets as he spoke.

I found this was a popular way of disposing of the hands, with sailors as well as landsmen.

" Naething at aw," returned the weaver, " only I'm just biden gude bye to thae folk ; I'm gaen hame the day with the Glasgow ship yonder, captain," and he pointed in the direction ·of the ship, which had now considerably increased in her proportions.

" Oh ! ye are, are ye ? and who told you it was a Glasgow ship ?"

" I didna need ony body to tell me that," replied he, warned by a look from his friend, who stood in front of the weaver, and a little behind Captain Russel.

" Aye, and what way did ye find it out ?"

" That was vera easy ; I ken the mak o' a Glasgow ship ; that's nae the first ane I ever saw."

His courage seemed to be failing a little, but he was quickly
reassured by a look from his friend in rear of the captain, and
plucking up heart he continued,

" I'm sayen, captain, I'll be obleeged to ye, to gar ane o' your
lads tak doun a boat to pit me on board wi.''

" Oh ! man," said the captain, enjoying the joke, 'there's no
ane o' thae boats that would hold a pail-full of water, we have
had such a long tack o' dry weather, they're cast every one o'
them."

" Weel, captain," replied the weaver, with a more determined air than I thought he could put on, " it's no a likely like
story at aw your boats hae gaen gizen ; but whither or no, I'll
nae bide anither nicht on this ship, gin ye wad gee me the
rights o' her for biden, I hae aw my claes packed up, and
I'm nae gaen to loose them out again for naebody."

" If that's the case, I fear ye'll hae to swim to the Glasgow
ship, as ye call her."

" Na, I'll nae do that either, captain ; I hae the law on my
side, I ken that, and sae its better for you to pit me on board wi'
quateness."

The captain called to the mate to bring him the spy glass,
and putting it to his eye, he said, " Sandy, that's a French
ship."

" It's nae that, captain ; ye canna make a fule o' me. bit I'll
tell ye what, ye needna be feart for me seeken the siller back
at I paid for my passage ; I'll never look after a bawbee o't ; an'
mair than that, gin ye like ye can keep it to yoursel, and nae
body at the office will be the wiser ; I'm sure I'll never say a
word about it as lang as I live, sae pit it in your ain pouch, captain."

The captain laughed heartily, and putting his hand on Sandy's shoulder, said, " Ye'er no a bad chap after all ; but the

worst of it is, they have the siller at the office, and I'm afraid they'll no ge'et to you or me either."

E'er long it was found that the ship was on another tack, and it sailed away, without coming within hail.

The poor weaver could not be prevailed upon to unpack the paper parcel containing the flute, for three days, waiting in full confidence of another Glasgow ship passing ; most likely he did not unpack the carpet bag during the whole of the voyage.

Mrs. Lessely and I, by dint of perseverance, found out the 'open sesame' of the back door of the saloon ; this done, it was an easy matter to lift the trap door, which shut in poor Tom, who was confined in a part of the hold where a ray of light never reached him, except when his bread and water was brought morning and evening.

Unless the captain's presence was required on deck, he always went to bed, from two o'clock until four in the afternoon; during this period, Mrs. Lessely and I regularly visited Tom, bringing him pieces of pudding, bread and ham, hard boiled eggs, crackers, &c.

Mrs. Lessely used also to give him good advice, and speak to him of the love of Christ and of his gospel, telling him the wondrous story of that birth, and life, and death, which the angels of God, bringing light with them from their home in the high heavens, came to announce to a few shepherds keeping watch o'er their flocks on the dark plains of Bethlehem, in the solemn midnight, centuries ago ; and she told him of the love which that God-man bears to every wayward or forsaken brother, wandering in doubt and darkness here below, and that even while she was speaking, he, the blessed Saviour, unseen of mortal eyes, was stretching his arms of love and mercy to the dark hold where Tom was chained, and calling him to come up to the holy heavens, and join the songs of the angels, and eat of the fruit given for the healing of the nations, and walk by the river, the streams whereof do make glad the city of our God.

And by degrees she led him on, and told him of the brightness of the great white throne, and the Ancient of days, whom the sun-eyed seraph host behold with awe and fear; and of the golden crowns, and the glassy sea, and of all the wonders which were shown John in the lone desert of Patmos more than eighteen hundred years ago.

Tom always listened to Mrs. Lessely without the frown he usually wore on our first visit to the trap-door; he told us he recognised her as the lady in white, who pleaded so earnestly for him on the night of the storm, when he was consigned to the hold, and he used to gaze with open mouth and eyes, while she told of the wonders of redeeming love; she felt sure an impression had been made on his heart. I was not so hopeful.

He told us that when we came to the first port he would be taken to prison.

Mrs. Lessely promised to intercede with the captain for him, but he shook his head and told her it would be of no use; the poor fellow probably remembered how little impression her former intercession in his behalf had made. One day we had nothing but crackers to bring him, and we asked the steward to give us some slices of cold beef.

" If I gave you a biscuit for Tom," said he, " and Captain Russel were to hear of it, I would be confined in the hold myself in ten minutes afterwards."

We were now within a day's sail of the coast, we had for a time remarked the clear blue of the sky, the apparently increased size of the moon and stars; the sun also rose and set here with a radiance never known at home; clouds of deep purple, floating in a sea of gold, and the sun itself one mass of living fire. The morning on which we were told the glad news of our near approach to the land each of us were seeking, with such different hopes and fears, we came up with a ship we had seen the evening before, although then far ahead of us.

She seemed to be lying like a tub on the water, her motion so slow, it was scarcely perceptible.

The captain brought from his cabin a speaking-trumpet and spoke the ship in passing. What an unearthly sound that trumpet gave to the voice, it seemed as if the old genie of the sea had roused themselves from their long sleep, and to convince the unbelievers of the nineteenth century that they were still alive, were calling to each other from out their hollow caves and wondrous forests, of green and purple sea-weed, down in the fathomless deep.

In an instant every passenger in cabin and steerage was on deck, the latter placing themselves as close to where the captain stood as the mates would permit.

We learned the ship was the " *Home* from Dundee, out ninety days ; she had opened at the side, and they were obliged to have men at the pumps night and day : they had enough of provisions and water.

The conversation ended, our ship exhibited a black board, on which were marked the latitude and longitude, in large white figures, traced in chalk.—The " *Home*" replied by hoisting a similar board marked in like manner.

After this interchange of ocean civilities, our little bark sped swiftly on, each half-hour making the distance greater and greater between us and the poor " *Home*," until at last we lost sight of her altogether.

Late in the same afternoon, another sail appeared, about fourteen miles distant from our vessel : the stranger hoisted a yellow flag, as a sign there was sickness on board.

A few minutes afterwards, they hoisted several other signals : ours were taken from their keepings and unfolded in a second or two but the code of signals by which we were to arrange our own, and understand those of the other ship, was no where to be found, and neither captain or mate were able to tell what the signals hoisted on the fever-ship, as they called her, meant, or to hoist our own.

Mrs. Lessely asked the captain if he would not approach the strange ship near enough to speak her,but he shook his head, saying: "Depend on it, that poor craft has the ship fever, with all its horrors on board; were I to go as near her as you say, I would endanger the life of every man and woman on board my own vessel."

We gave many a look to the poor fever ship, as the shades of evening darkened around her, and distance at last hid hull, sail and pennon from our sight.

Next morning the glad cry of "land, land !" thrilled through every heart, and all rushed simultaneously on board to obtain a glance of that land we all so earnestly desired to reach. The land, which was greeted with such a joyous shout, could only be descried as a line on the verge of the horizon. What varied emotions the sight of that dark line must have awoke in each breast, filled with its different hopes and fears !

We had still many hundred miles of the immense gulf and the mighty river St. Lawrence between us and our haven of rest, yet all that day we talked of landing, as if it were to be on the morrow ! however, when the morrow came, we had settled down into our old routine again,

The next break in the monotony of our sea-life was our arrival at Grosse Isle, where we cast anchor in order that the doctor might come on board to give us a bill of health, without which we could not land at our destined port.

R

The doctor came on board, and dined with us; a good-tempered, gentlemanly man; and finding us all in good health, gave his dictum accordingly.

In three days more we had cast anchor opposite Quebec.

Scarcely an hour after our arrival, two men belonging to the water police came on board, and poor Tom was brought up from his dark abode to be consigned by them to the jail.

Mrs. Lessely begged of them to allow her to speak to Tom for a few minutes; they stared, as if they thought she was crazy, but nevertheless acceded to her request.

She drew him aside, and placing one hand upon his chained arm, spoke earnestly for a few minutes. Tom said a single word in reply, looking the while as if he thought she was an angel. The captain was at the other end of the deck; Mrs. Lessely signed to him, and he came up to where she and Tom were standing. I did not hear what Mrs. Lessely said, but the captain's reply was, " He shall remain on board if you will go security in ten pounds for him."

" I will."

The captain called to him the second mate and one of the sailors; another moment and Tom's irons were off, and he was a free man again.

His ugly face was much marked by the small-pox, and it had the peculiar grey colour which that terrible disease always leaves behind. He was a dogged-looking fellow, and I fancied that during his confinement his expression became harder, and I used to think that in his future life he would most likely go on from bad to worse. I didn't think so now —his pale, ugly face became almost handsome with the rich dark blood which mounted up to his forehead—his eyes filled with tears, and the first use he made of the freedom given to his hands was to seize one of Mrs. Lessely's hands in both his own great, rough-looking paws. It was doubtful what he meant to do; the unbidden tears fell from his eyes in showers, and letting her hand fall, he rushed to the other end of the deck. Poor boy, the sunshine had followed the rain too quickly, even for his iron nerves.

We were now anchored midway out in the river; the captain did this to prevent his men from running away, which they are very apt to do. Sailors are paid by the month, and when hired in Britain, seldom receive more than £4 a month as their wages. They are hired for the voyage, which generally extends over a period of ten weeks or three months, and they do not receive their wages until their return home. Thus, at the end of three months, a common sailor is entitled to twelve pounds, whereas, if he succeeds in running away from his ship in Quebec or Montreal, he can easily hire himself in one of the many ships which are built there every summer, and secures, for the return voyage alone, fifteen pounds. This is a great temptation to a man who is, or thinks he is, hardly used by his captain; hence, those captains who are not popular with their men take every precaution to prevent them running away.

Mr. Lessely wished to go on shore at Quebec, having business matters to arrange there, and the captain sent a boat for the purpose, Mrs. Lessely and I accepting very gladly his invitation to accompany him.

Quebec is built on the rocky and shelving sides of a hill, which rises almost perpendicularly from the river. It is divided, more in words than reality, into the lower and upper towns. The streets leading from the wharf to the upper town are so much up-hill as to be a perfect climb all the way.

We saw in some of the shop windows, as we passed along,

very beautiful work done by the Algonquin Indians, on the bark of the silver birch. This bark is a pale fawn colour, and forms a beautiful soft groundwork for the bright flowers and birds which they work upon it, with the fine sinews of the moose and other deer, which they prepare and dye of all colours, and of the most brilliant hues possible. It is the Algonquin women who make this beautiful work. They, indeed, are the busy-bees of the hive, tilling the ground, gathering the scanty harvest— the result of tillage entirely left to women—cooking the food; and in winter making bark-work, bead-work, and baskets; and then trudging long weary miles, on heavy snow-shoes, over trackless fields of snow in winter, or under the burning rays of the summer sun, laden with the produce of their industry, to sell in the nearest town; while their lords hunt and fish during the short season, and in the long intervals smoke or sleep away their time in their huts, or under the nearest tree, as their fierce Indian sun, or bitter Canadian frost, are in the ascendant.

We were shown, among other things, a portfolio, a little more than a foot in length, where the flowers were worked their natural size, and the colours of the most brilliant and beautiful description. The price asked for it was four pounds; how much of this money found its way into the poor Indian woman's hands ?

I have never seen anything in work which at all equals the brilliancy of colour the North-American Indians give to their bark-work, although the colours used by the Chinese in painting on rice paper certainly equal, perhaps surpass, those in common use among the Indians. The women of the tribes round Quebec and Montreal are dressed in a semi-savage style, their skirts reaching only a little below the knee. Of these they wear several—the lowest generally of some dark worsted stuff, the second, which is always a finger-length shorter than the first, is invariably of scarlet or crimson calico, the third and last skirt, being thin white muslin, sometimes scalloped and worked with coarse embroidery at the edge—this is, of course, the shortest of all; each lady has two or three necklaces, if possible—gilded beads, of a large size, being the favourite; on their feet they wear stockings made from pieces of cloth, and instead of shoes, moccasins, which they themselves make from the skin of the deer, and invariably ornament with bead-work : each woman, young and old alike, have blankets given them by the Government every year—these supply the place of both bonnet and shawl, being worn over the head and pinned at the waist. An Indian woman is seldom seen outside her hut without her blanket.

Mr. Lessely bought a basket, and then had it filled with the most beautiful apples I had seen since I was a child in France. There were on the counter a basket of tomatoes, which I also recollected as old acquaintances in my French home. They were thought early here, but in France we used to have them in July.

In the streets, almost every one we met spoke French. Mrs. Lessely turned to me with a sad look, saying, " How everything here tells us we are not at home—I hope Montreal will not be like this—I should tremble lest my children, brought up in a French population, as this seems to be, would forget the words of their northern tongue, and with that also the manners and customs of their native land."

I did not reply; French was my first language, France my mother's land, the land of my childhood, and hallowed by the memory of all my home joys.

Few thoughts of Willie came without bringing thoughts of dear France, and so the French accents falling upon my ears in the busy street, were to me like the sound of pleasant waters, the old, familiar tones of which made me involuntarily turn and look in the face of the speaker, as if there I ought to recognise one I had known and loved in the happy, careless time, before I had learnt to shrink from the harsh words and cold looks which my English speaking uncle so liberally bestowed upon me.

After an absence of nearly four hours we returned to the ship, loaded with fresh bread, butter, eggs and fruit, all of which Mrs. Lessely shared freely with every one on board.

When we awoke next morning we found our ship attached to a tug-boat and sailing up the St. Lawrence to Montreal.

The banks on each side were thickly studded with cottages and farm-houses, some of the latter large and handsome. The houses were invariably white-washed, as pure as snow, with green shutters outside the windows. Those of the better farm-houses have Venetian blinds instead of shutters. The roofs were all covered with thin wooden tiles, painted red; these latter, with the white walls and bright green blinds, giving a gay and picturesque look to the landscape.

As we approached Montreal, we observed the gardens and orchards becoming larger and better filled with fruit trees, thus betokening an improvement in the climate as we ascended the river.

By eight o'clock in the evening we were within a short distance of Montreal, and lay there for the night, close to a small island, called St. Helen's Island, garrisoned by the Royal Artillery. This island divides the St. Lawrence, and the current formed by this division is called the St. Mary's current; it is so strong, that a steam-vessel is required to tow a ship up the current from St. Helen's Island to Montreal.

Mr. and Mrs. Lessely and I sat on the deck for an hour or two after the ship anchored by the island, looking at the large, bright stars, larger and brighter than we denizens of the north of Europe had ever seen them, and the lights shining along the streets, and from the windows of the crowded town.

While we sat in the bright starlight, talking of the time when Jacques Cartier landed on these shores to teach the savage Indian to worship and to raise an altar to the Triune God, a cannon boomed along the little island by our side, and startled us not a little. We found afterwards it was fired every night to warn the soldiers garrisoned on the island it was time to retire for the night.

Before we parted for the night, Mrs. Lessely asked me to remain in Montreal with her for a week or two.

I gladly accepted her invitation, although for no specified time. I knew that my services would not be required at Algona for nearly three weeks, as school did not re-open at St. Bride's convent until the first of September; and besides the pleasure I anticipated from seeing the lions in the principal city of Canada, I had become attached to both Mrs. Lessely and her children, and felt loathe to part with them; they seemed to be the last link that bound me to home.

I now, strange to say, felt the greatest repugnance to entering the convent. Perhaps this feeling was induced by the pertinacity with which both Mr. and Mrs. Lessely, during the latter part of the voyage, endeavoured to persuade me from doing so; at all events, whether from this cause or my own natural love of freedom, such as I could not enjoy there, had my means and wishes agreed, I would rather have remained with Mrs. Lessely and taught her children for nothing, than go to St. Bride's for the large salary I was to receive there. I had another motive—by remaining for a week in Montreal, I could write to Gertrude and receive her reply before going to Algona, thus making myself certain of the welcome I was to receive there. It is true I had written to St. Bride's before leaving Scotland, accepting of the situation on the terms offered, and at same time advising Gertrude of my departure from Scotland ; but still, it would make assurance doubly sure could I again hear from the inmates of the convent previous to my leaving Montreal.

CHAPTER XX.

NEXT morning we awoke to find the vessel anchored at the wharf of Montreal, and people passing and repassing from the ship to the wharf.

I shall never forget the feelings of admiration with which for the first time, I gazed on this young and beautiful ' Queen of the West.'

The morning was lovely, the air fresh and pure, not such air as we inhale on the wharves in Britain—the sky one sheet of clear, unclouded blue—no smoke hanging above this beautiful city of the river, bringing uncleanness and sickness, with all their attendant evils, to those who live below. There it lay in all its beauty of situation and architecture, embowered in giant trees, with vine-shaped leaves, brown and scarlet and gold, gemmed by millions of dewdrops, under a sky as clear and blue as that of Italy. The bright morning sun, bathing river and mountain, trees and town, in a flood of living light, his radiant beams throwing such deep shadows of the passers-by on wharf and wall, that one might fancy the spirits of the Indians had donned the garb, and were following in shadowy guise the children of those who had driven them from their beautiful mountain home.

The day was one of the numerous *fêtes* of the Roman Catholic Church, and the wide-spreading-town, and the ships below, were alike gay with flags hung in every available space on the housetops, above bright tin roofs glittering in the morning sunshine. Streaming from windows, or suspended by cords hung from one house to another, across the streets, the tricolour of La Belle France, hanging in peace and amity side by side with the old lion of England, who in his dazzling golden dress pawed the scarlet folds surrounding him, and looked proudly down, as if guarding, and pleased to see the citizens in their holiday attire.

And almost encircling this emerald of his own, lay the mighty St. Lawrence, his rushing waters, with their pearl-crested waves, hurrying on to supply the wants, and rest in the bosom of his ocean bride, as they had ever done since the day when the Spirit of God moved upon the face of the waters, and as they will do until that other great day dawns when there shall be no more sea.

The island of Montreal is formed by the confluence of the rivers St. Lawrence and Ottawa, and is thirty miles long by ten broad. The town is built on the base, and extends up the sides of a beautifully wooded mountain, situated on the north shore of the St. Lawrence, called Mount Royal.

The mountain is formed, from the base to nearly the top, of large steppes, and on the broad table land forming the top of each are built the principal streets, which thus run parallel to each other; these being approached by cross streets reaching half way up the mountain, and in some instances much farther.

It possesses many fine buildings and several squares, in one of which is a large reservoir of clear water, supplied by several jets, which are constantly playing and diffusing a grateful coolness to the surrounding atmosphere.

The city contains upwards of one hundred thousand inhabitants, and appears quite immense from its being so scattered ; whole streets on the upper part of the mountain being built in detached villas, surrounded by large orchards or gardens. Several of the streets are lined on either side by trees, some of which are of no late growth. The poplars are, many of them, a yard and a half in diameter.

There are many fine churches, both Protestant and Roman Catholic. The Cathedral of Notre Dame, built on the street which bears its name, is the largest place of worship on the American continent with the exception of the cathedral in the city of Mexico. We found that whatever part of the town we were in, the towers of this cathedral were conspicuous objects in the landscape.

I have made a long digression in thinking of beautiful Montreal. I had almost forgot that I left my reader still on board ship. After breakfast we all prepared to depart. Mr. Lessely had obtained from a friend the address of a private boarding-house, to which we bent our steps, leaving our luggage to follow in the afternoon, when we were secure of an entrance.

Our residence for a few weeks was quickly arranged. My room was a very small one, looking out on the yard, but so white and clean, that I soon forgot all about its size and look-out.

In the afternoon Mrs. Lessely and I took the children out for a walk, Mr. Lessely going to the ship, and also to leave his card for the Rev. Mr. B., an Episcopalian clergyman, to whom he had an introduction from a friend who lived several years in Montreal, and was now in Scotland, where he had gone to enjoy the fruits of twenty years' labour ; instead of which his life was spent in vain regrets for the sunny skies and dry climate of Canada, that better suited his advanced years, than the chilly and damp atmosphere of his island home. The street Mrs. Lessely chose for our walk was a continuation of the one in which we lived, but called by a different name, where it diverged a little from the straight line : it was lined by large trees on one side along nearly the entire length of two miles.

This leafy covering overhead was very grateful, the sun shone with a fierce heat unknown in Britain, and we, not knowing better, had gone out during the very hottest part of the day.

We were in search of a registry office for servants, one of which we found on our line of walk. Mrs. Lessely requested the person in charge to send her a nursemaid in the course of the morrow, and in reply was asked—

" What wages do you give ?"

" I am a stranger in the country. I do not know what wages are given. But I will give whatever is necessary to obtain a tidy, trustworthy girl who can sew well."

" For such an one you will have to give from fifteen to eighteen pounds a year, hiring and paying her by the month."

What a price ! nearly the salary of an English governess at home. Why do not miserably paid Scotch girls come here where they will gain more in one year than they can hope to win by harder work in three years at home ?

Soon after breakfast next day, a gentleman was shown in who announced himself as Mr. B. He regretted being from home when Mr. Lessely called the preceding day, and said he came early to be sure of finding Mr. Lessely within.

We were all very favourably impressed by him ; he is of a serious, grave demeanour, has a fine face, large forehead, and an eye full of penetration and firmness ; his manner is calm and dignified, and he seems to possess the rare gift of shewing he takes an interest in your welfare, without intruding into your private affairs.

He asked Mr. Lessely if he meant to make a lengthened stay in Montreal.

Mr. Lessely at once mentioned the business which brought him to Canada, adding that he intended to remain in the country.

Mr. B., in the most friendly manner, offered him introductions to some gentlemen whom he thought might be able to forward his views.

This promise he faithfully performed, and these introductions were ultimately of the greatest benefit, in enabling Mr. Lessely to settle as he wished.

Mr. B. is the rector of one of the largest congregations in town, and from all we could hear, is the most popular Episcopalian clergyman in Montreal, and strange to say, nearly as much liked among dissenters as among his own people.

After his departure, our hostess entertained us for half an hour by repeating instances of his unwearied kindness and liberality to the poor of all denominations.

In the afternoon we had several visits from young ladies, as they invariably called themselves, who came from the registry office to be engaged as child's maid.

They were not, in either appearance or ability, at all to be compared with a respectable English or Scotch girl of the same class, and the most modest gave themselves airs that would not for a moment be endured at home.

The first, a great tall untidy-looking girl, came in saying, as she entered the room :

" Please, ma'am, I'm the young lady as came from the register."

According to her own account, she was perfect. She was told that in addition to attending upon the children, taking them to walk, &c., she would have to sew.

" Very well," she replied, " as the blind man said, we'll see. If I have time, I'll sew for you ; and if I have not, I won't ; so we'll let it rest there : but I think any girl as has two children to attend to, has enough to do, without sewing, if there's a reasonable woman for a mistress; and for me, I never stays more nor a month in a place, where they don't make me comfortable : I've seen me leave at five minutes' warning, when people goes contrary."

Mrs. Lessely did not seem to like the prospect of being left at five minutes' warning, and told her she would not suit. The girl took no notice of this, but said :

" I have decided to tell you my name. My name is Mary Barron, and you'll hear my ' *caracter*' at No. 10 Dorchester street."

Half an hour later, another " young lady," came on the same errand. On entering the room, she placed a chair for herself, and on sitting down, enquired of Mrs. Lessely—

" Are you the person who wants a young lady to help you keep house ?"

" I want a child's maid, who can give me a good character from her last place, and who is willing to sew in her leisure hours."

" There is my ' *caracter*,' " said the young lady, handing Mrs. Lessely a very nice, clean-looking envelope, containing the missive in question. " I can sew very well, and I suppose I'll suit you, if you'll suit me. Who brushes the children's shoes ?"

" I expect their maid to do everything for them."

" That's enough," was the laconic reply of the offended young woman, who got up, held out her hand for her ' caracter,' and was gone.

We had several other visits, but all with similar success. One of the damsels objected to sewing, as being double work ; observing " that as she made all her own clothes, she had enough to do in the evenings, without sewing for others. If people wanted a sewing girl, they ought to hire one, and not try to make slaves of others." And having decided that the place would not suit her, she turned to me and said in the same tone and manner as she would have addressed her fellow-servant—

" I would like to get a black silk thread, if you have one by you."

I gave her the thread, which she received without the slightest thanks, and taking a needle from her shawl, that seemed to be fastening that piece of dress, she lifted up the skirt of her gown, from which the braid-binding was unripped, and coolly sat down to repair the mischief.

" You had better go down to the kitchen and mend your dress there," suggested Mrs. Lessely.

"No, thank you," said the young lady, with great composure, " I'll not bother; I'll do it here for all that's of it. When I'm in place I won't have nobody coming poking into my kitchen, so I never does it to others."

She certainly completed her task in a wonderfully short time, and was evidently a smart girl, notwithstanding her dislike to sew for her mistress.

Having finished her work, she arose from her chair, and as a prelude to her departure, carefully arranged her dress above a set of most extensive hoops. While thus employed, the chambermaid came into the room, to take something from a cupboard. They at once recognized each other as old friends, the visitor exclaiming, with a bright glad look, as she held out her hand—

" Confounding to you, Susan Breet, are you here ?"

" Sure, that's not you, Bridget; did you hire ?" enquired the other, as they shook hands and laughed merrily with each other, ' sans ceremonie,' apparently quite oblivious of our presence.

" Faith, an' I didn't then," was the energetic rejoinder of her friend. " I'm not the fool she takes me for, to work all day worriting with children, and sew all night."

No one could be found to suit for several days, but at last, a nice, tidy-looking girl agreed to do all that she was told. She was very handy, and did her work cheerfully and well.

The fourth day of our residence in Montreal, the sun rose in clouds and rain; or rather, to our sight, he did not make his appearance during the whole day. The evening previous had been close and sultry; and during the night, at intervals, the awful thunder was heard lifting its deep-toned voice to God. This is always the harbinger of rain here, and our fellow-boarders warned us that we would most likely have three days of it.

This was not pleasant news for us, who had time, inclination, and opportunity for sight-seeing. However, there was nothing for it but to submit with a good grace.

We occupied ourselves in writing to those loved ones each of us had left in our home beyond the sea; father-land and friends now both doubly dear that they were so far away.

Later in the evening, Mr. Lessely took our letters to the post-office, and on his return, he brought with him a boy about twelve or thirteen years of age, who, in addition to being so wet, that while he stood in the hall, the water running from his clothes formed first a pool and then a stream which reached along the whole length of the place: he was clothed in a suit of perfect rags; had no shirt, no vest, and his trousers were suspended by a piece of rope untwisted, (I fancy that it might not cut his poor thin shoulders) and fastened on the left side in front, from hence passing over the righe shoulder, and finally tied into a hole cut in the band of tht trousers on the right side of the back.

Mr. Lessely had found him sitting on a neighbouring door-step fast asleep, and on shaking him up, and bidding him go home, had been told he had no home, but that he would wait there until the policeman came round, when he would be taken to the police office, and so have a shelter for the night.

Our good landlady was applied to, to permit him to remain in her house, and on the morrow Mr. Lessely would see what could be done for him. This was easily settled; she not only agreed to this, but gave little Joe, as he called himself, a suit of clothes belonging to one of her own children, and very soon his wet rags were thrown into the court yard, and the poor child clothed, most likely, better than ever he had been in his life. When he was brought in, he had no shoes or stockings, but both were provided by the kind-hearted motherly woman, by whose kitchen stove he was now sitting. These were the last articles of dress given him to put on, and before doing so, he put his hand into each stocking, and finding there were no holes in either, he fancied they must have been given him by mistake, and said to one of the servants, holding out the stockings as he spoke—

" Tell her they're new."

Poor boy, what a revelation he made of the vicissitudes of his short life ; he had no recollection of either father or mother ; he had been a waif on the ocean of life ever since he could remember ; he had often been in jail ; at one time going about with a blind man, who beat him for buying candy with one of the pennies that should have been handed to himself ; so Joe ran off and joined a train of four children begging with an old woman, who personated their grandmother ; at another, following a man with an organ and monkey, he was engaged to go round for the half-pence with the man's hat ;

later in life he was promoted to wandering about with a lot of strolling players; and again, happy time, which he still sighed after with vain regrets, he made one of a strolling circus.

One morning he awoke to find them all gone! horses and all! even the big dog, with whom he used to be such friends, went with the rest, and he was alone in the barn! His account of this was most pathetic.

He cried, and thought he would wait there always, until they came back; they told him they had been twice there before, they would be sure to come back; Tom Spring, the clown, told him he would keep him for a boy to himself; they had only gone for a day to some fair, and would be back at night; how sorry he was he had slept so soundly, but for that he, too, might have been at the fair; no matter, he would run about and pick berries, the night would soon come, and how he would laugh when he saw the horses and Tom Spring, and the great dog, come back again from the fair.

The morning passed slowly, it was late in the year, and there were not many berries, and he had searched all the shady places that no one else knew of but himself; but the birds ate such lots now, the young ones were so strong and ate so much, they had not left one.

He was very hungry, but it was noon; he knew that by the shadow of the great poplar falling just in the middle of the gap in the fence, through which the farmer's son brought the horses down to the water in the evening; that was a good thought, he would gather a lot of dry twigs ready to light the fire, and they would have such a roaring fire that night, and he would make Tom Spring promise to wake him when they went away early again; or, better still, he would tie a string to Bull's collar and then fasten the other end round his own waist, and so when Bull stirred he would awake; and he laughed when he found out this good plan ; what a lot of dry twigs he gathered ! and then he broke a great pile quite short; wouldn't there be a blaze! they would see it almost at the farm-house—the village people would see it well ; wouldn't they wonder!

" If he went to the farm-house now, he could have something to eat; the woman always gave him bread and milk ; and the little girl twice gave him cakes, and once a piece of a sugar-stick; but it took a long time to go to the farm-house ; Tom Spring and the master and all might be back again, and want the fire lit while he was away ; and they would be sure to want him to go for water to the stream; what could they have meant by taking all the pitchers to the fair ? if they had only left one, he would have it full of the clearest water from the top of the stream, ready for them when they came, and now they would have to wait, it took quite a while to go to the stream.

There is the farmer's son with the horses—the horses are not working much now, that is why he takes them all the way down here to the water."

" Hillo, Joe! why didn't you go off with the rest; what for did they leave you ?"

" I slept in, and so they forgot to waken me ; they have gone to the fair, and will be back to-night."

" What fair ? where is the fair ?"

" I don't know; I only know they have gone to the fair."

" Come along, Joe, and water the horses."

" No, can't go to-night, perhaps they'd come when I was gone, and nobody to light the fire."

" Never mind the fire, Joe ; it'll light itself with all that sticks; you've surely done nothing but gather sticks for a week!"

"I gathered them all to-day, and broke the little ones, too."

"You've worked well for your supper; come along to the water, Joe, and here's Lady Elgin for you to ride on."

Since the first day the circus people had lived by the old barn, Joe went regularly to water the horses with the farmer's boy, and a ride on Lady Elgin had been the great though unattained object of his ambition; but now he would not go, not even for that; he would not stir from the barn now, it was too late; they might come any moment, they would be sure to come soon; no, he would sit there, and look in the direction of the town all the time, and just as he saw the caravan on the brow of the hill between him and the sky, he would light the fire; wouldn't Tom Spring and the Golden Star laugh when they saw such a roarer of a fire! How long the farmer's boy stays away with the horses to-night! he used to come back whenever the horses had done drinking, but to night it seems as if he never would come—surely he has gone round by the other way—what a fool he is; the moon does not give much light, it is not nearly at its full, and the way by the smithy is two miles round, and so lonesome! yes, he has just gone round, there is something wanted to be done to one of the horse's shoes; ah, he is a sly cove the farmer, he always sends to the smithy at night, and so does not lose the boy's work during the day; them fathers always makes the boys work well. Joe was glad he hadn't no father; he remembers going round by the smithy one night with the boy, and coming back so late that Tom Spring thought he was lost.

" Ah-ha ! there he is coming back, Lady Elgin and all ;
he didn't go to the smithy !"

" What kept you so long at the water ?"

" I wasn't long; come, Joe, and sleep by the kitchen fire,
the circus folk won't come to-night !"

" Yes, but they will, they're having a lamp-light show, and
that's what keeps them so late : won't the Golden Star be
beautiful to-night ? won't there be crowds to see her ? I wish
I hadn't slept in !"

" I never seed the Golden Star ; that is like—I never seed
her in circus—what like is she, Joe ?"

" Like nothing at all as you ever seed, if you never seed
herself : and for seein' of her out here it's nothin'—she's no
more like herself out here than that old rotten stump is like
the big poplar with all its lots o' green leaves. At the circus
she's drest in a blue dress, wery short, and white trowsers (not like your'n, as you wears on Sundays), but beautiful white trowsers, wi' red shoes, and beads on her arms, and
three long red and blue and white feathers sticking up from
her head, the very same as the Prince of England wears on
his head—they calls them Prince's feathers, 'cause he wears
them—you see the Prince is King now, since the old Prince
is dead, and they as knows says as how he puts on them three
feathers so grand every mornin' afore he goes out, and never
takes them off till night—you see them grand folks don't care
for spendin'."

" But for why do they call her the Golden Star, Joe ?"

" O, I didn't tell you about that ; why, man, she has a
star o' gold, real gold, as big as that (and Joe put both his
hands together and spread them out) on her head, and another, twice as big, on her breast ; and when she has on the

white and red paint on her face you never seed nothin' so beautiful."

"I guess as how she's the master's wife, Joe."

"I guess she's nothin' o' the kind; she's Tom Spring's wife; the master's wife is no more like her than nothin'; the Golden Star is wantin' but an inch of six feet, and the master's wife is but five feet six; they was measured often, and often; and the Wanderin' Beauty has a squint in one of her eyes, but that's nothin', 'cause in circus she has a long red feather almost covers it; and she paints, o' my eye, as red as ripe cherries; and the folks think heaps o' her; but O! la, she's not the Golden Star paint and all, no how."

"And why did'nt the master marry the Golden Star hisself?"

"'Cause she would'nt marry him; Tom Spring is a real gentleman, and the master's not; in course the master's a gentleman, and so is they all, but not a real born gentleman like Tom Spring. Tom Spring's father keeps a grand hotel, an' place of entertainment for man and beast, ale and porter, wine and British spirits sold here. And Tom run'd off wi' the circus folk 'cause he likes a wanderin' life better nor waiten or measurin' o' spirits all the time. Tom tells me all about them things when we goes for fowls to the hen roosts; you see we has to go far off, 'cause we never takes no hens from the folks we lives near, and we has to go o' nights when its dark, 'cause Tom's too much of a gentleman to be carryin' of hens and turkeys on his back in the daylight."

It was getting dark; Ned must go with the horses, his father would wonder what kept him all this time.

"You'd better come along to the house, Joe, sure enough the circus folk won't come to-night; and the ghost with the ten bloody heads as always looks out o' the barn window there will be sure to carry you off."

"Oh! for any sake don't speak o' them things; I can't abide them; but I won't go no how. I'll never go out o' this till Tom Spring comes back."

The farmer's boy went away with his horses, and Joe watched them until they were lost in the shadow of the willows, which grew on the skirting of the bush, and stooped down to the ground with their long sweeping arms, as if to hide those who were passing underneath; and when he could see them no more, he listened for the tramping of the horses' feet, straining his ear until the last faint sound was lost in the distance.

"How lonesome it is to be out here alone; and it gets so dark; ha, there are the bull frogs, the jolly boys, croak, croak; they keep one's heart up, they'r a'most as good as some company; better nor sulky, one-legged Dick, as cleans the caravan and minds the horses, and won't let a body ride on a horse no how."

Joe wished he wasn't so hungry, but wouldn't he eat when they came home.

The night became darker, and darker; the sky so full of clouds, and only two or three stars; "last night there was so many you couldn't count them; the air was becoming quite cold; he would light a fire, just a little one; it wouldn't waste many sticks; and he had such heaps; and when they came it would be easier to pile a lot of sticks on the fire than to strike a light with the flint." So the fire was lit, and he warmed himself spreading his hands over the glowing flame. It must be very late now, the lights in the farm houses are all extinct, and he has fallen asleep once or twice, as he sits on the ground and looks at the fire; but he cannot go into the barn to lie down there, he still hoped they would come that night, and besides, did the farmer's boy not bid him beware of the ghost with the bloody heads; how frightened he was now that it was so dark, he could not bear to look in the direction of the window where the ghost always put out his head.

Poor Joe stretched himself by the little fire as close as possible; in the fire there was light and heat, and protection from the ghost; when the circus folk came he would be sure to awake with the noise.

But when he awoke it was with the song of birds filling the morning air, from every leaf-clad twig and bough; and the light zephyr passing by with accents of praise in the rustling of its wings; every fitful gust laden with fresh incense for the great altar. The gush of falling waters from above, the limped gurgling stream, just where the great grey-stones made a mimic rapid, whispering soft and low their morning matins. Poor Joe's voice alone was mute.

His fathers in the far past, and before they went to the land where there is no forgetfulness, had known this universal hymn; but each, in his time, had forgotten a little, and a little, until it was remembered no more; and their was no fear of God before their eyes.

And Joe, poor Joe; no one cared for his soul.

The farmer's boy came early and brought him bread and cheese; and Joe lingered all that day and made himself a broom of cedar, and swept the barn and tidied it up; but at night when the boy came again, bringing the horses to the water, he went home with him to the farm kitchen, and was warmed and fed; but he returned to the barn in the morning, and waited all that day; and so he did for many days, returning faithfully each morning to wait with wistful eye and listening ear for those who were never to come—until with the frost and snow the bitter conviction forced itself upon

him, that they had indeed gone to return no more. Even
then he believed most implicitly in Tom Spring's affection
for him, and relied upon his promise, "I will take you for
my own boy."

Joe knew why he had been left; " it was not Tom's fault,"
he would never have done it; but he remembered well the
day he went to the bush, and after many hours search returned with a basket of strawberries and a bunch of flowers, such
a big bunch as big as his head; and he gave all, strawberries
and flowers, every one to the Golden Star; the Wandering
Beauty beat Joe that very evening, and several times after
that, wished to turn him away, but his friend Tom Spring,
always came to the rescue; it was she who had contrived
that he should be left, O yes, he knew it was she."

The farmer's wife wished to keep him, but he could'nt
stay there, it was too lonesome, and he had to work; and he
didn't like work; not every day; one day in the week perhaps he would like to work; but at the farm they worked
every day but one; it wasn't like being with the circus folk
at all.

So one morning when the glad spring time came again,
and the trees were full of green leaves, and the birds were
singing all day, and the water so warm that you could stay in
for an hour and not feel cold, Joe slipt down from the garret
where he slept, and going into the best parlour, (where he
had never been but once before, when the boy took him in
to show him how grand it was,) he took a lot of nice things
for Tom Spring and the Golden Star, and he walked all that
day until he could walk no longer, he was so tired, and then
he crept into the bush and slept there; and ever since he had
been wandering from town to town, and from village to
village—every where that he heard there was a circus—in

hopes of meeting with Murphy's Royal Circus again ; he had lost all the nice things that he brought from the farm house, but he didn't care for that, he could easily find others if he could only find Tom Spring again ; this was all he cared for.

Two days before, he heard that there was a circus in Montreal, and it was this that brought him thither ; he had arrived the day Mr. Lessely found him; he had walked a long way; he did not know how many miles; he sat down on the step to rest and fell asleep.

Mr. Lessely intended to consult the Rev. Mr. B. as to what could be done for Joe, although it seemed a hopeless case. There was no place of refuge in Montreal, or indeed anywhere else, for such as Joe ; one who was old enough to earn his own bread, if he had only been brought up with habits of industry : but Joe's hands were as unused to useful labour as his mind was a blank. Joe had been taught nothing ; all he knew he had learnt of himself. Joe had as surely " growed" as any little negro Topsy, under the most careless master " down South." Joe never remembered living nowhere, only sometimes a woman would let him sleep with the other boys " o' nights," and he always got " bits o' bread round about;" an' when one folks was tired on him, he went round till he got some other boy as would take him home. Joe knew there was a good man up in the skies, and one woman told him some words to say to the good man ; but they was about a father, and when he left that house, he never said the words again. 'Joe didn't want no father ; he was glad he hadn't never had no father.' 'Joe didn't like fathers, they was always drunk, or sulky, or something. Joe could never go home o' nights wi' boys as had fathers ; fathers didn't like strange boys, and wouldn't let them come home o' nights, no, not if it was ever so cold.' In summer

Joe slept anywhere ; there was plenty places to sleep in then. He wouldn't sleep in a house in summer, not for nothin' ; oh, he didn't like it, only when it rained like to-night. Joe didn't like nobody but Tom Spring; the women in the houses he went home to o' nights, washed their own boys' faces, and combed their hair, but nobody never washed his face, nor combed his hair, but only Tom Spring."

Had Mr. Lessely been in his own house, he would have kept the boy, and endeavoured by degrees to win him from the semi-savage life he had been accustomed to, and delighted in ; but living in a boarding-house, and with his limited means, it was impossible. After a time, when he was settled in business, he meant to give Joe a trial. His devotion to Tom Spring had shown that he had strong affections, which, if they could only be turned into a proper channel, might be the means of making him a good member of society, instead of the little lawless vagrant he now was, utterly regardless of the rights of property, and ignorant alike of what was for his true well-being in time or eternity ; of the latter he knew nothing.

After tea we had Joe up stairs in the parlour; we were not surprised to find that, although he had some idea of a God, he had never heard of a Saviour.

There were a pair of old fashioned pistols lying upon the table, which Mr. Lessely had undertaken to convey to a gentleman in Montreal, from his grandfather, who was a General in the British Army, and in whose family they had been treasured as heirlooms for generations, tradition having pointed to their first owner as being coeval with, and a friend of, the Regent Murray. Mr. Lessely had unpacked the pistols for the purpose of conveying them to their destination, but was prevented from doing so by the rain which fell in torrents.

Mrs. Lessely gave Joe some candies, and while he enjoyed eating the sweets, he was bent on amusing himself by examining the various " nice things" which were in the room ; all at once he uttered an exclamation of joy, and seizing one of the pistols absolutely screamed with laughter, calling out, " Tom Spring's pistol, Tom Spring's pistol," leaping once or twice high in the air, and waving the pistol round his head, as he shouted at the top of his voice. We allowed his transports to subside a little, and then taking the pistol, (which he did not seem at all inclined to part with,) from his hand, Mrs. Lessely told him the story attached to it ; he shook his head incredulously, and lifting up the pistol, pointed with a look full of meaning to a large S. inlaid with silver on the side ; it was explained to him that that was the first letter of the name of the family it belonged to.

" It is the first letter of Tom Spring's name, and he showed it to me hisself, I have had it in my hand a many a time afore," and he looked as if he did not believe a word which had been told him.

We were sorry for this as it would doubtless have the effect of making him distrust what was said to him by Mrs. Lessely ; the pistol was again taken from his hand, and laid on the table ; he did not speak for some minutes, but at length said,

" If you tell me where Tom Spring is, I won't tell him you took his pistol."

" My poor child," said Mrs. Lessely, laying her hand kindly on his shoulder as she spoke, " we do not know anything of Tom Spring, we never saw him, never heard of such a person, until you told us of him this afternoon ; this pistol was only brought to Canada four days ago, and it was in Scotland, far across the sea, ever since it was made, before then."

"No it wasn't though," said Joe, and his countenance changed from its usually good-natured expression, to one of doubt and sullenness, " it wasn't in Scotland never, nor any way a near Scotland; and Tom Spring couldn't abear them Scotlanders nor Irelanders; Tom's father bringed it from England a many a year afore Tom was born, and he would never give it to Tom to shoot sparrows nor nothin', an' so Tom took it for hisself, and hid it safe in a place as the old man did'nt know of, and he gave Tom such a licking 'cause he wouldn't tell he'd took the pistol; an' Tom was real lonesome 'cause he'd no brothers nor sisters; so next mornin' afore the old folks was out on their bed, Tom runned off, an' he took lots of money wi' him; the money was all done, but he never lost the pistol till you took it."

Mrs. Lessely lifted one of the pistols from the table, and holding it towards him said, "take the pistol in your own hand and look over it carefully, and see if there is not something there," (pointing to the inlaid work with which it was nearly covered) " that you do not remember to have seen on Tom Spring's pistol."

He looked at the pistol as she held it towards him for a second or two, and then pushing her hand rudely away, exclaimed with impatience:

"You know well enough as how that's not Tom Spring's pistol, that pistol hasn't no moon, nor no sun, like Tom's pistol has, and them birds is swallows, and Tom's is red-breasts."

Mrs. Lessely and I compared both pistols examining them closely, and found that on one end in the inlaid work, was a small spot, not so large as a pea, while at the other, was one of similar size with diverging rays, most likely intended to represent the sun and moon, as Joe said, while the birds on the one without sun or moon, were swallow tailed!

There was a poser—we were at our wits end—Mrs. Lessely, probably thinking it better to end the conversation for the time, at least, told Joe that he might go down stairs, and that Mr. Lessely would perhaps talk to him about the pistol on the morrow.

By and bye we were joined by Mr. Lessely, who, on being told of the extraordinary scene with Joe and the pistol, said:

"This is one of those strange things which are ever taking place, and pass unheeded because we lack the key to unlock the mystery. General S——, upon entrusting those pistols to my charge, called my attention to those very differences in the embellishment, which you have just pointed out. Some forty years since, the General, who was then a young man, was with his regiment at Hill Sea barracks, near Southampton, in the south of England, and while there, had one of those pistols stolen from him, as he supposed, by his servant, an Englishman named Spring, who was one of the soldiers in his regiment; but as the man denied the charge with apparent innocence, at same time offering every facility for searching his person and kit, General S—— became ashamed of his suspicions and apologized for the injustice he had been guilty of. A large reward was offered for the recovery of the pistol, but without effect; subsequently, however, the valet absconded, taking with him money and jewels, the property of his master, to a large amount· There was no electric telegraph in those days, and it was supposed, that the thief made his escape to America. Some years since, General S—— found the other in an old curiosity shop in Paris, and so perfect was the similarity to his own, that it was only on his return to Scotland, when he had an opportunity of comparing the one with the other, that he made the discovery of the difference pointed out by Joe ;

until then, he was satisfied he had recovered his lost pistol. How certain is the law of retribution," continued Mr. Lessely, leaning back and resting his head on the easy chair in which he sat, while his countenance assumed a graver look than usual : " A young man steals a pistol in England, flies off with his booty to America, and, it may be, prospers there, spreading his roots to the waters, as a green bay tree ; but time goes hurrying by ; and his only child sees and covets the stolen pistol ; again a little while, and pistol and son are both lost to the man, who perilled his soul, and forfeited his Briton's birthright of freedom in his native land long years ago for the one ; so long ago that he had come to consider it as much his own, as if he had won the money which bought it by the labour of his strong right hand ; and for the other, could he but find him now, how gladly would he give all the ill-gotten gains he had toiled for and amassed during these forty years—poor lonely old man, does it ever occur to him that his sin has found him out."

On retiring for the night, Mr. Lessely took the pistols with him to his own room, and, placing them in a drawer, said, " he would go next morning immediately after breakfast, and deliver them to their owner." Mrs. Lessely observed, " That she would not feel easy after the exhibition she had witnessed this evening, until she knew they had reached their destination in safety."

Next morning during breakfast, Mr. Lessely was pleasantly surprised by receiving a note informing him, that the senior partner of a mercantile house, to which he had made application for a situation now vacant, was waiting in his office to make the wished-for arrangement, and that his presence was requested immediately, the gentleman in question being obliged to leave Montreal for Upper Canada within an hour.

This was indeed good news, and would put an end to much harrassing anxiety, and Mr. Lessely left us at once, going with the young man who brought the note, saying as he went out, that he would not return until one o'clock ; and bidding Mrs. Lessely and I go a house-hunting in his absence, adding, we will have a home now for Joe.

We gladly obeyed his injunction, and set out on our mission ; we were not long in finding a wooden cottage quite good enough for Mrs. Lessely's simple taste and straitened means. The cottage consisted of four rooms and a kitchen, to which was attached a small garden, containing several apple trees, which were loaded with fruit.

" The children will be delighted to find they have a garden, with lots of fruit to play in," said I.

" Yes," replied Mrs. Lessely " and how Joe will laugh : I hope it will assist in making him forget ' Tom Spring's pistol.' "

But the rent, when we came to inquire about that, forty pounds a year ! in addition to which were five pounds for taxes and three pounds to the water company ; in Scotland quite a large house might be rented for that sum ; however, on going to inquire the rent of other vacant houses, we found our cottage was the cheapest, and on the whole best suited for the purpose ; several brick housse, bold, staring upright things, without a tree or a foot of ground for the children to play on, were fifty pounds, " because they were brick." So we arranged with the landlord that he was not to let the cottage until the following day, when we would bring Mr. Lessely to give his decision.

On arriving at home, we found that we were a little late, and that Mr. Lessely had already dined ; he had entered on the duties of his situation, and was to return to his office at

two o'clock ; we told him what our success in house-hunting
had been, and he desired Mrs. Lessely to close the bargain
for the cottage, so that they might commence furnishing their
new home as soon as possible.

Before returning to his office, Mr. Lessely went upstairs
to bring the pistols, that on his way he might deliver them
to their owner ; he returned in a few minutes with one only,
the other, "Tom Spring's pistol was gone." Joe was called
upstairs, but did not answer to the call ; a search was made
in both house and court yard, no Joe was to be found ; no
one recollected to have seen him since ten o'clock, he had
been employed previous to that in helping the chamber-maid
to fill the water jugs, and seemed to like the work ; running
quickly and cheerfully from kitchen to bedroom with the
water pitcher ; the last jug he filled was in Mrs. Lessely's
room, the girl put some things in the drawer and saw the
pistols there. "She was not sure if Joe was in the room
when she did so ; she could not say if she left the drawer
open or not," at all events the pistol was gone, and so was
Joe.

Mr. Lessely went at once to the police office, and was
assured that the culprit would be found in a few days ; notwithstanding, he telegraphed in every direction, giving a full
description of both Joe and the pistol.

In three days Joe was found, tried in the police court,
and sent to prison there to await his trial before the Grand
Jury. This was done in order that he might be sent to the
Reformatory prison at Isle-aux-Noix, where he could not go
without a trial before the Grand Jury.

Fortunately for poor Joe, the Grand Jury were sitting at
the time, so he had only to wait two days in prison, until his
turn came to be tried.

T

Mrs. Lessely went twice to see Joe, and tried to make him understand something about God and the Saviour, but she was in a false position with Joe, he looked upon her as at least having a hand in taking Tom Spring's pistol, and all she said passed by him as the " light wind." Mr. Lessely had to appear as a witness on the day of Joe's trial, and as Mrs. Lessely wished to go there as a spectator, I had no choice but to accompany her.

We were by some mistake fully an hour in advance of the time for Joe's trial; the criminal at the bar was a young woman not over two and twenty years of age, who had stolen a sum of money in a house where she was employed to work by the day; she had three children under five years of age, her husband was dead ; she paid three shillings and nine pence a week for the room she and her children lived in ; she was paid two shillings a day for her work, and on an average had three days work in the week , she was a fair, delicate looking young woman, with large soft brown eyes and eyelashes that lay like a dark fringe on her cheek, as she closed her eyes languidly for a second or two, which she did often during the trial ; she must have been very pretty, before she was so thin, and as the blood mounted to her pale cheek (on hearing her sentence pronounced), suffusing it with the glow of health, and she raised her dark eyes for a moment to the ceiling, as if she sought there for the God that is so hidden ; I could not help mentally exclaiming how beautiful ; she was sentenced to two years confinement in the penitentiary at Kingston.

I wondered what was to become of the three children ; were they to become three little Joe's ?

And poor Joe, his sentence was five years residence in the reformatory prison. I hope he may reform in constant intercourse with those who are probably wiser and older in the ways of sin than himself.

Both crimes were legally established, the jury found the criminals guilty, in the sense that the law requires, and the spectators were satisfied that the criminals had been dealt with according to law, and that the law itself, was a just and necessary one—just at least as far as the objects and the nature of human laws admit of being just—but did the question never arise in the minds of the actors in this scene, how far the criminal as a matter of retribution, deserved to suffer ? Is it not felt amid all the formalities of trial ; all the precautions, by which the possibility of injustice has been fenced out, all the inquiries, with which truth has been sought ; all the machinery, by which the effects of ignorance or partiality on the part of his judges have been excluded, is it not but too evident, that amid all this, the real guilt of the criminal, as a moral agent, his desert of suffering as a retributive measure, is a point that has been comparatively unattended to. That not one circumstance has been mentioned in the course of trial, otherwise than incidentally, which would enable us to form a judgment in this particular.

And if the criminal has been under the influence of powerful temptation—powerful either in the attractions of the tempting object,—the dire necessity, which prompted the theft, or the peculiar constitution of his mind, this last acting as a more powerful incentive than either of the others, do we not consider these as alleviations of his guilt ? And moreover, if we are satisfied that the temptation operated with increased effect from his want of moral principle,—a want, not the effect of a wilful abandonment of former virtuous habits, but of neglected or perverted education, of constant familiarity with vice, and evil company, exemption from discipline and want of instruction (still allowing him to be aware, that he was committing a crime,) should we not pity him on account of these circumstances?

And can we avoid believing, that when he comes to be tried at last by the Omniscient God, He who " searcheth the hearts and trieth the reins of the children of men," his sentence will be past on very different grounds from those on which it has been founded by an earthly tribunal.

I cannot help thinking, that there is much thoughtlessness and want of consideration, and benevolence, in the feelings with which the respectable part of mankind, (which means in fact, the fortunate and comfortable part,) behold the crimes and punishments of the more wretched of their brethren.

How a person living in comfort and independance, holds up his hands, at the grossness, the deceit, the ingratitude, or violence of those whose crimes are exposed and avenged by public justice. How just, how well deserved does he think the punishment? How does he congratulate himself, that his conduct is so different.

But have you considered also the difference of your circumstances? Sated with enjoyment ; with every desire gratified, every joy of life tasted, until, perhaps the appetite has become palled ; with the ministers of pleasure, ever ready to attend your call, how little can you understand the avidity with which an occasional, it may be an unlawful gratification is grasped at, how little need you wonder at the gross excess in which it is indulged ! Unruffled by disappointment, undisturbed by anxiety, unexposed to rudeness, contradiction, anger, flattered into complacency, by the respect and obsequiousness of inferiors, and the elegant mildness of equals ; never hearing a word uttered that is not, to say the least, either subdued by mercenary submission, or smoothed by artificial polish—how little can *you* comprehend, the temper of him who is soured by misfortune, maddened by the prospect of hopeless, helpless, poverty, and an entire exclusion from all the enjoyments or even comforts of life ; exasperated by the neglect and contempt of those, who have been only more fortunate than himself, hardened by continual contact with the discontent, the fierceness, the rapacity of those who have been as unfortunate.

Placed in the midst of abundance and security, satisfied with the present, and at ease about the future, feeling no embarassment, no want ; so circumstanced in short, as that dishonesty is either impracticable, or if practicable would be utter madness—would be disgrace and ruin without a motive, how little can you imagine what it is to be without a morsel of bread, without a covering against the inclemency of the weather, without a home, without a friend ; or harder still to bear, to have those, who are dearer to you than life, pining with sickness, in a bare garret or damp cellar, shivering with cold, and asking for bread in vain, and to feel that you are utterly helpless, that to-morrow and to-morrow must be the same, until this weary life has passed away; and it may be with no hope for the unknown, untrodden land beyond the dark river; but in its place, " a fearful looking forward too of punishment " for crimes, the temptations to which were irresistible ; how little can you imagine, what it is to ask for work, bare work, for scanty wages, and to be refused with coldness, perhaps driven away with suspicion ! how little need you be surprised that he, whose very misery often procures for him the reputation of being dishonest, should yield to the temptation of really deserving such a character.

Undoubtedly crimes must be punished, whether committed with or without temptation—with or without excuse; if it is not morally just that the criminal should be punished, it may at least be necessary that he should be restrained or even extirpated, and this, if only for the safety of others; but one cannot help thinking, that if a part of the time, the ingenuity and expense, that are employed to detect and punish crime, when committed, were employed to remove the causes that led to crime; if some part of the time, which legislators spend in first, second, and third readings; in committees, speeches and debates, motions and amendments on criminal laws, were applied to discover and remedy the circumstances which form the criminal; if some of the expense, that is incurred in counsel's fees, officer's fees, in courts, judges and juries, were given to supply the want which prompted the theft; nay even if the purse, or the jewels, or the plate, or some portion of the value stolen, had been expended in benificence; if the same ingenuity that is used in examining evidence to ascertain the point guilty or not guilty, were applied to discover how the criminal became guilty? how was he ignorant? how was he become hardened? how came he to be in want, in destitution, in desperation? and above all other questions, let us each ask ourselves, how came he to have no faith in the God, who is so near his people, who cry unto him? and no hope of the land, that is very far off, and is yet so near, so sure—the land that was bought with toil, and with sorrow, and with blood, in distant Asia long ago, for the thief on the cross, for the poor charwoman with her three children, for little Joe, and for you, and for me? If some part of the maintenance allowed to the criminal had been allowed him before he became a criminal; if the massive edifices constructed to secure him, had a little sooner been offered to shelter, surely some part of the vast degradation, suffering, and guilt, which abound in this and in every civilized land, would admit of being removed. In the mode of our managing such things, surely there is something like beginning at the wrong end !

CHAPTER XXI.

WE went on Sunday morning to hear Mr. B—— preach, he spoke well and earnestly, as the expression of his countenance betokened he would ; he seemed never for a moment to forget that he came there bearing a message from God to man, or to be highly conscious of the awful responsibility attached to his office, and the deep importance of how this message was delivered and how heard.

We had many delightful walks in the shady paths leading up the sides of the beautiful mountain, on which Montreal is built, and in the public gardens and squares, where gigantic trees, many of them upwards of a yard in diameter, formed a shade for delicate flowers, whose gorgeous dye and profusion of blossom are unknown in our northern clime.

We laid aside one afternoon to visit the "ship" as we denominated the Winged Zephyr, it was our ship, we knew no other.

I do not know, whether it is from having no home of my own, and so very few to love, or an innate feeling which clings to all of us, and creates a fondness for familiar things, giving to them a grace, and beauty, and attraction, which they do not of themselves at all possess, but I have never lived any where for even a week or two, without feeling a fondness for every thing around me; so strongly is this feeling implanted in my nature, that I have at times suffered exquisite pain, in parting from scenes and people, who a month previous were unknown to me ; and so before leaving Montreal, I wished to bid good bye to the ship, and speak once more to the kind simple men we lived among so happily, while crossing the ocean. The captain was not on board, but the mates and sailors came forward to meet us as kindly as if we had been old friends of their own. The steward was gone, he went out to the wharf one evening three days before, telling Jack to put a candle in his pantry, as he would be back in three minutes; but the three minutes lengthened into three days, and the steward came not; I suspected he would run away. The captain often scolded him, and one day during dinner, on the steward's replying rather pertly, the captain said, " no sauce; repeat that again, and I'll send you down below," (meaning to the hold, beside Tom.) After dinner the steward came into the saloon, where Mrs. Lessely and I were seated, and occupying himself in arranging the room said, " The skipper said he would put me in the hold, he'll not have the chance going home."

The Glasgow weaver was still on board, and we asked him in joke " if he meant to stay there."

" Oh! aye," said he looking as if he was surprised by the question, " did ye no ken, I'm gaen hame we her again; I canna abide America, its the lonesomest place at ever I was in."

" Have you been through the town, Sandy?" asked Mrs. Lessely.

" I was na aw through the town," was his reply, " but I gaed aye day up the first street there, and that was eneugh, I did na see ae gude shop in't aw, or a hous at a Glasgow gentleman wad bide in, bit I dar say the place is weel aneugh for the folk, they did na look as gen they war great things."

" But, Sandy," said Mrs. Lessely, " you have only been along the street fronting the wharf, where of course, you could see nothing, there are shops filled with beautiful things up in the town, and finer streets than you have ever seen in Glasgow."

" Gen there be let them be," said he, " I'll nae file my sheen gaen to see them, I've gotten my sick sairen o' the sea an America baith, bit it was aw my ain faut, I was weel, an I wad na bide weel; mony a decent man gangs tae their bed, whan the wife flytes, an never lats on at they hear her, as my father, honest man, did mony a day; bit that wadna dee for me, na, I ma'an be aff till America; less wadna sair me, sae lat me tak fat I got; gin I ever won hame again," continued he, and his countenance assumed a most doleful aspect; " it'll learn me, whan the wife flytes to jouk an lat the jaw ower."

" What are you to pay, Sandy, for your passage home ? " inquired Mrs. Lessely, I suppose thinking he would be short enough of funds.

" I'm nae needen to pay ony thing, I got the steward's place fan he desertet ; deed I was rale glaid, whan I heerd at he ran aff, I gaed tae the Captain that menit, an tellt him I wad dee the wark for naething gen he wad only tak me hame ; its a rale gude birth I'm only feart at he'll come back again."

"Has the steward left any of his clothes ? "

" Nae ae screed o' them, he did na leave as mukle as the paren o' a nael at wis his ain on board."

Mrs. Lessely had a conversation with Tom, and then distributing some fruit which she had brought on purpose, we bade farewell to all on board, and received from them a hearty good-bye. On our return, I found a letter awaiting me from St. Bride's, in reply to one I had written the day after my arrival in Montreal.

My letter was from Gertrude ; she was in great joy because

of my arrival in Canada, and all impatience to see me. The
Superior requested that I would leave Montreal on the day
after the receipt of her letter, giving me the name of the
steamboat I was to sail with, the time it left Montreal, and
the name of the wharf, it started from; the boat stopped at
several places on the way, and in consequence would not
reach Algona until the evening of the second, or the morning
of the third day; when the boat arrived at Algona, I would
find a conveyance waiting on the wharf, to bring me to St.
Bride's.

Mr. and Mrs. Lessely both expressed themselves sorry to
part with me, requested that I would write to them, and
offered me a home, in case I should not feel happy at St.
Bride's.

I felt very grateful for this offer; a presentiment of evil
seemed to haunt me, when I thought of St. Bride's, and I
would most willingly have declined going, were it in my power,
but I had made the engagement, and in addition to that I
was in Mrs. Livingstone's debt, and I knew that the money
Willie would make in summer, would not be more than half
what he would require for his expenses during the winter
session of college.

However, Mrs. Lessely's kind invitation had made me
more independent, and tended to reconcile me, not a little,
to going to St. Bride's; if I did not like my new home, I at
least knew where I could remain, until I found another, and
I had still Mrs. Livingstone's five pounds untouched in my
pocket. By Gertrude's letter, I was informed that my passage money from Montreal to Algona was already paid, and
a passage ticket was enclosed in my letter, for me to shew
when I went on board the vessel.

Both Mr. and Mrs. Lessely accompanied me on board the
Lord Elgin, and I parted from them with much regret.

After gazing from the deck, where I was standing by the bulwark, until the very shadows of my kind friends were lost in the distance, I went to the ladies' parlour to secure my berth. An American lady was seated by the table feeding a fat little baby, while a boy of four years of age was exerting himself to the utmost in dragging about the various band-boxes and packages—and they were by no means few in number—belonging to his mother, screaming as he did so with never-wearying lungs.

"Whatever are you about, Nally?" said his mother, in a beseeching tone of voice, and looking at me, continued, "I don't know whatever he means; I suppose it's because he's among strangers; he's always so quiet at home."

"No, I ain't, either," said the youngster, "I always makes a noise when I chooses to."

And he choose to then, and pulled about the boxes more vigorously than ever, to the great annoyance of his mother, a pretty good tempered looking woman, who evidently was too much accustomed to noise to suffer from it herself, but did not like I should be troubled.

I said a few words to put her at her ease, and having chosen my berth, and in token thereof, placed the satchel containing my night clothes, brushes, &c., in the one I had selected, I again sought the deck.

Having found myself a comfortable seat, I opened the book my kind friend, Mr. Lessely, had presented me with for the purpose of making my time on board pass more pleasantly, but I had scarcely read a page when I was interrupted by some one at my side, whose presence I was previously unconscious of, saying—

"This is a fine morning, Miss!"

I looked up and found that the speaker was a fat, short,

very plainly dressed lady, between thirty and forty years of age, who, with her little daughter, a pretty slight child, apparently about eight years old, were seated on the sofa behind me.

I replied in the affirmative, and then I was catechised as to where I was going, if my parents lived in Algona, whether I had been long in Montreal, and several other questions equally pertinent, all of which I answered with, at least, an air of patience. In return she informed me that she was Mrs. Butters, of Boston ; the child interrupted her mother by saying, " No mamma, of Stoncham."

" Sadia, let me speak," hastily exclaimed her mother, and turning to me, added, " I always say of Boston, because I have lived so much there ; I went to school to Boston, and after I left off school, I lived quite a while there with my uncle, Mr. Silas Stimson, of Boston, you have heard of him ; he was my mother's brother. I suppose you know he made his fortune in the shoe trade ? I always call myself of Boston because Stoncham is such a small place, and every one knows Boston ; this is my daughter, Miss Sadia F. Butters, of Boston ; she is our only child, and we think everything of her ; that gentleman walking with his hands behind him, is Mr. Butters, Algernon Brutus Butters, Esquire, of the firm of Butters & Winks, in the shoe trade ; do a large business every year in Montreal. Mr. Butters is a senior partner, and he makes one journey to Montreal every year himself. I will introduce you when he comes up to here."

" Where did you live before you came to Canada ?"

" In Britain."

" Well now ain't that far away, in Britain ; you ain't Scotch ?"

" Yes."

" Well now, I'm real glad ; Mr. Butters' family are Scotch ;
his grandfather, I think, came from Scotland ; the Butters
property is one of the largest estates in Scotland ; Mr. Butters is a descendant of Mary, Queen of Scots, she is dead
you know long ago ; yes," continued she, as if she was considering some doubtful point, " I think it's Mary, Queen of
Scots ; she's not bloody Mary, is she ?"

I assured her that on the contrary, Mary, Queen of Scots,
had a great horror of shedding blood.

" Had she ? O then it's she ; I was sure I was right, yes,
it's Mary, Queen of Scots ; grandmother Butters bought
her picture at a sale, because she was a relation ; it had a
shocking shabby frame, and was real old itself, but grandmother Butters had it varnished and put into a gilt frame,
cost ten dollars ; you wouldn't believe it was the same."

Mrs. Butters stopped, perhaps exhausted from " much
speaking," and Miss Sadia F. Butters took up the strain.

" Did you ever live at Stoneham ?"

" No, I never was so fortunate."

" Would you like to live there ?"

" I am not sure ; were you sorry to leave Stoneham ?"
asked I of the child, questioning in order that I might not
be questioned.

" I felt real glad ; I've been there all my life, and I was
real tired of it."

The child said this with the look and air of a woman of
thirty. I looked at her but did not reply.

" You should go to the land of Stoneham only to see it ;
Pa's store is there, and cousin Althine lives there, too ; I'd
give you a note to introduce you to her ; they're so rich
you'd like them of all things. I wish I saw her now, I'd give
her a real good hug."

At the first landing place, one or two gentlemen went on shore, and a lady, with two grown up daughters, came on board. The young ladies were showily dressed in blue silk dresses, with feathers in their hats to match, which, with their scarlet cloaks, made them look, at least, conspicuous. They found some acquaintances among the gentleman on board, and after walking about for some time, both sat down to the piano in the deck saloon, and played duets for fully two hours.

Mrs. Butters was at first pleased with the music, if such it could be called, but at last she became quite indignant, said she wondered if they thought no one on board could play but themselves, &c., &c.; she looked at her watch, it was near the dinner hour, and addressing the child, she said :

" When you finish your dinner, Sadia, you come right up here and sit on that piano stool and don't leave it till I come up stairs; I want to play as well as they do;" turning to me she said, inquiringly :

" You don't play, do you ?"

" Not well enough to play in public."

" Well, I dare say ; you see it takes a deal of money for people to learn to play as they'd like to, not that I call that good playing," nodding her head towards the performers. " What I call good playing is slow airs played with expression and pianaissima."

After dinner Miss Sadia Butters did exactly as she was bid—went up stairs and took possession of the music stool, there to await her mamma's appearance in the deck saloon.

The young ladies in blue gave themselves a great many airs, and so did their mamma, although her airs did not sit so easily upon her as theirs did. Their party was quite a large one, the young ladies having attracted all the beaux on board, and the ease with which they became intimate was, to my unsophisticated eyes, quite marvellous. They were seated opposite to Mrs. Butters and I; they evidently took us both for Americans, and looking at us, talked to each other and their beaux of their dislike to Yankees, speaking in whispers not very low.

When they had satisfied themselves by giving this proof of their high breeding, and so made sure that they themselves would not be mistaken for Yankees, they indulged in pleasant reminiscences of their school days, which were, they said, in a very loud key, passed in one of the first boarding schools in Paris, where, happy coincidence, Lord Doodell's four elegant daughters were being educated at the same time. They were untiring in their descriptions of the beauties and accomplishments of the four honorable Miss Doodells, and Miss Elvira Todd showed, and kissed as she showed, her darling Beauty, who was a pup of the honorable Miss Rosina Doodell's Beauty, and given to Miss Elvira as a parting gift by that young lady; later in the day, the mamma, oblivious of Beauty's former history, told the large price which was paid for the poodle to a dog fancier in Montreal. I am sorry to say that I discovered, by "the accents of the mountain tongue," which still hung on their mamma's speech, that she was a countrywoman of my own. Miss Todd had the kindness to inform all at the table who were not deaf, that her father's family was one of the first in Belfast. I can fancy now, how an Irish gentleman would laugh, and his lady open her eyes upon hearing such an announcement.

In due time Mrs. Butters was led to the piano by her husband, Augustus Brutus Butters, Esquire, who stood behind her chair, or rather piano stool, for an hour, during which time his lady tinkled Hail Columbia, Ben Bolt, and

Home Sweet Home, going over each twice, and playing them in succession all very slow, and I suppose with expression; but the most delicious sweets will cloy, and having tired herself and her listeners out, Mr. Butters turned solemnly round to where Sadia and I sat, (the child having taken up her former seat beside me, when her mamma replaced her on the music stool,) and beckoning with his fore finger, she at once obeyed the summons, and cast a triumphant look around the saloon, as she walked with a very upright gait towards the piano ; she then joined her mamma in singing The Star Spangled Banner, and various other popular songs, to the great delight of at least themselves and Augustus Brutus Butters, Esquire ; for my own part, I much preferred good humoured, sincere Mrs. Butters, and her tinkling music, to the vulgar assumed consequence and noisy thumping, without either time or tune, of my own countrywomen in the blue.

Mrs. Butters having finished her musical display entirely to her own satisfaction, left the piano, (which, without a moment's intermission, was occupied by the Misses Todd, who, as one of their beaux remarked, loud enough for us to hear, preferred playing as they did hunting (query—husband hunting ?) in couples.

Mrs. Butters seated herself again beside me, introducing her husband, and making room for him on the sofa betwixt herself and I, telling him at same time that I was Scotch, and knew all about Mary, Queen of Scots, which information he received with the same solemn air which he beckoned to Sadia with.

"I guess," said Mrs. Butters, addressing her husband, " that if all the Butters family down at Scotland would die off, we'd be considerable richer; perhaps, my dear, we'd be obliged to go down there to heir the estate ; wouldn't it be nice ?"

" Well, it would be real nice," chimed in Miss Sadia.

" I guess I'd not live there, supposing I did heir it," observed Mr. Butters, looking very important, " it id inter- fere with my political principles; I'd not take up with the commonality, no how; and the lords is such bad men swearing and drinking; I guess they wouldn't one of them get a chance to be introduced to my family."

Mrs. Butters' broad face became broader still, by the pleased look with which she rewarded her husband for this speech, and leaning forward, so as to speak to me, in what she meant to be a whisper, said : " He's so awful particular."

Towards evening, the lady who had the fat baby and noisy sonny, as she called him, came on deck.

" Come and sit here Mrs. Chubbock," said Mr. Butters, " why didn't you come sooner on deck, we've been having such a good time, Mrs. Butters has been playing and singing all the afternoon."

"And so was I singing, too, pa," said Miss Sadia, not liking to be overlooked.

Sadia was eating some sweet cakes which her papa had brought her from the desert ; young Master Chubbock seeing this, placed himself in front of her, his little legs wide apart, and his arms akimbo, exclaiming : " I say, you young rat, give me a piece of poi."

Sadia seemed afraid of him, and raising her hands with a cake in each, until they were nearly above her head, called out : " Pa, pa, he's calling me a rat."

" So you are a rat and an ugly rat too, I say give me a piece of your poi;" and becoming more vehement, he stamped his little fat foot impatiently, saying, " give me a bit of your poi ; give me a bit of your poi."

I gave him some of the *bon bons* Mrs. Lessely had put in

my satchel, which he accepted, as if my giving them were a matter of course, and walked up and down the deck with a step like a little giant, his mother's eyes following him with delight for a second or two, and then turning to Mrs. Butters, she said : "Is'nt he stirring."

" He is," replied Mrs. Butters, with whom Nally seemed to be no favourite ; " but our way, we make our children mind better."

" I want to have you play with me, said Nally," coming up again to Sadia, who did not meet his advances as he wished, " mount my horse and I'll give you a ride, come hurry up your cakes."

But Sadia would not be entreated, so off he went, together with his horse, a toy half a foot in length.

" How did you come to baptize Nally, ' Ronaldo,' " asked Mrs. Butters, " I guess none of your folks have that name."

Mrs. Chubbock looked the surprise she felt, " why ! I like to know ;" I guess its a family name ; did you never hear Mr. Chubbock's name ? its Ronaldo; I'll tell you how the name came into the family. Grandfather Chubbock's a mighty learned man ; so after puppy (papa) was born, grandfather Chubbock was reading about Europe and France, and them foreign places, as he always do be ; so he takes right hold on two names, and makes out Ronaldo his own self ; so I reckon any how its a family name of the Chubbocks ; they have the best right to it."

The good tempered pretty woman having delivered this history of the family name, and well knowing the importance it would give herself in the eyes of her audience, looked pleased and dignified as she glanced from one face to another in expectation of the astonishment which the wonderful talents of her father-in-law were calculated to excite.

" My !" said Mrs. Butters, after a short pause, evidently greatly impressed with respect for her friend's father-in-law, " he must be a smart man, old Mr. Chubbock must."

" I guess, he knows a thing or two, does grandfather Chubbock ; well, that's nothing, he's reading all the time ; I reckon he has more than twenty books on his shelf, and every one he has read twice over ;" and turning to me, with her good tempered smile, she said : " I guess if he'd go to London he'd astonish you Britishers considerably, old Mr. Chubbock would."

And both ladies smiled and nodded to each other, in admiration of their country and its clever learned men.

" Does your Mr. Chubbock follow his father's reading ways ?" enquired Mr. Butters.

" He don't at all," replied her friend, drawing herself up with grave dignity, " he goes right off tother way, we havn't a book in the house but the Bible and hymn book, and some other book as is a pious book too ; you cant think, puppy's such a right down one for making money all day and every evening he goes to meetin' or lecture, or something; you should see the sight of money he gives to the chapel."

" Why ! I should like to know," said Mrs. Butter's, if possible more impressed with the devotion to business and high religious views of the son, than she had before been by the literary attainments of the father, " does he speak his self at meetins ?"

" I guess he does, and lectures too," replied the delighted Mrs. Chubbock, justly proud of the position she held as the daughter-in-law of the old, and wife of the young Chubbock.

Presently we were joined by Mr. Chubbock in person, a tall, thin young man, with long, lank hair of a dusty hue, and immense pale blue eyes ; it was painfully evident that

Mr. Chubbock had dressed hurriedly, he had quite forgotten to change his shirt collar, and to have his boots blacked, and as his trowsers were short, his unblacked boots looked conspicuous.

I was presented in form to Mr. Chubbock, who seemed to have one predominant idea, and that was a deep sense of his own importance.

The introduction was peculiar,—"Mr. Chubbock, from the United States of America," "Miss Keith, from Britain;" the words were peculiar, the manner in which these words were uttered, implied, "Mr. Chubbock, a free born citizen of the land which rules the globe," "Miss Keith, who has just crept out from a nut shell."

"So you'r from Britain?" said the gentleman, spitting a large mouthful of the tobacco juice he was chewing on one side as he spoke.

"I bowed in acquiescence."

"From Britain," repeated he, "what a long time since I heard that word; do you know ladies," and he turned to his wife and Mrs. Butters as he spoke; "it had gone sleek out of mind with me that there wor sich a place;" addressing himself to me, he continued, "I reckon you know how it is, we're the greatest and the largest nation in the world, and we rule the nation ourselves, and so we have no time to think on other folks as lives outside of us."

I felt humbled by the insignificance of Britain, and made no reply.

"What part of Britain do you come from, Belfast or Glasgow?"

"Neither."

"Wall now," said he, poising himself on his heels, his thumbs in his trowsers' pockets, swaying himself backwards and forwards and using the part of his hands which were free as fins to keep his balance ; " I guess there's not much else place to come from as ever I heard on."

" Why, now Puppy," said his better half, " aint there London, where the fashions come from, altho' I never have my things made but from a Paris or New York fashion book."

" Wall, I guess," responded her husband, " if a free born American lady can't find fashions enough in New York, she's considerable hard to please, don't you think she is, Miss Keith ?"

I thought to get out of the unpleasant position of arbitrer, by simply telling the truth, and replied that I had never seen a New York fashion book.

" My !" exclaimed both ladies simultaneously, " never saw a New York fashion book," and I saw, at a glance, that I had fallen in their opinion " considerable " below par.

" Wall," said Mr. Chubbock, " I see through it all, the London booksellers buy up all the New York fashion books as comes there ; if they did'nt, they'd be in a fix, they'd never sell one of their own."

" My, what a shabby mean set," said Mrs. Butters.

And both ladies exchanged glances full of meaning such as it was.

" So you hail from London, Miss Keith ?" Mr. Chubbock recommended.

" No, from Edinburgh."

" Why ! you don't say ; that's the place Mr. John Knox preaches in, I have his book to home, his confession of faith, I don't read much, cause I don't never see much to be got by it ; my father, I guess, has pretty nearly read all the books as is worth reading ; and I don't believe he ever made a red cent by it ; but I reads Mr. Knox's book on Sunday afternoons when there's no meetin, and I reckon it's better doing of that than wanderin about in the vain fields, or shootin sparrows." He paused for a second and then continued, " I guess when you'r to home you go pretty much to Mr. John Knox's meetin, I take it he fixes them pretty sleek ?"

" I said, in reply, that I had never had the pleasure of hearing John Knox preach, but that I was aware of his being a famous preacher."

" Wall, now, if that aint like a Britisher; when there *is* a man among you as can preach the gospel, you'r afeared to go and hear him, cause he'll tell you your sins and no mistake ; I guess if he'd come to the United States, he'd have full meetins every night of the week."

I also " guessed " he would, but I did so without saying why.

We had quite a scene on the evening of the second day.

Miss Elvina Todd took off her hat, and placed it on the sofa where she sat, reading, unconscious that Beauty, feeling lonesome as Nally expressed it, took the hat in his mouth, and by way of sport had torn the straw apart in several places. Nally, however, who was constantly on the trot in search of amusement, saw what happened, and brought both dog and hat under the young lady's notice. She was very much annoyed, as well she might, having no other hat on board ; but the mamma's lamentations were loud and long ; that short stout lady, displaying more energy than grace, ran in pursuit of the hapless Beauty up and down the deck, and having at last succeeded in capturing the recipient of her daughter's yesterday caresses, bestowed upon him marks of disapprobation, in the shape of several hearty cuffs, to which

Beauty replied with loud whines, setting the spectators almost in fits with laughter; this done, the mamma lifted the dilapidated hat, mourning over its " glory gone," and related to a crowd of eager listeners, the trouble bestowed on its formation and the price it cost ; the hat, ribbon, and lace having cost seven dollars, while the feather, which inconsiderate Beauty had snapt in two places, cost eight more, in all fifteen dollars ! Miss Elvina looked as if she could die with vexation, and so excited the sympathy of Nally, that in order to comfort her, and with a view to repair the mischief, he proposed that she should give the hat to her Pa to mend.

Oh ! the storm, which instantly ensued, the young lady slapt him more than once, calling him an impudent brat, the old lady seized and shook him with a will, which equalled the energy she displayed in the pursuit of Beauty round the deck, and doubling her not very small hand, bent down and shook it in the child's face, telling him with scarlet face and stuttering utterance, that she would teach him to keep his ill bred Yankee tongue within his teeth.

Mrs. Chubbock flew from the ladies saloon, where she was putting her baby to sleep, to the rescue of sonny, who was now bawling lustily ; and certainly the Yankee lady behaved with a coolness and moderation which, under the circumstances, few would have exercised, showing herself to be by far the best bred woman of the three.

One of the beaux, who was an acquaintance of Mrs. Chubbock's, came to lend his aid in consoling Nally, and when peace was once more restored, accounted for the violent emotion which Nally's advice had given rise to, by telling her that Mr. Todd (the Papa) had made his money as a tailor in New York. Instead of hating, they should have loved the Yankees, who doubtless helped to raise their Ma and themselves so much in the social scale.

My two days sail passed wearily enough, between listening to the peculiar style of music both young and old ladies chose to entertain us with on the one hand, and on the other, Mrs. Butters and Mrs. Chubbock's descriptions of their household, furniture, dresses, family connections, riches and last and favourite theme, the vast superiority of the United States of America and its inhabitants over every other country and people, or rather over all other countries and people put together on the face of the globe.

As to reading, I found this was impossible; Mrs. Butters considered herself guilty of great neglect if I was allowed to read quietly for half an hour.

When I came on board, it was with a feeling of great reluctance. I dreaded going to St. Bride's for I knew not what ; now I looked forward to our landing at Algona, as a relief from the danger of having my skirts spit upon by the men, or the disgust of seeing men, women and children heap their plates with beefstake, fowl, pie, green peas, preserves, fish, in short, everything within reach. The second day, at dinner, the gentleman who sat next to Mrs. Butters emptied the dish of green peas into his own plate, although she was unserved, saying as he did so :

" I like green pease a'most better than green corn."

We reached Algona about two o'clock in the afternoon ; our luggage was all on the deck, at one end, and I easily secured my two trunks, so that they might be ready when the person who was to come for me arrived.

I had not long to wait ; the gangway, which connects the vessel with the wharf, was scarcely a minute arranged, when two nuns, accompanied by a young lady, came on board ; I knew well who it was, although I did not see her face.

I was seated on one of my trunks, with the other by my

side, taking care of both lest they might be carried off by mistake. The group passed without observing me, going in the direction of the deck salooon. I went softly after them and put my hand on Gertrude's shoulder. I shall ever remember the look of happiness her face lighted up with when she found who had touched her.

" Oh ! darling," she exclaimed, as she clasped my hand, and touched my cheek lightly with her lips. How much that one word and light touch expressed ! it was something to cross the Atlantic for, to see and hear Gertrude speak and look thus. The nuns stood smilingly by, looking at us both as we spoke for a few minutes, and I saw at a glance, that they did not understand a word we said ; they were happy and good-tempered looking, and not in the least like my preconceived ideas of a nun, except in their costume.

In a few minutes we were seated in a light-covered carriage, with a square top, such as I had seen at Montreal, my trunks being disposed of under the seats.

Gertrude introduced the nuns as Sister St. Hermonie and Sister Marie ; the former a woman of fifty years or upwards, and the latter, not older than myself.

As we were about to start Master Nally came rushing from the vessel, calling out, " Come back, come back, you shan't go off !" and as he came near enough to see the nun on the side of the carriage next to himself, he added, " with that old ugly rat."

" Nally, you must go back, like a good boy, to your mamma," said I, not a little frightened to see the child in the crowd ; but in a second his mamma came in person, still wearing the same calm, good-tempered face.

" Nally, you ain't a going to leave puppy and mummy, puppy says you're to come and walk on deck with him."

" No I ain't, either ; I's a-going in the buggy with her."

" Why, Nally ! Miss Keith 's going to the small-pox hospital."

" No, she ain't, them old rats ain't sick."

" Well, I guess she's going into town to buy some more candies, and she'll be back in half an hour, but, I reckon, if you hold on so to the buggy, she can't go ; come to puppy and let Miss Keith go for the candies."

" I guess I'll go too."

That was an unlucky thought of his mother. Nally now tried to climb into the carriage, to the great astonishment of the nuns, who did not understand a word that was said, and consequently could not comprehend what the scene meant.— Nally had just succeeded in seating himself on my knee, when his puppy made his appearance, and poor Nally was borne back to the ship, screaming and kicking with all his might.

As we drove into the town, Gertrude called my attention to an irregularly built, immense house, with wings and additions innumerable, surrounded by a high stone wall.

" That is St. Bride's Convent," said she. " We don't live there in summer; I mean the boarders do not; the community have another convent, called St. Mary's of St. Bride's, where part of the nuns always reside : it is about two miles out of the town, and the Superior thinks it more healthy for the boarders to spend the summer months (which, in this country, are always very hot) in the green fields, among the trees and flowers out at St. Mary's : we are driving there now. I hope to see the day when we will live always at St. Mary's."

The road by which we left the town wound by a gentle slope to a high table-land above. The country was richly wooded, and the fields white with harvest ; we were constantly passing large orchards full of apple trees, so loaded with fruit that the branches were bent almost to the ground. The fameuse apple reminded me of my early home, this being the first time I had seen it since I left France; it is one of the most delicious variety of that useful fruit, bright red outside, and when cut, as white as snow. The striped immense St. Lawrence, and the rough *pomme grise*, were in the same abundance; while here and there the *cérise sauvage* hung its lovely pale green leaves, and long clusters of grape-like crimson fruit, which the slender twigs they hung by, seemed scarce able to bear; and the wild vine towering queen above all the rest, her broad shiny leaves of pomona green lined with grey velvet, softer and more beautiful than human hands ever wove, as if nature made them so, to protect the rich bunches of purple fruit, with its soft downy bloom peeping out from under the thick covering which strove in vain to hide them alike from sun and passer by.

The air seemed all life, hundreds of birds, many of almost Indian brilliancy of colour—the wild canary and blue bird making the woods ring with their song. A clinging plant with scarlet blossoms hung every now and then from the great arms of some gigantic forest tree as we passed, and there we were sure to see the little grey, or green and scarlet humming-bird, with its butterfly-like motion, darting in and out among the bright flowers; no lack of butterflies, purple and brown, red and yellow, several varieties so large that they quite eclipsed the dear little humming-birds in size. The wild bee, humming as she goes round the flower-cup, as if considering whether she would enter or not, and then diving inside until she almost disappears, was there also, not a solitary labourer as we see her in Scotland, but six or seven at a time working in community, out-of-doors as well as in their own mossy home.

We stopped in front of a great gate made of wood, and studded with round pieces of iron as large as a half-penny, giving it an appearance of great strength ; the gate was about ten feet high, and was placed in a stone wall fully three feet higher. A few yards from the gate, on either side, was a round tower, built into the wall, and so placed that half the building was inside and half out; both towers were at least six or eight feet higher than the wall, and were each surmounted by a stone cross ; they were exactly alike, and had each one narrow window visible from the outside, about a foot and a half long.

The driver descended from the carriage on our arrival, and rapped at the gate by means of an iron knocker, which made noise enough to be heard a quarter of a mile off. I was looking at the right hand tower, when the man knocked at the gate, and almost immediately saw the window open, and a man's face put out and drawn in again in a second, and when the gate was opened I recognized the face of the man who opened it as being the same. We were drawn up a broad walk which went straight from the gate to the house, a long way off.

What a scene of beauty that high stone wall and great wood and iron gate shut in! the greenest and most beautiful grass, closely shorn, formed a ground work, on which were placed plots, in all fantastic forms, none of which were larger than two yards square, filled with flowers rich alike in blossom and perfume, and growing so close to each other, that each little parterre seemed like a huge bouquet, lying under the warm air in its own green mossy bed, and dazzling the eye with scarlet, purple and gold. These beautiful little gardens, whose name was legion, lay shaded from the hot summer sun by grand old trees, larger than any I had ever seen, and which must have taken many centuries to attain their present heighth and breadth. Hemlock and pine, whose heads seemed to soar into the clouds, giant elms, underneath whose drooping branches a small cottage might have been built ; cedars, a tree which in our cold clime is little more than a shrub, were here spreading their great fan-like branches out to the sun, which in their proportions, might vie with the cedars of Lebanon. I saw there, for the first time, the beautiful locust tree, its delicate tiny laburnum leaf and lovely white and pink blossom drooping, acacia-like, from their red brown stems, raising its lofty head up to the heavens, high above all the rest. Fountains, throwing up their pure silvery water high above our heads, played on each side of the walk, the water not flowing from the jets in a continuous stream, but springing up by fits and starts, and falling down in the basin below with a splash, as if it was there by its own spontaneous act, and for its own amusement, unaided by any help of man, and giving a delicious and fresh coolness to the air, which would otherwise have been oppressed with perfume.

The house was an immense place, built in the pointed Gothic style, and, like its sister, or rather mother in the town below, had evidently received additions at various times.

As we neared the house, fruit trees took the place of the denizens of the forest: apple, pear and plum trees loaded to profusion with their gold and purple burdens. Light wire palisades, over which were trained vines whose clusters of red and white grapes were giving a large promise for the coming wine month.

The house-door was rounded at the top, and placed in a deeply-groined arch similar to those used in churches, the door itself large and heavy ; the windows in front were also rounded at the top.

Besides the heavy door with its groined arches, I could see

nothing which I fancied convent-like, at least outside the house, and this, trivial as it was, lightened me in a slight degree of my recently acquired dread of convent life, which seemed to be a sort of intermittent fever of the mind, having its heats and chills, the former full of a fear I could not define.

The conversation of the nuns, too, as we passed along, was anything but what I had anticipated. They chatted cheerfully, as people do who are at ease with themselves and the rest of the world. Sister St. Hermonie particularly seemed to delight in saying smart things of the *habitans* as they passed by our carriage in their *charettes*, each lifting his tuque with great respect to the nuns.

Sister Mary knocked at the door, and then stepped back to allow Sister St. Hermonie enter first, which she did as soon as the door was opened by the porteress, a stout elderly woman dressed in black, with a small round cape on her shoulders, and a very white thick muslin cap. Sister Mary followed the elder nun, and Gertrude and I brought up the rear. When all had entered, the porteress shut and locked the door, and put on a heavy iron bar that we had heard her take off before she opened it.

Sister St. Hermonie led the way through a long passage to a large room, which Gertrude said was the waiting room, where visitors were brought to wait for whichever of the boarders they wished to see.

Gertrude and I were left there for nearly a quarter of an hour before Sister St. Hermonie returned. Sister Mary left us immediately on entering, and I did not see her again. Gertrude told me Sister St. Hermonie had gone for the Prioress, Sister St. Angelo, adding " you will soon learn to like her. I love her dearly, and so do we all, nuns and boarders and every one. When our Mother dies—and she is now old and frail; no wonder—she has been Superior forty years—before her no one ever held the office for more than half the time— Sister St. Angelo will be Lady Superior. I will be glad for her sake, and sorry for my own, and we all feel in the same way."

I asked why they would be sorry.

"Because," Gertrude replied, " we will see her seldom then, and she is always with us now, and creates an atmosphere of happiness around her. The Superior of a convent is as seldom seen by the lower nuns and boarders in the sisterhood, as the Queen of England is by the common people."

The room we were seated in was a large one, without a carpet, but the floor so clean that I feared to tread on it, lest my footsteps should be seen: a row of chairs on one side, and a row of benches on the other. The wall at the back of the chairs consisted almost entirely of glass, and inside this half-glass wall was another room, long and narrow, where three nuns were seated sewing. A half-glass door communicated with the receiving room. On the walls were several texts from the Scriptures, printed in type half an inch long, framed and glazed. One of these was " Charity suffereth long and is kind," another, " For every idle word that ye speak ye shall give an account at the day of judgment." There was a large crucifix, about a foot and a half long, hung at one end of the room, the cross of black shining wood, the figure of our Saviour of silver, and underneath the crucifix hung a small vase for holy water.

A glass door at the further end of the room led out to a gallery, and on the ground below the grass grew fresh and green. A plum tree was so near, that although I sat quite at the other end of the room, I could see the branches full of fruit leaning over and into the gallery.

Sister St. Angelo at last entered, and I was presented by Gertrude. The Prioress asked me about my voyage, if I was sea-sick, if my fellow-passengers to Canada were companionable people—who I had seen at Montreal—if I had been inside the Catholic cathedral?" and made me describe the altar-piece and the stations of the cross, asking the most minute questions as to the figures and painting, seeming to be much pleased when I told her it was the largest building I had ever seen, and by far the finest in Montreal.

"I have a dear friend who is one of the gentlemen of St. Sulpice," said she; " but I have not seen him for nearly thirty years. He must be an old man now, and growing grey like myself. They are the richest community in Canada. It is to them the cathedral belongs, although it is the parish church."

Sister St. Angelo was an Irishwoman by birth, but having entered St. Bride's at an early age, she now spoke good French and indifferent English. She and another nun who belonged to the lower convent, were the only persons who could speak English among a community of one hundred.

Sister St. Angelo was a middle-sized, thin woman, grey hair, grey skin, and sharp penetrating grey eyes, but her eye was the only sharp thing about her, with the exception of her intellect—that was clear and sharp as a Damascus blade. Her voice and manner were soft and ingratiating; and in after years when I came to know her well, I found her heart kind and true, her life pure and good.

Dear Sister St. Angelo, when I forget thee, and all thou didst for my sake, when passing through the burning fiery furnace, may my right hand forget her cunning.

She sat talking with me for half an hour, during which time Gertrude walked up and down the room fanning herself

v

with her hat. The sun shone with intense power, making the air outside hot in the shade, and even within the thick stone walls of the convent, and they were fully three feet thick, the heat was most oppressive, and were it not that decorum forbade an entire stranger like myself from doing so, I would gladly have followed Gertrude's example.

During our conversation Sister St. Angelo had informed herself of all the leading facts in my short life's history, that is, all I felt inclined to tell. She now knew I was an orphan, that I had an only brother, whose life made the sunshine of mine; that we had an uncle whom neither of us loved overmuch; that I was educated with a view to teaching, and had left my first and last situation suddenly. When she had fully satisfied herself that I had nothing else to tell, except what I absolutely refused to disclose, namely, the reason why I left Iona villa, where I lived so happily, and the inmates of which I loved so dearly, she desired Gertrude to shew me where to put my hat and cloak, and then bring me to the little refectory, where we would again find her.

I went with Gertrude to a long narrow room at the farther end of the passage, on one side of which were fixed pins for hats and cloaks, and on the other side, along the whole length of the room, was a table about a foot and a half broad, in which were sunk lead basins within half a foot of each other, each basin having a small tap attached to and above it projecting from the wall, by which it was supplied with fresh water, while a little brass drain at the bottom allowed the water to pass out again ; each basin was provided with soap dish, sponge and towel, while on the wall above each, hung a looking-glass eight inches square.

Gertrude took my hat and cloak, hung them up together with her own, and taking from her pocket a little dressing comb, gave it to me, that I might arrange my hair ; saying, " You will get one the same for yourself to-morrow."

I asked her to shew me to my room, where, by opening my trunk, I could find my own brush and comb, having placed my satchel, containing these necessary articles, in my trunk before leaving the vessel.

" I cannot shew you to your own room," she replied. " In the first place I do not know where your room is to be, and if I did, you could not go there at this hour ; we never enter our rooms from the time we rise in the morning until we retire for the night."

I did not like this, nor could I see any good end to be gained by such an inconvenient arrangement, but, of course, submitted with a good grace.

We retraced our steps, and entered the little refectory, a room next to the one with the glass wall.

The little refectory was a long narrow room, with four doors, all of half glass ; one door entered from the passage, two were on the side furthest from the entrance room, and led to other rooms, and the last led out to the gallery.

Along the whole length of the room ran a long narrow table about three feet broad, and on either side were ranged curious looking chairs made of common wood painted black, the seats of which were made from thick wheat straw, painted bright yellow ; the legs and backs were formed of wood cut square instead of round, as we have them, and about two inches in diameter, the front legs being raised fully two inches above the yellow seat, looking like little black posts, and very inconvenient they were for all except nuns and those who, like them, were innocent of crinoline. Upon the table were placed at one end, two covers, a jug of milk that in Montreal would be called cream, a loaf of bread, and a glass dish filled with raspberries.

Sister St. Angelo was already there, and invited me to eat something, as their evening meal would not be served for two hours, and she feared I might feel hungry after my journey. I was thirsty enough at least, and partook gladly of the fruit and milk. Sister St. Angelo left Gertrude and I alone, when we seated ourselves at the table, having, as she said, fifty-five things to do.

"That is almost literally true," said Gertrude, upon the nun's taking her departure, "never was busy bee more active than the Prioress, nothing can be done in chapel, schoolroom, hospital, field, garden, dairy or poultry yard, without her superintendence, and yet there is no novice in the convent more humble, few so much so; all her orders are given in the name of the Superior, who, poor old lady, would sink under one-fourth of the duties Sister St. Angelo has to attend to in the course of the day."

"I do not know if you are fond of pets," said Gertrude, as we rose from our delicious meal, ."Mrs. Moodie never suffered such troublesome things within the precincts of her dwelling. Here, however, it is very different, we have pigeons, rabbits, a tame racoon, families of tame squirrels, a couple of parrots, an aviary full of birds, two great St. Bernard dogs, which I pretend are my particular property, and last though not least, two pets belonging to a lady in Algona, who was herself educated at St. Bride's, and has now gone to England for six months, and before her departure brought her pets here for the Prioress to take care of in her absence ; and as Sister St. Angelo has so many things else to attend to, I have taken charge of these, always subject, however, to her directions. Come, I shall show you the new pets from Algona."

I followed her, wondering at the confidence of the lady

who could be selfish enough to ask a nun, with so much to occupy her time, to add to her other cares, that of taking charge of bird or beast, knowing they must be one or the other.

We passed through the door leading to the gallery, and along the latter to one of the wings, where, opening a door, half glass, like all I had yet seen. we entered a nice little square room, furnished with a table placed in the middle of the floor, half a dozen chairs, a work-basket containing work, a cupboard, and two strips of cotton carpet placed at a distance of half a yard from each other.

When we entered, Gertrude called out, " *Ma belle Donda, Donda,*" but no beautiful Donda appeared.

We then passed through a glass door to another room larger than the first ; in this apartment were two little French beds without curtains, covered with pure white quilts. This room had two windows trimmed with curtains of thin white cotton, reaching half way down the window, and finished by a narrow fringe ; these were stiffly starched and looked as if they had been crimped by a giant crimping iron, each fold being more than an inch broad. I observed afterwards that every window or glass door had either thin cotton or spotted muslin curtains plaited in this way attached to the two lower panes, and forming a sort of blind, and that all the windows opened in the middle, like doors.

Gertrude called " Donda" here again, but was again doomed to be disappointed.

We returned now to the gallery and, descending by steps to the green lawn, found ourselves at the east side of the house, and consequently in the shade, and there appeared Donda in the form of a beautiful little boy, about three years old, his short white frock shewing his fat neck, arm and legs to full advantage; he was assisted in his efforts to draw a little cart full of pine and cedar branches, by his sister, a child about four years his senior, both being cared for by a tidy looking girl who sat sewing on the grass, under the shade of a group of trees formed of the mountain ash and maple tree. The latter I had never seen in Europe; its leaf is shaped something like that of the vine; it was then of a beautiful light pomona green. I saw it in autumn scarlet, brown, crimson and bright gold colour, the most beautiful leaf out of fairy land; at the time I first saw it, forming a shade over the playground of those beautiful children, its leaf was pale green, and made a fine contrast to the dark feathery leaf and scarlet berries of the mountain ash.

Gertrude sat down on the grass, and in an instant, both the children came running up to us; she took Donda on her lap, and seating the little black-eyed sister beside herself, introduced me in great form to Miss Belle Morton; she then produced from her pocket some small round cakes of what looked like dirty gingerbread, and gave one to each of the children, and also to me, saying to me, " they were made of the sugar of the maple tree, which is tapped in spring as we do the birch." We in Scotland make wine of the juice so obtained, while in Canada they more wisely turn theirs into sugar.

The children ate the maple sugar greedily. I tasted it but could not eat it then; afterwards I learned to like it as much as the children did.

When Belle had finished her sugar, Gertrude asked her to sing, which she did in a clear sweet voice, and with a correctness of ear a young lady of seventeen might have envied. The rest of the song I have forgotten, but the chorus, which Gertrude helped her with, was, " Sliding swiftly down the hill, over the frozen snow, over the frozen snow," and the little thing sung with a spirit which was quite amusing when viewed in conjunction with the childish fat face of the singer.

By-and-by the two great St. Bernard dogs came and formed a part of our living group ; beautiful creatures they were ! immense dogs, longer and higher than a large New-foundland, the colour a fawn so light as almost to approach a cream colour, and so gentle were they, that they allowed Belle and Donda tumble over them, and pull them about as they would a pet lamb. We could also see in our vicinity a peacock and peahen walking about in great majesty, as if conscious that they were king and queen of the birds.

" Come into the house and you shall hear Belle exhibit on the piano," said Gertrude, leading the way with Donda in her arms, Belle following with a grave look in her pretty fat face that was quite amusing.

We walked round the wing of the house we were seated by, and entered by a similar gallery and glass door in another and larger wing. The door opened into a long passage, which divided this part of the building in two, and on each side of which I could see were several half glass doors. Gertrude opened one of the nearest, and we entered a large room, car-peted with the same strips of cotton carpet I had seen before.

This room was large and lofty ; all the furniture it contained was two pianos and a few chairs. Hung on the wall were texts from scripture, framed and glazed as I had seen in the receiving room, one of which, very different from all the others, was the work of a pupil, and dated twenty years back ; her name and age (sixteen years,) were there, and a short pre-face. " Pour faire plaisir à ma tante," and then the words of the text " Redeeming the Time." It was placed in a per-forated ivory frame, long and narrow, as suited the style of the work it was to preserve, and hung in the most conspicuous part of the room between two windows; the letters of the text six inches long, and of all colours.

" That," said Gertrude, pointing it out to me, " was the work of a favourite pupil of Sister St. Angelo. She died here at the age of sixteen, of a few hours' illness of inflammation of the lungs, and the good Prioress always talks of her as her daughter in heaven.

This little history made me go close to the picture, if so it might be called. On examining it closely, I found that the huge letters were composed of flowers, painted in water colour, of the most delicate outline, and the colours combined with exquisite skill. I do not know whether it was the taste of the young artiste, or that time had done his work, but the colours were all pale. Pink roses and blue forget-me-not, rose tipped daisies and primroses, clustered round the pale green wavy leaves of the meadow fern, and sensitive plant, the pure white blossoms of the rose of Sharon seemed to have been a great favourite with the young painter, who died one week after her work was finished. ·I fancied the flowers assumed their pale hues because the fair face they grew beneath would see them no more for ever. Here and there, wherever it was admissible, were placed birds and butterflies of the same tiny dimensions and delicate colouring as the flowers, projecting into the diverging silver rays which spread from each letter.

As I stood admiring a style of work I had never seen before, except in the title pages of prayer and other religious books, which had in my eyes, with very few exceptions, a gay, flaunting look, wholly unadapted to the character of the books they are meant to adorn ; this was very different, the artiste instead of being sixteen might have been sixty, from the beauty of execution and design.

Gertrude came and stood by me as I lingered, unwilling to withdraw my eyes from the picture, and taking my right hand in her left, as she used to do in our school days, she said:

" I will shew you her grave some day ; she was buried, by her own request, where her happy school days were spent, and where she knew happy girls would play in the fresh morning air, and the calm eventide, until He who cometh, hath come, and she, with them, shall rise to meet Him in the air."

CHAPTER XXII.

LITTLE Belle sat down to the piano, as if she was conscious she could perform her part well, and so she did, playing for half an hour, every thing she was bid; not one note by book, all by ear; when a running passage occurred, it had such a stuting sound that at last I went to the piano to look at her hands, when I found that these passages were all performed by one fat finger being passed quickly from key to key; the little thing had never received a single lesson, and this, I fancy, seemed to her the best method of performing a running passage.

You play a great many pieces, Belle."

" Yes," she replied gravely, " I play everything mamma and Miss Hamilton play."

A bell now rang for several seconds, and Gertrude giving Donda into his nurse's arms, said:

" This is the Vesper bell, we must go to chapel."

I went with her through several rooms and passages, until we came to the long passage running parallel with the door by which I had first entered the house, and quite at the eastern end of this passage was the chapel.

A long file of nuns, walking two by two, almost filled the passage; we kept back until they had entered, Gertrude standing all the while with her hands clasped in front and her head bent down, as in reverence of the sisters. When they had all passed in, we followed.

The nuns knelt on the bare floor occupying the space nearest to the altar; Belle and Gertrude knelt also, and I sat down on the bench in front of which the latter knelt.

The chapel was quite a large place, capable of containing at least five hundred people, and instead of the intense heat which pervaded every other place, outside and within, here it was cool and pleasant; the light streaming dimly through the painted windows, gave a look of holy calm, which must have been deeply felt by those who believed that God dwelt there.

The chapel had a very different appearance from the other part of the house which I had seen ; there everything was simple almost to nudity, here everything beautiful and suitable to the place, was in abundance : gorgeous colouring, painting, and sculpture ; flowers and incense ; every rare and costly gift they could offer to adorn the temple of the God they honoured. If we have a clearer light than they, surely the Roman Catholic places more of his substance on the altar he bows before, than we do. Do we ever ask ourselves the question is the money we thus spare devoted to God's service ? do we give tithes of all we possess ? do we feed the hungry ? clothe the naked ? visit the sick and in prison ? or on the other hand do we live in costly houses and fare sumptuously every day, while those of our father land, it may be of our kindred, nay, even of those who worshipped at the same family altar and played by the same hearth stone, who with those now at rest gathered shells with us on that very sea shore, perchance the very one we led by the little hand that sunny Monday morning, so many years ago, when she would fain have lingered in the green lane, and pulled buttercups and gowans there instead of going to school, and is now passing days of toil and weariness, and nights of tossing, wishing for, yet dreading the morning light; longing for the dawn, that the labours of the day may be commenced, that labour—which the sick and help-less household cannot live without—and which each morning is begun e'er the wearied body has had half repose, and while no eye is unclosed or window open in the long silent street, except those of other over-burdened ones, rising for the same purpose to prevent the day, yet, when the hour comes that men are stirring abroad, and the smoke rises from the chimneys opposite, and the doors are opened, and all is life and motion now in the busy street—one man going to his honest labour, in field or factory, another rid-ing to his counting house—then comes the time of dread, lest that knock which sounds so often by anticipation in the anxious ear, should bring the dreaded creditor, who, without rudeness, seeks only his own, and which, it may be, he needs so much, and has sought for so often in vain, from the tired eyes and over tasked brain, directing the ceaseless fingers which, with pen or needle, toil on, at half paid work ; unable, in homely phrase, to make two ends of the year meet : and the oft repeated excuse, " Oh ! I cannot pay now, but soon, when this work is done, and when the money comes, I will be so glad to pay," God knows so truly said from the inmost heart ; and the man looks at the faded black gown and the weary face, and he knows it is true, and he goes away say-ing " another time." He is poor himself, and the poor help the poor.

But the rent day comes, and the rich man sends for his rent, and there is none to give—not one pound, not one shil-ling. That last essay, which the poor trembling writer thought would pay so well, and which even the publisher of the magazine she writes for called a " great success," brought just five dollars ! that basket of needle work over which were shed so many bitter tears in the long, silent morning hours that were occupied in completing it, brought five shillings! and with the five dollars, there was bread and flannel and medicine to buy, which ten dollars would scarcely have done; and the five shillings, how can it be stretched out to buy fire and bread for so many, and clothes? Oh! what a mockery, the poor needle-woman buy clothes! She did long ago, when she had a man's strong arm and true heart to work for, and shield, and love, herself and the little ones, but now—

And how is the rent to be paid? the landlord has himself come, and the troubled heart, which fear has almost made cease to beat, must steel itself to listen patiently to all the harsh words that are poured forth, and ask for time, only a few weeks, or a few days, and then—

He is gone, but how will she smooth the anxious brow, so that the helpless ones around see not the grief they are powerless to aid? See how she looks so earnestly at the blue cloudless heavens, and turns with a shiver from what is so fair. Ah! Satan, how busy thou art. Yes, wearied one, there is rest there, and fulness of joy; but it only remaineth for the people of God, for those who watch and wait, not for those who rush uncalled into his presence. Bear all, believe all, " at evening time there shall be light."

* * * * * *

The chapel occupied the whole wing in which it was placed; there were three aisles, all of which were carpeted with rich crimson; on the two broad steps surrounding the altar, the carpet was of a darker hue; inside the altar rails, another and a darker shade, while a space three feet in breadth, close to the altar, assumed the deepest dye. The altar was white with a great deal of gilding; a large, lozenge shaped group in front represented the Holy family in *alto relievo ;* upon the altar were placed an immense gilt crucifix, three feet long, the arms of the cross beautifully covered with fret work ; candlesticks of the same material and proportions, and ornamented like the cross, stood on each side ; several marble and alabaster figures representing saints, and vases of wax flowers, conspicuous among which was the large white lily, considered sacred to the Virgin, covered almost entirely the top of the altar behind, and were so placed that a light from above fell on the painting, giving it a startlingly life-like appearance. It was a painting of the blessed Virgin, her hands clasped, and her beautiful head bowed down over the dead body of our Saviour, which lay below. The face of the Virgin was one of perfect beauty and sadness combined ; the picture was one which was not likely to fade from the memory. It was so real, it seemed a living, breathing woman oppressed with sorrow for her dead. I have more than once felt an impulse to take my handkerchief and wipe off the tear which lay upon her cheek.

The windows, of which there were five on each side, were of stained glass, each representing a subject from Scripture. Between the windows were large oil paintings, the figures in which were as large as life. They were considered of great value, and were beautiful beyond any I had ever seen; under the windows were a series of smaller paintings let into panels in the wall ; these represented what was called " *Le chemin de la croix,*" and consisted of fourteen different subjects, representing the incidents in the life of our Saviour, from his condemnation by Pontius Pilate to the taking of his body down from the cross ; this service of the stations of the cross, which Catholics consider a very sacred one, consists of repeating certain prayers kneeling before these pictures, each picture having certain prayers assigned to it; these stations of the cross are frequently given as a penance, and at other times enjoined to be performed as pleasing to Almighty God. In front of the altar, and just inside the rails, was a large gilded vase more than a foot in diameter, which hung from the ceiling by three chains of the same material. Suspended also from the ceiling, exactly in the same place, so as to hang above, and within a foot of the vase, was a small glass lamp of great beauty, the chains of which were like the others, but fine and thin; this lamp was constantly kept burning day and night in honour of the sacrament upon the altar, and which Roman Catholics believe to be the soul, body, and divinity of our Lord.

The roof was of carved oak, " beautiful exceedingly," the portion above the altar representing a group of angels surrounding the infant Saviour, carved in *alto relievo*.

At evening service the chapel was lighted by three large crystal chandeliers, glittering with hundreds of small flat pieces of crystal strung together, and formed into tassels and loops, having quite a dazzling effect, whether they reflected the rays of the sun, lighting them up with diverse colours, as it shone through the stained glass of the windows, or giving back a thousand little lights when the candles were lit for evening service.

The seats were of oak, finely polished, but without cushions or backs, unless a narrow piece of wood running along the back might be considered the latter; and every one always knelt on the bare floor.

We were in the chapel only a few minutes, when the priest entered by a side door, and passing within the altar rails, repeated a few prayers in Latin; afterwards a portion of the Vesper service was chanted by the nuns; the music was very beautiful, but of course the words of both prayers and chant being in Latin, were to me a dead letter.

I should think altogether the service did not occupy more than fifteen minutes. In coming out I observed a small stone vessel in a niche by the door, full of holy water, into which each person in passing out dipped her finger, and then with the water made the sign of the cross on the face.

On each side of the chapel door was fixed a round brass medalion, on which was moulded the head and shoulders of an old man, one hand resting upon a large round ball, and the whole surrounded by what looked to me like the waves of the sea. This was meant to represent God the Father: the ball, the world; the waves, the waves of time. In my Presbyterian ideas this amounted to something very like sacrilege.

At six o'clock Gertrude, Belle, Donda, and I, had tea, or, as they called it here, supper; it consisted of weak tea, milk, bread, butter and eggs. One of the nuns came into the room, and read aloud during the time we were eating; Gertrude said grace before and after supper, standing with her face turned towards the east, Belle and Donda bowing most reverently after she had finished.

After supper we again went to chapel to say our prayers for the night, this occupying about five minutes; this was the routine of every day when the pupils were in the house, and it was kept up now for the benefit of Belle and Donda!

     *   *   *   *   *   *

When I unpacked my trunk in Montreal, I took out and read the last letter I received from Willie before leaving Scotland, and when replacing it in my packet of letters, my eye fell on Robert Scott's letter, and I took it out intending to read it. This I did not do—I think I had not courage— but instead of replacing it in my trunk, I put it in an inside pocket in the bosom of my dress, which Mrs. Livingstone made and put there the evening previous to my leaving Edinburgh, that I might put my money in ; and there my letter still remained. I had cause to be thankful that it was so ; poor as I was, and much as I had suffered from Robert Scott's conduct, I would not part with that letter now for its weight in gold. Oh no, not now, when I was so far away from all I had loved and lost so recently. False as I knew Robert Scott to be, every word in that letter was truth to me, and itself a thing of life. In long years yet to come, when Willie has left our first little cottage, and I have his children as well as his wife and himself to love and to be loved by, perhaps, then, I will part with it voluntarily, but not now, not now.

At eight o'clock Sister St. Hermonie came and said she would shew me my room, and away I went with her, well pleased, not thinking I was to be put to bed, baby-fashion, at that hour.

We ascended a staircase at the east side of the house, and on reaching the third flat entered a long passage, on each side of which were placed half-glass doors at intervals of twelve feet ; the nun opened one of those, and on entering I found both my trunks and Sister Mary waiting our arrival.

Sister St. Hermonie asked me to give her the keys of my trunks, as she wished to tell the Superior what they contained. Gertrude had warned me of this, so I gave my keys at once. Everything was taken out, unfolded, refolded, and put on one side, until she came to the letters ; these were handed to Sister Mary, who prepared to leave the room, carrying my letters with her. I stopt her, saying, " they were my brother's letters, and those of female friends, and I would not part with them on any account."

W

"The letters will all be returned," said Sister St. Hermoine, "when our mother has looked over them—that is, all those written by your brother or any other relative."

I pressed my hand on my bosom above my letter; how glad I felt that it was safe.

Having finished her inspection of my trunk, the nun took up the paper that was laid at the bottom, and having satisfied herself there was nothing below, replaced it, and arranged my trunk in a neater manner than it had ever been done before, although I piqued myself on my love of order.

Her task completed as far as regarded my trunk, she set about opening Mrs. Livingstone's, which was a nailed box, and had not been opened by me. I told her I did not know what it contained, but she and Sister Mary were not long in ascertaining, with the aid of hammer and chisel, both of which were in readiness.

The box contained a large cake of gingerbread, a quantity of smaller cakes, a pot of marmalade, and a pot of black currant jelly; six pairs of white worsted stockings, and a dozen pocket handkerchiefs, hemmed, and marked in ink, Violet Keith.

"Dear, kind Mrs. Livingstone; my tears, which will never flow when I am in real trouble, and need their soothing influence, fell down like rain, when I looked at the contents of your box."

The good-natured nuns, seeing my tears, fancied they were those of disappointment, and the predispositions of each shewed themselves in the way they took to comfort me. Sister St. Hermonie fancied the cakes and preserves were not such as I liked, and assured me that the Prioress would exchange them for me; while Sister Mary being young, and, I fear, still leaning a little to worldly vanities, said, looking at the stockings and handkerchiefs, " that although not suited for this warm weather, they were very nice, and would come in well a few months hence, and was it not better to have a dozen pocket handkerchiefs, plain and good, like these, than one or two, however beautiful."

I explained to them that I was thinking of the kind friend who gave me the box and its contents, not of the things themselves, and that my tears were those of gratitude and affection, not of sorrow.

Both nuns looked at me approvingly, and then at each other, with an expression which seemed to say, " Is it possible an English woman can feel thus?" A French woman's emotions are almost invariably expressed as soon as felt ; hence, the more guarded English woman is generally looked upon as one who, if she feels at all, does so very slightly. They cannot understand how sorrow or joy can exist without giving birth to sighs and tears, on the one hand, or, on the other, making itself known to all around by smiles and song.

The Sisters then wished me good night, enjoining me not to go to bed before saying my prayers, Sister St. Hermoine enforcing her injunction by saying, that there are many instances of people who did so being snatched away, soul and body, in the night,—adding, " You will hear a bell at four o'clock, but do not rise then unless it is your own wish to do so ; that bell is to call the sisters to early mass ; the next rings at five, and by rising then you will have time to pre-pare for chapel at half-past ; you know the way to the chapel ?"

I bowed an affirmative, and they were gone.

I had now time to examine my room and its contents : at one side was a narrow flock bed, clean and white, at the side of which was a small basin-stand, a table of the same dimensions, a chair, a strip of cotton carpet, and my own trunk, completed the furniture, quite sufficient, too, for a room six feet broad by nine long. On the wall above the bed hung a small white crucifix, attached to which was a little cup of the same white material, for holy water.

Exactly in front of the bed, so as to strike the eye the first thing on awaking, was the same black glazed frame I had seen so often down-stairs, with texts. My text was, ". Whatsoever thy hand findeth to do, do it with all thy might," an appropriate text for the governess.

I now sat down by the window, took my Bible from my pocket, and read the life of my Saviour, until the light failed me.

I could not go to bed. I felt more widely awake than I did in the forenoon ; I undressed, and putting on my dressing-gown, seated myself again by the window, feeling pretty much like a wild bird in a cage. My thoughts wandered back to the first night I had spent at Iona Villa, and Harriote Scott's face and another came to me as vividly in the darkness of that convent cell as ever I looked upon them, when they lived and breathed beside me, and my tears fell fast on my bare hands, as they lay crossed upon my lap."

After a while I got up and bathed my face, determined to shake off all this folly. Iona Villa and its inmates were to me, now and for evermore, but as a dream. Were I back again in Scotland to-night, I would be, as to all intercourse with them, as far off as in Canada. I asked myself if I wished it otherwise ? I could answer my own heart truly, no ; knowing, as I now knew, were the one I loved best there—who was once the sunshine on my path—now beside me, I would recoil from his lightest touch as from that of a serpent.

I could not expect convent life to be congenial at first, but I would become accustomed to it, and perhaps like it as well as Gertrude did. At all events, three years would soon pass away; I would all the time be making the money, without which Willie must remain uneducated, and when the three years were over, I would return with sufficient to furnish our little home.

I knelt by my bed and prayed our Heavenly Father to " create a clean heart and renew a right spirit within me." I never had more need—the spirit of discontent I was indulging in was one foreign to my nature and painful in the extreme. I rose from my knees, feeling that it was already passing away, and assured that if my present situation would be less happy, it would never leave the life-long sting behind which the past year had done.

Next morning I awoke with the ringing of a bell; I knew it must be the first, as I saw through the grey dawn a single silver streak beyond the far purple mountains, and as I looked it broadened and became deeper, until lost in a wide ocean of red and gold, with light clouds of a crimson rose-tint floating along the golden sea; and then the window of my room was illuminated with a flood of living light, and, a moment more, another window of softer hue was thrown on the wall and part of my bed opposite, bathing my head in glory borrowed from the heavens.

I arose and dressed, inspirited by the good omen, and descended to the chapel ; the nuns had all gone, and I seated myself, taking my Bible from my pocket, which I read until Gertrude, Belle and Donda joined me ; his nurse having enough trouble to keep the latter quiet during prayers ; notwithstanding the awe he evidently stood in of the priest or his surplice, I know not which.

After breakfast I went with Gertrude to walk round the grounds. In this walk I found that I had at first entered by the door at the back of the house, the principal entrance being at the other side of the building, and very different from the other I entered by.   Here was a portico, the pillars of which, fourteen in number, were of a gigantic size, with beautifully finished base and capital.   Above the door, inside the portico, was a niche, in which stood a figure, as large as life, of the Virgin with the infant Jesus in her arms, and on either side, placed in smaller niches, were figures of St. Joseph and St. Bride—the patron saint of the convent.   Over the whole of the house in front were niches containing figures of saints or angels, the huge portico occupying almost the entire breadth, and with the broad steps ascending to it, giving quite a grand appearance to the building.   The western side of the convent was occupied exclusively by the nuns, and never entered by any one, except themselves and their visitors—the lay nuns doing the menial work.

When we returned from our walk, I told Gertrude she must find me some work, as I would get sick with *ennui* if I had nothing to do.

" You won't complain of that," said she ; " I shall bring Sister St. Angelo, and she will give you as much work as you have a fancy for."

The Prioress came, bright and cheerful as the day before, and with the same quick active step.

" *Bon jour, ma chère*," you want work, come with me and you shall have work to your heart's content."

We went through the receiving room, into the one beyond with the glass partition: there were two nuns seated there at work, and Sister St. Angelo took from a cupboard a basket with work, and giving it into my hands, said :

" There are some under-skirts for my children ; you will
find needles, thread, scissors, everything you require there ;
do as much or as little as you please. When you are tired,
put the basket again in the cupboard, and when you are
ennui you will find it there."

The work consisted of six under-skirts for little girls.—
Gertrude, who had followed me into the room and now sat reading, told me the skirts, which were of striped blue cotton, were
for some of the orphan children at St. Bride's convent in town,
of whom there were, generally, one hundred, sometimes more.

I sewed until we were called to dinner, and found the nuns
very companionable. They asked all sorts of questions about
Britain and France, were delighted to find I could speak good
French, as their former English governesses could speak
little more than was barely sufficient to make themselves understood ; and were charmed to find I had been in France *only*
eleven years since. One of them had left France forty-six
years before, and talked of her country as if it were a little
superior to Paradise, and what then surprised me, in a nun,
gave vivid descriptions of dances, pleasure parties, in wood
and on river ; she amused us for half an hour with a description of a pic-nic, which she had attended with her *cavalier*,
forty-seven years ago, in the forest of Fontainbleau. They were
both simple and child-like, and seemed to know as much about
the world as children of twelve or thirteen do. I asked the
youngest, a very pretty young woman, how long she had been
in the convent ?

" Ten years. I entered my novitiate when I was thirteen
years old," was her reply.

" And have you never been outside the convent since ?"

" Not outside the grounds. I am a cloistered nun," and
she said this with a look of great importance and satisfaction
on her pretty face.

" You have been at St. Bride's convent in Algona," said I.

" I never saw St. Bride's convent or Algona, either," she replied, with a look of even greater self-satisfaction than before.

" It must be a great sacrifice for you never to go outside these walls ?"

" Yes," said she, smiling complaisantly, as if I had paid her a compliment which pleased her, " a beautiful sacrifice."

" And how long have you been without going outside the walls ?" enquired I of the other nun, who was at least thirty years the senior of the first.

" I go when our mother desires me, I am not a cloistered nun," replied she, in a tone, and with an air, which told that she envied the self-denial of her companion, although she did not possess the resolution, or as she termed it a " vocation," to practice it to such a degree as would enable her to become a cloistered nun.

The pretty nun let her sewing fall on her lap for a second or two, clasped her hands upon her breast, and looked up to the ceiling, with what appeared to me a look of devout self-admiration !

The nuns left the room at eleven for dinner ; Gertrude, the two children and I did not dine until twelve. In the afternoon I asked Gertrude to give me a book, " I have not a book in the world," said she, " except my missal and vesper prayers. Mamma's Bible I keep in my pocket," she added, with a significant look, " but if you like you can have books from the convent library, by paying three dollars a year, it probably contains three hundred volumes."

I looked at the book she was reading ; it was a finely bound and illustrated copy of Paul and Virginia ! Every succeeding day was the same as the first and second I spent here, varied one day by seeing the dairy, the other the aviary, and so on ; the latter a little room, the windows of which were placed so closely together, as almost to form a glass wall. Orange and lemon trees nearly filled the room ; the former, with green and ripe fruit, and a profusion of white odorous blossoms. These were inhabited by several families of canaries, blue-birds and robins, the latter not the humble little bird we call robin red-breast, but a great magnificent creature, glorying in scarlet, black and yellow.

When I saw the library its contents were not such as to tempt me to spend three dollars in its perusal. Conspicuous there, was Lingard's History of England. I asked Gertrude if I was expected to teach his distorted views to the pupils ?

" You will not teach English or any other history, fear not," was her reply ; " you will never have a chance of imparting your opinions on history or biography either." I had not yet seen the Superior or heard any thing about my engagement, except what Gertrude had written to me ; these letters the Superior read together with Willie's, and returned to me through the hands of Sister St. Hermonie.

I asked Gertrude if she knew when I was to have my engagement arranged ; in two days more the pupils would arrive, and it seemed strange that I had never been spoken to on the subject.

Her answer was, " they are taking all the time they can to ascertain your character before making a regular engagement ; if you are not approved of, your term will be for six months, and very little to do ; if you are considered fit for a better position, the engagement will be for three years, and you will have no complaint to make of *ennui* from want of employment."

I had fancied myself quite a favourite with Sister St.

Angelo, she brought me with her every day to the dairy, poultry yard, pantry, cellar, sewing room, in short wherever she went, and more than once or twice, I was chosen to accompany her in her semi-weekly visits to the old men's hospital at St. Bride's.

It now occurred to me, that all our conversation was exactly such as was calculated to draw out my opinions and show the turn of my character and disposition, the Prioress frequently asking my opinion on the manners and customs of different nations, my views on religion and even on politics. Verily Violet Keith, with her one and twenty years, was no match for Sister St. Angelo; she knew me well no doubt—her fifteen days investigation had not been in vain.

As to myself, I liked Sister St. Angelo better by far than any one I had known for so short a time, and now that I knew she had been watching to find the flaw in my character, I still liked her, although this knowledge gave me an uneasy feeling I could not define. I was thinking over this when the Prioress came into the room.

" Come, Miss Keith," said she, in her usual pleasant way, " I want you to go with me for a long walk; our mountain porteress is sick, and I shall teach you how to prescribe in such cases."

Strange to say, I felt equally pleased to be her companion to-day as yesterday, although I knew every word I said was to be weighed.

I took the basket she carried from her hand, and following her we passed by the door opposite to the receiving room, and going round to the front of the house, with its beautiful portico and statues, we walked in nearly a straight line towards the gate at the upper end. This gate was built with towers, and in every way exactly similar to the one at the bottom of

the hill. As we walked along the Prioress said, " it is probable our mother will send for you to-morrow, to ask you how
long you would wish to remain among us." She paused, but
as I made no reply, she then continued :

" Our mother is old and frail, she is, therefore, often
obliged to intrust myself and sisters to perform duties which,
with her knowledge of human nature, she could perform herself far better than I fear any of us will ever be able to do.
When you arrived here our mother desired that I might have
you as much with me as possible, in order to discover
whether or not your disposition would be suited for our
retired life. I have satisfied our Superior on this point, the
next thing is to ascertain what your views are, whether you
would prefer a long or short engagement."

I replied, that if the duties required of me were such as
I would feel able to perform, I should prefer an engagement
for the term of three years, proposed in Gertrude's letter.

" The three years' term is, I know, what our mother would
prefer, and the duties required you will be able to perform
to her satisfaction ; the situation is no sinecure, but you are
no idler."

We had now arrived at the tower. The woman was ill with
violent pain in the side. Sister St. Angelo applied a mus-
tard blister, giving some orders to the lay sister, who was in
attendance upon her, in the same pleasant, cheerful way she
did every thing. It was evident she was as much a favourite
in the porteress' tower as in the convent.

On our way home, the Prioress took a different path from
that by which we reached the tower.

"-I am going," said she, " to visit the grave of a dear child
of mine, who I hope will be the first to meet me in paradise ;
if ever I win Heaven, so surely will I meet her there." We

had turned to the eastern side, and about half way between the tower and the convent, entered a grove of larch, the pale green tassels of which formed a pleasant shade from the hot rays of the afternoon sun. In the middle of the grove was a grassy mound, soft with moss, in which the hand sunk down among the violets and daisies, which peeped out like little stars from the dark green moss, in which their roots were hidden. The nun knelt in prayer for some time, and then lay down with her face buried in the moss of the grave.

It was long before she arose, and when I looked in her face, her lips wore the ashy hue of death.

"You are ill!" said I inquiringly.

She shook her head but did not reply, and we walked on in silence for some time. At length she said:

"In that grave lies the body of one who has been for twenty years wearing the white robe and the virgin crown, and strewing lilies at the feet of the blessed mother of God in paradise, while I, in my selfishness, would fain have kept her here. Her mother gave her into my arms when she was only a year and a half old, and after I closed the mother's eyes, I took the baby home here to be the star of St. Mary's. She was the light of us all, and in order that I might watch over night and day, our mother permitted me to leave my cell her and sleep in the same room with her. It was for her those rooms that little Belle and Donda now have were fitted up. All those fourteen years, I watched her every day and every hour. My beautiful, she loved me as no one ever did before, and never will again. She was ever by my side, even in my visits to the hospital she, too, must go; she would not suffer me to be absent from her for one hour. When her father came to see her, which he did every three months, travelling a long way to see his only child, she would say, 'I will never go home, papa, without my aunt.' Every one who saw her talked of her beauty and grace; she won every prize in every class she entered, and this without an effort. I would not allow her to study as she wished to do, lest it would injure her health, and she grew so strong in her young bloom. One evening she complained of pain after Vespers, and we had one doctor, and then another, and another, until five of the first physicians in Algona stood by her bed side, but we could not force the Blessed Virgin to leave her. From the commencement of her illness we had mass said in our own chapel every half hour, and we had grand mass said in every church in Algona, but it could not be. Half an hour before the Virgin took her she put her arm round my neck and asked me to have her buried in the grove there, and that when the time came for me to die, I would lay there with her. I promised all, although I well knew I had no power to do so, but I was crazed in my despair and in my rebellion against God. If she had asked me to put the morning star on her grave, I would have promised to do it. At four in the morning, the angels and she ascended together; I was a young woman then, and the little hair I was permitted to wear, was as black as a raven's wing; in that night, it became the colour it is now. Our mother applied to the Bishop to consecrate the ground for her grave, and it was done, and two years since I finished the work it was necessary for me to do, e'er I could have the dispensation given me to sleep beside her. It is five hundred years since a nun last asked to be buried out of her convent vault, and then it was granted to the prayers of a princess. The money consecrated for that dispensation, built one of the finest convents in Italy; and the one I now possess was obtained at the cost of thousands of pounds, besides eighteen years of hard work, and many prayers by night and by day."

CHAPTER XXIII.

ON the succeeding day, it was evident there were be to some grand doings at the convent. On entering the chapel, which I did every morning as soon as the nuns left it, reading my Bible until prayers began, I found the altars decked out with a profusion of flowers, making the whole place redolent of beauty and perfume. There were two small altars, one on each side of the chancel; these were undergoing some alterations when I came to St. Mary's, and this was the first day I had seen them dressed. They were in all respects like the Grand Altar, the same golden cross and candlesticks, flower vases, images, etc., but in smaller proportions. I saw they were dedicated to the Virgin and St. Joseph by their respective altar pieces, the one representing the Virgin with the infant Jesus, the other the angel appearing to Joseph in a dream, desiring him to take the young child and his mother and flee into Egypt. Above each picture were niches, in which were placed figures, as large as life, of the Virgin and St. Joseph.

In the afternoon Sister St. Hermonie came to bring me to the Superior. I had been warned by the Prioress to change my dress for the purpose, and I had done myself all the justice I could.

Sister St. Hermonie preceded me to the part of the convent occupied exclusively by the nuns, and, opening a door to the left, ushered me in to the reception room of the Lady Superior. No bare wall or lack of furniture here; all was profusion and splendour.

At the top of the room, on an elevated chair, and footstool of state covered with purple velvet, and fringed with gold, was seated the Lady Superior.

She was dressed in a long flowing robe of black velvet, which, notwithstanding her elevated seat, swept the floor on one side. Her head-dress consisted of a cap and veil of white silk, the latter divided in two and descending on each side of the head almost to the knee. Her hair, unlike that of the other nuns, was long, but braided back from her forehead, and was as white as the silk which covered it. She had the remains of a large, fine looking woman, but was evidently very old.

On each side of the Lady Superior were ranged three nuns, their dresses much finer and longer than those they usually wore, and their veils of black silk. A nun's veil is not worn over the face, but is either thrown back entirely, or is made to hang down on each side like a scarf. The nuns of St. Bride's wore theirs in the scarf style.

Seated on chairs placed in a row at the further end of the room, and opposite to the Superior, were six priests, dressed in the long black robe which they always wear in Canada.

In the middle of the room was an oval table covered with purple velvet fringed with gold. I saw all this at a glance, while Sister St. Hermonie opened the door, and pronounced my name.

Sister St. Angelo received me at the door of the room, and, taking my hand with a kindly pressure, led me to the side of the room, where I was relieved to see Gertrude. The room was dimly lighted, and everything around had an air of solemn grandeur, which for a few minutes quite awed me. When the Prioress left me, she went to the front of the Superior's chair, or, as I afterwards learned to call it, throne, and knelt down, bowed her head, on which the lady mother placed both her hands, repeating some words I could not hear, which was of little moment, as of course they would have been in Latin, and hence to me a dead letter.

The Prioress then rose and stood at one end of the table, upon which the priests came forward, surrounding the other. One of them handed a paper he held in his hand to his right hand neighbour, who immediately began reading from it in Latin ; and while he did so, I had time to examine the room.

There were three windows, all of which were draped with purple velvet, bound and fringed with gold. Inside the velvet curtains were others of soft fine lace, very full, fastened close to the windows, and falling in graceful folds down to, and upon the purple carpet below. The chairs were large and cushioned, with high carved backs. Every inch of the walls was covered with paintings from sacred subjects. Conspicuous above all the Virgin held her place. On a side table behind where the priests stood, were placed several small statues of alabaster, covered with glass shades : these were in groups, and of exquisite workmanship. Two jars of Indian china, painted in gorgeous colours, and nearly two feet in height, stood on either side of the table. The side of the room opposite to the windows was occupied by a low cabinet of ebony, the back of which was of plate glass ; the shelves were inlaid with mother of pearl, and on these were laid many uncut gems and rare specimens of Indian china. In the recess of each window was a small round table : two of these were of inlaid mosaic, such as in Britain we wear for brooches ; the other was of perforated ivory. On the latter was placed a thin book covered with scarlet velvet ; it was the only book in the room. From the richly fretted roof hung a crystal chandelier, similar to those in the chapel. The whole room had a look of sombre grandeur, which impressed me with a feeling of awe.

When the priest had finished reading, one of the nuns beckoned me, more by a look than otherwise, to approach the table. I did so, and one of the priests, speaking my name in full, asked me if I wished to become a teacher in the convent.

I looked up at the sound of the clear well-known voice—it was my friend and benefactor, Mr. Forbes, who addressed me, but not the slight-made, abstracted-looking man I knew in Ellenkirk ; but a strong, stately man, with a voice of power, and the eye of an eagle. It gave me strength to look at him, and I answered firmly " Yes."

The list of duties were then read over, and I was asked if I was ready to perform these. They had all been explained to me by the Prioress the evening before, and were such as I could easily undertake, and I again answered in the affirmative.

The Lady Superior was then asked if she wished to employ me, the terms and length of the engagement being stated.

Sister St. Angelo answered for the holy mother, and I now understood the meaning of her having been blest by the Superior at the commencement of the proceedings, and I fancied, by the way in which the Superior watched the lips instead of the eyes of the speaker, that she must be deaf. A paper was then handed by Mr. Forbes to the Prioress, and afterwards to myself for signature. This done, one of the nuns opened the room door, and politely bowed Gertrude and myself out.

Gertrude passed swiftly through the hall along a passage, which, by one of the usual glass doors, opened on the lower gallery. Down the steps we went, and were in the free air and sunshine, among the green grass, and under the great forest trees in a moment.

" Oh," said Gertrude, inhaling a long breath, as she

X

threw herself down on the soft grass, "how glad I am to be under the blue heavens, and away from these stupid old women and silly men."

"Gertrude!" I exclaimed, scarcely believing my own ears, "I thought you were a devout daughter of the Holy Catholic Church!"

"You thought right, so I am; but I cannot bring my reason to approve of all the idle forms, bowings and genu-flexions which her foolish sons and daughters choose to indulge in; they seem to me more like child's play than anything else."

"Why, Gertrude, you make me serious ; these were not your ideas when we lived together in old Scotland."

"No, that is true; but I am older than I was then, and I have learnt more in these two years than I would have known in ten, had I remained in Mrs. Moodie's. You know I read a Protestant Bible, and doing so can you understand my believing in such dogmas as the worship of the Virgin?"

"I will certainly tell Mr. Forbes," said I, laughing. She moved a little nearer to where I sat on the grass, and looking me in the face, said, with a voice and eye alike earnest :

"Mr. Forbes no more believes in the power of the Virgin to help us than I do."

"Then why does he remain in her church and preach a religion which inculcates her worship as one of its highest duties ?"

"Mr. Forbes is a priest of God, and his Church, and he never preaches the doctrine of creature worship; that is one of the abuses which have crept into the Church, not known in the early days of its purity, and Mr. Forbes has more contempt for those useless forms than I can have, because

he is so much wiser and better than I am. Did you not
observe when the address was given him to read, how he
handed it to the old man with the narrow forehead ?"

"No, I did not ; I scarcely looked at the priests until I
heard Mr. Forbes speak. What was the meaning of the
paper he read ?"

"I forgot you did not understand Latin; that is one advantage of being a catholic."

"The address commenced by telling the Lady Superior
with what pleasure the six priests then present obeyed her
behest in coming to St. Mary's of St. Bride's, and then
they complimented her on her various good qualities, the
half of which, most likely, the good old lady never possessed.
The idea of Mr. Forbes being expected to read such a rhodo-
montade of nonsense ! I could see it was with difficulty he
restrained his impatience while the other did so. He owes
much to his Roman breeding, it has taught him patience ;
but for it the thoughts burning in the breast of the perfervid
Scotsman would inevitably burst forth unbidden."

"And was it merely to engage me that these priests
came ?" I asked like a simpleton.

Gertrude absolutely screamed with laughter.

"Don't flatter yourself for a moment," replied she, still
laughing, while my face became scarlet, "you were never
thought of when the holy men were sent for ; no one knows
or will know for what they came, except those nuns who are
present—they are cloistered nuns and feel their own consequence on occasions like these, and would as soon think of
repeating a word they hear as they would of going to a ball
in Algona. In fact, they consider whatever is resolved on
to-day of as much importance as if it concerned the life and
death of hundreds."

" Sisters St. Hermonie and Mary and many others are
doubtless dying to know what the convocation of to-day was
for, but they never will more than you and I. St. Bride's,"
continued she, "is the head of a number of mission convents; the priests probably came to advise about work to
be done, at one or more of these, or perhaps to settle about
the erection of a new one. All the convocations are held
at St. Mary's of St. Bride's, because the Superior lives
here; at all events, we are all glad when they come—we
will have a fine ceremony, with a beautifully-sung Te Deum.
They will not eat half of the creams and jellies prepared for
them, and which at this moment they are busy with in the
Superior's dining-room. So we will have a share of these
at supper to-night, and then the flowers in the chapel will
last for some days, so you see we are gainers in every way."

Shortly after the bell rung for Vespers. Gertrude was
right in saying that we would have an imposing ceremony
and fine music; as I listened to the grand swelling notes of
the organ, the deep, full voices of the priests, relieved every
now and then by the clear, silvery tones of the nuns, I
could not help wishing that the service was in a language I
understood, and contained no creature worship, as Gertrude
termed it.

When Vespers were finished, Gertrude remained in chapel
to make her confession, and I went into the vinery, there
undisturbed to think over the events of the day.

What Gertrude had just said on the subject of religion,
although it astonished, did not take me entirely by surprise. Even when in Scotland I could see that her faith
in the Virgin was partially shaken; but if the surmise with
regard to Mr. Forbes was right, what results might not flow
from that? a man of such large brain, who seemed intuitively

to hold unresisting sway over all he came in contact with
—whose eloquence entranced his hearers, as much as ever
did Guthrie in one church, or Millman in another;—a very
Whitfield in his devotedness to the God he worshipped, and
the Church whose doctrines he believed in : were this man
to leave the worship of the saints and Virgin, he would not
do so alone.

I was greatly relieved by my agreement being completed;
I was now secure of my salary for the next three years, if I
lived and had strength to work for it, and the work appointed
me was neither difficult nor laborious. I had been tormented
for the last few days by fears lest I should only be kept for
six months ; these fears were all at an end, and I could now
begin my work cheerfully and with an easy mind ; I was getting accustomed to convent life, and by-and-bye the disa-
greeables would fade away.

I had waited an hour for Gertrude, but she had not yet left
the church ; ten minutes used to suffice for her confession in
Scotland—perhaps they had prayers before and after confession, which occupied more time here.

I would wait no longer; I went into little Belle's parlour,
and finding that the nurse and her charge were both out, went
to the dressing-room for my writing materials, where I had
left them in the morning, that I might write to Willie and
Mrs. Livingstone, which I had not done since I came to St.
Bride's. Having possessed myself of my portfolio, I returned
to the children's room, shut the door carefully, and sitting
down with my face towards the door, finished Willie's letter,
and was busy writing to Mrs. Livingstone, when a light hand
was placed on my shoulder. I looked round and saw Sister
St. Angelo. My face must have expressed the surprise I
felt ; but the nun had too much policy to notice what was not

more openly expressed. How she entered I cannot tell; the door was shut as I left it.

"Do not seal your letters until the Superior has seen them," said she, in as cool a tone as if she had asked me to open the window.

"They are for my brother and two old ladies," said I, unwilling they they should be read.

"My child," replied the Prioress, "if they were for the blessed Virgin, our mother must read them."

This was conclusive, and saying so she went out by the door; it puzzled me to think how she came in, at all events she left fetters for me to write in.

I read over what I had written to Willie, it could never be shewn to the Superior, or rather to Sister St. Angelo; perhaps she had read it already, as she stood looking over my shoulder; if so, the boldness of some of the remarks therein must have been anything but in my favour.

I now tore what I had written in shreds, and wrote shortly to each of my correspondents, mentioning in each letter the reason they were so short; this was a trifle, but it troubled me, taking away almost entirely the greatest pleasure I had. These little annoyances are like little sins, "the little foxes which spoil the vines."

CHAPTER XXIV.

By the tenth of September all the boarders had returned, and many new pupils been added to the establishment.

They were divided into three classes. The elder girls, who had been at the convent three or more years, were called " the Children of Mary" (of course the Virgin;) those who had only been a year or so were " Aspirants," that is they aspired to be children of Mary; while children under nine years of age were " Children of Jesus."

There were four dormitories.

That in which the " Children of Mary" slept, was carpeted with fine crimson carpet, white cotton-fringed curtains for each bed, a wardrobe between two girls, and the walls entirely covered with coloured prints, framed in light coloured wood; these represented, in every instance, passages from the lives of the saints or the Virgin, none of which, however, were taken from Scripture. There were five pictures of the Virgin; two of these nearly as large as life, were placed each in a recess, with an altar in front, decorated as nearly as possible to resemble those in the chapel; here the young ladies placed fresh flowers every morning in summer; in winter, these were replaced by paper flowers.

The " Aspirants" had two dormitories—they were the largest number—these were carpeted with cotton carpet in stripes, no curtains on the beds (a decided improvement in my opinion) and only a few common wood-cuts on the walls, with two very plain altars in each dormitory.

The dormitory of the " Children of Jesus," was furnished like that of the " Aspirants," only that the wood-cuts were coloured and represented the fourteen stations of the cross; it had one altar adorned with a wax figure of the infant Jesus asleep.

My duties were to teach English, spelling, reading, and grammar. There were two nuns in every class room, who did nothing but see that the girls attended to their lessons ; the most perfect order prevailed, and there was never any thing like harshness or severity used to enforce commands ; everything seemed to be effected by the law of love.

The girls, with few exceptions, were French; they were, as a general rule, quick and easily taught, and, taken all in all, my duties were very pleasant.

It was late in October before I received a letter from home, as I loved to call Scotland, although I could not point to any particular spot there and say, " that is my home." Well, perhaps I would possess a home there in the days to come.

I received letters from all my friends this month. Willie was well, and still much pleased with Doctor MacDonald's family ; he promised he would take care to attend to my instructions with regard to the Scotts when he went back to college.

Mrs. Moodie's letter contained the intelligence of the death of my uncle's son ; he was only a fortnight ill previous to his death, and his father had never crossed the threshold since the day of his burial. She added, " I was in hopes Willie would have got the property, but it seems that it goes to his eldest daughter upon the death of her father."

" Poor fellow ! I loved my cousin as little as I loved my uncle ; I had received many a cut from his whip, but never a kind look or word ; indeed, I am not sure he ever addressed me except to bid me get out of his way ; but now he was dead, I wished him alive again ; his mother was ever my friend in my short visits to my grandfather's home (I liked to call it so), and I knew she would mourn sadly for her only son, and he himself—there is something in death which cancels all animosity— he was dead ; we have no quarrels with the dead.

Mrs. Livingstone's letter was such that, had it not been opened before it was given me, I would have felt great delicacy in showing it. She expressed great indignation at the impudence of the old wife, (as she called the Superior) in reading the letter I had written to her, but it was just what she expected, Catholics were the same over all the world, they were fit for anything ; she had warned me what they were before I left Scotland, that she trusted, although I was now a dweller in Mesech, I would worship the God of my fathers in purity, and never be tempted to let even the sole of my foot enter their Temple of Baal. In her whole life she had known only one good man who was a Catholic, and he was faithful among the faithless. There was one righteous man in Sodom. She added, I have outwitted them, however ; they won't read my letter if they have read yours, I will send this to your brother and he will send it to you enclosed in his own ; they will never dare to read his letters ; he's not the man that would let it pass with them if they did, and quite proper. She then gave me a long scold because I left my watch. The last paragraph of her latter, ran thus. " Deacon Scott came three times to the house last month, but I was out every time : twice at the market and once at a prayer meeting in the Independent chapel ; the third time he asket at Jean if she saw you or kent aboot you, but she said, you had never been in our house after Mr. Keith left it ; the lassie kent nothing aboot your being here, and only told the truth as she thought : I was very glad I was out; I wouldna like to affront Deacon Scott, and I wouldna break my promise to you."

The day I received my letters, I made a scapular of a large size, and in the bright moonlight I took Robert Scott's letter from the pocket in the bosom of my dress, read it over, and then sewed it into the scapular and hung it round my neck.

I was obliged to do this by moonlight; I was never alone by day now, and we were only allowed ten minutes to undress and go to bed, after which the nuns came round to take away the candles.

I lay in bed until the moon rose ; the moon and stars are always larger and brighter, and the sky clearer in Canada, than they are ever known in Britain ; I can understand here that the stars give their aid in warming the earth. In October we have the hunter's moon, and it shines so bright for the hunters to find their prey, and the skies are so cloudless, that without an effort we can read or write, or indeed do almost any thing we can by day ; so when the moon was high in the heavens, I rose from my bed, read my letter, and sewed it in my scapular. What a long time I must have taken in sewing it in, the bell rang for five e'er my task was completed, when I hung it round my neck, dressed myself, and went down to the chapel to read my Bible. I had not slept all night, but I was never less weary; had I the ability I would willingly have joined the birds in their flight and their song, as they flew, singing in their morning gladness, from tree to tree, among the fir tops outside the chapel window ; I felt as fresh as if I had been bathing in the clear sea on the yellow sand down at Portobello.

CHAPTER XXV.

MR. FORBES said mass once a month at St. Mary's; he used to come early in the morning, sometimes at four o'clock, heard confessions (Gertrude always confessed to him as also Sister St. Angelo, and one or two other nuns), said mass, took breakfast—always a grand breakfast in the Superior's breakfast room—and was gone back to Algona before seven o'clock.

It was now the end of November; he had been four times at St. Mary's since I came, yet I had never spoken to him, except the few words which passed in my engagement on the thirty-first of August. I was often sorry for this, and wished I could speak to him, if only for a few minutes; but it must be by his own desire, I could not propose such a thing; it would have been looked upon, even by my friend Sister St. Angelo, as the height of assurance, had I done so; Mr. Forbes in Ellenkirk and Mr. Forbes in Canada were two very different persons. He was a great man in St. Bride's, a great man in Algona: if Sister St. Angelo was right (and she had a brain as large as his own, and was no cloistered nun) he would in a few years be a great man through the length and breadth of Canada.

The first week in December he again celebrated mass, and before his departure, Sister Mary came to say he wished to see me in the sacristy; I was very glad, and went down the stair-case with a light heart and step.

On entering the sacristy, I found Sister St. Angelo and Gertrude there, sitting on the only two chairs in the room.

Mr. Forbes stood leaning against a cornice, made exactly like a mantle-piece, on which was placed a marble statue of the Virgin; how handsome and grand he looked, dressed in the flowing robe of his order, which, unlike the other priests, he wore open, its folds thus forming a back-ground to his tall and well-made figure; how different he was to every other priest I had seen in Canada or anywhere else!

He turned towards the door as I entered, and coming towards me, took my hand with the same calm smile he used to greet me with in the old time, when I was a girl in Mrs. Moodie's. He asked me how I liked convent life, said he was happy to find I was a favourite with the Prioress, that he had wished to see me each time he came to St. Mary's, but his time was so limited he could not always do what he would; asked when I heard from Willie, and told me he had a letter from Mrs. Moodie within the last few days.

Gertrude offered me her chair, and he walked back to where he stood when I entered the room; he spoke a few words to Sister St. Angelo, and then inclined his head with a sort of half bow to Gertrude; she immediately came forward and knelt down before him, he placed his left hand on her head, and lifting the other to heaven, he prayed the Heavenly Father, in a voice clear and strong yet full of emotion, to bless her, in her whole soul, and body, and spirit; to shed on her the peace he giveth through His son; to lift up the light of his countenance upon her, that in that clearest light of his, she might clearly see light.

There was a moment's pause and he was gone, departing through the door which led from the sacristy to the chapel. Sister St. Angelo took my hand and we left the sacristy, shutting the door quietly as we went out; we left Gertrude on her knees, as the Prioress remarked, praying to the blessed Virgin, before whose image she knelt; praying, indeed, but not to the Virgin; I knew more than the grey-haired nun, with all her years and wisdom.

" She will make a beautiful nun," said the Prioress as we walked along the passage. I did not reply, I thought her very beautiful indeed; I had never seen one who at all equalled her, but I did not wish her to become a nun, or was it at all likely with her changed views that she would become one.

On the first Monday in December I received my first quarter's salary; it came to fifteen pounds sterling, the currency here being sixteen shillings sterling to the pound; I did not know this when I came here, so that my salary was fifteen pounds less than I believed it to be; however, it was still more than I could have expected to receive at home, and I was comfortable and contented.

When I received the money, I got a draft on the Bank of Scotland in Edinburgh for the whole sum, and sent it to Willie, desiring him to give ten pounds to Mrs. Livingstone in part payment of my debt, the rest with the remains of his own salary, would suffice until March, when I would again remit him the same sum; I told him of Henry Keith's death, and of the distress my uncle suffered in consequence; I also mentioned that on my uncle's death Haddo would go to Lizzie, his eldest daughter. I feared poor Willie might, like Mrs. Moodie, imagine that he was to be the heir. I enclosed a letter for Mrs. Livingstone, and this done, presented both to the Prioress for her perusal. Early in January I received an answer to my letters: Willie had passed his examination with tolerable credit, as he expressed it, and was now busy night and day; Robert Scott called at Mrs. Livingstone's and also went to college to see him, but Willie was absent on both occasions; he then received a note saying that he (Robert Scott)

would call at Mrs. Livingstone's on any day and at any hour
Willie would appoint; they saw each other next day, and I
give the rest in his own words.

"Mr. R. Scott asked me why you had left Iona Villa so
suddenly; I told him I was entirely ignorant of the cause;
he then inquired where you were, and requested me to give
him your address; I refused to answer his question then, but
promised to ask your permission to do so."

I did not answer this letter until March, when I again
remitted my quarter's salary: in the intermediate time I
took up my pen for the purpose, at least every week, and
laid it down again,—at last I decided my answer would be
no. It was evident Robert Scott was not tired of his lost
toy, but I was determined there should be no second part in
that dream which had ended so bitterly. Whether he was
innocent or not of the charge brought against him by his own
father,—that father was, without doubt, my bitter enemy,
and I could only become Robert Scott's wife by sowing the
seeds of discord in his family, and false as knew Mr. Scott
to be, the earnest, truthful expression of his countenance while
he uttered his abhorrence of the disgraceful conduct of his
son, had made an impression on my memory which could
never be erased; no, that dream life of mine was now of the
past; it was true there were words and looks there which
came back uncalled for, and, when least expected, as fresh as
yesterday, and weak woman as I was, I lifted them up as the
rubies and pearls of my existence, strung them together and
hung them round my heart; these I would never part with,
they had become part of my very being, but Robert Scott
himself I would not willingly hear from or see again. When
I had finished Willie's letter, I added a postscript thus—" Do
not give my address to any one."

This month the snow, which had merely covered the ground before Christmas, and even on New Year's Day only reached a few inches in depth, now began to fall in earnest, not in beautiful large flakes, such as we had during the last two months, but little tiny things, just like a shower of grated crystal, or the moats we see floating in the sunbeam; there it falls so fine, yet so thick, that soon every crack and cranny is filled up; every tree, each little twig is laden with its pure beautiful burden; these tiny flakes are greeted with joy, as the snow which will rest on the ground and make the roads fit for sleighing.

The fine snow came down almost without intermission for three days, and then the sleighs were passing along the road that lay by the tower-gate, half-way down the mountain, their bells ringing merrily in the frosty air, the snow now fully four feet in depth.

The scene round the convent was lovely beyond anything I had ever seen or could conceive ; the great building itself, its roof one sheet of pure white, every window, every niche, each figure of saint, or head of angel draped in the soft, white, mossy snow, while each tree seemed to keep its individual character ; the giant pine with its great branches, green alike in winter's snow or summer's sunshine, so bent under the weight it carried, in flat shelving—like rows, one above another, that branches which were towering above our heads a week previous, were now bent to the ground, while elm, mountain ash and fruit tree, were clothed alike in their white garments, each separate twig or bunch of berries, or seed pod, with its pure feathery dress, telling almost as surely as in its leafy verdure, who it is you look upon.

The fall of snow over, the sun shone out with a dazzling brightness, such as in Britain we only know at midsummer,

I doubt if we know it even then. The Prioress was going to St. Bride's, and as it was Thursday—(the holiday in the convent)—offered to take me along with Gertrude (who always accompanied her when the day was fine) for a sleigh drive. I gladly agreed; it was my first sleigh ride, and I do not know that I ever enjoyed drive or ride on horse back or in carriage as I did my first sleigh ride over the frozen snow.

We had a double sleigh, with two fine horses full of spirit, and on we went, swiftly and smoothly, along our pure white path, as if we had borrowed the wings of the wind for our journey; the sun shone brightly over head, not enough of wind to stir the lightest snow flake, the crystal trees lining each side of our way, making the whole seem like fairy-land; below lay the town with its hundreds of sloping tin-covered roofs, glittering in the sunshine, while far above all the rest rose the square towers of the oldest Church in Canada, dedicated to Notre Dame de Douleur.

We drove through St. Benedict street that we might see a new church, which had been built for the wants of the increasing population. Mr. Forbes had lately been made parish priest there; it was now the most fashionable church in town, and great things were hoped from his popularity, he being considered the most eloquent preacher in Algona, many said in Canada, and daily attracting crowds of Protestants as well as Catholics, who each went home wondering at the startling truths he taught, and asking each one of himself if indeed it were so?

We stopped there and went into the church, as the Prioress said, " to say our prayers ;" I fancied the good nun wished to see the altar decorations, which we had for a long time heard spoken of as something extraordinary; whatever was the motive of the half hour we spent there, certainly not over three minutes were spent in prayer.

It was an immense place with a great deal of decoration ; the pictures representing the Stations of the Cross were so large that, even seen from below, they seemed as large as life. Some of these pictures contained eight or nine figures. There were three altars, all of which were fitted up with great magnificence, the mellow light from the painted windows coming in softened and subdued, suited with and heightened the gorgeous effect of painting, sculpture, and altar decorations ; there were six confession boxes, in several of which there were priests hearing their penitents—we knew this by the doors being shut.

"Ah !" said the Prioress, "would that the good time were come, when every Protestant in Algona will each in their turn fill these confessionals." She and I had different views of what would constitute the good time coming. There were several people in the church scattered here and there saying their prayers, nearly all of whom seemed very devout ; one old man, however, on his knees, with his beads in his hand, was intently watching all our motions as we walked from picture to picture, his lips never ceased praying or his eyes from following our steps ; we passed close by where he knelt, and I saw by the way he held his beads, he had not said more than half. I hope he found other amusement after our departure.

On arriving at the convent, we went with the Prioress at once to the hospital. There were about thirty in the men's ward. Sister St. Angelo had a kind word for every one, and each had something to say to her, very often some little complaint to make, which was listened to patiently, and redress promised or the grievance put an end to at once.

Everything was strictly clean, notwithstanding that all these people were more or less helpless ; one old paralyzed

Y

man, quite foolish, had been there in that condition for thirty years ! many had lived there for ten and twelve years ; an old man whose chair was placed within six feet of the stove, was constantly trying to sit under it, and in consequence was fastened into his chair by a broad belt; he complained of this, and the Prioress had the belt removed ; in less than two minutes he was below the stove ; he must have been a salamander, six yards off was quite near enough for me.

Two old men, both above eighty years of age, were taken by the Prioress a month previous from the jail, where they had been put to prevent their starving, as there was no house of refuge in Algona. She visited the jail every month in order to rescue such cases ; they both looked as if they had known starvation by bitter experience ; one of these men had a look of deep thought in his almost skeleton face, and his eye was bright and penetrating ; he had a small white hand, and as he leant his head on the hand, the arm of which rested on the side of the easy chair he occupied, his air and look told through all his misery he was not one of those he lived among. As we walked about among them, the Prioress said, " I have an affection for this room, although it was the scene of my labour most mortifying to the flesh. For eighteen years I came every morning from four o'clock prayers to clean this room, and here I worked for two hours before I breakfasted; my work was always disagreeable, sometimes most revolting, but God accepted my sacrifice and gave me strength for it ; in all these eighteen years, I was never absent for one morning." We were called to see an old man who was dying ; he lay calm and peaceful, his hands clasped on his breast; he was evidently passing fast to the better land.

" He is a countryman of yours and a Protestant," said the nun, turning to Gertrude and me.

" Do you receive Protestants here ?" I asked.

" If they are poor and old or sick, we never ask what religion they are of. This poor man was educated at the University of Glasgow as a student of Divinity, and became a licentiate of your Kirk of Scotland, but I believe he was unsteady and hence was not ordained ; he came to Canada forty years ago, and through misfortune became silly; but for some weeks I have observed a great change in him ; I do not think he is silly now."

I went beside his bed, and stooping down close to his head spoke to him in a low tone. I told him I was a Protestant and very lately from Scotland ; he raised his heavy eyelids and looked in my face with an eye full of intelligence, but did not reply ; I took one of his hands in mine and pressed it; he returned the pressure; his hand was quite cold ; I said so to the Prioress, looking away from the man and in her face as I spoke ; with her eye she directed my attention again to his face ; his eye was fixed, his fingers had relaxed their hold upon mine, his spirit had passed away. Poor man, this was another victim of the great Goliath intemperance.

On our way home, I asked the Prioress when we were to go into St. Bride's to live, adding, " when we go I should like very much to help you in the hospital."

" The pupils will never go to St. Bride's again, it was with this view we had the additions made to St. Mary's last year. St. Bride's is small enough for the poor and sick, St. Mary's, too, is more pleasant and healthy for the pupils ;— that was true enough—but," added she, " if you wish to help with the hospital work, you can come with me every Thursday now, and in summer you may come twice or thrice a week ; I am always back at St. Mary's by eight ; you must not keep me waiting, I start at half past four precisely."

I agreed to all this very readily ; the monotony of convent life was to me becoming almost insufferable ; this would make a great break in it, and I would have an opportunity of making myself useful in a way very congenial to my nature, and I proposed that I should at once begin going to St. Bride's in the morning, and so it was arranged.

On the following Monday morning I commenced my hospital work, as the Prioress called it, rising at four o'clock for the purpose, and I continued to do so all the time I lived in St. Mary's, and these were my happiest hours. These lovely morning rides in the starlight or moonlight did more for me than all the education in the world could have done ; they, together with the habits of reflection and promptitude which were nourished and called into action in my attendance on the sick and dying, gave me an energy of body and mind which made me pass unscathed through trials, which but for the strength thus obtained might have been fatal in their effects, on both mind and body.

CHAPTER XXVI

THE snow passed away neither so silently or so agreeably as it came; it passed in broad streams running down the mountain, that almost seemed like little rivers, rendering the walks in our convent grounds impassable for all except geese and ducks; however, it went so rapidly that the ground became green almost while we looked at it.

The month of May came with its green leaves and flowers, it was also the month of Mary, that is, it was dedicated to the Virgin Mary, and service was held and the church dressed in honour of her every day.

Early in the morning of the first day of May, Gertrude and I were sent out to gather snowdrops for the Virgin's altar; it was a difficult task, the flowers were still very scarce, and to find enough, we had to wander all round the grounds, at the same time taking care not to pick buds, as these would be required for next day.

"How tiresome this silly work is," said Gertrude, "picking flowers at the rate of one every three minutes, and for such useless nonsense."

"So you consider it useless nonsense to pick flowers for adorning the church?" I asked in some surprise.

"If they were for adorning the church as the house of God, I would not consider it useless; when I am desired to aid in dressing the altar for Trinity Sunday, or any other fête in honour of God, or our blessed Saviour, I consider myself honoured in being chosen for the work; but these flowers are placed on the altar as a mark of devotion to the Virgin Mary, and in my opinion, it is very doubtful whether she knows anything about their being there or not."

" Go on, Gertrude," said I, " I see you are in a fair way of being excommunicated."

" I do not believe in the power of any human being to excommunicate me," said she, looking up through the leafless trees we were standing under, to the clear blue Canadian sky above. " I believe that neither height, or depth, or length, or breadth, or any other creature is able to separate me from the love of God, which is in Christ Jesus my Lord ; and I believe, if ever I shall walk in the streets of the New Jerusalem, it will be by my faith in the blood of Christ, shed for me, and the atoning sacrifice made by my Redeemer on Calvary, and not by the filthy rags of my own righteousness or that of any created being, whether saint or angel."

" What would the Prioress say, if she heard you speak thus, you whom she expects to become one of her best and favourite nuns, when she is Superior ?"

" With one exception I would rather please Sister St. Angelo than any human being under God's heaven, and it is my love for her, and the knowledge of what I owe to her, that has kept me silent for months back ; yet I often think it would be better for her, as well as for myself, perhaps both in time and eternity, had I the moral courage to say now, what must be said some day—the want of moral courage is the great fault in my character."

" Holding such opinions, I cannot understand your remaining in the convent ; it is impossible for you to feel happy."

" I am not happy, but there are many reasons for my remaining here. In the first place, where am I to go ? I do not know one person in Canada outside the walls of St. Mary's

and St. Bride's. During papa's lifetime, the few acquaintances I had were the wives and daughters of the officers 'in
his regiment; these I only knew slightly; we had nothing in
common with each other, and I did not cultivate their friendship; I know no one either here or in Scotland except Mrs.
Moodie, and were I inclined to go there (which I am not)
what could I do without money; I have never more than
twenty dollars at one time in my possession, how long do you
think that would last?"

" Not long, certainly; but how is this, why have you not
the power over your own money? You are surely old enough
to be able to manage your own affairs, why do you not do so "?

"Because Sister St. Angelo and papa thought it best. I
think papa, during his illness, conceived the idea of my becoming a nun, and of course, the Prioress considered that life
the happiest and best I could lead. Papa's will ordered that
I should remain at St. Bride's until I was twenty-five years
of age; that the Superior was to receive a hundred pounds
a year for my board: if I became a nun, the whole of my
fortune would be at my own disposal, if not, five thousand
pounds would go to St. Mary's of St. Bride's, the remaining
five to me."

" What a strange arrangement! were you cognizant of the
terms of the will at the time it was made?"

" Yes, and very much pleased with it. I then thought the
life of a nun the happiest I could lead in this world, and one
by which I would most surely win eternal happiness in the
next."

" Have you no relations?"

" Not any that I am aware of, except my mother's brother,
Colonel Fanshaw, of the 6th, and it may be stationed in China
or Timbuctoo, for aught I know; besides, papa and uncle

were not on good terms at the time of mamma's death, and never corresponded afterwards, hence if I could find him out, I do not know how welcome he would make me."

"Gertrude," said I, "the 6th regiment is stationed at Algona at present; I have observed that was the number on the cap of every soldier we passed going or coming from town this winter."

"That may be, but it does not make the least difference in my case. Uncle certainly would not care for an addition to his family, in the shape of a grown-up girl of three-and-twenty, who most likely would not have wherewithal to purchase clothes with. I do not know that I am entitled even to pocket money, were I to leave St. Mary's before the time specified in papa's will. I do not think my taking such a step was ever contemplated. A year ago, I did not think it possible I should ever wish to leave these walls."

July came and brought to us the vacation, and with it came Mrs. Morton to bring Belle and Donda home. She arrived at Algona the previous evening at eight o'clock, and was at St. Mary's to early mass. I shall never forget the joy of both mother and children on seeing each other; poor little Belle clung to her mamma as if she was afraid she would again leave her for another year. Mrs. Morton spent the day with her children at the convent; she said it made her feel young again, wandering about in the grounds where her school days were spent; every vine and tree were old friends reminding her of some girlish joy or sorrow.

She amused Gertrude and I, who were appointed by the Prioress to be her entertainers, by describing, with a ready wit, the places and people she had been thrown among in Scotland while visiting there. She made us laugh more during that day, than we had done during the previous year.

Sister St. Angelo came now and then into the room, remaining for a few minutes, laughing at our guest's wit, and
was off to her work again; she called Mrs. Morton, Annie,
and Annie was evidently a great favourite with the Prioress.

Mr. Morton came before six o'clock in the evening to bring
his wife and children home, but ere then it was arranged
that Gertrude should go with them, and spend at least part
of the holidays in Algona ; she did not return until the first of
September, and without her the time hung heavy enough on
my hands, although not for lack of work; I was supplied most
liberally with that.

The autumn passed, and the winter was passing away
pretty much as it had done last year. In February I observed that Mr. Forbes did not come, as was his wont in the
beginning of each month, to say mass and hear confessions.
March also came and passed and no Mr. Forbes. What a blank
his absence made ! The priest with the narrow forehead, who
read the Latin address to the Superior, the day of my engagement, came in Mr. Forbes's place, and Gertrude would not
confess to him ;—there was trouble in the convent, Sister St.
Angelo's pale face became many shades paler and grayer,
the lines on her forehead also became closer and deeper ; I
would have asked her what was the reason of his absence,
if I could have seen her alone, but such a thing did not take
place now once in six months ; there seemed to be a restraint
and gloom thrown over the convent that I could not comprehend. In our semi-weekly rides to Algona, we were always
accompanied by one or other of the nuns. A nun never leaves
the precincts of her convent without another of the sisterhood along with her. It was late in March ere I had an opportunity of asking Gertrude—we were never allowed to be alone
together now. My question was useless, Gertrude was as far

at sea as myself, and more anxious to know. April, May, and June passed away, and still he came not. I often asked myself was it possible he would never come again.

One morning in the latter end of June, Sister Agatha, a cloistered nun in St. Brides, came into the hospital seeking the Prioress. I had seen this nun before once or twice, and felt an instinctive dread of her, which I could neither account for or shake off. She was a tall, dark, hard-featured woman, with a sullen, defiant look; she seemed to me as if she was always plotting mischief. She entered the ward in which the Prioress and I were occupied, walking with great strides and a heavy step, more like a man than a woman, coming up to the sick bed where Sister St. Angelo was employed bathing a large tumour on the cheek of a poor boy who was suffering great pain; she laid her hand on the Prioress' shoulder, quite regardless of the patient, and said almost fiercely:

"Listen to this."

The nun turned towards her, and soon the patient was forgotten, even by the benevolent heart and kind hand that were ever ready to soothe the afflicted; every feeling and thought seemed absorbed in listening to the astounding intelligence Sister Agatha had to communicate. They spoke in Spanish; the grand accents of the language flowing with elegance and rapidity from the lips of Sister Agatha, while the Prioress spoke with difficulty,—Mr. Forbes was the subject of their conversation, Sister St. Angelo deeply lamenting his fall; the other, with a wicked, triumphant air, saying, she knew he was a heretic in disguise from the first moment she saw him; he could not hide his cloven foot from her; she saw the bold devil in his great eyes and brazen forehead, while others were lauding him to the skies. She hated the Saxon and his hissing language, which Satan had sprinkled so well with his own

initial; could she now set hands on him, the worthy represen-
tative of his devil-worshipping Saxon face, she would tear
him limb from limb.

When she had calmed down a little by giving vent to her
rage, she told the Prioress that information was received at
the monastery of St. Benedict the previous evening, that he
was daily preaching to congregations of three thousand people
in the Public Halls of New York, those who wished to obtain seats going an hour in advance of the time in order to
secure them, that he was everywhere received with open
arms, each great man in the city endeavouring to persuade
him to make their house his home, or at least that he would
become their honoured guest for a few hours, and worst of all
he still declared himself a Catholic, a member of the Catholic
Church as it was in the days of its purity.

"Poor misguided man," said the Prioress, "may the
blessed Virgin bring him to repentance and amendment of
life."

"Repentance," replied her companion, with a diabolical
sneer, "if he could live a thousand years, and spend it all,
day and night, in one long act of penance, it would not
atone for the evil he has already done. On his first declaration
of heretical opinions, he should have been buried alive, and
if I had been Bishop of Algona it would have been done; allowing him to escape was the greatest act of madness; he
knew well whom he had to deal with, or he would never have
dared to preach the damnable heresy he did, for months previous to his declaration to the Bishop. The priests here," continued she, drawing herself up with a fierce wild look, which
for the moment made me fancy she was really insane, "are a
poor, pitiful, weak set, unfit alike for good or evil, and wholly
unable to combat with the cunning atheistical Saxon. Oh! if

they were in my land," and she ground her teeth in her rage, "had he been in Spain with its men of might, who let not their right hand know what their left hand doeth, he would long since have been wagging his tongue to the dungeon walls."

The Prioress clasped her hands and, shutting her eyes, said with ashy lips and a voice trembling with emotion:

"Holy St. François Xavier pray for him, that God may pardon and grant him repentance."

Sister Agatha seemed beside herself with rage; she clench-ed her hands, and pushing them before her, while her face became purple, screeched out in a loud shrill voice, "repen-tance, repentance, what makes you harp on repentance, do you not know that we are explicitly forbidden to pray for the forgiveness of the sin he is now committing? were he hanged to-morrow, and his vile body eaten by dogs, I would long for the Death Angel, that I might look from the gate of heaven, and see him suffering in the hell he deserves so well. Were I not a cloistered nun, I would dog his steps from America to Europe, and if need were, from Europe to Asia, until I could drag his false heart from his reeking body, and dash it in his face." Having said this she strode from the ward, with the same long heavy step as she entered.

It was eight days afterwards e'er I had an opportunity of relating this scene to Gertrude, and even then I could only tell a part of what I heard.

Little Belle Morton had been for six months past a boarder at the convent, and Gertrude was to accompany her home, and spend the holidays at Algona, as she had done the pre-vious year.

On the morning of their departure, I was sent to the dor-mitory of the Children of Jesus, to pack up Belle's clothes in her trunk. While I was thus occupied, my head bent over the clothes I was arranging, I told in a low voice to Gertrude, who sat beside me, a part of the coversation I had heard in St. Bride's. She made no reply, and I dared not look up for one in her face. There were sliding panels in every room in the house, through a slight opening in which we might be strictly watched without being aware of it ; and it occurred to me afterwards that I was sent to pack Belle's trunk in order to discover whether Gertrude and I had any secrets, previous to allowing her to go to Algona.

When Mrs. Morton came to bring Gertrude and Belle away, we had an early dinner of fruit. A dish of fine straw-berries was placed before Gertrude, and lifting up the dish she came to the end of the table where I sat, and while pre-senting it to me, said in a scarcely audible voice : " It is well with him."

Gertrude had been gone three weeks, when the Prioress and I going into St. Bride's, for our Thursday visit, encountered Mrs. Morton, Gertrude, Belle, and Donda, accompanied by a young lady from the United States, on their way to St. Mary's, that the latter might decide whether or not she would enter as a boarder in September. We stopped our horses to exchange civilities, and Gertrude insisted on coming into our carriage, and going to St. Bride's instead of accompanying Mrs Mor-ton and the others, saying that Sister St. Angelo was the only one she cared to see at St. Mary's, and therefore she would go with her to St. Bride's.

The Prioress urged her to continue her ride with her friends, pretending to be angry, but a child might have seen she was highly gratified.

Gertrude kept by Sister St. Angelo all the afternoon, and while we were driving to Mrs. Morton's to leave her there, she sat by the Prioress, holding the nun's hand fast locked in hers all the time. After she had descended from the carriage, she jumped up again, put her arms round the Prioress' neck, and kissed her many times; and as we drove on, we saw her watching us from the steps of the door, until she and it were lost in the distance. "My darling," said the nun, while more than one tear of joy coursed down her pale cheek.

Time did not pass very pleasantly at the convent without Gertrude, I was terribly *ennui*, and counting the weeks, and at last the days, until she would come again. At last the first of September arrived. I was in the parlour where the pupils and their parents were received at the beginning of the term; two nuns and I attended there during the first three days in September, in order to receive the pupils. When a new pupil arrived the Prioress came to make the arrangement; those who had been previously at the convent the nuns in attendance received.

I waited impatiently enough for Gertrude's arrival, at last in walked Mrs. Morton and Belle.

"Where is Miss Hamilton?" I asked.

"Why?" exclaimed Mrs. Morton, "is she not here? she left us a week since."

I did not wait to hear any more, but went at once in search of Sister St. Angelo, to whom I repeated Mrs. Morton's words. She did not at first speak, but her face and lips became almost livid, and holding by the bureau, at which she stood writing when I entered, sunk rather than seated herself on the nearest seat. In a second or two she raised her face and clasped her hands, saying in a voice choked with emotion:

"Mary, Mother of God, shield her young head!—Mary, Mother of God, help me now and at the hour of my death."

I gave her a glass of water, and presently she rose and went slowly, but with a firm step, towards the parlour.

From Mrs. Morton Sister St. Angelo learnt that during the seven weeks Gertrude spent in her house, she had been a frequent visitor at her uncle, Colonel Fanshaw's, with whom, as well as his wife, she seemed to be a great favourite. The evening previous to her departure from Mrs. Morton's, she said, quite unexpectedly—

"I must go to-morrow."

Mrs. Morton pressed her to remain for the rest of the holidays, but she said it was impossible. On the day she left Mrs. Morton's house, that lady proposed accompanying her to the convent, but she preferred going alone, as she said she intended visiting her uncle's family and spending the forenoon there. After the first week of her residence in Algona Miss Hamilton received letters every other day, and her evenings were mostly spent in writing ; Mrs. Morton had no idea who were her correspondents, as she regularly put her own letters in the post-office. This was all Mrs. Morton could tell.

The Prioress heard all in silence, spoke a few words to Belle, asked for Mr. Morton and Donda, pressed Mrs. Morton's hand kindly and was gone.

In less than ten minutes Sister St. Angelo, accompanied by one of the other nuns, were being drawn rapidly towards the town in a carriage and pair.

They did not return until long after convent hours that night, and on the following morning they were off again before five o'clock, returning late as on the previous day ; the next day and the next were alike spent in town, and then all things settled down again as usual, but there were more lines of care on the Prioress' brow; her face was paler and her step slower from that day henceforth. It would have been useless to ask any of the nuns who were engaged in teaching a single question regarding Gertrude, I well knew they would never hear a word spoken on the subject. There were only six cloistered nuns in St. Mary's; it was possible they knew, most certainly none of the others did.

Two months passed ere I had an opportunity of asking the Prioress what had become of Gertrude. Her answer was: " Never speak to me on that subject again, it is owing to my carelessness that she is now a companion of those who make a scoff of the religion she was born and bred in. I made a most solemn promise to her father on his death-bed. Alas! alas! how have I fulfilled that promise. Every time I speak on this subject I do double penance for the share I have had in this sad story."

There was no need of her imposing penance on herself, it was but too evident to the most thoughtless inmate of St. Mary's convent, that the Prioress did involuntary penance in mind and body, since the day she first knew of Gertrude's flight.

CHAPTER XXVII.

THE third New Year's day I spent in St. Mary's I received a letter from Willie, containing a photograph of himself. It was nearly three years since I had seen him last. What a difference these three years had made. The boy of nineteen was now a man of two-and-twenty, dark, tall, and slight, as his boyhood promised. I pressed it to my lips. How happy the possession of it made me ! In the morning I felt so sad and spiritless—my lonely isolated situation pressed so heavily upon me, life was to me a very weariness, a scene of constant effort, a dull round of monotonous duties, without even the hope that when the day closed, a loved or kindred voice would sound in mine ear, a gentle hand touch mine—and beyond this life, what of that ? Ah ! that was the worst of all—thoughts of doubt and darkness ; and with a strange energy I asked myself the startling question, " What, if this life past, death should only bring annihilation ?"

But now at the sight of my handsome brother, new life seemed to run through every vein. My loneliness, clouds, and darkness were all forgotten, and the sun was above the horizon, and was pouring its glorious beams into my heart of hearts.

Taking up my picture, I pressed it again to my lips, admired every line and expression of eye, and mouth, and brow, until all was engraven on my heart. I opened my letter. I will give it in his own words.

" This being my last year, I am now no inapt hand, and

z

having come in contact with Dr. B—— once or twice, I had the good fortune to please our king of surgeons, and have been appointed one of his dressers, during his visits to the hospitals. I can scarcely tell you the advantage this has been to me; and apart from that, it has introduced me to an old friend of my father's, and one who is inclined to be a friend to his son.

· I had been dressing for Dr. B—— for some weeks, when he asked me to sit by the dying bed of a favourite patient of his during the night, desiring me, in case the pain of dying should be severe, to use a certain opiate which it would not be safe to put into the hands of a nurse. I fulfilled my mission—the spirit passed at eight next morning in a quiet sleep; and according to promise, when all was over, I called on Dr. B——, and told him of the perfect success of his prescription. He was at breakfast and alone when I entered. He asked me to take breakfast with him, to which I gladly agreed. When he had done the honours of the table, he said :

" ' When I was a boy at the high school, I had two companions, brothers, of your name, and I have often fancied you are like what the eldest would have become. They were sons of Keith of Haddo, near Ellenkirk. I spent a vacation there, and we had merry times trout-fishing in a little river which runs through the place. My friend Charlie, who was the eldest, was a famous rower, and we used to sail down the river for miles, merely to have the pleasure of rowing up against the stream, but we could never tempt Dick into the boat.'

" I replied his friend Charles Keith was my father, but that he was dead many years ago.

" ' You are not the eldest son, I suppose, from your having chosen to study a profession. I am sorry to say our lairds prefer becoming the drones of the hive.'

" ' I am Charles Keith's only son, but you are mistaken as to his being the eldest. My uncle Richard was the elder of the two, and is now in possession of the property.'

" He threw himself back in his chair, resting his forefinger upon the table, and, putting an emphasis on almost every word, said : ' Charles Keith was the eldest brother by at least two years, and if you are his only son, you are the rightful owner of Haddo, no matter by what chicanery you are now kept out of it. And for Charlie's sake, with whom I slept in one room for five years, I will help you to make good your title to your land, my boy. Write to Dick by this evening's post, and tell him what I have said ; and you may add that John B—— keeps his promise now as surely as he did when he thrashed him for clashing to the head master nearly forty years ago.'

" I wrote to my uncle that day. His reply came in course of post: it ran thus :

" ' Your father was, as Dr. B—— says, my eldest by two years. I did not conceal this from you as you impudently assert, but I allowed you to suppose he was a younger brother, because I fancied this would be more satisfactory to yourself, and place you in a better position with the world at large, than a knowledge of the fact that you are illegitimate.'

" I knew and felt that this was false as hell, but how was I to prove that it was so ? I carried my letter to Dr. B——. He read it carefully over, and then desired me tell him the history of my young days, during my father and mother's lifetime, as far as I could recollect.

" I did so, and mentioned my recollection of mamma's receiving letters from our paternal grandfather and grandmother after papa's death, and also of mamma's sorrow when the intelligence of the death of her father and mother-in-law, which happened within three weeks of each other, reached her.

" When I had finished my narration, Dr. B—— replied : ' There is not the least doubt but Dick's story is as false as himself : he lied like a trooper at school, stole tops and marbles *ad libitum*, and, unless the janitor maligned him, he did not hesitate to appropriate odd shillings and sixpences when they came in his way. The boy is father of the man, and he who stole tops in youth has no doubt in his manhood stole your land. However, there is law enough in Scotland to win it back, and make Dick refund the money he has been spending these ten or twelve years. The question is, how to set about collecting materials for the lawyers to go to work upon.'

" ' But, Doctor,' said I, ' my sister, who is two years older than myself, and I have both to work hard to pay my college fees. How are the lawyers to be paid ?'

" ' Leave that to me. Depend upon it Dick will be very glad one of these days to settle the whole affair with very little law ; and even if it were otherwise, I know a dozen honest men of law in Edinburgh, who will take your case in hand, without asking you for a penny until you are in possession of your property. And if we had not such men as these among us, rogues like Richard Keith would ride rampant through the land. But,' continued he, ' you say your sister is two years your senior ; you must write to her, and request that she will make a list of every visitor, French or English, male or female, whom she can recollect seeing in your early home ; and, if possible, let her state where these visitors lived ; old servants also are most valuable in such cases. You say there are no letters or papers of any kind, no books with presentations upon them ?'

" ' None ; my uncle arrived in time for mamma's interment, and doubtless possessed himself of everything that could be used in the way of testimony to the truth of our case, or falsehood of his. The day after my mother's funeral we accompanied him to Scotland, and during the journey he never addressed one word to either of us. We brought with us a great quantity of clothes and my mother's Bible, one given to her by my father before their marriage, with her maiden name written in it by his pen ; and that is all we possess which ever belonged to father or mother. It was a good thing for us we had so much clothes. When we outgrew them, and before we could earn more for ourselves, we were supplied very sparingly. Yes,' said I, all at once recollecting your watch, which Mrs. Livingstone insisted upon my wearing ere her debt was paid; 'there is my mother's watch, which she put round Violet's neck some time previous to her death;' and I placed the watch in his hands.

" He looked at it, carefully removing the cap, I fancy in search of name or initials, which might be of service, and then returning it to me, said :

" ' What a buck you are ! sporting a watch set with pearls ; so it seems your uncle did not supply the means even to enable you to learn your profession ?'

" He was already aware of how the case stood, and I replied to his last observation by a look.

' Aye,' replied he, ' Dick the boy is Dick the man ; when he bought candy with his penny no other boy got an inch. Ah !' looking at his watch, ' I have lost nearly an hour of my visit time, I must be off; and go you to bed for a couple of hours.'

" I had passed the night in the hospital attending a case of hemorrhage, which could not be left in unskilled hands, and

Dr. B—— had confided to my care. I laughed at the idea of going to bed in the day-time, saying that I made up for a night's sleep by a bath and a long walk. He looked at me approvingly.

" ' A good plan, my boy; day-light sleep does us little good.' And taking his notebook from his pocket, wrote the address of three of his patients thereon, and handing it to me, gave in a few minutes a synopsis of each case. ' When you take your walk, (mind you take it before eleven o'clock) pay those visits for me, and in the afternoon bring me the account of your labour !' "

Willie then continued : " Our most sacred duty in life is to establish the fair fame of our parents in defiance of the tongue of the slanderer. I trust that your memory may help us in our need. Do you remember if Philomene's parents lived in Marmaude, or where ? I think her surname was La Forte."

When I had finished Willie's letter I laid it down with a feeling akin to despair. No wonder I felt so depressed in the morning. Surely we have forebodings of the evil that is about to overwhelm us. Our only earthly treasure was an unsullied name, and that was taken from us at a stroke. I well knew that it was of no use trying to recollect the names of visitors. We had none. During papa's life-time his health was so bad, that mamma was constantly occupied in nursing him; and this close confinement to a sick-room induced the disease under which she eventually sunk. As to Philomene, she only entered mamma's service a short time previous to our coming to England, replacing the nurse, who had been our *bonne* from our childhood, and possibly could give valuable information ; but she had gone on her marriage, which was the reason of her leaving mamma's ser-

vice, to live in a distant part of the country, where her
husband's relatives resided, and I had not the slightest recollection of his name. I had often heard mamma say that her
marriage was a private one. I had seen the dress she wore,
and the jewels my grandfather sent her as a marriage gift;
but what would this amount to? absolutely nothing. I took
up my letter, and going into the chapel, which was now
deserted, the principal services for the day being over, I
knelt down, exclaiming aloud in bitterness of soul, " All
these things are against me."

I prayed my Heavenly Father to help me in this great
woe, and, if it were possible, to make the innocence of my
parents clear as the noon-day. When I rose from my knees
my first impulse was to seek the Prioress. She had read
my letter already. I was sure of that, and if she could not
shew me a light in the dark path I now trode, she would, by
her sympathy, help me to bear my burden. I had another
motive lying deeper in my heart, and stronger than any
feeling merely connected with self could be. I wished to
tell her all the reasons I had for knowing that my uncle's
tale was false, as if Judas had been its inventor.

I found the Prioress ready to hear me at once, an unusual thing with her. I shewed her the letter, which she
would not read, saying she had done so already, expressing,
at the same time, a hope that I would be able to recollect
the names and residences of those who could confute my
uncle's story.

I told her no ; I knew not a human being who I had the
slightest hope would know anything of the matter, adding a
description of the isolated life we led.

Her countenance fell ; she evidently thought my case a
bad one. She spoke to me about submission to the will of

God, and that now was the time to prove my strength and truth of mind, and to rest in Him with holy confidence. She might as well have said to the raging winds, " Peace, be still."

All at once I recollected my interview with Mr. Weimes, the gentleman I met at Iona Villa, and, as far as my memory served, I repeated every word he then said. Her clear head at once saw light amid the darkness.

" Your way is very plain," said she ; Mr. Weimes and his sister were both present at your father and mother's marriage ; he must be found, that can be done through his friends in Edinburgh. From him you will learn the name of the parish where, and the priest by whom, they were married. No doubt your brother will be a rich man yet."

I had quite overlooked the prospect of Willie's becoming proprietor of Haddo in my misery at the slur thrown on the fair fame of my parents, and, in truth, I cared not for it ; we had nearly climbed the steepest part of the mountain unaided, and I thought if Willie had his bread to win, and a position to make for himself, his mind would become larger and stronger for the struggle, as I knew my own had done. I did not know then, what I have learned since, that whether we have to earn our wealth or only to spend it, if our position be high or low, the battle of life is to be fought, and those who would end wisely must fight bravely.

I sat down to reply to Willie's letter with feelings very different from those I had experienced an hour previously. I felt as if I had been rescued from death and the grave—as if I had trodden a path of darkness hemmed in on every side by great perpendicular rocks, which seemed almost to reach to the black, starless sky above—when, in an instant, my eyes were opened, it was past and gone—I knew it was a dream—and I sat on the smooth, green sward—under the broad, blue vault of heaven, and at my feet the river of hope was running softly by. The daybreak had come and the shadows fled away, and I hied me to the mountain of myrrh, and to the hill of frankincense; spikenard and saffron were there, calamus and cinnamon, with all the chief spices. I sat in a fountain of gardens, a well of living waters, and streams from Lebanon.

I told Willie of Mr. Weimes, of his being my father's groomsman at his marriage, that his sister was my god-mother, and that I thought his address would be obtained from Mr. Erskine, whose guest he was at the time of his visit to Iona Villa.

Having finished my letter, I brought it to the Prioress for her inspection, asking her, at the same time, if Gros Pierre, or his son, the man who kept the lower gate, would be permitted to take it to town, as this was the English mail day.

" Go and put on your hat and cloak," said she ; " I will go into town myself and take you with me, and we will our-selves put your letter into the post office."

In half an hour Sister Nativity, Sister St. Gabriel and myself were seated by the Prioress in a large double sleigh, driven by Gros Pierre, and passing swiftly into Algona with a bank of snow five feet high on either side of the road. The snow had fallen in great quantities during the whole of December, almost every second day of which there were snow-ploughs along the road.

We became terribly chilled during our drive, and Sister St. Angelo thought it best for us to drive to St. Bride's; and while we warmed ourselves by the great stove in the receiving-room, Gros Pierre was sent to the post-office with the letters.

The Prioress sent for Sister Agatha, and they talked together in Spanish during the half hour we were there.

Sister Agatha said Mr. Forbes was in town, and preaching to crowded audiences every night in the largest Protestant church in Algona—that the evening before he held a meeting, at which there were three thousand people, and there he openly denounced asking the intercession of the blessed Virgin as idol worship, denied the authority of the Pope extending beyond his own diocese, called the granting of indulgences a license to commit sin, said that St. Peter was a married man, and lived with his wife after he became an apostle. At this the Prioress lifted up both her hands and eyes to heaven, exclaiming, "Holy Saint Antoine, what will they say next!"

"Anything the devil bids them," replied Sister Agatha. "If I had him," continued she, "I would put his head down on that floor and tear his guilty tongue out."

"Much better for us all to join in a novena to the blessed Virgin for his conversion." A novena is a certain number of prayers to the Virgin, or any of the saints, which continues for nine days, and if strictly held, is kept with fasting.

"A novena for him," replied Sister Agatha, with a sneer, "I would not waste my prayers on such a wretch; far better for me to keep a novena for myself."

I agreed with her there. Mr. Forbes was one of the best and holiest men I ever knew; Sister Agatha was not the best or holiest woman.

"Colonel Fanshaw is in Algona with the renegade priest," said Sister Agatha, "but his wife or Miss Hamilton are not with him."

At the mention of Gertrude's name Sister St. Angelo's brow became troubled and sad, and in a few minutes she hurried us away.

In our way home we passed through the street where Sister Agatha said the Protestant church was in which Mr. Forbes had preached the previous evening.

There was a great crowd in the street coming to meet us, as if the people were dispersing from a church. As we approached the church the crowd became less; however, we had still to drive very slowly, because of the number of vehicles and also of people. My attention was attracted to a group on one of the side-walks, in which a colonel in his scarlet coat and sash formed a conspicuous figure. Three of the others seemed to be clergymen, one of the latter wearing the hat and undress of a priest. They shook hands and parted, the officer and the three clergymen coming toward us. The one wearing the priest's habit was Mr. Forbes; the Prioress and I both recognized him at once, and involuntarily looked at each other. I did not like the part of listener which I had again sustained during her second conversation with Sister Agatha in Spanish, and said, using that language,

"How strange it seems to see him there." The nun turned upon me that sharp, penetrating glance which seemed to read one's very soul, saying, at the same time, "You speak Spanish?"

"He taught me," was my reply.

CHAPTER XXVIII.

IN the end of February I heard again from Willie; he had seen Mr. Erskine, who undertook to obtain Mr. Weimes' address, if the latter was still alive, of which, however, he expressed great doubts. He had not heard anything of him since the previous summer; he was then in France in very delicate health, and obliged, notwithstanding, to go back to India, in order to withdraw his name, if possible, from a bank, which threatened to involve its shareholders in ruin.

Mr. Erskine promised by that mail to address a letter to him at his French residence in Caen, and, if he had no answer in the course of a few weeks, to write to Lord B——, who was also a resident there, and from whom he hoped to receive intelligence of Mr. Weimes' whereabouts.

This part of the letter was anything but satisfactory, but my faith was strong as to our ultimate success, and I was willing to leave it in the hands of Him, without whose permission not " a sparrow can fall to the ground."

Willie's college days were drawing to a close; he was studying hard, and in addition to this, one day in every week, sometimes two, he spent the forenoon visiting such of Doctor B——'s patients, as the latter could intrust to him.

He said the whole of next month must be devoted to hard study; he was sure of his degree, but he wished to do something more than merely pass.

He gave me a piece of information, at which I did not feel surprised. Poor Mr. Scott was the inmate of an asylum for the insane. What else could be expected from the fits of uncontrolled passion he allowed himself to indulge in ? He had been under restraint for upwards of a year. It was said that Miss Hariote was soon to become Mrs. Erskine. I cannot understand why this did not take place long ago; maid or wife all happiness attend her.

March, April, May, went by, and brought only one letter from Willie ; he had passed and with *éclat*. After securing his degree Doctor B—— offered to take him as his assistant, but he would not accept the situation without consulting me, as it involved his living in Doctor B——'s house; his salary was to be a hundred pounds a year.

This situation, I was fully aware, would be of the utmost consequence to Willie; his success in life would most likely be insured by a residence with Doctor B—— as his assistant; by this means all the heart sickness, longing and waiting for patients, which falls to the lot of most young medical men, would be obviated, and provided that his talents were equal to the task, the time would in all probability arrive, when the assistant would become the partner ; and a course of honour and independence secured with less trouble than falls to the lot of most men.

On the other hand this would put an end for the time, perhaps for ever, to all our former plans of cottage life. I was heartily sick of the convent; Gertrude had taken away with her every tie which bound me to it ; except Sister St. Angelo there was not one I cared for in St. Mary's or St. Bride's; indeed, I scarcely knew another. The nun I saw and spoke to to-day while we sewed or made wax flowers, (a great branch of industry in the convent, and one much required ; as we not only supplied our own altars, three in St. Mary's and three in St. Bride's, but also the altars of St. Benedict, and as they were never covered, they were constantly in want of renewal) I would not speak to or almost see for three weeks, hence I was a stranger in the midst of a crowd; it was true I had lived calmly and comfortably while there, but that great wall seemed as if it shut me out from communion with my kind, and in reality it was so. I would rejoice at regaining my liberty when the first of September arrived, and would not live another year in St. Mary's on almost any terms. I felt as if I would like, on regaining my freedom, to rush into the woods, and live there wild and free from all restraint.

But there was no reason for my remaining at St. Mary's because it was thought expedient for Willie to live as assistant to Doctor B——. I could take another situation in either Britain or Canada, the former if possible, (I need have no fear of poor Mr. Scott shooting either myself or his son now,) and in a few years we would be quite rich, by that time Mr. Weimes would surely be found, and then—

I wrote to Willie inclosing a draft for the past quarter's salary, which I had just received; he was to add this to our little store, the last money due me by the Superior, I would draw on the thirty-first of August, fifteen pounds sterling; this would I knew from experience, bring me from St. Bride's to Mrs. Livingstone's land, with its comfortable parlour. How I longed to be there once more, once more to listen to the kind words dictated by her large heart, and above all I longed to see and make the acquaintance of Willie, who would be quite a stranger in those great black whiskers.

I told him all this and advised him to accept of Doctor B——'s offer. If I did not hear of a suitable situation in Canada, previous to my leaving the convent, I would at once return home, perhaps go to Mrs. Moodie's although I had still my former objection to going there.

At the commencement of the holidays, two of the nuns belonging to St. Mary's and I were to go, at the request of the Prioress, for six weeks, perhaps two months, to St. Bride's ; a couple of new dormitories had been added to the hospital, and we went to assist in making mattresses, sheets, pillow-slips, towels, in short all that was required for furnishing forty beds ; a grant had lately been left to the Prioress for the purpose, and by it she was enabled to take in a class of needy poor, who had been formerly excluded, namely the sick apprentice or servant. girl, who wanted a home and medical attendance during illness.

I cannot say I liked the change from the fine house, beautiful grounds, and fresh air of St. Mary's, to the low-roofed rooms and paved court of St. Bride's, but I was glad to spend the few weeks left of my convent life in working for the Prioress, who had done me so many kindnesses during my sojourn at St. Mary's.

The room assigned me was, if possible, smaller than the one I occupied at St. Mary's ; the bare walls were whitewashed ; not an inch of carpet, and the window consisted of nine panes of glass placed high up in the wall, so that when I wished to look out I had to place the only chair in the room close to the window, and stand thereon ; the bed was covered with a blue striped counterpane, everything clean, but not inviting. The morning after I had taken up my abode at St. Bride's I was surprised to see so many nuns when I went to morning prayers at four o'clock ; they were mostly old women, with the exception of the novices ; the younger and stronger must have been sent on missions ; they had all, with the single xception of Sister Agatha, quiet, subdued, almost unhappy ooking faces. I did not wonder at this after I had spent a week or two at St. Bride's, the long day there seemed as if it would never pass; to me such a life would have been one of extreme penance. The two nuns from St. Mary's and I sat in the new building, which our work was to furnish, sewing, busy as bees, from five in the morning until six at night, with the intervals necessary for meals and worship. The windows looked out to the paved court, surrounded by a high wall; the only break in the monotony of our lives being when the gate was opened to admit a cart with hay or straw for the cows, and twice a day when they were led out to or brought from pasture. It was well that it was not to last long, I believe six months of it would have made me crazy.

On going to my room at night I regularly placed my chair by the window, stood on it, and placing my Bible on the broad sill, formed by a wall four feet thick, I continued reading until the light failed me; and then I stood looking at the bright stars as they came out, one by one, in the silent night, my thoughts wandering away to that far land which contained all I held dear; no not all; Gertrude, I often thought of her, and wondered whether I should ever see her again, and Sister St. Angelo with her ever active body and mind, used to cross my mind's vision, like the angel who stands between the living and the dead.

One night, a week after I came to live at St. Bride's, the moon shone bright in the heavens, making my little cell almost as light as day. I had wearied myself reading and yet felt no inclination to go to bed; my spirit went back as it always did to my Scottish home; I thought of Willie and the new life he was entering on, and I praised the Lord in my heart for raising up to him such a friend as Doctor B——, and then I thought of another whom I had promised myself many times never to think of more, and of the first earnest look with which his eye met mine in Mrs. Livingstone's land, that look which sunk deep in my heart then, and now, when nearly four years old, was as fresh as yesterday, clear and bright as the dew drop glistening in the morning sun, and with more than a quarter of the globe between me and the dark eye which gave it me, making my pulse beat with accelerated pace. I put my hand on my bosom as if I could press down the painful thoughts which rose there, and under my open palm was the little silken scapular with its precious contents.

In a moment, before I gave myself time to think what I was doing, the silk bag was unripped, and the letter spread out before me; and as I stood there, reading under the convent roof, in the cold midnight, the strong words of the good true heart and firm hand that traced them, I felt sure as if an angel spoke, I had been the dupe of a madman; that in my pride and folly I had thrown away the noblest, truest heart that ever sought woman's love. With this conviction came the knowledge, sharp as the forked lightning, that the words traced by my own hand had placed a gulf between us which must roll on in its darkness for evermore. My cheek burned and my temples throbbed as I pressed my brow to the cool stone window sill of my cell, and wept in my lonely wretchedness. My cell became intolerable; I could not breathe; I must have air and space. I went through the long corridor and down the staircase leading to the hall where the poor dined; there the air was close and hot, not a window open. I turned towards the chapel, there to pray to Him who alone knew my soul's bitterness.

As I entered, the moonlight streaming in through the painted windows, shed a dim light around, aided by the perpetual lamp that hung before the great altar in front of the host, I was startled, on walking up the aisle, to see a coffin laid on trestles placed under the holy lamp. It was covered

by a long black cloth pall, which swept the ground except at
one end, where it was folded back about half a foot. My
curiosity was excited. I had heard of no death among the
nuns; and if any of the poor people had died, they would certainly never have been brought to lay all night in the chapel.
I approached, not without a feeling of terror, yet impelled by
an irresistible impulse I could not control, and going up to
the end where the pall was folded back, I there discovered
Sister St. Angelo fast asleep!

Doubtless this was a self-imposed penance to win Paradise
for some careless soul, dear to the loving heart that in its
unselfishness could do and dare for ever for those it loved.

Next morning I was in the chapel before four o'clock mass,
and watched the face of the Prioress both as she came in and
went out: it wore the same pale hue and anxious expression
which it had done ever since Gertrude's departure, not one
shade more, never one shade less. I felt restless and uneasy
during the day. I had not sewed my letter into the scapular, and I longed for the night that I might do so. I wanted
to make it quite safe once more.

At eight o'clock, the usual hour, I entered my cell. After
completing my arrangements for the night, I got up to my
window—the moon large and bright like a silver shield, as on
the previous night, not a cloud to be seen, the " bonny lady
moon" sailing in her majestic beauty, queen and mistress
there. It was the eve before a great fête of obligation, and
I had just finished sewing my scapular, and tied it round my
neck, when the bells rung in the fête at midnight.

I did not go to bed. I was excited. I knew I could not
sleep, and it was much more pleasant to stand by the cool
window, looking out into the solemn night.

The bells ceased one by one; first, the great bell of Notre

Dame des Neiges halted with a heavy clash, as if calling upon the others to follow in its wake ; then the three bells of St. Benedict rung out their last note. St. Peter's, St. Patrick's, and St. Bride's, each in their turn, stayed the glad notes, as it were in obedience to our Lady of the Snow.

Silence once more reigned queen of the night; the hum of the busy town was still, all around sunk in deep slumber. I was alone with the moon and stars, those old sentinels, who sang at Adam's advent, and rejoiced with him in his joy, when he received his bride fresh from the hands of the Creator ; who have been watching those six thousand years so replete with sin and sorrow ; who have heard all the sighs and seen all the bitter tears his sorrowing children have shed, ever searching with wandering foot and weary breast for the barred gates of the Paradise of God.

I was tired now ; I had only slept two hours the previous night, and I turned more than once to leave my window and lie down on my little bed, but I felt as if I were fascinated by the pale face of the moon, climbing heaven companionless amid the millions of stars around her. I determined at last to go, and leave her to complete her journey alone, when my ear was caught by the sound of distant wheels. They must have been far away at first, it took such a long time for them to reach the convent wall, and there they stopped. Could it be possible ? The great gate was opening, and from the outside, what extraordinary thing had taken place to bring visitors to the convent at such an hour ; and visitors, too, who could open the great gate for themselves. Verily, wonders will never cease. Yes, most surely there it was opened from the outside, and the carriage passed into the court.

I now heard the house door open, but I could not see it from where I stood. Two priests alighted from the car-

riage, and then helped a lady to descend. She wore a hat
with a long black feather. It must be some boarder for St.
Mary's, but why come so late ? The lady took off her hat
and swept back her hair as if she felt too warm, and then
looked up to the heavens. The moon shone full on her face.
It was Gertrude! pale as death, but surely Gertrude. There
was something, I could not tell what, fixed across her mouth,
but there was no mistaking the rest of the face, and, as if to
make me perfectly certain, she again took off her hat, and
carried it in her hand.

All this passed in a few seconds. They were joined by those
who opened the convent door. The priests again entered the
carriage, and were drawn out. I then observed that it was
a priest who drove. Sister Agatha—I knew it was she by
her height, half a head taller than any nun in both convents—
shut and locked the gate, after which they all entered the
house. I slipped out into the corridor ; they were talking,
several voices, not in anger—Sister Agatha, and, thank God,
Sister St. Angelo.

CHAPTER XXIX

NEXT morning I was at early mass with the nuns, but saw or heard nothing of Gertrude ; I tried in vain to speak to Sister St. Angelo for several days, in hopes she would say something of her, but now I scarcely ever saw the Prioress except at early mass, and immediately after the benediction she was gone ; I knew it was of no use asking any of the nuns about the matter ; the cloistered nuns very likely could tell, but I had never spoken to a cloistered nun in St. Bride's ; even at St. Mary's, where I lived three years, I had only spoken to two of the cloistered nuns, and I must say both of them were humble, self-denying women, endeavouring, as far as they had light, to live up to the precepts of our Saviour when he said, " be ye perfect as your Father which is in heaven is perfect." That all cloistered nuns are not so, I had ample proof; Sister Agatha was a cloistered nun, but she was neither self-denying, gentle, or humble. I never encountered her glance without receiving a scowl which made me shudder and think of an evil spirit.

Ten days had elapsed since I saw Gertrude enter the convent at midnight ; when I again saw her at vesper prayers she came in with the nuns; on seeing me she smiled gladly, and in going from chapel asked me when I came to St. Bride's ; why I was there, &c. She did not appear to be under the least restraint ; she looked very pale ; I asked if she had been ill.

" Yes," was her answer, " very ill. I came home ten days

since; I was then suffering from the effects of fever; this is the first time I have been in chapel; if I feel as well to-morrow as I do to-day, I will come and help you to work. Sister Agatha told me of the new wing, but did not say you were working for it; she probably did not know I knew or cared for you." This may have been the case; she stood behind Gertrude while we talked to each other in English, a language of which she understood not one word, her eyes fixed on my face with a searching glance; if she understood mind-reading she would not have her love of human nature as represented in my person strengthened by that scrutiny.

Every day after that interview Gertrude came to the new wing twice, each time spending an hour or two helping us to sew, or sometimes reading, but she never alluded to her absence from St. Mary's or her return to St. Bride's; I also saw her several times a day in the court yard, sometimes with her hat on, sometimes off, but in her hand; she never came to the work room, or even the chapel, without her hat; she wore deep mourning, fashionably made, and of handsome materials, but she never changed her dress; I asked myself once or twice if she had another in St. Bride's, but whether she came to sew in the hospital or walked in the court, she was always attended by Sister Agatha. The nun never left her for a moment, yet with a policy quite in keeping with her character, she did not allow her presence to seem obtrusive. In the hospital she would come to give orders or cut out work, an office previously left entirely to Sister Mary; in the yard she would bring one of the lay sisters to clean the steps, or call the man who attended to the court to pull out the tufts of grass growing between the paving stones, or some such thing, and she would superintend; all the while, however, watching Gertrude as a cat does the tame bird it has determined to pounce upon.

One day Gertrude told me she was in mourning for her uncle, Colonel Fanshaw; that he died about a month before, leaving the bulk of his fortune to his wife, a woman young enough to be his daughter, and that the latter had gone to England, having left Canada on the day of his funeral; immediately after the reading of the will.

During this recital Sister Agatha's eyes glistened with curiosity; at last she left the room, returning immediately with another nun, who she doubtless hoped would be able to interpret. Alas! as poor Burns says, "the best laid schemes of mice and men, gang aft agley." So do the schemes of nuns. Sister St. John Baptist's knowledge of the English language extended to the ability to say, how do you do, and good-bye, which she often misplaced, saying good-bye when she met me, and how do you do when we parted; but she was proud of her English, and never failed to use it when we encountered each other, this forming her only opportunity for doing so.

It must have been the frequent mention of Colonel and Mrs. Fanshaw's name which excited Sister Agatha's curiosity, as she could not possibly understand the import of another word we used, and yet I did not dare to ask Gertrude where she had been or when she came back; the same feeling, it may be, prevented her from telling me.

There was in St. Bride's a silly creature, quite decrepit, and very old; she was said to have numbered more than a hundred years, who still wore the purple dress of a novice, and when asked her age, invariably answered "fourteen;" her thin gray hair was parted on her forehead, and not cut like that of a nun; she had a soft brown eye, and old as she was, had the remains of beauty. She spent a great deal of her time with us in the new wing, attaching herself particularly to me ; she was always well received by us, her visits, idiot as she was, relieving the terrible monotony of our lives.

She had an idea that she was going home on the morrow, and each day washed either an apron or handkerchief, which she would draw out, fold, unfold, and refold again for hours, observing occasionally during the operation, that she would willingly help us with our work, but as she was to leave St. Bride's on the morrow, she would require all the intervening time to make her apron ready. Sister St. Angelo always spoke to her kindly when she found her with us, Emma regularly bidding the Prioress good-bye, as she would be gone before her next visit to St. Bride's; she did not at all like Sister Agatha, a shade always coming over her face when " *La mauvaise*," as she called her, came near. She told me that when " *La mauvaise* " met her in the passages alone, she always kicked her, but said she in a whisper, " when I bid good-bye to the Superior, I shall tell her all; she is old enough, and ugly enough to know better." Emma used to say she was to leave the convent because she had no vocation to be a nun ; she told me there was a baby boy at home, who was just a year old ; he was two months when she came to St. Bride's; she was sure she would not know him, he would have grown so big and fat, but he soon would know her ; she would feed him with such nice things every day, very soon he would love her best of all; and then her poor mind would wander off to the chapel and prayers, the image of the Virgin, and the flowers on the altar, all mixed up with the proper way to fold her apron, which ever occupied her busy fingers.

No one now in the convent remembered Emma except as the poor silly old creature she now was ; every day for more

than eighty years back washing an apron in anticipation of
to-morrow ; she had outlived every friend of her young days :
the baby boy she loved to talk of, had doubtless grown a man
in the far past, pressed babies of his own to his lips and bosom,
and forgot while he did so all about poor Emma and her loving heart, that had even in her madness never forgotten him ;
and while she still talks of her baby boy, he, a grown man,
lies sleeping, the sleep that knows no waking ; and even those
who knew her in middle age had long since laid themselves
down to rest, and were numbered with the other dead sisters
in the great vault below the convent, while she wandered
restlessly in the sunshine above their heads, ever preparing
for the morrow, in the very rooms they knew so well, where
they lived and died, the walls of which witnessed their few
joys, and happily their few sorrows also. The only thing
known of her now was a tradition that, more than eighty
years before, she became silly in the tenth month of her
novitiate. It was easily accounting for this being handed down,
when she was asked how long she had been in the convent,
her answer was always the same, " ten months." For the last
eighty years she had been bequeathed by one Superior when
dying to the care of another, with the solemn injunction ever
accompanying the charge, "that Emma be carefully and
tenderly dealt with for the love of the Holy Cross."

There were a great many alterations going on at St.
Mary's ; there was to be another room added to those now in
use for the class of aspirants, as the number of pupils in that
class would this year exceed by thirty what it had ever been.
The class of children of Jesus also was to be much larger, and
the arrangements for these fell entirely on Sister St. Angelo.
In consequence of this she was now very little at St. Bride's.
One thing Gertrude and I observed, she used to come twice

a week, late in the evening, after convent hours, to St. Bride's, slept there, attended first mass, and was off to St. Mary's again by five o'clock.

First mass was at four o'clock, and although not fond of early rising, Gertrude always attended the first service, that she might kiss the nun's pale cheek, which every day seemed to become older and more careworn, and speak a few words to her in passing from the chapel.

I told Gertrude of my having seen the Prioress sleeping in the coffin in front of the chancel; she seemed inexpressibly shocked, and for some time made no reply, at last she said, with an abstracted air, as if her thoughts were far off:

"Dear Violet, will you go again when the Proiress comes here at night and see if the coffin is again in the chancel; it is impossible for myself to go."

I knew it was.

Several times after this I went at midnight to the chapel. I never saw the coffin there again. Each time I went to look for the coffin I told Gertrude of my visit; with her lips she made no reply, her eyes thanked me in the fullest sense of the word.

I had no letter from Willie for a long time ; I knew he was waiting for a satisfactory answer to the letters respecting Mr. Weimes. I was not impatient, my convent life would be over in a week or two, and I had resolved to go home. I had written to Mrs. Moodie telling her this, and that I would go to her for the first year at any rate ; I knew she would be pleased, she had told me so several times in her last letters.

I asked Gertrude what she intended to do when her convent life was over, if she would go to Scotland or remain here, her answer was, that she had not made up her mind, she would talk to me on the subject another time.

Three days more, and my engagement would expire. I had
been counting the days for some time, and now I had scarcely
patience to sit at my work ; I used to go twenty times a day
to the window, as if there was anything to be seen there. Gertrude came and read for an hour that forenoon, and then
Sister Agatha said "it was time for her to take her walk
before dinner." Very delightful walk it was indeed, round and
round the paved court yard; I could not understand why Gertrude did not go to St. Mary's ; I was sure she could if she
would ; living there was like being in Paradise in comparison
to St. Bride's.

Of course Sister Agatha went to walk in the court also.
There is a strange perversity in our human nature ; I despised
walking in the court, and yet now the others were gone I
should have liked to go too, only had I done so, I would have
laid myself open to a rebuke on account of my idleness, which
Sister Agatha would not be slow to give; it seemed to afford
her great pleasure pointing out, and enlarging upon, any
little deficiency or short-coming of mine ; constantly impres-
sing upon me, the wholesome truth, that they who were
obliged to earn their bread, should have no will of their own,
even in thought. Notwithstanding the knowledge that Sister
Agatha's eye was upon me, I left my sewing and stood looking at them from the window ; two of the other nuns came
from the back of the court, where the clothes were bleached,
and joined them, and they all stood on the right handside of
the great gate, chatting and laughing; even Sister Agatha's
risible faculties seemed excited in an unusual degree. The
great gate bell rung, and the porteress came from the convent
with her keys to open the gate; the person who rung was a
man with a load of hay. It was a large gate, which opened in
the middle, and it required both sides open to let in the hay

cart; the nuns and Gertrude were at the right side of the gate as I said, and just as the cart was entering, the mid-day bell rung for the nuns' dinner. I have often heard the other nuns joke about Sister Agatha's love of good eating and the quantity she could consume ; it was she who said grace, and they used to allege she was always first in the refectory, and instances were said to have occurred, when so anxious was she to eat her dinner, that she said grace to bafe walls, and commenced supplying her own plate before one of the other nuns had appeared; of course this could only take place in the absence of the Superior and Prioress, in this case Sister Agatha always acted in their stead, and, it is likely, considered herself entitled to do as she pleased, at all events I was amazed to see the hurry she was in to enter the house; she passed the back of the open gate, in which stood the hay cart —something had gone wrong with the wheel, and the man was putting it to rights ; it looked as if the linch pin had fallen out— the other nuns followed. Last of all Gertrude, when she came to the edge of the gate instead of following the others in the direction of the house, she turned and passed out into the street by the narrow passage, that was formed by the load of hay and the outer side of the gate, the porteress meanwhile talking to the man at the opposite side of the cart as he endeavoured to arrange the wheel. The space between the gate and the hay cart was so narrow, that I involuntarily clasped my hands and uttered an exclamation of terror, lest by the least hitch of the latter, she should be crushed between the heavy gate and the load of hay. As the nuns stood at the door waiting for it to be opened, they observed that Gertrude was not with them, and were back at the gate talking with the man and the porteress in a moment, both of whom were evidently denying what the nuns said, pointing to the cart, which by a movement of the horse now leant against the open gate on one side, and they themselves on the other. As a proof that it would have been impossible for any one to pass, the habitant pointed to the side of the convent where the nuns and Gertrude had been before the gate was opened. The man had evidently told them he saw her go round the house in that direction, as they immediately posted off with lightened faces in the way pointed out. They were back again, however, in a moment, and down at the gate, which by this time the porteress was closing. She opened it again, and she, the two younger nuns, and the habitant, went out, Sister Agatha taking her post at the back of the gate, regretting, I fancy, for the second time in her life, that she was a cloistered nun, which was equally effectual now in restraining her from joining in the pursuit of Gertrude, as it had been on a former occasion, in preventing her from following the footsteps of Mr. Forbes from Canada to Europe.

In a few minutes they returned, shaking their heads, and all talking at once. Their search had been unsuccessful. No wonder, Gertrude was at least five minutes in advance of them. There was a cab-stand not ten yards from the convent gate. She would most likely take a cab, and even the man who drove it would not, in all probability, know where she came from. At all events she was gone. As the nuns passed the window where I stood, Sister Agatha looked up with an expression of countenance so full of diabolical rage, I could not help laughing. Her face became at once purple and livid, and her whole frame shook with ill-suppressed emotion. She clenched her hand and shook it in my face. In a second she recovered herself, probably ashamed of having shown such emotion in the presence of one whom she considered so much her inferior in all things, and whom she hated most cordially. That laugh cost me dear.

There were three doors to the room in which we worked, and where I then was. I heard all these locked so quickly, the one after the other, that it would have been almost miraculous if the work of one hand, which, however, I did not doubt it was. However, it troubled me not; I did not care much for being locked into a room. I seldom left during the day. In three days I would leave it and St. Bride's for ever; and I rejoiced that it was so. I was heartily tired of convent life; although I did not regret having entered St. Bride's for several reasons, one of which was, I had gained a knowledge of convent life I could not have acquired except as a resident. I had become convinced, both by the seeing of the eye and the hearing of the ear, that the ideas I had formerly entertained of the happiness and tranquillity enjoyed there were entirely fallacious. I knew by experience that there were little annoyances occurring daily and hourly in the convent, as well as in the world; and there these locusts, which spoil the grain and eat up the flowers and tender buds of our every-day life, are more poignantly felt, because petty things assume an importance there which we would never accord to them in the outer world. I have known a broken figure of St. Joseph to be the fruitful cause of bitter tears and many falsehoods during a whole month, which, if the good, kind man himself had been on earth to witness, would doubtless have grieved him far more than breaking all the trumpery images representing him in the convent. I had learned that gossiping arrogance and avarice were rife here as in the world, and I well knew there were breaking hearts wearing out a hopeless existence that bitterly regretted the irrevocable step they had taken.

I sat down to my work and sewed for more than an hour. Surely they were n t going to keep me here without dinner!

I became hungry with the idea. No matter, I could fast a whole day very easily, and not suffer in the least from it. What could be keeping my companions ? they never used to stay so long at dinner, and I was sure their minds would not be disturbed by hearing of Gertrude's flight. No one within the convent walls would hear of that except those to whom it was absolutely necessary it should be divulged. Even the few who already knew of her departure were bound by a solemn oath never to disclose the secrets of their convent; and the least sign, the uplifting of a finger from the Superior, was sufficient to ensure their everlasting silence.

The clock chimed; I looked up from my work, it was two o'clock, and still they came not; three, four; they would not come now—that was certain; and if my dinner had not been forgotten, I was to be punished for laughing at Sister Agatha by an enforced fast. Be it so, it would do no harm; in two days and a half I would be as free as the wind, with fifteen pounds of my own earning in my pocket. No one would lock me into a room alone then. How I laughed at the childish way she took of punishing me! I knew that I could very easily have her punished for acting so without the per- mission of the Prioress; but I would never think of disturb- ing dear, good Sister St. Angelo with any such nonsense.

I had been standing by the window, counting the number of paving stones within a given square of the court—I often caught myself engaged in this profitable mental employment since coming to St. Bride's—and tired of that, had returned to my seat and begun my work again, when suddenly I was startled by seeing Sister Agatha by my side. The doors of the room were full in my view—she could not have entered by any of them; she must have come by a sliding panel, such as Sister St. Angelo doubtless entered by, when she surprised me in appearing so suddenly one day during the early part of my residence at St. Mary's. What the Prioress meant by this I never could devine. Sister Agatha's motive was easily fathomed. On the one hand, it would show me I was never secure in thinking myself alone, and thereby perhaps terrify me a little; on the other, her sudden appearance would probably startle me into some observation which might betray my knowledge of Gertrude's abode; anything, however slight, which would weaken or startle my mind, if only for a time, and enable her to obtain the slightest ascendancy over me would, of course, forward the object she had in view. I felt certain, from the time she shook her hand so significantly, that she considered me an accomplice in Gertrude's flight, and that, as far as she dared, she would wreak her vengeance upon me. Let her do her worst, I feared her not; the time was too short—she was quite powerless to do me evil. She remained without speaking for several minutes; at last she said, "You have made a good day's work."

I misunderstood her, and wondered how she knew that I had sewed so little, fancying she commented ironically on my idleness. After a pause, finding I did not reply, she asked, "Where is Miss Hamilton?"

"How can I tell?" was my answer.

She seated herself on the other side of the table opposite to where I sat, and replied, with a self-command and coolness I did not give her credit for possessing, "You can tell, because it was by your advice and instructions she left the only safe home she has in the world."

"I never spoke to Miss Hamilton on the subject of her leaving the convent since I came to St. Bride's, nor did she speak of her future plans to me."

"Do you mean to tell me that you and Miss Hamilton never talked over and formed plans for the time when both you and she would leave St. Bride's?"

"I do not know," replied I, with a firmness which astonished myself (for I feared as well as disliked the nun), "what right you have to put such a question to me, but, notwithstanding, I will answer it truly. Some time since I asked Miss Hamilton if she intended going to Scotland after the period appointed by her father's will for her residence in the convent had elapsed. Her answer was that she had not made up her mind, but would again talk to me on the subject."

"A very plausibly got up story, provided you could get me to believe it; but these Protestant prevarications will not avail with me," said the nun. "I am too well aware that your convenient creed, by which you are self-relieved of the necessity of confession, makes it a small matter whether you utter truth or falsehood. Your dread of punishment in what is to you a far-off and very uncertain future being too weak to deter you from committing crimes, and lying to conceal them, which a Catholic would shrink from."

"If that is your opinion," replied I, "there is no use in your asking me questions, or in my replying to them."

"As to that I am the best judge," said the nun, with more heat than she had yet shown, "and your impertinence only adds to your crime, but, let me assure you, there are means within these convent walls to enforce a confession of the truth, and I now warn you that your only safety consists in telling now what you know, and all you know. Depend upon it, it will yet be wrung from you in a way you little think of."

"I neither fear you nor any means you dare employ," I

replied, fearlessly, my courage rising with the occasion ; " my engagement with the Superior terminates in two days—tell her to keep whatever she may consider sufficient to recompense her for my services during that time, and let me leave the convent to-night, or as soon as you can obtain her permission for me to do so."

" A very good proposition," said she, with apparent composure, although I could see the storm was rising, " and very convenient for the maturing of plans which have already succeeded so well ; and then you would join Miss Hamilton in whatever horrible low haunt you have appointed as your place of rendezvous, and by your further advice and assistance you would make her seven-fold more the child of hell than yourself. No," continued she, in a voice so replete with rage as to sound almost sepulchral, " she will wait from morn to night, and from night to morn again, and long for your coming, with aching head and weary breast—it may be, until her hair grows gray with age and watching, but you and she will never meet again ; until she is within these walls you shall never cross the threshold. But I need not draw such a picture—it is only fancy ; perhaps, ere the stipulated time is over, Miss Hamilton will have tired waiting for one she knew too well to value highly. Friendship cemented by intrigue and sin is under the curse of both saints and angels, and lasts no longer than the devil, who made it, thinks necessary for the accomplishment of his own purposes. Perhaps, while we are speaking, Miss Hamilton may be on her way to some of her heretic friends, whom she prefers to Miss Keith."

I looked at her with all the contempt I could throw into my face, but did not answer.

The nun rose from her seat, and placing one hand on

the back of the chair, drew herself up to her full height, looking grand in her great stature and black robes. I thought of Jezebel as I looked upon her. She stood for fully a minute without speaking, and then said, " Would you like to become such an one as the fool Emma ?" I answered not, but kept my eyes firmly fixed on her face. " There are means down there to make you so,"she added, pointing with her long arm and the outstretched finger of her right hand to the floor, and as she spoke she looked on me with a solemn, warning air. " You have heard of such things, and so did Emma. You have treated all such tales as the visions of a disordered brain or weakly-organized nervous system ; while you vainly think, that to you, with the sceptical creed and calculating brain of a Scotchwoman, they would be as the passing wind, which you regard not. Have a care lest, when too late, you find ' there are more things in heaven and earth than thy philosophy dreams of !' "

I kept my eye and face as immoveable as possible, while I said firmly and fearlessly :

" If it were so, the God whom I serve is able to deliver me out of the burning fiery furnace."

Her whole body, and particularly the arm she still kept pointing to the floor, shook with a rage she was scarcely able to control, as she said, speaking slowly and distinctly, yet her frame quivering as she spoke :

" I desire again, in the name of the Lady Superior, that you tell where Miss Hamilton is, or if you like it better, where you think she is ?"

" I have already said all I intend to say on the subject," replied I, " and I demand my liberty ; I did not come to St. Bride's to listen to vain threats, which had you the power you dared not put in force, or to be locked up in a room without food, on suspicion of having aided in the escape of a young lady of fortune from these walls, who was brought back and kept here against her inclination, and depend on it you shall repent having done so ; I have more than one male friend in Scotland who, if I do not arrive there in six weeks from this date, will stir heaven and earth to find me out living or dead, and avenge my cause on those who have done me wrong."

" Your Scotch friends will have difficulty in finding any trace of you," said she, with a composure of face and a calmness in her tone of voice, which reminded me forcibly of the unnatural hush pervading all earth and heaven previous to a thunder storm. " You shall have food, but as to leaving the convent, were you to live a hundred years, you will never put your foot outside the walls until Miss Hamilton returns. You shall live and die here, and your bones will be thrown to whiten on the dunghill, when your guilty soul and polluted flesh have left them ;" and lifting up both her hands and eyes to heaven, she added, " I make this solemn vow to the Blessed Virgin and all Saints ; may they help me to keep it."

As I looked upon her repeating her evil vow, I shuddered to think how easily she might keep it, and yet when I thought of the Prioress, I was reassured ; I knew her too well to entertain for a moment the idea of her giving countenance to any such deed of darkness.

The angelus rang for evening prayers, and she left me without another word, opening the door as she went out with a key which she took from her pocket.

Half an hour afterwards she came again, bringing with her a cup of mint tea—a convent beverage which I disliked very much—and a slice of coarse bread. I had fasted from six in the morning, and I ate it greedily. I had scarcely finished eating when I felt the most irresistible inclination to sleep, and notwithstanding all my efforts to keep awake fell asleep sitting in my chair, Sister Agatha's eyes fixed on me like those of a basilisk.

The last thing I can recollect before falling asleep, was the regret I felt because I knew Sister St. Angelo would not be at St. Bride's before Thursday, and it was now Monday evening; there were three days to wait. For several weeks past she had only come on Sunday and Thursday, Sister Hermonie coming twice a week to attend to the old people in her stead.

CHAPTER XXX

WHEN I awoke I found myself lying on the floor, or what, I fancied was the floor; but the darkness was too intense, I could only ascertain by feeling around me. I found that by putting out my hand in a direct line from where I lay, it came in contact with what seemed to me damp earth. I then recollected that there was a large jug of water on the work table. In my sleep I must have fallen from my chair, and probably in my fall shook the table and so upset the jug; wherever I was I determined to remain until daylight. I felt sure I was not in my own room as it would not be so dark there; in the work room where I sewed a gallery covered the top of the windows; this accounted for the great darkness, the convent wall shutting out the light in front and the gallery at the top: if I rose I might hurt myself by coming in contact with the table or one of the chairs, and the floor was the only place to lie down on; I was still very sleepy, I knew by this as well as by the darkness it could be no later than midnight.

I awoke again, I think long after; the room was still as dark as midnight, darker than any midnight I had ever known before, and yet I was quite awake; I was sure I had slept enough; not that I was refreshed by my sleep—my bed was too hard and cold for that—but my eyes were wide open and I was tired of inaction; I sat up and put out my hand in the direction I had felt the damp floor when I awoke the first time. It was still damp, but surely it was earth, could it be possible? I scratched it with my nails, yes, it was earth, damp earth. I asked myself in horror, " where am I ?" I put out my hand on the other side, it came in con-tact with a stone wall, cold and damp ; the nun has too surely put her threat in execution. " Heavenly Father, do thou, for thine own name sake, and for my Saviour's sake, send thine angel to comfort and strengthen me in this place of dark-ness."

I stood up and raised my hand above my head. Within a few inches of my head my hand touched the roof of the place. I feared to move lest I might fall into a well or pit. I came close to the wall again, there were boards there, per-haps these had formed the bed of some other poor unfortu-nate like myself, who it may be had died here, and whose bones were thrown to whiten on the dunghill, as Sister Agatha had said mine would be. I thought of poor Emma, with whose fall the nun had threatened me, and my soul shrank with terror at the long dark future which might be in store for me. I now recollected while at St. Mary's lis-tening to stories of wicked people, who had died long ago in the dungeons of St. Bride's, and whose spirits still haunted the place which had formed their living sepulchre ; then, I laughed at Sister Mary for believing that on stormy nights their voices might still be heard wailing in the midnight wind, and asking with accents of piteous woe for the prayers of the Church, for the sin, which can never be forgiven—not in this life, not in the life to come—the sin against the Holy Ghost, that of wilful disbelief in the power of the Virgin Mary as the mother of God. I asked her if ever she had seen these dungeons? She answered, " No," with a shudder of horror, " had I ever been there, I would not speak to you now ; no one ever comes back from these dungeons to tell what they have learnt in the eternal darkness there."

Gertrude and I talked of this afterwards, and I pitied the simple nuns for believing such tales of terror, which most likely had no foundation, except in the vivid imagination of some one, who long ago wished to amuse herself by witnessing the wonder which such revelations from the world of spirits would excite in the simple ones by whom she was surrounded, and said I did not believe there were such places under the convent.

I recollected now Gertrude's grave look as she said, " there are such places branching off from the vault, which contains all the bodies of the nuns who have lived in St. Bride's for nearly two hundred years. I have never seen them," she added, " although I have several times been in the vault. The grated doors leading to the dungeons always filled me with more terror than I can describe, and the black darkness beyond the gate seemed the embodiment of the darkness which can be felt. In the vault, among the dead nuns, I felt the awe the presence of the dead always inspires ; but there the lamp shed its light, dispelling in a measure the surrounding gloom, while in the dungeons no eye could pierce the darkness."

And to this darkness I was most surely consigned, with how little hope of ever escaping from it. Sister Agatha had warned me I would never leave the convent unless Gertrude returned. What probability was there of that ever taking place ; warned by her former captivity, was it likely she would again fall into a second snare. I could now understand why she preferred living at St. Bride's. There the event had shown escape was possible ; while at St. Mary's, with its guarded gates, and long way from town, there was little hope of such a thing.

I knew that in three days the Prioress would be at St. Bride's, and she would then hear of Gertrude's flight, if she was not already aware of it, which was most likely. I was sure Sister Agatha would not dare to conceal from her where I was, and I was equally sure she would release me at once. She was truthful herself, and would give me credit for being so also. I knew she would not miss me at first. In the search for Gertrude everything else would be forgotten; but on Thursday she would visit the work-room, and then Sister Agatha would tell the truth: one good thing she dared not lie to the Superior or to the Prioress, more than she dared to her confessor.

But the question occurred to me, was it possible Sister Agatha would starve me to death before the Prioress came. This seemed most likely; long weary hours passed away, and the horror I felt at first increased so much, that I lay down covering my eyes with my hands, so that I might not see the darkness. As I lay there, I wondered if I should not live till the Prioress came; if Willie would ever find out what had become of me. Oh, no; he would no doubt be written to in answer to his next letter, and told, I was dead; but he would never know of the horrible death I had died, in a cold damp dungeon, surrounded by darkness and starved to death. There was consolation in that; it was much better he should not; a knowledge of the truth would embitter all his future life. Again, I thought of the Prioress coming, and I felt as if I was so strong I could well live three days without food. I called to mind all the authorities I could recollect having seen quoted in support of the theory, that life might be prolonged many days by a strong will, without nourishment of any kind, and I tried to remember all the anecdotes I had heard of people living several days without food. I had read in my school days of a woman who was buried in a wreath of snow, who lived eight days, but she had a small piece of bread and some onions, and she ate the snow to quench her thirst. As I lay thinking thus, I began to feel sleepy, and concluded from this, that it must be near the end of my first day's imprisonment. I lifted up my dress over my head so that I might be warm; it was a thin muslin, but it would shelter me a little from the damp of the place. I wrapped myself up as well as I could, and, lying down again tried to compose myself to sleep, but it would not do. Thoughts of home and those so dear to me far away, came fast and strong, and the well-known faces were close to me in the darkness, and I almost touched the hand I had clasped so oft in many a midnight dream. I remembered my reluctance to enter the convent, and it seemed to me now like the warning voice of my guardian angel. I fancied I saw a light amid the darkness; it could only be fancy. No, there it is again. Strange to say, I felt terror-stricken, and shrunk under my uplifted dress. I knew it was something from the world of spirits, a thing of terror, perhaps the very evil one, whose scowl seared away poor Emma's wits. No doubt now remained on my mind, that the poor crazy, restless thing had once been an inmate of this very dungeon. The spirit, who brought madness to her eighty years ago, was so surely bringing it to me now. What was eighty years more than yesterday to one who had passed the barriers of time. I bit my lip in my agony, lest I should scream out in my horror of that light, as it flitted about, within the space of a few feet; now seen, now gone. I remembered the legion of Ehrenbreitstein, and knew that my only safety was in silence; on it came, nearing me every time by an inch or two. I clasped my hands on my eyes; I could endure it no longer; I fancied the spirits of the dead nuns came trooping round me in hundreds; and the light I had seen was gleaming from their eyes. One of them called out to me to come. I screamed in answer. I knew I was going mad, and would soon join them in their horrible dance of death. They laughed loud, and called again; the voice resembled that of the nun Agatha; the call was repeated a third time. It was indeed Sister Agatha calling me to come to the grate, if I wished for the bread and water she had brought me.

" Thank God! thank God! for the sound of the human voice. These words, spoken by the only woman I ever hated, was the sweetest music that ever sounded in mine ear.

I uncovered mine eyes, rose and went in the direction of the light I had so much dreaded.

Sister Agatha stood outside the grate, which was formed of bars of iron, very rusty, and reached from the top to the bottom of the cell. She held a cup of water and a piece of bread in one hand, and a dark lantern in the other. The lantern was hung on a large ring, and by giving it the least touch, she could throw the light into the cell and out again in a moment. She had studied her business, and might well laugh at the success of her stratagem.

The nun asked me if I would now tell where Miss Hamilton was.

I replied, " I know nothing at all about Miss Hamilton, and when the Prioress comes she will believe me."

" You shall never see the Prioress, unless you give me such information as will lead to the discovery of Miss Hamilton. When she comes back you will be allowed to go free if she does not come, you never shall."

" I have no fear of that. On Thursday, when the Prioress comes, she will release me at once."

She laughed aloud—such a fiendish laugh; while her black

eyes glistened with a look of triumphant malice. The lantern threw its light on the lower part of her face, while the upper half was in shade, little more than the glitter of her eyes being visible. I never saw anything more ghastly and horrible than she looked, as she stood laughing outside the dungeon grate, her eyes and large wide-set teeth looking as if they were part of a skull with the skin tightened over it. I shuddered as I looked. She mistook the cause of my emotion, and said :

" Well may you shake in anticipation of the fate which is before you. You can utter lies with your tongue, but the fear which consumes you will appear. You have good cause for fear ; a few nights more in that dungeon will do its work either on mind or body. Do not trust to the Prioress ; she was here last night, and was told by Sister Mary, who I sent to St. Mary's for her, that you left the convent while we were searching for Miss Hamilton, locking the work-room doors before you went.

" How could Sister Mary dare to lie to the Prioress ?"

" Sister Mary never lies," said the nun, as coolly as if she herself was a personification of the truth. " Sister Mary was told to say so, and believed she was telling the simple truth, having been shown the locked doors, in confirmation of your having gone."

How I despised the contemptible false woman. I turned away. I fancied she held the bread and water only to tempt me.

" Here," said she, putting the cup with the bread placed on the top, through the grate, " take this, it is the last food you shall ever eat on earth, unless you divulge your guilty secret."

I took it from her hand, and before eating, thanked God

for that bread and water, more fervently than I had ever done in all my previous life.

The nun lifted up the lantern from the ground where she had placed it while speaking, and holding it above her head, departed. I then saw that the light flitted backwards and forwards as it had done coming to the grate, when it frightened me so much.

During the time the nun stood at the grate, there was sufficient light thrown into the cell to show me that it was a narrow strip, the entrance to which was the grated door, through which the nun put the bread and water.

When the last faint gleam of light was gone, and I was again alone, with that thick *darkness, I knelt down, and thanked my Heavenly Father for having in the same moment relieved me from that most hideous of all terrors, the fear of the hidden things of darkness—the spirits of the dead (which I, in my folly, had so often laughed at in others) and the dire hunger and thirst which consumed me; and I prayed earnestly, beseeching Him to shield me from this horrible fear, and again I prayed for the presence of His Angel, that for my Saviour's sake, he might be sent to comfort me in this abode of darkness; and he did send His angel to strengthen me there, and I arose from my knees with the full conviction that He would in His own good way and time, take me out of the dungeon. I remembered Daniel of old, and I knew the God of Daniel was mighty to save now as then, and alone there in the darkness of that dungeon cell He gave me faith to believe that I would yet stand in the free air and blessed sunshine, and sing of His mercies with a sound mind.

" I will love Thee, O Lord, my strength. The Lord is my defence, my Saviour, and my God, in whom I will trust. The horn also of my salvation and my refuge."

"I will call upon the Lord, so shall I be safe from my enemies."

"The pains of hell came about me, the snares of death overtook me. In my trouble I will call upon the Lord, and complain unto my God."

"He shall send down from on high to save me, and will take me out of many waters."

CHAPTER XXXI

I SLEPT soundly on the boards in the corner of the dungeon cell, in the full assurance of the Lord's help and omnipresence, and I lived on the strength of His help long, long hours of bitter hunger and thirst, and I knew it was time for my tormentor to come with bread and water, but she came not. Could it be that she would fulfil her threat ? I knew she would not come that night ;—but her master Satan, that old serpent who tempted our mother in the Paradise of God, came in her stead, and he who counselled the angels and made them fall from their allegiance, ere yet the earth was formed, spoke to my soul and counselled me, and he told me there was no God, and no hereafter; and he bid me bite my own flesh, that I might drink blood and quench the burning thirst which was consuming my very vitals. But God's angel came also, and I knew there was a God, " mighty to save to the uttermost." I remember, how he had heard and helped me, when cold, and sick, wet and weary, alone in a dark staircase in the crowded city of Edinburgh, and I knew that " His arm was not shortened that He could not save," or " His eye dim, that He could not see," No, no, " He is God and there is none else ; in all the universe there is none other ;" He is omniscient and omnipresent still, and will yet save me out of this dark dungeon in Canada ; and in my Redeemer's holy words I shouted with all my strength, until the dungeon echoed back the sound : " Get thee behind me, Satan," and the Holy one who spoke to me more than three years before, spake again in the same clear, distinct voice, each low tone sounding in mine ear, sharp as a silver bell ;—

" Fear not, thou worm Jacob, by my power thou shalt thrash the mountains."

I laid myself down to sleep, praising my Father in Heaven, in that he had heard and answered my prayer, and I awoke thrice from that heavy sleep only to sleep again, and hunger and thirst were no more.

I slept again, and in my sleep I dreamt there were spread before me all manner of baked meats, fit for Pharoah's table. I was about to eat when I fancied the nun called me. I heeded her not, I would eat and be satisfied ; again and again the voice of the nun Agatha sounded in mine ear. I awoke, and knew by the light streaming through the grate that she was there in reality. The smell of the baked meats was still strong in my nostrils. I sat up, but felt so weak I did not answer at first. The nun called again, and louder than before, and then said in her native Spanish :

" Body of Christ, the heretic devil has gone to the hell she deserves so well."

" Truth is green," replied I, answering her in the same language, and using one of the proverbs of her own tongue.

" Holy Virgin defend me," said she, " Satan teaches his children all languages ;" and still continuing to speak in Spanish, she called me to come to the grate if I wished to eat and drink that night.

On my coming to the grate, she gave me a smaller slice of bread than before, covered with fried ham. Ah ! the wicked one, how well she knew to serve her master.

I took it from her hand, and lifting the ham from the bread (it felt warm in my fingers, it was not probably five minutes off the fire), I threw it on the damp floor and trod it down with my heel.

" Good night," said she, with a quite composed air, taking not the least notice of what I had done. " This is Thursday evening, the Prioress is in the convent, she has not yet gone to her cell, before she does so, of course, she will come to release you ;" and she walked away taking with her the cup containing the water.

I had not yet tasted the bread ; when I did I found, what I might have expected, that it was impregnated with the salt from the ham ; I endeavoured to rub off the particles of salt but without effect ; my hunger was terrible now, and I could not resist eating it. God, who " tempers the wind to the shorn lamb," had not forgotten me. I ate the bread and felt little thirst. On my knees in the dungeon there I thanked God for this mercy, and lay down, " So giveth He His beloved sleep."

I must have slept many hours. I awoke with a raging thirst, and without opening my eyes put my tongue to the stones of the damp wall at my side ; it was a blessed thought given of God, the wall felt so cool and pleasant to my parched tongue. I repeated this many times, changing the place as the stone warmed under my fevered tongue, until I felt strong enough to open my eyes, which I was too weak to do when I first awoke.

A faint light gleamed from the side of the dungeon opposite to that on which the grate was placed ; the light was steady but at a distance, yet sufficient to show me that it came through another grate the bars of iron being distinctly visible. I arose and went towards it ; hoping against hope, that the bearer might aid in setting me free.

I found that the light came through a grated door, similar to the other, and on looking through, I saw that it came from the vault containing the bodies of the dead nuns. I shrank back with the instinctive horror we all feel of the dead, whom in life we have not loved or known, but immediately recovering myself, I took hold of the grate endeavouring to open it, knowing that this might be my last chance for life and liberty.

The door opened with little trouble, the rusty padlock falling to the ground like powder. Upon entering the vault the first object that met my eyes was the coffin on tressels, covered by a pall, exactly as I had seen a month previous, in the chapel, at midnight. I went close up to it, the end of the pall was folded back as before, and there lay Sister St. Angelo fast asleep.

I fell on my knees—I could not utter one accent of praise, the mercy was too great ; no words could give utterance to the gratitude which filled my heart to overflowing, but my soul lifted itself in silence up to Him who searcheth the hearts of the children of men.

While on my knees I felt the vault shake as if from above, and I fancied I heard noises, which must have been louder than the loudest thunder, ere they could reach these dungeons beneath the cellars of the convent.

I rose from my knees, and folding back the pall, touched Sister St. Angelo ; she sighed but moved not. I bent down and kissed her forehead. She then opened her eyes, fixing them upon me with a wild stare of astonishment. I knew the lie she had been told, and said, " I have been confined here since Monday, and am dying of thirst."

Without speaking she raised her arm, and pointing to where the light was placed, motioned me towards it. On going in the direction indicated, I found the lamp placed in a niche, built into the wall, for a statue of the Virgin, before which stood a stone vase filled with holy water. I put my face into the vase and drank that stale salt water as if it had been nectar; again and again I drank, and while doing so, another heavy shock came upon the vault. I looked towards the place I had left the Prioress, but, in turning round, saw that she was by my side. Just as my eye met hers, a roar, as if of a thousand waves came down above our heads, with exactly the hurling sound accompanying it, which we occasionally hear emitted by thunder.

"God have mercy on us," said the Prioress, "the convent is on fire—come while we have a chance of escape," and snatching up the lamp, she led the way through the windings of the vault, all of which were filled with the dead. In the last was a broad staircase consisting of seven steps, wide enough for several persons to descend at once. We ascended to the top of the staircase, it being within several feet of the roof of the vault, which latter was much loftier than the dungeon. Sister St. Angelo then pulled a couple of pullies placed there for lifting up a trap door—it did not move; she pulled again, exerting all her strength, but without effect, when she first tried the pulley, she gave me the lamp; I now laid it on the floor, and took one of the pullies, while the Prioress took the other; all our efforts were unavailing, a child might as well attempt to stem the tide of the mighty St. Lawrence, as we to lift that trap door.

"May God have mercy on our souls," said the nun, "the convent is on fire, and part of the building has fallen into the chapel above our heads."

As she spoke, another roar louder, and another shock more felt than the former, seemed to come, as it were, down upon our heads.

"Let us pray to God," said the Prioress, "He alone can help us to escape from the most horrible of all deaths."

We knelt down beside the staircase, the Prioress praying for more than an hour, during which time two other shocks occurred.

When she arose from her knees she sat down on the steps, making me do the same ; she then said :

" If we live until they clear out the debris from the chapel, we can make ourselves heard, but the virgin only knows if our strength will last until then ; tell me how you wandered into this place ; your undue curiosity has perhaps cost you your life."

I told her everything which had occurred since Monday morning; she heard me without speaking a word, until I told her of Sister Agatha bringing me the fried ham, and then clasping her hands and looking up as if her eyes would pierce through the roof to the firmament above in search of the God who hides Himself so wondrously, so as even to make His own people think, in their hours of doubt and temptation, that there is no God, said with a solemn voice, " may the virgin mother of God have mercy on her unshriven soul this night."

After a pause, during which the tumult above our heads seemed to have stopped, the Prioress said :

" You must try and bring me to the cell where you were confined; I will find bread near it," and saying so, she retraced her steps to the part of the vault where the coffin in which she had slept lay ; she then observed the open grate of the cell, and turning towards me with a strange wild look, said : " It was surely not in that cell you were ?"

" Yes," replied I, " it was through that door I entered the vault," and carrying the light, I preceded her into the cell; when I had gone a few steps I observed that she did not follow, and turning round, I waited for her with the light. She stood looking at something above the door of the cell; when she had finished her scrutiny she said: "Holy Jesus—the wicked woman, she is unworthy the name of a nun—she, indeed, put you into the cell of the Inverted Cross; if she and I live to meet in this world, her nun's robe and veil will be stript from her dishonoured head and body in the presence of every novice belonging to St. Bride's by the gate porteress, while the priests of St. Benedict will be called to witness a sight, and the Bishop to confirm a deed, which no eye ever saw in St. Bride's from its foundation, two hundred years ago. She is the first nun of St. Bride's who has disgraced her robe; no marvel that the convent is on fire when such a deed of darkness has been committed under its walls." As she spoke, another loud roar, which sounded nearer to us, but unaccompanied by the shock which had either preceded or come after the others, recalled her to the necessity of searching for the bread, and taking the lamp from my hand, she entered the cell with a look of horror, and shuddering as she did so ; as we passed through, I looked with interest at the place where I seemed to have spent a life time, and there, within four feet of the boards where I lay, was an uncovered well, the water in which rose to within a few inches of the floor of the dungeon. The angel of the covenant had preserved me from sundry kinds of death.

We left the cell by the grated door, through which the nun Agatha gave me my bread and water. In going out I looked for and showed to the Prioress, the ham, lying half imbedded in the damp earth; the grate opened with little effort, being merely kept by its rusty hinges; we passed through two other dungeons, the doors of which were wide open, and while passing through, the Prioress raised the lamp she held in her hand in order to shew me a plate of knotted glass, about a foot long, in the roof of each ; by this a dim light would be afforded to the dungeon from the cellar above—verily the nun chose the worst place for me—they were also, comparatively speaking, dry; however, this fault was in my favour, I would have suffered more from thirst in a dry place, and had I been in either of the others, I could not have seen the light which led me to the Prioress ; in the third we found a niche similar to that in the vault, but without a statue, and there was a loaf of bread from which had been taken the two slices I had eaten since I was a prisoner, and the pewter cup, still filled with water, which the nun had carried away with her on her last visit. At the sight of the bread, I felt hunger return with almost irresistible force ; the Prioress knew this would be so, and at once lifted up a slice and gave it me ; the loaf was cut into eight pieces—there must have been ten in all.

For some time the tumult above head had, in a measure, ceased, but now another shock occurred that seemed to rock the convent from its very foundation, and was succeeded by the roaring noise : now, the roar did not cease in the course of a minute or two, as it had formerly done, but continued, almost without interruption, for what seemed to us fully half an hour. We gazed at each other speechless, the Prioress' lips ashy white, I myself appalled with terror.

Sister St. Angelo lifted up the bread and pewter cup, from which I had already drank the contents, and hurrying out by the same way as we had entered, came again to the vault with the dead. "We are safer here," said the nun, " the dungeons are not arched with stonework as this vault is, and were they to fall in we would be smothered with the falling debris in a moment."

She deposited the bread on the niche beside the figure of

the Virgin, and taking the cup, bade me carry the lamp and follow her, saying she would show me the well. It was in a small recess off the dead vault, not larger than a deep cupboard, and covered by a stone fitted into it, so that it turned to one side with very little pressure; an iron chain with a hook was attached to the well, and a small wooden bucket lay on the stone cover; the Prioress drew water with the bucket, and then filling the pewter cup, gave me to drink, smiling at the eagerness with which I took the cup from her hands.

Such delicious, pure, cold water, how it sparkled in the lamplight, showing other tiny lamps down to the bottom of the cup, I could not help saying as I finished drinking, having drained it to the last drop, " what a delightful drink, I never tasted such water before."

" Yes," said the nun, her grave face looking more serious as she spoke, " fresh, pure water must, indeed, be delightful to you, who have drank only, during three days, salted water that has been drawn and lying in these cellars for months— I am sure poor lost Agatha never would trouble herself to bring you water from the well here or from the convent above; no doubt she filled the cup from one of the holy water fonts."

We returned with the lamp to the Virgin's shrine (each niche containing a figure of the Virgin is considered a shrine from the sacred character of the statue it bears), and sat down on a stone bench exactly opposite, where the coffins containing the dead were always placed for six weeks previous to their being put into the recess assigned to each nun the day she takes the black veil.

The vault was a long narrow place with many turnings, more resembling a very wide passage than aught else, with hundreds of recesses filled and unfilled, covering the walls on either side.

" We have bread here to last for three days," said the nun. I looked at it as it lay on the shrine opposite to where we sat, and thought I could eat it all at once. " Water will sustain life at least two days without any food ; but I do not anticipate being left so long; they will dig out the debris as soon as possible, to secure the valuables which the fire cannot destroy. Those are all in the chapel, and we are under it. The trap door is in front of the chancel before the great altar, and when they find the trap, curiosity will make them open it.

" Strange to tell," continued she, " forty years ago I was in Mexico, in a convent belonging to our order there, and for a very little fault I was sent to do penance in the place of sleep. I was young then, and so full of fear that sleeping among the dead seemed to me more terrible than death itself. That night the convent was burned to ashes over my head, and every soul within it perished. I, down among the dead, alone was saved of sixty nuns, who dwelt there. Well did I know the meaning of that dread shock and the loud roar which followed. I had listened to the same awful sound on my knees and alone in the darkness for long hours that dismal night, thinking, in my agony, that the spirits of evil had left their abode of horror, and were striving in their rage to enter and destroy the place where the holy nuns rested.

" I was saved then for a long pilgrimage. Be St. François Xavier ever blessed. He helped me to spend and be spent in the service of the Holy Trinity, and I have had much comfort by the way, more than falls to the lot of most women. It is true that at times the smooth grass became thorns and sharp rocks beneath my bleeding feet, but it was only for a short distance, and the fresh daisied sward appeared again, and was softer and cooler than ever from the contrast, and I went on my way rejoicing."

A louder and nearer crash than before startled us from where we sat. I had been saved from a horrible death, one the most revolting to human nature. The convent walls had fallen into the dungeons, and through the grate, which it had pushed open, there poured earth and stones as if it were a torrent. We both stood awestruck, I expecting every moment that the vault would be filled up and we buried alive. How gladly would I have exchanged death by hunger and thirst for the awful death we were threatened with. I became breathless, and shook with terror. The Prioress was calm. "No fear," said she, "the aperture is too small, the earth entering there could not fill the vault, and if it did, there is a long way behind where we could go. The masonry is too strong above the vault to fear its falling through; and I wish to remain in the vicinity of both trap doors" (as she spoke she pointed with her finger above her head a little to the right; my eyes followed her uplifted hand, and I saw there another trap door much larger than the one with the staircase), "so as to be seen, or make ourselves heard as soon as possible." After the lapse of ten or twelve minutes the debris ceased to pour into the vault, although every now and then a few handfuls would slide down from an insecure resting-place, and at intervals we were conscious of portions of the walls or other heavy material falling into the dungeon. How mercifully the Lord had dealt with me! Had the fire happened the night previous, I would surely now have been numbered with the dead; and of such a death who can tell the horror?

The Prioress knelt down before the Virgin's shrine, and,

taking my Bible from my pocket, I read the deliverance of Peter by the angel of God, and I knew if it were necessary He could send His angel now to save us from the death which seemed so certainly closing in around us.

As I read, my hands and the Bible they held, fell on my lap, my eyes closed, and I slept soundly as ever I had done under the birch trees, that waved their towering tops and shed sweet fragrance around my room in Portobello; and in my sleep my spirit went back there for the first time since I left it, and I trode on the light heather bell—the low murmur of the waves sounding like home music to mine ear—in the grey mist of early morning, and one walked hand in hand with me there, whose dark eye I would never see, or whose hand would never touch mine again. When I awoke, the Prioress was still upon her knees. I slept again, and the second time she still knelt, and prayed as before. I must have slept many hours. I awoke refreshed, and feeling that I needed sleep no longer.

The pewter cup was placed in the niche beside the Virgin full of water. I longed to drink, but dared not approach, for fear of disturbing the nun. I now believed what I had been told of nuns passing whole nights on their knees praying.

It was an hour after ere she rose from her knees, and when she did, she went to the coffin, folded back the pall, and, ascending by two steps which it concealed, lay down, placing the pall with the end turned back as I had first seen it.

When I thought she had fallen asleep—I did not move before in case I might disturb her—I went to the niche, and drank such a long delicious drink, and then I prayed and read my Bible for several hours.

How strangely the mind adapts itself to the circumstances in which it is placed. Now that I had light and the presence of Sister St. Angelo I was far from being unhappy. I had little fear of our being ultimately rescued from the living tomb we now occupied, provided we had strength to sustain life with the small portion of food we could afford to eat each day. What the Prioress had said of a search being made for the altar jewels and plate, was enough to satisfy me that in a few days the vault would be opened. St. Bride's altar was the richest in Canada ; the jewels hung round the Virgin alone were worth more than twenty thousand dollars, while the value of the altar plate was enormous, the greater proportion of it being in gold. A service of that precious metal, worth twelve thousand dollars, was left some ten years before by one who had lived anything but a pious life, in hopes of buying heaven. Even if the nuns had all perished, a thing very unlikely to happen, the priests of St. Benedict were doubtless well aware of the immense value of the jewels and plate kept within the chancel of St. Bride's, and would take immediate steps for their recovery. Our release was almost certain to follow. Hence my mind was almost easy on this point ; the vault was not cold and damp like the adjoining cell, and darkness and thirst were no more.

I wandered round the vault, looking at the coffins, each exactly like the other—no name, or age, or date, but a white cross, the sign of their salvation, placed on the black cloth, which alike covered all. Everything here was as purely clean and in order as in the chapel over our heads—no smell, and, stranger still, no feeling of confined air.

The Prioress must have slept many hours ; on awaking, she sat up and crossed herself, and then, descending from the coffin, she again knelt before the Virgin's shrine and prayed.

When her orisons were over, she took the pewter cup and, signing to me with her eye and finger to bring the lamp, went to the well, drew water, and gave me to drink ; and, having drunk herself, filled the cup and brought it to the stone bench. She then took from the niche two slices of bread, and, placing them beside the water, stood with her face to the east, crossed herself, and, pronouncing a blessing on the food, sat down with me to our humble meal.

Having ate our bread with thankful hearts, the Prioress returned thanks to the Giver ; she then asked me if the noise continued after she went to sleep, and having been answered in the negative, she crossed herself and lifted up her hands and eyes to heaven, uttering a few words of praise, adding, " I do not doubt that the clearing away of the earth and stones in search of the altar plate will be commenced immediately ; we must try the pulley of the trap door every hour, when the debris which now covers it is removed, it will open with the least touch."

We passed long hours without hearing the slightest sound ; I knew afterwards that during all that time of silence, night and day, by torch light and sun light, there were men with warm human hearts and strong arms working above our heads, any one of whom had they known we were there, would have risked their lives to save us ; they were so near and yet so far ; that pile of earth and stones above our heads, although only a few feet in depth, forming a greater barrier than miles of space would have done.

We tried the pulley often and often, but in vain ; once we fancied for a long time, fully a day, that at intervals we heard a human voice, and we watched and listened for it so eagerly, with hands firmly clasped together, ear and eye alike strained in the direction from whence it came, waiting in silence and with beating hearts to catch the slightest sound ; at last, we distinctly heard a shout as if of one calling to another ; we both rushed to the grate in the direction from whence the sound proceeded, and almost instantly a loud crash of falling debris shook the convent, or rather the foundation, as had occurred once before.

This was the last sound we heard, no voice or motion ever again broke that dread silence, save our own voices or the dull tread of our footsteps, as we in our weariness paced to and fro in the vault, when we had both lost all hope, but dared not say so to each other.

Once or twice the Prioress spoke of those around us : " Look at this," said she, putting her hand behind one of the coffins and taking from between it and the wall a bunch of faded roses ; " I often bring a bunch of flowers and place them here, by one who, in her life time, loved them so well ; she came here to hide from the world, the torn heart and pale cheek given by one she loved most undoubtingly ; and for eight years bore her worldly cross in this convent. If these walls could speak they might unfold sad secrets of blighted hopes and crushed affections ; I doubt much if these feelings which spring from the deepest source in the human heart are ever, while we are in this earth, altogether obliterated. Poor Sister Valleiry, I fear long after she was the bride of heaven, her very soul was centered in him, who had been at once the star and curse of her existence. We wished her to go on a mission far away to some distant land, distance and change would have wrought a good work in her, but she would not consent to go, and unfortunately the Superior issued no command. Sister Valleiry could not consent to tear herself from where he lived and breathed, although her own vows and the convent walls had placed a barrier stronger than death between them. Ill-judging people from the world came now and then, and I know they told her how he lived and looked, and of his words; and at last they came and said that he had brought to Algona one young and beautiful as she had been eight years before. She repeated their words to me with a smile, but I knew through the thin disguise that a terrible struggle was at hand; and that night I obtained leave from the Superior to visit her in her cell. She lay weeping bitterly, the handkerchief she held in her hand soaking wet; I took it from her unresisting fingers and put the towel in its stead, e'er I left the cell it also was wet enough to wring.

" Next morning she went into a retreat of three days, but before the third sun rose, our blue eyed sister lay prostrate before the Virgin's shrine, her rose leaf cheek turned to marble, cold and dead. Our mother was dreadfully shocked, and from that time forth would allow of no retreat within the walls of St. Bride's being made with fasting. It was neither the retreat or the fast that killed fair young Sister Valleiry."

In different parts of the vault, wherever it branched off into a separate compartment, there was a niche with a figure of the Virgin, and in front of each figure was placed an unlit lamp; the Prioress said that the reason why these lamps were there, was that on certain days, such as the anniversary of the death of St. Bride, Good Friday, and also the anniversaries of the death of each Superior, who had ruled in St. Bride's, there were processions made by all the nuns and novices passing through each winding of the vault, and on such occasions the lamps were all lighted up. In the part of the vault where the foundress lay, the figure of the Virgin was of white marble with a lamp on either side, twice as large as the others, and the shrine was exactly in front of her coffin.

When the oil in the lamp we used became low, we lit

another, Sister St. Angelo putting the extinguished lamp in the place from which she took the one in use, with the same precision as if everything was going on in the convent above, as it had done for ages.

I asked the Prioress, if the anger she expressed against the nun for putting me in that particular cell, was on account of its darkness or because of the well, which exposed me to the risk of instant death in case I moved about.

" For neither of those causes," said she. " There is a tradition in the convent so old, that no one knows its origin, that the dungeon you were confined in is haunted by an evil spirit ; in the history of our convent, mention is made almost from the first year of our community settling here, of nuns at their devotion in the vault being disturbed by wild cries immediately succeeded by a loud splash in the well, as if a heavy body had fallen into the water ; the cell has been exorcised more than once, but it was of no avail. Not more than a hundred and twenty years ago, a pious missionary of the order of Passionists, who had walked barefooted over every part of the globe where Catholics have raised the standard of the cross, essayed, together with two of his brethren, to drive away the evil spirit, but it is there still ; we know that too well. It is thought that some terrible deed of darkness was done there by heathen hands in the days of the early Christian settlement, and that there are heathen spells still around the well. I myself have heard in stormy nights in winter what might well be imagined the wail of an evil spirit striving with the blast around the north-east wing of the house above that dungeon.

" Eighty-six years ago, poor silly Emma lost her senses there ; she was then only fourteen years of age, and in the tenth month of her novitiate ; she had a most insubordinate

temper and had absolutely refused, first to the nun in
charge of the novices, afterwards to the Prioress, and at last
even to the lady Superior herself, to perform some irksome
duty on which she was ordered. It is no light ordeal a
novice has to undergo before she can acquire a right to
assume the nun's robe and veil here on earth, together with
the full assurance that if that robe and veil are kept spotless
until the day when they are resigned for ever, together with
the poor, decayed cerement they were made to cover, the
renewed soul will then appear in its pristine glory in robes whiter
than the driven snow, and for the nun's humble veil receive a
crown of purest gold ; there to dwell at God's right hand
where there are pleasures for evermore, and to follow the
Lamb withersoever He goeth ; this is the promise given to
those virgins who have not defiled their garments. 'They
shall walk with me in white,' are his own blessed words, but
they who would inherit the promise must first strive, that
they may win the fight, ever bearing in mind that the kingdom of heaven is only for the poor in spirit, and that none
but the pure in heart shall see God. This ordeal is too
grievous for many—all who run do not obtain the prize; it was
too hard to be borne for poor Emma's proud spirit. The
Superior had great patience, and warned her that if she did
not comply with the nun's command within six hours, she
would be imprisoned for twelve in one of the dungeons, and
afterwards expelled from the convent as unworthy of becoming a nun. She would not submit, and in consequence was
sent to the dungeon ; the nun, who was appointed to conduct
her there, was unfortunately one who had only arrived from
one of our convents in Europe a few weeks previous, and
knew little of our convent, and nought of its traditions, and
not knowing what she did, put poor Emma in the haunted

cell. In eight hours, not twelve as was threatened, the Superior went herself to bring her out, and to her horror found a raving maniac! Superior Bourgette from that day until the hour of her death, twenty years after, never permitted a lamp to be lit in her own cell, also passing two hours of each day in prayer for Emma down in the vault. Emma was not then the silly, comparatively happy being she is to-day, but at times raving mad, tearing her clothes in shreds, and when the fit was over, so fearful that the least unwonted noise, even the shutting of the convent gate, would throw her into an ecstasy of terror. At such times she would fly to hide herself beside the nearest nun, covering her head with the Sister's robe, while her screams echoed over the whole convent, calling out with piteous tears to the Superior to save her from the demon of the inverted cross; every doctor within hundreds of miles, who made insanity his study, was called to minister to her relief—special masses were said for her—every effort was in vain, God at last granted her recovery to peace of mind, to the prayers of Superior Bourgette; she has had none of these violent fits for sixty-eight years past. The day on which the Superior received the last sacrament, she told the Superior of St. Benedict, who was her confessor, that it had been revealed to her in a dream, that on the day of Emma's death, the convent of St. Bride's would fall to the ground; but Emma lived so long (a hundred and two years if she is now alive), and the old convent was so strongly built, that a saying went among the nuns that she would never die. The convent of St. Bride's has fallen to the ground, that is most certain, and in all probability Emma is under its walls."

We had exchanged our lamp six times, and our bread was reduced to one slice. I was becoming very weak, and at times felt so giddy, that I was obliged to sit down on the floor to prevent myself from falling ; but what distressed me far more than aught that concerned myself, was the conviction that the good Prioress was sinking fast into the arms of death; no wonder, when I, with youth and health on my side, felt weaker almost every hour, that she with her many years and painful fasts and vigils should sink beneath this sore trial. She said that she knew by the burning of the lamps that nearly three days had passed since we heard the voice calling near the dungeon grate, that last sound which we had welcomed with such joy, not thinking that it was the last we should ever hear from the outer world, and the knell presaging the doom which awaited us.

I had only seen her eat once ; twice when she gave me the bread allotted to me, she carried her own to the well to eat it there, and the last time she drew water, she filled the bucket and put it outside the well, desiring me to carry it to the niche, saying, " that she feared if she was unable to help me I would find it hard to draw water with no one to hold the lamp."

She also made me bring, one by one, six small and the two large lamps from the white Virgin's shrine, and put all in the niche. I knew well what all this betokened, my companion in captivity, my kind good friend, the self-denying, true hearted nun, was going away to that far heaven her soul had longed for these many weary years of self-inflicted penance ; she had been many hours in the coffin; I leaning upon and supported by it stood beside her. She asked me to bring her a drink, I took the cup and went to the well, that the water might be fresh, and there on the stone cover were laid the two slices of bread I thought she had eaten ! unselfish unto death, that my life might be prolonged a day or two longer, she had voluntarily laid down her own.

I brought the water, taking the bread also with me, and shewed it to her, by this letting her know that I was aware of the sacrifice she had made. I could not speak, but I felt as if I would gladly lie down in the coffin there and die beside her.

I raised her head and she drank enough of the water to moisten her lips, but no more ; a faint smile came over her dying face, and collecting all her strength, she said, " When you are out in the world again, go to the Superior of St. Benedict and tell him I am here, he will have me removed to sleep with my darling under the green grass and forest trees at St. Mary's."

I kissed her cheek, and, with saddened heart and faltering voice, told her that if ever I left the vault alive, I would never leave Canada until I had seen her laid in her dear one's grave, and with my own hand planted the shamrock of her native land there.

She looked in my face and tried to smile, but death was too near. I stood there, her lessening pulse sinking below my touch, listening to the failing breath, and watching the last faint life-streak flying, flying. I stooped down and put my lips to her forehead. I started at the touch, I was alone with death.

I could not leave the coffin where Sister St. Angelo lay ; I could not realize that she was gone from me ; when by her body I felt as if she were still here, and beyond were the dead nuns, and they were now become things of fear, as they had been when I was alone in the adjoining cell.

It is a common saying : " It is a solemn thing to die." To me it has always seemed a far more solemn thing to live. What a mysterious influence soul exercises over soul, while it still inhabits the body ; no matter how weak or powerless, though unable to make itself understood by word or sign, the body is cared for with tenderness and affection, its slightest motion attended to and interpreted as love suggests to be best,—the feet are wrapt up lest they be too cold, the hands fanned lest they be too hot, and the lips carefully moistened long after they have ceased to emit a single sound ; a wealth of love is lavished on all its members ; but the last sigh is breathed, and the soul, a moment so low, so agonized, is now beyond the stars, the influence it once possessed for good or for evil all gone. Yesterday, a word of his might have turned the current of our lives, made us less selfish, less worldly, more inclined to make the cause of the poor and needy, the wronged or oppressed, our own. Was that admonition given or withheld ? Each of us stand in the same position—each living soul has power to influence, for good or evil, some other soul. The body we so loved yesterday is now, even while we kiss the cold lips and pale forehead in our woe and weeping, become a thing of dread. So will it be with us to-morrow. Let us then arise, be up and doing, ere the day breaks, and the call is given for us also to pass over to the shining shore.

I remained leaning over the body, and gazing on the calm, worn face until I could stand no longer, and then I folded the pall over her face and lay down on the ground by the side of the coffin. I was weak from want of food and worn by long watching, and my Heavenly Father sent me long and refreshing sleep. I must have slept many hours— the oil in the lamp was quite low when I awoke.

I tried to light one of the large lamps, but I was too weak, and it fell to the ground. I drank a cup of water and ate all the slice of bread which remained on the niche. I could not touch the others ; they seemed to me to be the price of Sister St. Angelo's life.

I then kissed the dead face of the Prioress many, many times, covered it with the pall, and lay down again beside her coffin. I was unable to stand, and tottered, rather than walked as I came from the niche.

I must again have slept several hours. When I awoke I was again in the darkness ; but I cared not, all things were alike to me now. I was too weak to think, and closed my eyes in the hope of awaking in the spirit land, where Sister St. Angelo had gone before me, and I tried to think of the happiness of seeing my mother again.

I was roused from my lethargy by loud voices, and opening my eyes, the light from the open trap-door so dazzled me that I was obliged to press both my hands on my eyelids. I tried to rise, and also to speak, but was too weak to do either.

I remember no more until I was in the open air, borne in the arms of strong men, one of whom said :

" Call a cab ; I will go with her to the convent of the Holy Assumption."

I called out, with all the strength I had left,

" No ; I am a Protestant."

I saw and heard no more for many weary days and weeks. I was only conscious of restless tossings to and fro ; my head burning with pain, and my eyes so dazzled with the bright sun, that shone day and night alike upon the bare, white walls around me—its sharp, lightning darts piercing like pointed arrows into my brain—that I fancied I had no eyelids, and could only shield me from its fierce glare by keeping both hands constantly upon my eyes.

While I lay there, every public print in every land where the English tongue was spoken, told the sad story of the burning of the old convent of St. Bride's, where sixty nuns,

and three hundred paupers—little innocent children, paralyzed old men and sickly women—every soul in that great
nunnery, perished in the flames ; and of the frantic, unavailing efforts of the town's people to save them ;—strong men
attempting to scale the burning walls within which sisters
and daughters were consumed almost before their eyes.
Two men, with love and courage stronger than death,
ascended ladders placed against these burning walls, and
paid their daring with their lives. Priests, men devoted to
the cause they served, and believing that those unshriven
souls were passing into doubt and darkness, striving to reach
those whose cries of despair filled the air, were every moment
driven back by the smoke and flames, which were bursting
out in all directions. The rest I copy from an old newspaper, which I have treasured " 'mong my things most precious" for many years :—

" The fire commenced in the lower part of the building
where the old people resided, most likely occasioned by some
of the old men smoking in bed, a practice which all the
vigilance of the nuns could not prevent. The dense smoke
ascending must have choked the children and many of the
nuns ere the fire reached them. Before the town's people
were aware of the fire, it was illuminating the country for
miles around, the alarm having been given by a countryman coming into town for a doctor, who saw the light against
the sky from the cross-roads on the mountain three miles
off, and when he reached Algona, found the inhabitants
sleeping in fancied security, with the fire raging in the
midst of them.

" In a few minutes there were hundreds of people on the
spot, and when the alarm spread that St. Bride's was on fire,
there were few men in Algona who were not beneath its

walls, each striving to save one or more who were called by his name. There was no water except what could be drawn from wells; fire-engines were brought, and when used, found to be burst in several places, and to be wholly ineffi- cient. They endeavoured to pull down part of the masonry —alas! it was built as strong as stone and lime, with iron bars, could make it; St. Bride's was a doomed house, and its inmates were to perish with it. One poor nun, a tall woman, whose proportions seemed greater than that of most men, ran from window to window of the up- per story, shrieking for the help it was impossible to give. Ladders were placed against the walls and ropes thrown up to her aid, but in vain, there were strong iron bars fixed in the firm masonry of those windows, which would take hours of hard labour to dislodge, under the most favourable circumstances. One man after another ascended the wall with a sledge hammer, and working for a few seconds, was forced back by the flames and smoke issuing from the window. At last she called loudly out, her strong voice making itself heard above the roaring of the fire, beseeching a priest to be sent up to her, as she was perishing in mortal sin. Several priests made the attempt, and were each in their turn driven back by the fire, which was burning below and around, ere they could reach the window in the roof where she stood. At last her cries and pleadings were so piteous, that the Prior of St. Benedict declared he would shrive her or die in the attempt; and tying a handkerchief across his mouth, ascended to the top. She stood in the window, her hands having firm hold of the iron bars, her head and body down to the waist being in full view. The priest reached the window, and she was seen speaking to him for a second, when her body disappeared, and nought could be seen but part of her face and hands, which still clung to the iron bars; an instant more her hands relaxed their hold, and she sunk amid the burning ruins, with a shriek which few who heard it will ever forget. The roof of the chapel was one of the first things to give way, it having fallen in at an early stage of the fire. Fortunately the plate and altar jewels were all saved before the chapel was entirely destroyed, the falling in of the roof having stayed the burning for a time, thus giving an opportunity to save them.

"Four days after the fire, the Superior of St. Benedict returned from a missionary tour, in which he had visited all the convents of his order on the continent of America. He did not hear of the fire until his arrival at Algona, and at once ordered fifty men to be sent to open up the convent vault, to work night and day, and be relieved every hour, he being cognizant of penance done there during two nights in every week by the Prioress of St. Bride's.

"The vault in due time was opened, and the nun found lying in a coffin, dressed in her veil and robe, cold and dead. Beside her in the vault an English girl lay dying. Near the latter were found a bucket of water and two slices of mouldy bread. The girl had still strength enough left to tell that she was a Protestant! and was carried to the English hospital. Neither the priests of St. Benedict nor the cloistered nuns, who alone were left in St. Mary's of St. Bride's, knew who the girl was, and the poor emaciated creature herself is quite deranged. The only clue by which her friends may identify her is a letter found in a large scapular, which was tied round her neck. It is dated Perth, May 18—, and was evidently written in Scotland. The signature is Robert Scott."

CHAPTER XXXII

WEEKS were wearing into months, and I was still unconscious of the care strangers were taking of me; my senses must have returned to me by slow degrees. At first I was conscious of lying in a room where there were several other beds, and I fancied it must be the dormitory of the aspirants at St. Mary's, and wondered what they could mean by putting me there, but what puzzled me was, that it was neither a nun or convent servant who attended to my wants—I knew this by her cotton clothes as they touched me when she smoothed my bed.

I was then conscious of being visited by a man, who I knew was a doctor by his talking of medicine and feeling my pulse; but I saw neither he or the nurse for I never opened my eyes. I feared the sun, and fancied if I did so its fierce glare would strike me dead; I used to lie thinking over one thought—about the woman's dress being cotton, or there being no prints on the walls, and why it was so for hours, until my head ached as if I had studied too much. After a time I used to fancy the Doctor was Willie, and again he was Robert Scott; I knew that neither my head or my mind was as it had been in the old time, but it seemed so long ago, that I could not remember it, and I did not care to do so; I felt contented if the pain came not back to my head again to lie there always.

After a long sleep I opened my eyes, and before I recollected that the sun would kill me, I saw that there were no other beds in the room, and there was a paper on the walls, and then I saw there was a carpet on the floor and Willie's dog Carlo was lying sleeping on it stretched out at full length. I knew that this was all fancy, I had been accustomed for a long while to fancy many things, which had no existence in reality, and I knew this was one of them, that in reality there was no carpet, no Carlo in the room, but there was one thing, which was always real, and I shut my eyes fast when I thought of it. I knew the sun was coming and he would look through my eyes into my brain, and make it burn and whirl round and round as it had done all the long weary time that was gone. I lay very still with my hand pressed down on my eyes to keep out the sun; the Doctor came and stood by my bed, and took my other hand, which lay on the bedquilt, and felt my pulse; the woman said,

"She had her eyes open for two or three minutes just before you came in."

He answered, "Thank God," in Robert Scott's voice. How well he imitated it! it startled me and made my heart beat quick at first, until I remembered that he did that to make me open my eyes. I must have dreamt that he did so once before. He then put his hand on my forehead, and instead of his own thick-fingered warm hand, he made it feel like Robert Scott's long thin fingers and cold hand, and he said speaking still in Robert's voice as before :

" Her temples are quite cool."

But I kept my eyes shut; he could not deceive me. The Doctor went to the other side of the room and spoke to the nurse, and then he came again and leant over me and said, " ma Sœur, ma Sœur," imitating Willie's voice; I put both my hands over my eyes, and turned away. In a moment all the memory of my early days came back again, and I wept

long and bitterly. He came round to the side on which I had
turned, and tried to take my hand, but he had given me too
much misery already, and I pushed his hand away with all
the strength I had ; the woman then came and made him leave
me. I felt more grateful to her for that than for all the
kindness she had bestowed on me in the troubled time that
was past, of which, indeed, I had but a very indistinct idea ;
looking upon her more as a piece of furniture, that was always
there than as a kind hearted woman, who was unremittingly
ministering to my wants. When he was gone, I put both my
hands on my eyes again and wept myself asleep.

When I next awoke I felt so well and strong that I sat up
and looked round the room. I was not in the dormitory of the
aspirant's or in any room at St. Mary's; the walls were covered
with paper and a carpet on the floor, and the woman was
sitting knitting by the window, dressed in a white cap and
lilac cotton gown.

When she heard me move she came towards the bed, and
without speaking, brought me a basin of fresh water, and
washed my hands and face; she then smoothed my pillows,
asking me to lie down in the way she would have done to a
child—by-and-bye she brought me some tea and bread. I
kept my eyes open all the time. I had forgotten about the
fierce rays of the sun, perhaps the fear of it was gone. She
wished to feed me as she would a child, but I took the tea
cup in my own hand, and asked for a glass of water; I heard
afterwards that these were the first words I had spoken for
many weeks. Some one knocked at the door, and when the
woman opened it the dog of my last day-dream entered; I
held out my hand and said Carlo; he came to the bed and
put his head in my hand, wagged his tail and put up his forepaws on the counterpane, endeavouring to evince his doggish

pleasure at being noticed; he remained beside me, his head resting on the bed, and looking as if he knew I was ill, and a stranger, and that I fondled him for the sake of one like him I had known in my own land. I closed my eyes and slept; I felt tired with speaking to the dog and thinking of home.

When I again awoke, Willie, my own darling brother was by my bedside, not the slight boyish Willie I had left at home, but a tall, strong Willie, six feet high, with great whiskers. And another came and pressed both my thin hands in his own, and his voice uttered no sound, but his dark eye told me the ill I had done to myself in all those years of estrangement, distrust, and doubt.

I might have seen them both long before if I would have opened my eyes; perhaps it was well I did not—I think we need to be stronger to bear joy than sorrow—my heart beat almost audibly, and my cheek burned so that I had to take Willie's cold, large hand and put it alternately to each side of my face; the nurse became very fidgety, came by my bed, smoothed the counterpane and pillows, said the " room was too warm,—there were too many breaths in it,—that the air was all consumed,"—went to the window, opening it wide,—came again by my bed and objected to my talking so much, (I had not spoken two words) at last finding that hints were of no avail, she bluntly observed, " you can come in the evening, gentlemen, but you have been too long here already just now."

She was in the right, my head had begun to ache, and very soon I felt as if my bed was swung backwards and forwards by no gentle hand.

When they left the room she darkened the window, so that she had only enough of light to ply her knitting by sitting close beside it; she was a good kind woman and knew her business well, and I owe my ultimate recovery out of that time of darkness principally to her unremitting care.

Next day I was so much better that I sat in an easy chair by the window, wrapped in a blanket, while my bed was made; four days from that, I was lying on the sofa, clothed and in my right mind.

The nurse had already told me that on the arrival of my brother and Robert Scott, I had been removed from the public ward to the private room I then occupied, that they had been beside me almost every hour for ten days before I recognized them; she thought they were both my brothers. and in talking of their distress at the state they found me in, she said " your youngest brother would come and kiss you twenty times a day, speaking to you in French so I could not understand him, but, poor young man, it was easy to see his trouble was nearly as bad as your own; they had a consultation of the first medical men in Algona the day they arrived, and your younger brother went into the consultation along with the rest of the doctors; from that time the treatment was entirely changed, and your brother took the case in his own hands; your elder brother never spoke a word, and he kissed your forehead only once, but if I can read the heart from the face, his was the sorest of the two, poor man; when his wife dies he'll never mourn more for her than he did for you, he looked as if his heart was breaking, the doctor, (this was what she called Willie) used to take his book or his newspaper and amuse himself with that; but I never saw either book or paper in the other's hand; your face was his book, he never took his eyes off you, and he never spoke but to ask something about you or to answer a question."

That day Willie brought mamma's Bible and laid it on my

lap. I was not able to read with him as we used to do, but he
read to me, and so fulfilled mamma's behest: he told me he had
read from it every day by my bedside since his arrival.

When he had finished reading, I took it from his hand;
the poor, old cover was much worn now, and getting very
shabby, and I determined the first day I was able to sew, I
would put a new cover upon it and so surprise Willie. I asked
if Mr. Weimes had answered any of the letters yet? his reply
was no. Some days after when he thought I could bear it
better, he told me Mr. Weimes was dead, and with him had
perished all hope of being able to prove our father and
mother's marriage, at least for the present. It might be, he
observed, in years to come, some one, who was in a position to
bear witness to the fact, might cross the path of one or either
of us as suddenly as Mr. Weimes had done. We knew it
would be even as He hath said, who ruleth all things, and to
Him we were willing to leave it. I myself had a perfect confidence that I would live to see the truth made clear to the
world as the noon day. " Now that you are well again," said
Willie, " I do not care a fig for anything else; before I heard
of your illness I wearied myself day and night in devising
schemes for proving my right to Haddo with an unsullied
name, and gloried in the revenge I would take of uncle
when I was installed lord there; every night e'er sleep visited
my pillow, I, in imagination, varied the process of humiliation
I would subject him to; now I am a wiser and, I hope, a
better man: should Haddo ever be mine I shall certainly
rejoice for more reasons than one, but if it never is, I will not
trouble myself, it has been like an *ignus fatuus* to me during
the last year; I have spent more time upon it than I could
well afford, and certainly my meditations on the subject have
neither enlarged or improved my mind. Seeking the wealth

that is in the possession of another, whether you have a right to it or not, has in my experience a most deteriorating effect ; and now that this trouble is over I should thank God for its having occurred. While you were lying there, I saw in its true light the little happiness which wealth or rank, without one we love to share it with us, can afford; and were I to fritter off my time in fruitless endeavours after, and idle speculations upon what may never be mine, as I have been doing for many months back, instead of applying myself industriously and giving my attention to my profession, I would be laying but a poor foundation for my future life."

On the same day he told me it was Robert Scott who shewed him the account of the burning of St. Bride's; they had not spoken to each other for two years and a half, although Willie was aware, through Mr. Erskine, that it was principally to Robert's untiring exertions he owed Mr. Weimes' address. On the morning of the day on which they left Edinburgh for Canada, he came to Dr. B——'s, and without sitting down or even speaking, he shewed Willie the newspaper paragraph containing the account of the burning of St. Bride's, the English girl's removal to the hospital, and the subsequent discovery of the letter to which his signature was attached. He then told my brother of our engagement, adding, " I have already made my arrangements to leave this for Liverpool by the night train, from thence I will sail by the first steamer for Canada, fortunately she will sail in a couple of hours after the arrival of the train, and whether I find Violet sane or insane, I go to claim my wife, and bring her to her own land."

It was at once arranged that Willie should go also; that afternoon Doctor B—— held a consultation with two of the first physicians in Edinburgh, who made insanity their study

—the result was the course of treatment which Willie on his arrival pursued so successfully.

On the voyage out, Willie repeated to his companion the words I used in writing to him of the way in which I believed myself to have been treated by his father and himself. Robert told me afterwards that not receiving any answer to the letters he wrote regularly for a fortnight, he wrote to Hariote, and from her received an account of my departure in nearly the same words used by Mr. Scott when desiring Simpson to pack my trunk ;—when I recognized him on the wharf in Glasgow, he was on his way home to ascertain himself what had become of me, and no one expressed more sorrow for my distress, whatever it might be, than Mr. Scott.

A few days later, I was able to bid good-bye to my kind nurse and leave the hospital where I had been cared for so well. Our plans were to remain for a few days in a hotel and then proceed to New York, where we would embark on board one of the steamships for Britain.

CHAPTER XXXIII.

THE day after I left the hospital I became Robert Scott's wife, at the Church of St. James-in-the-fields; this was the first and last time of my being in a Protestant church in Algona. Next day we all went to St. Mary's of St. Bride's, to visit the grave of my dear, dear friend Sister St. Angelo, and I there performed my promise by planting the shamrock, so dear to every Irish heart, on the grave of the holy nun and self-denying woman, who slept beneath—she whom I loved in life and in death.

I did not enter the convent, it would have been a painful visit full of sad reminiscences. The night of the burning of St. Bride's, every uncloistered nun, including the Superior, were there; it was the eve of the festival of St. Bride, on which the fire took place, and all those nuns had taken the veil in the old convent, and consequently wished to spend the *fête* there. Of the two cloistered nuns whom I knew, one of them died while I was at St. Mary's, and the other I had only spoken to once. St. Mary's convent, where I had passed so many quiet, peaceful hours, would be a sad desert to me without the active step and quick eye of her who had been my friend even unto death; and I did not think it wise to subject myself to painful emotions, which were unnecessary. A shower of light snow, fine as powdered pearls, such as we never see in Britain, and in Canada is hailed as the snow that will lie on the ground and bring winter, had fallen in the morning, and formed a slight covering for the otherwise bare, deserted-

EE

looking ground; but in the grove where lay all that earth held of the Prioress, and her darling, the snow had not penetrated through the thick inlacing boughs above, protected by the shade they afforded alike, from winter's cold and summer's sun. The grass there was still green, and some of the daisies were still struggling into blossom. I picked one for myself and one for Gertrude, and placing both within the leaves of my pocket-book, turned away with a sadder heart than yesterday I thought I would ever feel again. When I arrived at the hotel I put my own daisy in my Bible, and I laid aside Gertrude's to be companion for one or two little reminiscences of Canada, which I knew she would like to have. I felt sure Gertrude was in Britain—if she had been in Canada she would have sought me out while I was in the hospital.

The evening before our departure from Algona, my husband and brother went to buy me some Indian work like that I had seen at Quebec, worked by the Algonquins.

I was too tired to go with them, and set about making a cover for mamma's Bible, with a piece of crimson silk I had already provided for that purpose. I had a good deal of trouble in removing the cover, which was folded down inside each of the boards, it being glued to the book. When, at length this was effected, there fell into my lap several papers that had been placed between the boards and the cover. The first I examined was the certificate of my father and mother's marriage! to which was attached, each with a wafer, the certificate of my own and Willie's birth.

"O Lord God of truth, thou hast not shut me up in the hand of the enemy, thou hast set my feet in a large room, the thing that is hid bringeth He to light."

There was also a copy of my father's will, and three other papers which seemed to be receipts for money; all the documents were written in French. The marriage was performed at the church of Notre Dame in Paris, my mother having been a Catholic at the time of her marriage. There was also a second certificate attached to the first from the chapel of the British Embassy, where the marriage was performed a second time on the same day. I read both certificates over and over again, as if to convince myself I saw aright, my whole frame trembling with emotion I could not repress; I felt as I had done when I discovered that Sister St. Angelo was with myself an inmate of the vault. My feelings were not those of joy but of such deep thankfulness, I had no words with which to express myself. I knelt before the Lord, my lips uttering no word, my heart conceiving no thought—I knelt there in silent gratitude and adoration to Him who had taken us from " the horrible pit, and the miry clay." When Robert and Willie returned, I put the whole of the papers into their hands.— Those I fancied were receipts for money, were bills to the amount of ten thousand pounds, which were left to me by my father's will. Willie's long minority would entitle him to a like sum, the rental of Haddo being sufficient to provide amply for us both, besides paying mamma's jointure until Willie had attained his majority.

When mamma was dying she tried several times to speak, and finding herself unable to do so, she signed to me to give her the Bible, which I having done, she put her hand over it twice or thrice. We thought that she wished us to promise to read it, as she had made us do before, and we reiterated the promise. She then endeavoured to shew us that the cover was glued to the boards; and we still misunderstanding her, promised to take great care of it and always keep it covered. Just then the fit of coughing, in which her life passed away, occurred.

I was surprised how coolly Willie took his elevation and independence. Robert said " he was sure that my uncle would at once give the property, but as to anything in the shape of restitution for the rents, which he had defrauded Willie of for so many years, he considered it very doubtful his having anything to give."

Willie called Carlo without making any reply, and taking the dog's head in both hands said :

" So, Monsieur Carlo, we will go to Haddo, both of us, without leave from the master."

I tried in vain before leaving Algona, if it was possible, to hear anything of Gertrude, but no one seemed to have heard that a young lady had left St. Bride's without leave from the Superior. I might have known that such would be the case, Gertrude would fear its being known lest she should again be brought back, and on the other hand anything which at all involves the credit of the convent, is never talked of, or, if possible, allowed to be known inside the nunnery ; far less could it escape and become the subject of conversation outside the convent walls. I went to Mrs. Morton's, but found that she, her husband and family had all of them gone to England in September. I felt sure Gertrude was there; not with them, but there, in Britain somewhere, in England or Scotland.

We went by rail to New York, and in driving to the railway station, we passed the blackened and roofless walls of St. Bride's. How I shuddered as I looked for the last time at the place where I had suffered a living death, and lived long years in a few days ; one of the windows in the roof still stood, the glass and wood-work gone, but the stone window frame and strong iron bars were there, as firm as they had been a hundred years ago ; I knew that window well, strange to say it was the one at which, by moon-light, I had read Robert's letter one night, and the next had seen Gertrude brought back at midnight. I had put a nail in the wall, and there hung a calendar, a little thing not more than six inches long. I used to leave my window open all day, and to prevent its being blown from the wall, I fastened it securely by knotting the string round the nail, and there hung the little calendar still swinging backwards and forwards on its nail, while every living thing in the convent was burnt to ashes. The driver of our vehicle stopped his horses for a few minutes, that we might look at the ruin, and pointing with his whip in the direction of the window, said " I saw there the most awful sight that ever was seen in Algona, one of the nuns, a woman bigger than myself, made her last confession there, and before the priest could open his lips to give the. absolution, the flames came round her like tongues of fire ; she was holding by the iron bars, but the flames and smoke were too much for her, and she sunk into the fire with a cry, that sounded loud above the roaring of the fire and the noise of the falling stones ; many a night since then I have started from my sleep with that cry ringing in my ears, and making my flesh creep and my heart quake as nothing else ever did before ; the burning of the convent was nothing to that wild yell of despair ; every one who heard it trembled and shook like little children, it was the cry of no human being that—they who know about these things, say that it was the demon of the well, who took the form of one of the dead nuns, and tried in this way to escape from the dungeon in which he has been confined for two hundred years—the burning of the convent, and the bursting of the dungeon doors, broke his chains, and he knew if he could get a priest to assoilzie him he would escape into the world. The priest who absolves a demon, is in his power, and the evil spirit thought to leave the body of the dead nun and enter that of the holy man, who would be bold enough to climb that burning wall. There were many priests there, who hearing her cries, tried one after the other to ascend the ladder, but the Holy Virgin sent the smoke and flames to drive them back; at last the Prior of St. Benedict, shocked by the cry that never ceased to pour forth from the lips of the nun: 'I lose my soul, I lose my soul, I perish in mortal sin,' said, ' I am an old man, I have numbered my seventy years and ten, I have finished my course, I have kept the faith and, with the help of the Blessed Virgin, I will shrive that nun or perish in the attempt; and he took off his Prior's cap and knelt on the ground before one of the priests, and said, ' assoilzie me quick;' the young priest put his hand on the gray head of the old Prior and set his soul free, and the frail, gray man went up the ladder with the step of youth, and stood like an angel of mercy on one side of the burning wall, and the demon on the other. It was an awful sight to see in the dark night, the pretended nun, whose size alone might have told it was no nun, her body and head almost filling the window frame, speaking fast into the ear of the aged man, who clung with holy hands to the same bars, as she held by in her wickedness, both seen as clear as a picture up in that giddy height by the light of the flames that towered high above their heads and behind them. She stopped speaking, and the priest made the sign of the cross —the demon was vanquished; with a howl of despair, she sunk into the midst of the burning convent; the Prior loosened his hold and would have fallen to the ground, but we were prepared for it, and there were piles of straw and beds under him; his little finger was not hurt, and he walked home that night to the convent, but in seven days the great bell of St.

Benedict tolled the knell of his departed soul; the holy man had gone to his reward among the angels, while the demon he conquered, was sent howling to his place of torment. You see," continued he, " no one can live more than seven days after speaking with an evil spirit."

I, if neither of the others did, listened with interest to the wild tale of superstition, which the death of poor sister Agatha, woven in with the old belief of the common people, that a demon dwelt in the dungeons of St. Bride's, had given rise to; I myself could well imagine the wild cry she would give in her dread despair, as she sunk amid the flames and smoke to rise no more until she meets before the judgment seat of God, those whom she tormented in life.

We embarked on board the Steamer *Asia* in the end of November; we had a pleasant although cold passage home, and I attribute regaining my strength so soon to the cool sea breeze fanning my pale cheek, and giving strength to my weak limbs in those delightful walks on the deck of the *Asia*.

It was in this pleasant time that I learned how foolishly I had acted in believing the accusations made against my husband, without even allowing him an opportunity of defending himself; I indeed had been signally punished for my imprudence and mistrust; and he, in coming to seek and claim me for his wife, while I was enveloped in clouds and darkness, had given the most noble proof that his love was " passing the love of woman."

He told me that he had never doubted my faith for one moment, that he had watched the unfoldings of my character during the fourteen months we ate at the same table, and worshipped the God of our fathers at the same altar; and the result was that, in his thoughts of, or fears for the absent one, his trust in her firm faith knew neither change or wavering.

Willie had told me of the death of Mrs. Scott, which took place only a few weeks after that of her husband, and also of Hariote's marriage to Mr. Erskine, and I knew little more of the changes at Iona Villa until I was on board ship.

The Erskines lived in a fine house with enclosed grounds in the village of Portobello, where Mr. Erskine had been born and where his parents died. In his bachelor days he let the house, and Georgy had pointed it out to me in one of our walks; I recollect Hariote saying that if ever she married she would prefer living in Portobello to anywhere else.

"I am a social body," said she, "I like to be among neighbours, and Portobello is woven up with all my young memories. I fancy that I could not feel at home anywhere else." They were rich people, the Erskines, but they lived as quietly as we used to do at Iona Villa. Their carriage was kept for comfort not state.

Mrs. Murray, with her husband and two baby boys, lived almost entirely in Edinburgh, and Georgy passed most of her time there. My pulse beat quicker, as he told me that long after my departure Georgy's eyes would fill with tears when my name was mentioned.

Harry was still with Mr. Watts, but had now overcome his aversion to Latin, and was preparing for college. Simpson, under the guidance of the widow who nursed me during my short illness at Iona Villa, was still there, doing her best to make the old house seem like a home to Robert, who was now master.

I was Robert's wife several weeks before I summoned courage to tell him of the scene I had in parting with his father. Had the old man been alive I would have felt less delicacy; but the dead seem to be holy things, of whom we care not to speak lightly, far less do we like to repeat the wrong they have done us. I said as little on the subject as possible, repeating of his words only barely what was necessary ; but I felt, although unasked to do so, that Robert was entitled to an explanation of the sudden manner in which I left his father's house.

He replied, " Had Hariote been at home, this could not have taken place. My father was, all his life, a violent tempered man ; and until the very last, we had no suspicion that those fits of passion were the result of disease. Years ago it was discovered that Hariote had certain powers by which she could control him in his worst of moods; but for this she would have been John Erskine's wife long since. Hariote's presence was necessary to our peace at home, and she, unselfish as ever angel was, sacrificed her happiness for years, that she might be the spirit of peace in the household.

" Our cottage," said he, looking in my face under my hat as he spoke, " is the scene of much happiness. Ellen Syme, as Lady Enderby, lives there with the fondest of husbands, and her two lovely little girls, dressed like fairies, in scarlet and green. They hired the cottage to spend a quiet summer near Hariote. Miss Syme is married to a younger brother of Sir Harry's, who is at the English bar."

Upon our arrival in Liverpool we went direct by rail to Edinburgh, and at the depot were pleasantly surprised to find Mr. Erskine waiting for us. He seemed shocked on seeing my thin pale face, and the dark circle under my eyes, which all the fresh air of the Atlantic had not been able to dispel ; but quickly recovering himself, he welcomed me home to Scotland, addressing me as Mrs. Scott. It was the first time I had heard my new name, and the feelings it called forth were those of gratitude and unmixed happiness. I had much cause. The last time I stood on that spot I was on my way to Glasgow, to seek work in another quarter of the globe, where the sweet words of my northern tongue were smiled at as the uncouth accents of a strange language. I went escorted by and with money borrowed from my brothers' landlady, unaided by whom I could not have gone to win bread for myself, and an education for Willie, amid strangers in a strange land. And now I was rich in my own right, beyond what I had ever thought of in my wildest dreams, and far above all, I was the wife of one whom I loved better than the daylight, who realized, centered in himself, each high idea I had ever formed of man's excellence in mind or body. My darling brother had passed through his course of study with honour, and if not now, would soon be the proprietor of the lands of our fathers. Verily, I might well say with the Patriarch of old, " with my staff I passed over this Jordan, and lo, I am become two bands."

We drove down to Portobello, or rather to Iona Villa, in Mr. Erskine's carriage, under the bright starlight of a frosty December night. Robert almost lifted me into the hall where I was first as a stranger received so kindly. How dear each seemed to be as they pressed rejoicingly around to bid me welcome home as their old friend and brother's wife.

Mrs. Murray alone spoke. " Welcome, welcome home again. We have been watching for the sound of wheels stopping at the door for an hour back. How awfully pale and thin you are. You seem all eyes, and look twenty years older than when I saw you last."

Mrs. Murray, whom I had not seen since her marriage, had not changed. She was still the same matter of fact person, saying what she thought, and never waiting to consider whether it would be pleasant or not.

Hariote interrupted her with heightened colour and flashing eye, saying :

" Yes, we all look wretched after a sea voyage of only two or three days, what must a voyage from the other side of the Atlantic do ?"

We had tea in what used to be the school-room, but had been lately fitted up as a library. Robert told me he lived there when he kept bachelor's hall; adding, "It is not an elysium living alone, particularly when you have been accustomed to live with sisters, who watch your looks and spoil you."

How beautiful Georgy had grown; she had exchanged her sallow sickly look for the rounded rose-leaf cheek, which only health can give, and her blue eye had a softened air, which to me is beauty's self. Poor child, she had doubtless paid dear for the latter. She was her mother's darling, and all her little joys and sorrows were calmly listened to and sympathised in, when confided to her who was, in this respect, at once mother and sister.

After tea Mr. and Mrs. Murray left us, Mrs. Murray's baby making it impossible for her to pass the night from home. Georgy, at her own request, remained with us.

When they had gone, Robert, into whose keeping Willie had given the papers found in the cover of the Bible, put them all into Mr. Erskine's hands, requesting him to read them there and then. When he had done so, he placed them on the table, folding each to the length and breadth of the other, saying, in his calculating Scotch way:

" Ah ! the old rascal, these are the papers he talked of as being missing. It was a loss to him he did not get a hold of them ; he would have made a sure thing of it if he had got these certificates and bank shares into his hands at once ; he told me he had searched every drawer and desk in the house, from top to bottom, and no marriage certificate or paper worth two-pence was to be found. I believe him now ; then

I thought he lied like a trooper, and I felt inclined to tell him so."

Addressing himself to Robert, he said :

" We will have a good scene when he comes now. Last time he went off with flying colours, acting the part of the virtuous and indignant gentleman beating off the attacks of wily lawyers and poor relations, trying to extort money under false pretences. I knew he was a rogue when he tried to bully me into giving up the case. It is my opinion he knew where the marriage was celebrated. It was on what bears most strongly on this very point I told you he contradicted himself. His first story was that Colonel Keith first met Miss De Salaberry in Paris. The next, that she was the daughter of an obscure peasant and never was in Paris in her life. The cur! I felt inclined to kick him out of the office for daring to lie in my face, and I told him so. But from the very first, when I heard of him consulting a pettifogger like Renney, instead of the Robertsons, who have had the Haddo business, father and son, for more than sixty years, I knew he was false as hell, and so was the story he trumped up. He no doubt feared the Robertsons had heard something of his brother's marriage, and that the want of a marriage certificate would be no valid reason in their eyes for denying the existence of the marriage ceremony. I saw Robertson and spoke to him on the subject, he says : " Old Haddo died suddenly and without a will; that he saw little of them for several years before the old man's death, and nothing since, as the present proprietor manages all his own affairs. He knew Colonel Keith was dead ; supposed him married, but without children." However, we will settle the whole affair very easily now. I will write to him by to-morrow's mail, and doubtless we will have him here in a day or two, with his hat in his hand.

Willie had not told me that Mr. Erskine was the lawyer employed by Dr. B——, but I was very pleased when I found it was so.

In the afternoon of next day, I went up to Edinburgh, to see my friend, Mrs. Livingstone, it being arranged that Robert, who left me at the door of her land, would call for me after office hours. I had warned Willie to keep away from the high street, as I wished to give her a pleasant surprise.

It was the old lady herself, who opened the door to my knock. "May I be kept and guarded," said she, with unfeigned pleasure and surprise manifested in her face and manner, "is this you come o'er the sea again; come awa ben, but whar's your luggage ?"

"I will tell you that by-and-bye," said I, entering.

"Sit down here, and warm yoursel, ye'er vary caul like, ye hae nae been weel, I rekon;" and she placed a chair in front of the fire, at the same time taking my hat and cloak in the old kind way.

"Aweel, its a sight gude for sair 'een to see you ; I was aye hearin about ye fae Maister Keith, but he's nae at hame the noo, he has nae been here for sax weeks an' mair; an' I could nae think what was keepin' him, for he aye brings up his socks here, whan they want a steek, an' comes to fess them hame himsel again ; and he thinks his poetry books wi' red boards are safer an' cleaner here than among the fingers o' Dr. B——'s servant lasses, he aye makes the auld place a kind o' hame ; sae whan I mist him 'at he didna come for hale aught days, an' he wasna in the kirk on Sabbath ither, I put on my shawl an' gaed away doun to the doctor's tae speir for him ; sae I was lucky enough to meet the doctor himsel just comin' out at the door ; an' he's aye very civil, for I kent him weel whan he was a lad, an' he tellt me at Maister Keith was out o' the town, and wadna be back for sax weeks or may be twa month; he laught and said, ' 'Deed, Mrs. Livingstone, its my faut at ye didna ken he was awa, for I promised to sen up word, and I forgot aw about it;' the doctor's vera jokie," continued she, " an', says he to me in his ain pawky manner, ' you weman folk are aye ailen and that keeps me rinnen, an' sae I whiles forgets the things I wad like best to mind.' I said it was sax weeks sin sine, but, 'deed, I'm weel sure its mair than twa month since I gaed doun to the doctor's, sae I wadna say but he's at hame noo; at ony rate we'll see afore nicht."

By the time she had given me this information, the table was drawn to the fire side, and covered for tea; I did not object to these preparations, I knew the trouble she was taking was nothing to the pleasure she felt in the exercise of her hospitality.

Seating herself opposite me, she put her clasped hands on the table, and first returning thanks to the great All Father, for his merciful kindness in sending me again to my own land, she prayed for a blessing on the absent one, and that we might eat and drink to His glory, who had once more brought us under one roof.

" Maister Keith took his dog wi' him," observed she, as she poured out the tea, " I wanted to tak him hame whan his maister was awa, for serven lasses are whiles nae ower fond o' dogs, an' altho' I dinna set muckle store by him mysel, I kent vera well it wad gee a sair heart tae some body gin he was lost, but the doctor tellt me he was awa wi' his maister, and said it was him at garet Maister Keith tak Carlo wi' him, for he thought he wad maybe be o' great service whar he was gaen; but it wadna be easy to tell what service the puir tyke wad dee. I'm thinkin' the maist o't wad be haden his maister out o' langer. Ye hae come hame at a bad time for meetin' aw your friends; your auld joe Deacon Scott has been awa I reckon, near han as lang as Maister Keith, at ony rate he hasna been in the kirk for a lang time, I heard tell at he had gaen to America. Ye did nae see him there, did ye ? but na ; America 's a wide word, he might be in aye town an' you in anither, an' the ane nae ken at the ither was there."

"I bade Maister Keith," continued she, "be sure an' tell you aw about the auld man's death. O sirs, bit that was a sair thing, the father o' a family tae pit a han in his ain life, mad or nae mad, an' his puir wife never liftet up her head after she heard o't; they tried to keep it frae her, but the youngest lassie heard it and told her mither, unwritten to the rest, an' sae puir Mrs. Scott jist gaed aff like the snuff o' a candle twa days after. Little doubt but the auld man was as mad as a March hare whan he flytted wi' you about his son. A weel," said she, sighing, her dislike of the man having been buried with him, "its aw ower noo, an' I trust the Lord has had mercy on his soul, he'll neither flyte or fecht wi' ony body in this warld mair, an' gin Deacon Scott be worth your pains, he'll mak up to ye now whan there's nae body to gang atween ye, and gin he doesna he's nae muckle worth, your better wantin' him ; there's mair lads in Edinburgh, and ye'll get a better than him."

I said nothing, but I doubted very much in my own mind if there were any such.

I did not know that Mr. Scott had committed suicide until now, and I felt truly shocked.

Mrs. Livingstone resumed, "Ye maun tell me now your ain story ; I doubt ye'ev had hard wark makin' aw the siller ye sent hame, ye'er white face and thin hands tell that plain enough ; but I'll tak ye down to the braes o' Ballquider wi' me in the summer, and ye'll grow as strong there as ever ye were."

I took off my left glove, which I had kept on on purpose, and showed her my ring.

" Ye dinna mean to say," she exclaimed in surprise; and pausing for a moment, " weel, I'm sorry for't; I aye thought ye wad be Mrs. Deacon Scott some day, an' wha's your gude man ?"

I took from my pocket the first present I received from my husband; it was a small pocket-bible bound in white enamel with gold clasps, and opening it at the first leaf, put it into her hands.

She took her spectacles from her pocket, and rubbed the glasses with her apron, all the time wearing the same grim look I had seen on her face, and gazed on with such anxiety the first evening we met. She then took the book from my hands, and read with a slow, distinct pronunciation, her countenance gradually changing its expression as she read :

" Presented to my dear wife, Violet Scott, on her marriage day, 10th November, 18.. Algona, Canada."

She read the inscription twice over, as if to assure herself she read aright, and then laying down the book, and taking off her spectacles said :

" An, he gaed aw the road to America to seek you; weel, its just what he should hae done, though its nae aw body at would hae done it, but I aye thought I could nae be muckle mistane in young Deacon Scott."

I told her as much of my three years' experience in Canada as I deemed necessary, and no more. I told her also of the prospect there was of Willie's becoming Laird of Haddo, and of the money found in my mother's Bible.

" And that's the auld reprobate that hounded the dog after Maister Keith," said she, looking very grim as she spoke, " weel, weel, the Lord has his ain, and Satan has his ain in ilka tribe and tongue. I heard the godly minister o' Gallasheels say forty years sine, 'at in the judgment, it wad be seen at ilka family had its ain black sheep, and your folk maun be warl

like ; the great rascal, to keep his brother's orphan lad sae lang
out o' his birthright ; he has wrought weel for the gallows, an'
its a pity but he got it, only it would affront decent folk at bears
his name. I'm nae rich, but I wad be willin' to pay ony ane
that would hound him wi' dogs through the Cannongate at five
shillings the score ; hech sirs it wouldna be every day at we wad
see a sight like that."

And the old lady laughed heartily as in imagination she
saw an old gentleman, supposed to be my uncle, running
down the street with dozens of boys and dogs at his heels ;
having satisfied her indignant feelings by thus expressing
herself, she took out her knitting and sat down with her
usual industry.

I now produced a watch and chain which I had bought on
purpose for her, and throwing the chain over her neck, put
the watch into her hand.

" I brought this from New York for you, and I hope you
will wear it in remembrance of all the kindness done to one
pennyless and friendless but for you."

She looked at both for a moment without speaking, but
her face was the most easily read of all books, and reading
there, I knew the pleasure my gift created.

" An' ye brought this aw the rood frae America tae the
auld wife in the high street o' Edinboro' : weel, ye was very idle
to ware your siller on ony sic nonsense ; do ye no think it
would be very gluicket-like o' an auld wife like me, at never
had a bit o' gowd about her aw her life, only the ring her
gude man gae her to be marriet wi', to gang to the kirk
decket out wi' a gowd watch and chain, as gin she thought
she'd grown a lady : hech sirs, there wad be mony a laigh
laugh and a touchin' o' elbows in the kirk that forenoon ; I
wad get mair to look at me, I'se warrant, than would hearken

FF

to the minister; I wad nae wonder," continued she, with a grim but pleased smile, "but yer ain gude man wad be drawen me up for't."

I shewed her that her shawl would cover it in the church, and that her friends would know that it was a present from one whom she had befriended in poverty and loneliness, and there were few things could give me more pleasure than to know it was put on the first thing after dressing in the morning, and put off the last thing at night.

" Weel, my bairn, I'll nae take it aff the noo, at ony rate—it's very bonny, and ower gran' for the like o' me, but may be I'll wear't whiles for a' that, and at kirk or market I needna speir the hour fae nobody."

Robert came to bring me home, and Mrs. Livingstone wished him joy in the authorized form.

A few days later Robert sent me a note in the forenoon, informing me that Mr. Erskine, Willie, and my uncle, would accompany us from town to dine with us. In due time they arrived, my uncle wishing me joy as if he had been one of my best friends in all time past; while we were in the drawing-room before dinner, he asked me where I went on my marriage tour—regretted I did not come to visit them at Haddo, &c., &c., all with a suavity of manner and expression perfectly amazing. He surely must have thought I had been drinking of the waters of Lethe; nothing exhibited his craven soul more than that short interview; the gentlemanly urbanity he thought proper to assume towards me in my own house was, if possible, more irksome than the harshness with which he always treated me at Haddo or Ellenkirk, and I would have told him so had he not been a fallen foe; I knew he would make peace on any terms.

He did not require to be asked to give up the estate—he was perfectly willing to do so at once; he pretended having within the last few days found a letter of my father informing their father and mother of his marriage; this he produced in testimony of the truth of his assertion; Willie took it from his hand, and looking over it, said with great coolness :

" I'm astonished you did not burn this ; had the certificates never been found, this letter might have done damage to your grandchildren.'

He was quite unable to make restitution of the money he had been drawing from the estate for so many long years. He was a lazy man, and had given up his profession upon the death of his father, from which time he had been defrauding us. He would now be wholly dependant upon his wife, whose private income amounted to two hundred a year.

The mean-spirited fellow looked and spoke as if he would lick the dust beneath Willie's feet, caressed Carlo, who growled in return, and, I verily believe, would have signed himself rogue and knave to escape the peril he had incurred by his misdeeds.

It was finally settled that John Erskine, Willie, and my uncle should go down to Haddo by the night train, Willie to be put in possession of, and he to vacate the premises and resign his false title. Fortunately his wife and daughter were spared the humiliation of this scene, they being on a visit to some of their friends in England.

A few days after my brother's departure for Ellenkirk, Robert told me that Mr. Forbes was preaching in the Free churches in Edinburgh, and attracting great crowds. He declared himself still a Roman Catholic, but denounced the temporal power of the Pope and transubstantiation, the belief in the intercession of the Virgin and other saints, and the granting of indulgences. He preached the Gospel with eloquence and fervour, and was talked of by many as in his own way a second Whitefield. He preached in Protestant churches because none other were open to him, and he hoped to win those of his own creed, who came to scoff, or from curiosity, to remain to pray.

We went to hear him from two motives, one to hear the preacher, whose name and praise was in every mouth ; and the other, and with me stronger motive of the two, that I might learn from him where my earliest friend—the one I had known the longest and esteemed the most—was to be found. I was sure he knew. She would have communicated with him as soon as possible.

We went early and yet with difficulty obtained a seat, and long before the service commenced, every seat and aisle was crowded to suffocation. When Mr. Forbes entered the pulpit, I was grieved to see the change which had taken place in his appearance. When I last saw him without his hat in the sacristy of St. Mary's, I thought him one of the handsomest men I had ever seen. His dark hair, which he did not cut priestly fashion, forming a strong contrast to a forehead white and smooth as a girl's. Now, his hair was nearer white than black, and his forehead full of lines, which the expression of his eye told, were graven more deeply in his heart than on his brow. After service was over, we waited that we might speak to him. We had considerable difficulty in getting access to him through the crowd by whom he was surrounded. When at last I found myself near enough, I put out my hand with a smile. He looked at first as if he tried to recollect who I was, and then said, " Miss Keith," his countenance not for a moment changing its solemn, sad expression.

I expressed my pleasure at seeing him again, and then asked whether he could tell me anything of Gertrude. " Yes," he replied, compressing his lips and brow as if in pain while he spoke, " she is beyond the stars, and her body lies in the cemetery at Ellenkirk."

www.ingramcontent.com/pod-product-compliance
Lightning Source LLC
Chambersburg PA
CBHW022009110726
47901CB00006B/1447